Raves for Mercedes Lackey's Valdemar:

"Lackey's delightful world of magic is inhabited by strong and believable men, women and creatures, the most enchanting being the gryphons."

—*Publishers Weekly*

"First-class fantasy adventure."   —*Booklist*

"Lackey's back doing what she does best, and the result is affecting and compulsive reading."   —*Locus*

"Lackey's world remains rich in ideas and personalities, and the magic she imagines continues to be complex and often innovative. Come the next stormy night, admirers will enjoy curling up with this temptestous work."

—*Publishers Weekly*

"Leaves us simultaneously satisfied—and longing for more. Not an easy feat. . . . Once you jump into this world, you'll find yourself immediately involved, surrounded by new friends, and glad you made the trip."

—*Realms of Fantasy*

"Ms Lackey's Valdemar series is already a fantasy classic, and these newest adventures will generate even more acclaim for this fantasy superstar."   —*Romantic Times*

And for *The Valedemar Companion:*

"Exceedingly well done, it helps keep readers unconfused while wandering the enormous fictional terrain the Valdemar oeuvre covers."   —*Booklist*

*Coming Soon in Hardcover from DAW Books

THE
VALDEMAR

COMPANION

A Guide to Mercedes Lackey's World of Valdemar

EDITED BY

JOHN HELFERS and DENISE LITTLE

DAW BOOKS, INC.

DONALD A. WOLLHEIM, FOUNDER

375 Hudson Street, New York, NY 10014

ELIZABETH R. WOLLHEIM
SHEILA E. GILBERT
PUBLISHERS

http://www.dawbooks.com

DAW Book Collectors No. 1205.

DAW Books are distributed by Penguin Group (USA).

Book designed by Stanley S. Drate/Folio Graphics Co., Inc.

DAW TRADEMARK REGISTERED
U.S. PAT. OFF. AND FOREIGN COUNTRIES
—MARCA REGISTRADA
HECHO EN U.S.A.

PRINTED IN THE U.S.A.

Dedicated to Mercedes Lackey, for creating such a wonderful world for people of all ages to wander through and lose themselves in.

———————————

And to the fans of Valdemar, for embracing this world and taking it with them on their own journeys.

The Editors would like to thank the following people:

Betsy Wollheim and Debra Euler for their inspired and invaluable editorial assistance, and to them, Sheila Gilbert, and Martin H. Greenberg, many thanks for believing in this book.

Teri Lee at Firebird Arts & Music for her many contacts and her assistance.

Larry Dixon and Daniel Greene, for their incredible artistic achievement.

Kerrie Hughes, without whom this book could not have been completed.

CONTENTS

THE
VALDEMAR

COMPANION

OFFICIAL TIMELINE FOR THE

by Mercedes Lackey

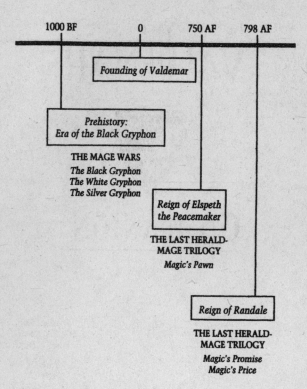

1000 BF   0   750 AF   798 AF

Founding of Valdemar

Prehistory:
Era of the Black Gryphon

THE MAGE WARS
The Black Gryphon
The White Gryphon
The Silver Gryphon

*Reign of Elspeth
the Peacemaker*

**THE LAST HERALD-
MAGE TRILOGY**

Magic's Pawn

Reign of Randale

**THE LAST HERALD-
MAGE TRILOGY**

Magic's Promise
Magic's Price

BF *Before the Founding*
AF *After the Founding*

HEROS OF THE VALDEMAR SERIES

Sequence of events by Valdemar reckoning

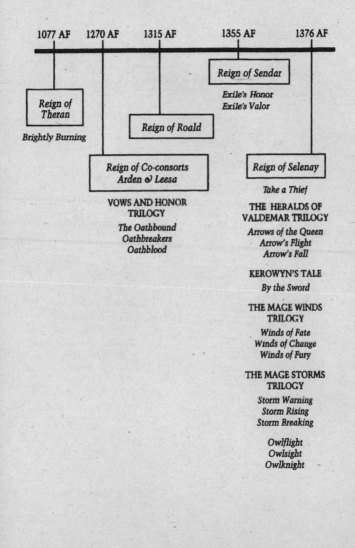

| 1077 AF | 1270 AF | 1315 AF | 1355 AF | 1376 AF |

Reign of Theran

Brightly Burning

Reign of Co-consorts Arden & Leesa

Reign of Roald

VOWS AND HONOR
TRILOGY

*The Oathbound
Oathbreakers
Oathblood*

Reign of Sendar

*Exile's Honor
Exile's Valor*

Reign of Selenay

Take a Thief

THE HERALDS OF
VALDEMAR TRILOGY

*Arrows of the Queen
Arrow's Flight
Arrow's Fall*

KEROWYN'S TALE

By the Sword

THE MAGE WINDS
TRILOGY

*Winds of Fate
Winds of Change
Winds of Fury*

THE MAGE STORMS
TRILOGY

*Storm Warning
Storm Rising
Storm Breaking*

*Owlflight
Owlsight
Owlknight*

GIRL MEETS HORSE (SORT OF)

Mercedes Lackey

THIS is the worst cliché in the world: Valdemar started with a dream. Really.

In the dream, I was Talia; it began at the point in *Arrows of the Queen* where Talia runs away from the prospect of marrying at the ripe age of thirteen, and continued to the point where Selenay explains what she is and what she *will* be, and in some osmotic way I picked up the arrow-code at the same time. Then I woke up.

All things considered, that's not a lot to base an entire series on—and if I had a nickel for everyone who has come up to me with a mystical expression on his/her face and began to tell me about this wonderful dream they had that they were (someday) going to write a book about, I would be able to buy Stephen King, John Grisham, and J.K. Rowling and still have change left over. But there was something about the atmosphere of that dream that felt very compelling and very inviting, and I had been writing short stories for some time, without ever having a solid base to use for a novel. The projects I had started were, frankly, way too ambitious for someone at my (then) current state of development as a writer; I just didn't have the tools yet.

This was a simpler story; no great world-shaking conflicts, no cast of thousands, just one girl with powers that one day *would* be extraordinary, with a helper who already was extraordinary, and a difficult, but not impossible, task ahead of her. This was something that I could handle.

I had already begun the Tarma and Kethry short story series, and it seemed to me that on the whole they were more suited to that venue—like Fafhrd and the Grey Mouser, their adventures were by their nature episodic. Mind, there is nothing wrong with an episodic novel, but Tarma and Kethry were also mature women, and I was just starting to figure them out. You can handle characters like that easily enough in short stories, but not in a novel.

So Talia was the perfect character to begin a book with; she wasn't "finished" yet. And I could develop her character over the course of the book.

However, there was one tiny little problem. I am the world's worst typist.

But I really wanted to start on a novel, and I didn't want to try and write it longhand in a notebook like all my other previous novel attempts, because if anything, my handwriting is worse than my spelling. Although I had a job where I worked on a computer, I didn't want to take a chance on getting in trouble by using "company resources" even after-hours. So I gritted my teeth, took out a loan and bought a PC. And this should prove that I'm older than dirt—it was one of the very first non-IBM PCs, it had a whopping 16K—that's "K," not "megs"—of memory, and it had two single sided single density 5 1/4 inch floppy drives. And let me tell you, it was state-of-the-art. Whatever program you were running went in one floppy drive, and the disk you were saving to went in the other. I didn't even have a word-counter or a spell-checker; I had to do both by hand until a friend wrote me a program that counted the words for me. I still had to spell-check with a dictionary in one hand and the prose on the screen. But at least now I could work without interference from my lousy typing.

And work I did. I ate, drank, and slept Valdemar; I was working things out in the back of my head all the time. I rewrote that first book—which covered the territory of what became all three books of the trilogy—at least three times by myself, all the while continuing to work on short stories.

But I knew it needed more before it was ready to be seen by a book editor. And about this time, as luck would have it, I met C.J. Cherryh, who at that time lived in Oklahoma, at a convention. She admired my song lyrics, asked if I was working on a book, and offered to look at it. I thanked her, but said no—because I wanted to make sure she wasn't just being polite.

Well, she wasn't; she meant it, and she helped me through seventeen rewrites of what became a trilogy. In fact, she was the one who said, "commit trilogy." The number of times stuff went back and forth in the mail was phenomenal, and the number of times I spent the weekend at her house was equally so.

During the course of all of this, I had to figure out exactly what *was* a Companion, why were they in Valdemar, what was Valdemar all about anyway, and why did it have Heralds? And what were the Heralds all about, anyway? The role of the Monarch's Own seemed pretty obvious and necessary to me, quite frankly. Every leader should have someone around that he can trust, who will also keep him honest. But what was the job of a Herald going to be besides being the Monarch's messenger and mouthpiece?

Once that was figured out, I had to lay out Valdemar in my mind—and let me tell you, that was no great joy, because I hate, loathe, and despise maps. Rather than take a single semester of world geography in high school, I took world history instead for *two* semesters. For no other reason than because it was nifty, I made Lake Evendim round—I decided I could figure out why it was round later. I also came up with the Pelagiris Forest full of weirdness, because every country needs some weirdness on its border. Every country needs an age-old enemy too, so I came up with Karse. And at that point I figured that I might as well shoehorn the Tarma and Kethry stories into the same world, so I brought up Rethwellan.

Then there were the whys—I didn't want Valdemar to have "real" magic, or at least not yet. I wanted to concentrate on psionics instead. However, after the book was sold, my editor, Elizabeth "Betsy" Wollheim insisted on having real magic, and a lot of it, right at the beginning of the book. So I put it in the story that Talia is reading and made it very clear that the soon-to-be-dead Herald Vanyel was the *last* Herald-Mage. That gave me the chance to put real magic in later, when I was ready to juggle a few more balls.

I hope at this point you can see that I was deliberately creating a very "open" world, with lots of ways to move and lots of directions to go in. I was hoping that this would turn into a long, long running series—each piece of the series standing alone, of course—and I didn't want to find myself boxed in by some limitation I'd set early on. That just made no sense to me. So I built in a great deal of vagueness, and to be honest, I still do. I know that some readers get frustrated that *all* of their questions aren't answered in a given book, but more often than not it's because I haven't figured out the answers myself yet.

Eventually the first book of the trilogy was ready to be seen and I sent it to C.J.'s publisher, DAW Books. Betsy Wollheim liked it, but pointed out that it still needed work, and that she wanted a *series*, not just one book. I was so happy about the second part of this that I put my nose back on the grindstone, and now there were manuscript copies and versions of the trilogy going back and forth between DAW and me. Betsy is a suberb editor, and I learned a lot from her. When that first book came out, with that wonderful cover by Jody Lee, I was just about ready to burst with excitement. Alas, it did *not* make any best-seller lists, but it got nice reviews and it did well enough to be encouraging and to prompt questions from DAW about what I was going to do for an encore. Well, what I was going to do—was the Tarma and Kethry stuff. By now, I knew them, and I had enough material from the short stories that I had sold to *Fantasy Book Magazine* that I had a good start on a novel. Best of all, I knew how I could work them into the same world as Valdemar, precisely *because* I had left myself so much maneuvering room.

It's a good thing to do that, if you're going to have a

long series. Unanswered questions create some wonderful plots. Sometimes I've let other people answer some of those questions, especially if they're minor points. Teri Lee and Juanita Coulson would call me up and ask about things like food or what fabrics there are during the course of creating this volume, and I'd tell them, "Make it up and I'll retrofit it." In the volumes of short stories, I've let people come up with entirely new sets of characters and situations that sometimes added to the "canon." But a couple of times some of the other contributors have wanted to do this or that, and I've had to say, "No, please don't do that. I haven't decided myself what I want to do there and I don't want to get boxed into an awkward position later down the road."

I tend to think of Valdemar/Velgarth as an actual world somewhere, a world that I'm only writing the history of. It had a long and detailed history "before" Talia, and hopefully will continue to have a long and detailed history. Although I am not sure yet what I'll do after the next two books—*Take A Thief,* the book about Skif before he met Talia, is just out, and *Exile's Honor,* the book about Alberich, Selenay, and the Tedrel Wars, will be out in fall of 2002—it will probably have something to do with Valdemar's "past." Larry and I would like to do more *Owl* books as well. But there are also all the intriguing possibilities of Valdemar's present—what's going on with Hardorn, for instance, and just what *is* it about Iftel? All of those Change-Circles and other uncontrolled magics have mucked things up all over the place, including within Valdemar itself, so it isn't the safe and cozy kingdom it once was; there are perils in the heartland now, and people (and Heralds) are going to have to deal with them. The Artificers will be plunging Valdemar straight along into a Steam Age if they have anything to say about it, but is that altogether a good thing? And there is still an Eastern Empire out there, with a very ruthless man on its throne. . . .

I haven't figured any of this out yet. It's all sitting in the back of my mind, simmering. At some point, something will emerge; I'm just not sure what it will be.

It might not be earthshaking. It might just be a simple story about one person who has a lot of problems to take care of—but a lot of friends to help. It will *probably* be about a Herald, but it just might be about a Healer, or a Bard. At one point I was going to alternate stories, doing an equal number of books about members of all three Circles, but the Heralds seemed to be more versatile as characters.

In the meantime, while I'm pondering the next installments in the Valdemar series, I hope you will enjoy this book, which probably *won't* answer all your questions and probably *will* just raise more in your minds. And I hope you enjoy the story of Tafri, who is, unlike Talia or Vanyel, Elspeth or Lavan, Skif or Alberich, a perfectly *ordinary* Herald (if there can be such a thing). Perhaps I should say, a *typical* Herald. He doesn't have any great MindMagic, he doesn't have any real magic at all, but he has that special something that makes a Companion Choose someone, and he manages to solve problems which, if they aren't exactly earthshaking, *are* important to the people he serves. He and his kind are the glue that holds the Kingdom of Valdemar together, and I, for one, am deeply appreciative of them.

—M.L.
2001

A HERALD'S JOURNEY

A NEW VALDEMAR NOVELLA

Mercedes Lackey

ONE

A Journey Begins

TWELVE-YEAR-OLD Tafri Tallyman tightened his knitted muffler around his neck and carefully tucked his brown woolen breeches into his worn boot-tops. Snow had been falling on the village of Delcare since last night, and by now it was deep enough to be a considerable nuisance.

Tafri had already been out once this morning, in a pair of old, threadbare, colorless breeches of his father's, discarded as too worn for patching. It had been his task to shovel the path that led from the door of his cottage to the village street, getting soaked to the skin in the process, for his father had to leave at dawn for his job. No fool Tafri, with only two pairs of winter breeches of his own, he didn't want to have to spend the rest of the morning shivering in wet clothing when there was a pair of discards in the ragbag that would do as work clothing. Nobody was going to be looking at his breeches while he shoveled, after all! And if they were far too big for him, well, that was all right; it meant that the worn places were not anywhere that it would count!

Now changed and dry again, with a bowl of hot bread-and-milk inside him, he was ready for his day to begin— lessons at the village temple of Kernos. He dressed for the weather. A heavy knitted sweater over his tunic, his muffler, a pair of mittens and a knitted hat pulled down over his ears would get him from the cottage to the temple without freezing to death. These articles were so multicolored that he could have been a jester, although his mother had done her best to try and make some semblance of patterning in them; she knitted them out of the odds and ends she bought from other women who had already finished more uniform projects.

He had no coat this year. The only coat the family could afford was reserved for his father, who worked out-of-doors as a carter all day—Tafri had completely outgrown his coat last year, and there was no money to spare for the woolen fabric for a new one this year. Perhaps next year—or perhaps someone at the inn would spoil a blanket that his mother could bring home and piece into a new coat or cloak for him.

His mother had a cloak cleverly made of tiny pieces of whatever woolen fabric came into her hands pieced together with embroidery stitches. She was so clever in her handiwork that it was, in Tafri's opinion and that of his father, a veritable work of art. She had just finished it, fortunately, before this latest snowstorm. She had offered to make another for Tafri, but—he wasn't interested. That cloak was too feminine a garment for a boy; he would rather shiver than wear something that fussy and girlish.

"Have you got your luncheon?" his mother called behind him as he reached for the wooden door-latch.

"Right here," he replied, turning to hold up the rag-wrapped bundle of cheese and yesterday's bread for her to see.

His mother smiled at him from where she was scouring the dishes with sand and hot water, next to the fireplace that served them for heating and cooking together.

Tafri thought she was the most beautiful woman in the world, and not a one of the fine ladies that stayed at the inn where she worked as a maid could touch her. Her brown eyes were always merry, and she was never without a song on her lips from morning to night. Her employer, the local innkeeper, was a clever woman named Lilly, a stranger to the village who had arrived several years ago looking for a suitable site to build a new inn. This worthy woman thought that Shanda Tallyman was as much a treasure as her own family believed, and although Shanda might only be the inn's maid and occasional server, she got an extraordinary number of benefits besides her wages. She'd been encouraged to bring her child along with her when Tafri was too small to go to school, a concession that was completely amazing. In addition, she had the right to as much leftover food as she could carry home in a basket every night, the right to any ordinary clothing left behind if it had not been reclaimed in a year, and the right to torn or worn linen from the inn's beds. Lilly was a generous employer, and the Tallyman family was well aware how lucky they were that she employed Shanda.

"Mind the priest, and do what he tells you to do," Shanda told her son, as she did every morning, raising her round chin a trifle and tucking a strand of goldbrown hair back into the scarf tied about her head.

"Oh, mama!" Tafri replied; he was old enough now that the morning admonition was, well—*unnecessary.* He wasn't a little boy to be told to mind every morning!

"No sauce, now!" Shanda said, but with a smile, and a shooing motion of her strong, square hands. Gratefully, Tafri opened the door and escaped into the snow.

Their cottage was at the heart of the village, although it was tiny—just one room with a loft over the kitchen area where Tafri slept. Larger and more expensive houses stood on either side; the slip of land the cottage stood on had once belonged to the farmhouse to the right, and had been parceled out for a hired-man's cottage back in some long-ago time when the village hadn't held more than a dozen homes altogether. To get to the street, a path had been made along the garden wall of this larger home, and that was the route Tafri took now, with piled-up snow on his left and the snow-topped brick wall on his right.

This brought him to the single road that ran through the village of Delcare. There was no village square in Delcare; all gatherings and celebrations were held on the village green just on the other side of the road. The Halchers, prosperous merchants, lived in the big, half-timbered house on his right; they had a maid and a man-servant to do their chores for them. This morning their man-of-all-work was out shoveling their path, and he waved to Tafri as the boy reached the road. Tafri waved back, but didn't stop for a chat; shoveling had taken time and if he paused he'd be late for school.

All children went to school in the Kingdom of Valdemar; the school term lasted from the end of harvest to spring planting. Some, in the tiniest of villages, were taught by old folk, widows mostly, who would hold school lessons and be paid a little for each child by the Crown. But most lessons were taught in the temples of whatever religion one belonged to, it being considered that priests and priestesses in general were better educated than old women who might be a bit hazy on their arithmetic in numbers higher than twenty, and rather vague as to spelling. A child who didn't live on a farm, or who didn't hire out for light chores during farming season, could get additional lessoning all during the spring, summer, and fall, if his family agreed and he was willing and apt to the task. And of course, any child whose parents could afford it could have tutors or share a highly educated teacher with others whose parents had the means. *Very* occasionally, where there was one of the Houses of Healing where several Healers were stationed, a Bardic Retreat, or a Herald's Resupply station, children might get their lessons from a Healer, a Bard, or even a Herald. That was rare, though; most relied on the homely resources of their own neighbors.

Tafri envied those children; he would have given a great deal for access to such tremendous sources of learning.

Once a child could read, write, and figure to the teacher's satisfaction, his mandated education was over. Tafri had passed that point last season; now he kept up with his lessoning because he liked it and his parents were willing to forego the added pennies he might have brought in doing odd jobs. Once the priest was done with him for the day, however, he would present himself at the inn to help his mother, and perhaps, if he was lucky, earn a copper bit or two as well doing extra chores for guests or for Lilly.

The temple of Kernos lay past the village green in its own little grove of trees; it didn't look a great deal different from any of the larger houses in the village in size or general shape. The roof was made of native slate, the chimney and walls of stones, which came out of the fields every spring with exasperating regularity. There was a stone porch at the front of the building, and around at the side was a second cottage where the priest actually lived. Smoke arose from the chimney into the grey sky, and Tafri hurried up the path to that promise of warmth.

Once he reached the porch, the first difference between this place and an ordinary house was evident. The door was big; taller and much wider than normal. It was also carved with the head of a great stag. He pulled the door open, and entered.

Here is where the temple really differed from the other large buildings in the village; it was one huge room. Stone-floored as well as having stone walls, here inside the walls had been lathed and plastered, then painted with scenes from the Holy Books. The roof above, wood planks supporting the heavy weight of the slate roof tiles, had great beams that had been carved with vines, flowers, and stags' heads. A wide hearth with a cheerful fire now burning on it had been set into the wall at the left; at the rear, decorated with evergreen boughs and expensive wax candles, was the altar. More candles, tallow this time, stood in wooden sconces mounted on the wall, but with all of the light coming in the real glass windows, reflecting off the snow outside, they weren't needed this morning.

This year Tafri was the oldest child being schooled here. Priest Dofren looked up and smiled to see his favorite pupil enter; he and all the pupils were seated at a wooden table and benches placed before the fire for warmth and light. But he didn't pause for a moment as he coaxed Sera Hopewell through her stumbling recitation of the alphabet. He simply nodded at Tafri's place at the end of the dark, well worn table, and the open book waiting there for him.

It was history today, Tafri saw as he sat down in his place. The priest had marked where he was to begin and end with clean straws, and he read diligently while the

younger children were drilled in reading, writing, and
sums. There was a two-year gap between him and the
next oldest, a ten-year-old. Of the eleven other children
his own age that had begun their lessons with the Priest,
all the rest were elsewhere this winter. Jem, Kaleb and
Cortny were helping with farmwork; Jillian, Geoff and
Dugal learning their parents' crafts. Marak, Tovy, Kyle
and Wyatt had all been apprenticed outside their parents' crafts because they were second and third children.
And lucky, lucky Sushanna had been sent away to a real
board-school, where the girls lived while they studied,
and only came home on holidays; some, so Sushanna
had told them, were even highborn. She said that this
school was going to teach her fine and fancy needlework,
the special manners that important people seemed to
require, and something called "deportment." Why anyone thought such things were necessary, Tafri had no
idea—unless it was to make her suited for a marriage
with someone above her in rank, wealth, or state. But
Sushanna's parents were the richest in the village and
she was their only child; nothing but the best was ever
good enough for her. She wasn't exactly spoiled, but
Tafri didn't regret that she was gone. She'd always held
herself apart from the rest of them, as if she was made
of some delicate material and was afraid to get smudged
by their commonness.

The book in front of him was not going to be one of
his favorite texts; it was fairly dry and didn't give him
much of the sense of what the times it described *felt*
like. Still, Tafri carefully committed the details of the
chapter he was reading to memory; books were precious
things, and many of them went the rounds among the
various Temples in the region as various children were
deemed ready for them. Once he had finished this one,
he might not ever see it again.

When he finished the end of the passage, and had
gone over it another two times to make certain that he
had it all firmly in his mind, he signified that he was
ready by closing the book and sitting quietly with his
hands folded on top of it. The priest looked up, saw that
he was ready and nodded. Within a few moments, while
Tafri watched the flames dancing on the hearth and be-

came ever more aware of the fact that it could not be far to lunchtime, Priest Dofren finished with the child he was working with and came over to Tafri.

Taking the book from him, the priest opened it at the marked page and began asking questions about the chapter Tafri had finished. Tafri didn't get them all right by any means, but those he answered incorrectly the priest corrected him on, and then went on. Priest Dofren was very good at this sort of teaching; Tafri had found that those things that he'd been corrected on tended to stay with him as well as the ones he got right.

They were not quite finished when the noon bell rang at the baker's shop, signifying that those who had left their luncheons there to be baked or heated along with the day's bread, pasties, and cakes, had better collect them. The Priest put the book down on the table, and smiled at the children, who now looked at him as attentively as any circle of puppies who had heard the word "cookie."

"Right, off with you!" he said, and there was a flurry of arms and legs, then the children were gone, out the door, heading to their homes, their lessons over for the day. None of them had the kind of hunger for knowledge that Tafri had always shown, so (as Dofren wisely said) it was no use in trying them past their patience. Their afternoon would be spent in chores and play— more of the former than the latter. In a village like this one, children did *some* work at least from the time they could be trusted with tasks.

While Tafri moved over to the hearth to eat his bread and cheese, the Priest dipped up a cup full of cold water from the pail for him, then went off to get his own luncheon, leaving him the only occupant of the Temple, which echoed with every pop and crackle of the fire, every time he shuffled his feet. Tafri didn't mind eating alone; if he really *wanted* company, he could find one of his old schoolmates enjoying his or her own lunch where they now labored beside their parents or at their new apprenticeships.

When he finished his meal, he got up and stretched, then decided to go outside for a little before settling into the afternoon lessons, which would probably be advanced ciphering. This would allow him to do a bit more than simple accounting; it wasn't a favorite lesson, but he was good at it.

The day was still gray, the air a little damp, with a hint that there might be more snow to come. That was all right; more snow would mean that the people stopping at the inn might have to stay overnight or longer, and that meant possible tips and even a bit of work for him. He wandered down the path, across the green, and down to the road, to see what there was to be seen.

The snow creaked underfoot—another sign that there might be more of it forthcoming. At the luncheon hour it was unusually quiet; no clanging and hammering from the blacksmith, the carpenter, or the cooper, no wood-chopping. A few women were about, making purchases at the baker, the butcher, or the one shop in the village, but otherwise there wasn't anyone to be seen.

No one on the road, either, which was something of a disappointment.

No, wait—

Tafri saw distant movement, he thought, though it was hard to be certain against the white of the snow. Was there a rider coming?

He peered down the road; noticing his intent gaze, the few villagers out on the street also peered in the same direction.

And after a few moments, it dawned on all of them that they were, indeed, seeing something coming toward the village, but it wasn't a rider. Or, rather, the steed coming toward them wasn't *carrying* a rider.

And no wonder it had been hard to make out—white steed against white snow, saddled and bridled but not ridden—

This was a Herald's Companion, and if it wasn't being ridden by a Herald, then it was on Search!

Tafri had only seen a Herald, those dispensers and enforcers of the Queen's Justice, a few times in his life; he had never seen a Companion out on Search before. He only knew that the Companions Chose their Heralds, and that the people Chosen went to the far off capitol city of Haven, to learn the things they needed to know to be Heralds.

Heralds—so much in Valdemar depended on the Heralds! They could do all sorts of things, and virtually everything important in Valdemar involved them and depended on them. All Heralds had magic of some sort or other, but they didn't all have the same sorts of magic—their Companions, although they might *look* like beautiful white horses, were nothing of the sort. They had magic of their own, so it was said. . . .

But now the Companion was close enough to see clearly, and he—for it was a stallion—claimed every bit of Tafri's attention. He had never seen anything so gorgeous in his life!

The Companion stood a little taller than most of the village horses, but his head was bigger, his forehead broader, and his eyes were set a little further forward on his head than a horse's, giving him a very intelligent look. His coat was as white as the untouched snow, his mane and tail like twin waterfalls of ice spun into the finest possible thread. He wore a saddle of blue leather with silver ornaments, a bitless bridle to match, and a saddlecloth of deeper blue trimmed with silver embroidery. His hooves were silver, too; he set them down as delicately and carefully as if he were dancing, and the nearer he came, the more Tafri stared. He drank in the sight; he wanted to remember this for the rest of his life, for he might never see a Companion on Search again—

Companions came looking for "their" Heralds when the time was right; that was what being "on Search" was all about. Usually the Chosen was a child, but not always, and no one really knew what it was that the Companions looked for—or waited for—or how it was that they Chose one particular person above all others. Until that moment they lived at Herald's Collegium in Haven; after that they never left their Heralds until they died.

Oh, to be Chosen as a Herald! Only in a few, wild dreams had Tafri ever indulged in such a thought; he was perfectly ordinary in every way, the common son of a common carter and a village-inn maid-of-all-work. Children like *that* were never Chosen; if anyone in this village would be Chosen, it would be someone like Sushanna. But he couldn't help it now, as the Companion drew closer and closer, he was consumed with the longing that the stallion would stop in front of *him*, look deep into his eyes—aching with the wish that it would be *him* this time, that for once in his life, he would be touched, himself, by that special magic . . .

The Companion stopped in front of him. As the nearby villagers gasped, the stallion bowed his head down to Tafri's level, breath steaming from his nostrils, and Tafri looked deep into eyes that were bottomless, sapphire treasures holding warmth, and wisdom, and—

—and he was falling into them; they filled his gaze, and he didn't want to ever stop falling into them. With a shock to heart and soul, he felt an empty place he hadn't known was inside him suddenly fill with warmth and joy.

And he felt something inside *himself* rushing to fill a similar place inside Adelayan. For *that*, he knew without knowing how he knew, was his Companion's name.

His Companion.

:Your Companion, Tafri. I Choose you. You will be my Herald.:

TWO

On the Road

TAFRI pinched himself, for he could not believe that he, possibly the least important and certainly the poorest child in his village, had been Chosen. But here he was, sitting in Adelayan's saddle, on the way to the Collegium in Haven. He, who had never ridden anything except the carter's placid old horse at an ambling walk, now sped over the snow-covered roads as if he was flying.

He had not been permitted to leave the village unacknowledged, however.

He and Adelayan had been surrounded by an excited crowd who cooed over the Companion and thrilled to the fact that *any* of their number would become a Herald. Before the excited villagers had allowed him to leave, he'd been redressed from the skin outward. From

one family had come new smallclothes, from another, a
nearly new pair of moleskin breeches in good condition
and just a little too big. Sushanna's parents provided a
knitted sweater of lambswool, too small now for their
own daughter. The cobbler gave boots that had been
intended for another boy with that lad's father's blessing,
and his wife a pair of woolen socks she'd just finished.
From his own neighbors came a wonderful tunic of soft
buckskin meant to go hunting in, and from Lilly, the
innkeeper, the Midwinter gift she'd been saving for him,
a wonderful thick woolen cloak. She put it over his
shoulders with tears in her eyes and a kiss on each
cheek. "You have to show us all proud, young Tafri,"
the village mayor had said, clapping him on the back.
And then, with virtually everyone in the village putting
in something, two bulging packs of provisions and more
clothing had been added to the back of Adelayan's
saddle—including fresh socks, smallclothes and a change
of sweaters and shirts. "You've a long way to go, and
there might not be inns when you need to stop," the
priest told him, once he was newly clad and sitting above
everyone in Adelayan's saddle. "Your Companion will
take you to Waystations to sleep at night if there are no
inns at the end of the day. If there *are,* you just present
yourself at the door and tell them that you've just been
Chosen. They'll put you up for the night, and give you
a little marker that will tell the Collegium that they
helped you. You give those when you're asked for them
at the Collegium."

Tafri just nodded, completely overwhelmed by all this
attention. His mother and Lilly stood together, both with
tremulous smiles and tear-streaked faces; his father,
summoned on the run by his employer, beaming.

The priest stood back, and his mother rushed forward
for another kiss, his father for another embrace. "They'll
let you come home, now and again," his mother whis-
pered, and he felt a rush of relief. At least he wasn't
going into exile! "Now, you be good, and show us
proud!"

"He will, lovey," his father said, hugging them both.

Adelayan's skin shivered and he shifted his weight

from foot to foot, clearly impatient to be off, and when Tafri's mum and da stepped back he shook his head and neck so that the bells on his bridle rang.

"Time for him to go." Tafri's father was the one who made the pronouncement, and no one contradicted him. Without pausing a moment for anyone to change their minds, Adelayan stepped out smartly. As Tafri turned in his saddle to wave goodbye, Adelayan moved from a walk right into a canter, and the village and all its madly waving inhabitants receded behind him until a turn in the road hid them from his sight.

He was torn between excitement and tears, and scrubbed some of the latter from his cheeks with mittened hands.

:Ah, Chosen, you'll be back for a visit before you know it,: Adelayan said in his mind, startling him and making him look wildly about for a moment before realizing that the words had not been *spoken,* precisely, and had come from his Companion.

:Oh, yes, Tafri,: there was a feeling of a chuckle in the words. *:Companions can talk to their Chosen, mind to mind. It is called MindSpeech. Just think what you wish to tell me if you wish it to be private, but otherwise speak as you would to anyone.:*

Mindspeech! "Is this—magic?" he asked cautiously.

:Mind-magic, yes. There is Mind-magic, and there is the magic of the Mages and Herald-Mages. I hope you will not be disappointed, Chosen, but you do not have it in you to become a Herald-Mage. . . .: Adelayan's ears swiveled back toward him.

"Oh no!" Tafri exclaimed. He couldn't imagine how anything could be better than *this.* Why would he want to fling magical fireworks about? He'd never fit in at Delcare again if people thought he was likely to go blasting things to bits in a fit of temper!

:There is that,: Adelayan said, with a deep whicker that *definitely* sounded like a chuckle. *:I must admit, that sort of reaction has happened in the past; most uncomfortable for the Herald in question.:*

All this time, the Companion sped on, his pace so smooth that Tafri had no fear of falling off, though he'd never sat so high or gone so fast. Nor had he ever been so far from home; the few times he'd gone out with his father, they'd traveled no further than the nearby farms.

The excitement kept him looking in every direction as they rode, and he couldn't help notice how people kept looking at *him*. In farmyards, driving wagons, and through the tinier villages he passed, people saw him, smiled broadly, and waved. He always waved back.

"Do they know—"

:That I was on Search and Chose you? Of course. Until you earn your Whites, you will be in Trainee Grays—: A picture flashed into his mind of a boy his age, wearing a shirt, tunic, trews, and boots all in matching gray. *:—and you are far too young to be a Herald, anyway. So when people see a youngling who is not in Grays riding a Companion, they know he must have just been Chosen.:*

"No one like that ever came through our village," Tafri said, shifting a little in the saddle. As comfortable as the Companion's pace was, it was *still* the first time he'd ever done any amount of riding, and he was frankly getting tired, and sore.

:Not within your memory, perhaps, but surely within the past ten years,: Adelayan told him. *:Your village may not be on a main read, but at least it is on a road. There are many places that are barely linked by goat tracks, and Heralds have come from them.:* Now Adelayan wasn't just chuckling, he was laughing, but Tafri knew that the Companion wasn't laughing at him.

When they stopped—and to Tafri's great relief it was in a village, and not at some empty Waystation—he was very sore indeed. But the Companion might well have known exactly what kind of folk ran this particular inn, for Tafri found himself whisked out of Adelayan's saddle by a great, friendly bear of a man and bundled into the inn, where he soon found himself soaking in a tub full of hot water beside a fine fire in a little room all to himself. And both a pot of liniment and a hot meal waited for him when he got out. He was certainly in need of both, and went straight to bed, sleeping as soundly as he ever had in his life.

The next several days were a repeat of the first, as he went farther and farther from his home, out of an area of flat farmland and into one of rolling hills and roads lined on either side with tall hedgerows. He was glad of the extra provisions, for he seemed to be hungry all the time, but when those were gone, Adelayan made sure he got more from the inns where he stayed overnight. He'd been hesitant, but Adelayan had insisted, and to his surprise, his hosts, after having fed him, housed him, and gone out of their way to take care of his aches, *then* went on to stuff his packs with additional food. Why, they didn't even *know* him!

It took him seven days to reach the great city of Haven; seven days during which he saw villages both small and large, towns that could have planted his village in their market square with room left over, and a city so big he thought it surely must be his goal until Adelayan told him otherwise. Adelayan talked to him the entire time, too, telling him what he could expect when he reached the Collegium, which kept him from being too homesick. And although he had at first dreaded the coming of night, thinking he would surely lie awake in his strange beds, missing his parents dreadfully, he was so tired at the end of every day's ride that he went right to sleep, sometimes even falling asleep over his dinner.

Then, one day, Adelayan didn't stop before sunset— he kept right on going, as the sun dropped below the horizon, and the moon rose, reflecting off the snow-covered fields and providing a silvery and mysterious light. Here and there, warm yellow lights glowed in square or rectangular shapes from out of irregular dark hummocks—farm houses, off in their fields.

:We're nearly at Haven,: Adelayan explained. *:Don't worry, we're expected. I can reach quite some distance with my Mind-speech, and I've warned the Collegium that we're coming.:* He shook his head, and continued apologetically, *:I'd have stopped tonight and brought you there in the morning, but there's another pair of new Trainees coming in then, and having so many arrive at the same time sometimes makes for some confusion.:*

All that Tafri could say was, "Oh," but he wished, as the air grew colder, that they were at their destination *now*.

At least he was used to riding, now. And the road was

very wide, quite wide enough for four carts abreast. It wasn't as if they were likely to get lost.

Then they topped a rise—and there it was. A sea of yellow lights, stretching out as far as he could see.

:That is Haven,: Adelayan said, proudly, and they followed the road down into the great capitol city.

And within moments, Tafri was overwhelmed.

The streets had been swept clean of snow here, and Adelayan's hooves rang on the cobblestones like bells. Even though it was well after dark, there was still plenty of traffic, both mounted and afoot, as well as a few carts or carriages. It was difficult to tell just what sorts of buildings they were passing; there were streetlamps, but they didn't do a great deal to illuminate the building fronts, and anyway, by this point Tafri was getting very weary indeed. The people here didn't pay a great deal of attention to them as they rode past, but then again, the people of Haven must surely be so used to seeing Heralds by now that they were as usual a sight as geese on the common in his home village.

At one point they rode beneath a huge wall with armed men—Guardsmen, he thought—atop it and four more beside the tunnel going beneath it, but they simply waved the two of them through.

Adelayan was rather preoccupied with picking his way through the traffic, finding ways of getting around slower-moving objects and threading between carriages. They had gotten into a particularly congested area where a great many people seemed to be trying to get into or out of a huge building with painted cloth banners flapping on either side of the door. The Companion, however, found places to eel through that Tafri didn't think a donkey would fit into, and got them through it without much delay.

There were still a great many people, though. It seemed as if they must have gotten themselves into a part of the city where there were a *lot* of inns. Doors opened and closed, spilling people out into the street, talking, singing, staggering, hanging over each other's shoulders. When doors opened, besides the people spilling out, snatches of music and the aroma of a hundred different kinds of food spilled out as well. Adelayan now adroitly maneuvered his way around the people who wandered out into the street without really looking where they were going.

He rounded a corner, and came into a quieter area, for which Tafri was very grateful. All those people made him nervous, and as for the scent of cooking food, well, his stomach kept growling.

Back and forth they went, taking streets in no particular pattern that Tafri could make out. He was totally confused within moments.

And he was really, truly, coming to the end of his endurance.

:Cheer up, Chosen, we're almost there, I promise.:

He didn't notice just when the houses stopped being "houses" and started becoming eye-poppingly huge mansions, but he did manage to take note of the moment when the mansions vanished from the right side of the street and an enormous wall took its place, just as tall as the first one they'd met up with. And finally, Adelayan slowed his pace to a walk as they approached a small gate in the wall, with a single Guardsman outside of it.

This time, the Companion stopped. The Guardsman had gotten a board with a piece of paper clipped to it and looked up at Tafri when his Companion paused beside him.

"Adelayan and Chosen?" the Guardsman asked. Tafri nodded wearily. "Go on, youngling, they're waiting for you," the Guardsman said, with a sympathetic smile. He pushed open the gate and Adelayan trotted through. Tafri's first sight of the Palace and the four Collegia was impressive—but truth to tell, he was far too tired to appreciate it. It was mostly just overwhelming. Huge, huge buildings, with hundreds of windows all alight, and grounds that glimmered under the moonlight, lit in some places with huge torches, dark in others.

Adelayan stepped up into a trot again, and Tafri clung on for all he was worth, until they reached an enormous building, a stable the size of his entire village, with a loft over it, that was lit up as brightly as any human habitation.

Adelayan stopped at last in front of a cluster of people; folks who helped him out of his saddle, asked for the bits of metal that the innkeepers had given him, and took him straight to a room in one of the huge buildings. There a couple of youngsters near his own age helped him out of his clothing and into a flannel bedgown two sizes too big, sat him down on the side of a bed, and pressed an enormous mug of thick ham-and-pea soup on him. He was achingly grateful for it, and even more grateful that it didn't have to be cut up and chewed. He could hardly keep his eyes open by this time.

"Drink this—" someone said, when he was relieved of the empty soup-mug, and a second cup was pressed into his hands. It was herb tea, thick with honey, and he drank it without a protest over what would otherwise have been too cloyingly sweet a liquid for him to swallow. Then, without prompting, he laid himself down, felt someone pull the blankets over him, and nothing more.

THREE

Directions

WHEN Tafri awoke the next day, it was to the sound of a bell.

That he woke in a strange bed and a strange room didn't trouble him; he'd been doing *that* for days. But this was the first time that he'd been in a place where a huge bell sounded overhead to rouse him from slumber.

When he opened his eyes, it was to darkness—except for the coals in a tiny fireplace opposite his bed, and a thin line of yellow light under a door just past the foot of his bed. He yawned and rubbed his eyes sleepily with one hand, then sat up in bed.

His first thought of *where am I?* was answered almost immediately with memory. He was *here,* in Heralds' Collegium, in the huge capital city of Haven.

He cautiously put a bare foot over the side of the bed; the floor was cold, and he shivered as the second foot joined the first and he opened his door.

Outside was a hallway, brightly lit, and other doors were opening along it as other boys used the hall lanterns to give them the light they needed to find candles and kindle them at the coals of their fireplaces. Tafri did the same, once he saw what his neighbor across the hall was doing.

The candle showed him a simple room, about the size of one of the private rooms in Lilly's inn. Bed, desk, chair, bookcases and a wardrobe, with a tiny bedside table, all well worn, were the furnishings. Beside the fireplace was a basket of logs, and Tafri, shivering, quickly built up the fire while still in his too-large bedgown.

With light from candle and fireplace to guide his steps, he closed his door again. He felt suddenly shy, and certainly wasn't used to undressing in front of strangers.

His packs were beside the wardrobe, and although the clothing he'd been wearing last night had been taken away, his boots were still there, and so were the clothes packed in those bags. He changed quickly in front of the fire, and pulled on his boots, then wondered what he was to do next.

He was answered by another bell. Outside in the hall came the sound of several pairs of running feet, and then a diffident tap on *his* door.

He opened it quickly. Waiting outside was a boy—or young man—who looked about sixteen or seventeen. He was raw-boned and gangly, brown-haired and brown-eyed, and Tafri sighed with relief because he looked just like the blacksmith's eldest son and apprentice.

"Hullo, Tafri!" said the boy, who was wearing an outfit of trews, tunic, knitted sweater and boots all in a uniform medium-gray color. "I'm Adan, and I'm your mentor. I'll take you around and get you set up, and from now on if you need anything all you have to do is ask me." He grinned, and Tafri grinned back; Adan's generous mouth revealed a set of white teeth that would make any horse proud.

Adan patted the door. "This is your room, from now until you leave the Collegium on your Internship Ride. I'm right next door to your right, and to your left is Lerek. He's fifteen. Your two yearmates are due in this morning, and they'll go just down the hall, but right now I need to start you off with breakfast!"

"Oh, yes, please!" Tafri said, suddenly aware that he was ravenous. Adan laughed, and gestured for Tafri to follow.

Nothing loathe, Tafri closed his door and trod in the wake of his new friend. They headed down the hall toward a door in the end of it, but before they reached it, Adan unexpectedly turned aside.

There was another door here, one that opened to let another gray-clad boy out, along with a cloud of sage-scented, humid warmth. "Wash up, first, Tafri," Adan said catching the door and holding it open.

Tafri remembered not to gape, but he had never seen anything like the room he entered. Several china wash-basins were mounted on the left wall, and he wondered how they were supposed to be emptied until he realized there were pipes coming out of the bottom of each of them and leading down through the floor. There were three enormous copper bathtubs along the right wall, with more pipes running to them and a huge copper boiler next to them. And there was a swishing, watery sound as they entered and a boy emerged from one of four small doors along the back wall, heading for the basins; as the door closed behind him, Tafri got a glimpse of something and only then realized that it was one of the indoor privies—*water closets,* they were called—that only one house in his entire village had.

There were piles of snowy white towels everywhere, and boxes of pale green, soft soap. Adan rolled up his sleeves, put a bung in the hole in a basin and filled it with water from two little spigots of the sort that *he* was more used to seeing in the side of a beer-cask. Cautiously, Tafri imitated him, discovering that one spigot dispensed hot and the other cold water, and the bung kept the water from running down the pipe.

With hands and faces scrubbed, Adan showed him the chute to drop the used towels down (to *where?*) and led him to the common room.

It was just like the common room in the inn, only much bigger. There were two fireplaces, many tables and benches, and a hatch in one wall from which girls and boys, all in Trainee uniforms, were bringing steaming plates, leaving them on the tables so that those sitting there could help themselves.

Adan brought Tafri to the only table without benches around it, and the two of them took clean spoons, forks, knives, plates and bowls from stacks in the center of the table, putting them on trays.

They took their trays to the nearest table with empty places at it, and following Adan's example, Tafri helped himself. No bread-and-milk here, oh no! This was the sort of food that he imagined Sushanna ate every day for breakfast! Hot porridge with honey, dried fruit or preserves, toasted bread, scrambled and fried eggs, butter, bacon, sausage—more good things than he would ever have expected in his dreams! He stuffed himself unashamedly, while around him a babble of talk went on, none of which he understood.

When he was finally replete, he followed Adan with his dirty dishes, leaving them beside the hatch where the food had come from. He noticed then that there were perhaps a dozen Heralds eating along with the Trainees. Adan followed his glance, and shouted over the din.

"Those are all Heralds who've finished their Circuits and haven't gone back out again. The teachers have already eaten."

Tafri nodded to show that he'd heard, but Adan just shook his head and gestured to him to follow him back out into the hall.

The door shut on the noise and Adan sighed with relief. "All right, that was the common room. The girls' side is on the other side of it on the same floor. Now, we all have to do chores—well, you saw the Trainees doing the serving. There are more down in the kitchen to do the washing up, and there were some helping the Cook earlier. So, first we'll go to Housekeeper Seshel and she'll get you uniforms and set you up with your chore schedule."

Within a candlemark, Adan and Tafri were back in Tafri's room, laden with piles of clothing and other articles. By now the sun was well up, and the little room was full of light. Someone had come in to mend the fire while they were gone, but otherwise everything was as it had been when he left, including his unmade bed.

Adan *tskd* over that. "Bad form; as soon as you're out of it, they want the bed made up and neat," he told Tafri, who hastily complied. They put Tafri's new clothing away in the wardrobe, all but the boots he'd been measured for. The Housekeeper (who had, Adan confided, replaced old Gaytha two years ago but could have been Gaytha's younger twin for attitude) had deemed his new boots adequate until the ones in Trainee Gray arrived, along with some soft shoes and dress boots. Adan advised a bath before he changed into a new set of Grays, so nothing loathe, Tafri took himself and a change of clothing to the Bathing Room while Adan went on some errand of his own.

Adan was waiting for him when he emerged, hair wet and slicked back and feeling like an entirely new boy. The boots he'd been given back at the village didn't go too badly with the new Grays, being a sort of charcoal color themselves. Adan gave him a once-over and nodded satisfaction.

"There now, you look a proper Trainee. Now to Dean Teren. He'll be seeing what you know and reckoning which classes to put you in." With a wave of his hand, he beckoned to Tafri to follow. "I'll give you more of a tour on the way."

Adan was as good as his word; first they went up a floor and Tafri got a quick lecture on the Library. "This isn't the only one, but you have to get special permission to use the Palace Library, the Library at Healers' is pretty boring, the Library at Mages' is absolutely off-limits to anyone who isn't a Mage, and as for Bardic—" he shook his head "—too crowded for me."

"Mages'?" Tafri asked inquisitively as they clattered down the stairs to the as yet unseen first floor. "Is there a *Mages'* Collegium now?"

"Aye. Not very big yet. Herald Elspeth and her Hawkbrother started it a year after the Mage-Storms finished. *Mostly* it's got Heralds in it, but there's a couple of priests and some people that don't seem to be anything *but* Mages. She told the Queen that it seemed to her we were either going to have to have a Collegium for them or take our chances on what they turned into on their own." He opened the door at the bottom of the staircase for Tafri. "So they got the old Guard Barracks as soon as a new one got built. So far the teachers they've got are that old man from the Eastern Empire, the gryphons, a couple of Sun-priests from Karse, some mage that used to be with Herald Kerowyn and a couple of his friends, and Hawkbrother Darkwind."

"Gryphons?" Tafri gasped. "There's gryphons here?"

"Oh, aye, four of 'em, but you probably won't see 'em much, no more than you will the other Mage-teachers— or the Bardic and Healer teachers for that matter. They're pretty busy and *we're* pretty busy. Now this is where all the classes are—"

Adan dropped his voice in the open hall, and the drone of voices behind the many doors lining the hall showed that classes were definitely in session. Now that it was day, light for the hall came from open transoms above each door, which allowed the light from the windows of each classroom to shine into the hall.

"All our classes are held here, and we share some of them with Bardic, Healer and Mage students, and some that aren't any of those," Adan said quietly. "Those are the ones in the blue uniforms. Some of them are high-born that don't have their own tutors; the rest are here because they're really good at something, like reckoning and artificing. There's a couple here because they're really good at *teaching*. Anyway, they've all got uniforms like ours, in their colors."

"We're Grays, what are the others?" Tafri asked, as they walked quietly down the hall toward a door at the end.

"Well, Bards are scarlet, so their Trainees are sort of rust-colored. Healer-Trainees wear pale green. The Mages kind of decided to wear a golden-brown, so their Trainees are in yellow, and the students that aren't Trainees from any of the Collegia wear blue." Adan paused at the door, and turned, gesturing to Tafri to do the same. "It's almost time for class-change, so see for yourself."

Just then one of the ubiquitous bells sounded, and all of the doors on the hallway swung open. Tafri gaped at what seemed to be a horde of youngsters, mostly in Grays, but with perhaps half in uniforms of the other four colors poured out of the classrooms and milled around in the hallway. Adan grinned at him, and gestured to him to follow through the door that he held open.

The peace and quiet of the hall on the other side of the door came as a relief to Tafri's rattled nerves.

"This is Heralds' Wing," Adan told him. "This is where all the Heralds that *aren't* stationed somewhere else permanently have at least a room, and the ones that live here have suites. Like Dean Teren—he's the Herald in charge of our Collegium, and he's a teacher too. But he's always in his office the candle-mark before and after lunch."

The Dean had a suite of rooms halfway along the corridor, and Adan pushed Tafri in ahead of him through the door that was three-quarters ajar.

The Dean was a plain man who reminded Tafri of a hunting hound going a little gray; friendly, a little stiff and not quite as fast as he used to be, but still eager and enthusiastic. His warm brown eyes welcomed both of them as he gestured, inviting them to sit in his neat, tidy office.

"I can't stay, Dean, I have kitchen duty," Adan said regretfully. "But I'll be back to get Tafri for lunch if you want me to."

"No, I'll take him in," the Dean replied easily. "You can take him around after; we'll have his schedule then."

Adan left then, but Tafri couldn't feel in the least uneasy around the Dean, who questioned him carefully about all the things he'd been studying, interspersing academic questions with ones about Tafri's parents and home village. Tafri was very glad he'd been diligent in his studies, even of things he didn't much like. He thought he was able to give a pretty good accounting of himself.

Dean Teren made notes as they spoke, and when the bell rang again, he smiled at Tafri. "I think you'll be able to fit right into our schedule without having to scramble to catch up, Tafri," he said with great cheer. "Now, how about a meal?"

Lunch was much like breakfast, except for the variation in menu, and that the participants were considerably more awake. To Tafri's relief, Adan was waiting for him, and brought him over to a table at which a boy and a girl dressed in ordinary clothing sat. "These are your yearmates, Tafri," he said without preamble. "This is— Holly, isn't it? And Hadrin. Twins, in the ongoing tradition of twins at the Collegium." He winked, but it didn't seem to make the two who sat there any less nervous. "Our Dean is a twin, as are two of the Queen's Own's year-mates."

"Heyla," Tafri said diffidently, but with the confidence imbued by having *been* here for half a day already and gotten into uniform. "Where're you from?" He couldn't make out anything from their clothing; less shabby than his had been *before* he was Chosen, but if their neighbors were anything like his, they'd showered these two with gifts before they were allowed to leave.

"Hunsted," said Holly, after a pause. " 'Tis a Guard Outpost, on Hardorn Border."

"We just got here," Hadrin added—which might account for why they both looked so pinched and pale— it was with cold, probably, rather than with shyness. "Papa's with the Guard."

Tafri and Adan exchanged a wordless glance, and Tafri nodded when Adan told the twins, "Well, if you just got here, then stay where you are and thaw while we get you your plates."

With food and hot cider inside them, the twins took on a healthier color and a livelier outlook. Tafri trailed along behind as Adan ran them through the same routine he had with Tafri that morning—down to House-keeper for uniforms and chores, then up to the Trainees' floor for rooms. The only difference was that after leaving Hadrin in *his* new room, the moment Adan and Tafri appeared with Holly on the Girls' Side, a girl about his own age popped out of a door and took Holly in hand, shooing the "aliens" back to their own side as if she was shooing hens.

Adan left Tafri alone in his own room while he guided Hadrin through the intricacies of getting cleaned up, into uniform, and down to Dean Teren for evaluation. Tafri used the time to put his things away properly, including all of his gifts from home and the precious little pouch of coins that Adan had explained was his "stipend," spending money allotted to each Trainee at quarter-year intervals, so that they *all* had spending money alike. Then he stared out his window, down into a snow-covered bit of garden and across at an L-shaped building he supposed must be Healers Collegium from all the green-clad bodies going in and out.

:And how is your first day as a Trainee, Chosen?: asked Adelayan out of nowhere.

He jumped, but grinned immediately, and concentrated on *thinking* his answer rather than saying it out loud. *:If I could have Ma and Da here, it'd be pretty near perfect,:* he replied truthfully.

:If we had everyone's Ma and Da here, there'd be no room for Heralds, and no work for all the Mas and Das,: Adelayan pointed out. *:You'll be busy enough you won't miss them too much, I think. And if you get lonely—you have me.:*

Warmth filled Tafri, and a feeling of utter contentment. Because, of course, that was true, the truest and the best thing that had ever been said to him. He had Adelayan, and he *was* a Heraldic Trainee, and at some point in the distant future—well—he would be a *Herald!*

FOUR

Trying the Paces

"**S**O there you are. I'm to be your mentor—I'll show you around and if you need anything, all you have to do is come find me," Tafri said to the youngling standing uncertainly beside his new Companion in the aisle of the stable. The youngster—Rojek was his name—was unusually tall for his age (thirteen), and very thin; with his unruly puff of white-blond hair he looked like a dandelion gone to seed.

Rojek blinked eyes as blue as his Companion's, and suddenly smiled. "Guess I look like I was rode hard and put away wet," he drawled. "Thenkee, Tafri. I can use a helping hand about now."

Tafri laughed. "We all can when we first show up here," he said cheerfully. "Are you up to the work of cleaning—"

:*Civera*,: Adelayan supplied.

"—Civera?" Tafri said smoothly, without a noticeable pause, "Or are you about ready to drop?"

"Both." Rojek squared his narrow shoulders and raised his chin. "We're horse-folk, born and bred. No matter what, see to your mount afore you see to yourself."

"With a hand, then," Tafri said, and helped Rojek to take the tack off Civera (a neat-footed little mare as long in the leg as her Chosen was) and give her a good nose-to-tail grooming. Then because Rojek was clearly coming to the end of his energy, Tafri fetched one of the Companion-grooms to make sure she got a good feed, and took the latest Chosen off.

It was long after supper, but there was a cupboard especially for raiding by hungry Trainees in the kitchen, so Tafri took his charge there, watched him inhale vast quantities of ham, bread, and butter, and then took him first to the bathing room and then to the nearest empty room he could find. The poor lad was asleep before his head hit the pillow; Tafri saw to it that his room was marked and went off to find some of his friends.

As he expected, they were up in the Library, commiserating over a particularly hard assignment in History. The twins, Hadrin and Holly, had been his best friends since they all started here together, and Jisette and Borek, though one was a Blue and the other a Bardic Trainee, were from the same year-group and had gravitated toward the Heraldic trio as if they'd all been friends for life.

"I just got the new Trainee, and I need to swap kitchen duty or something with one of you," Tafri said, as soon as all four of them finished picking his brain for clues as to what Herald-Chronicler Myste wanted in their essays in the History class they all shared. He was the best of all of them at History, and he'd finished the assignment the day it was handed out, instead of waiting until the night before it was due as his friends had. On the other hand—*he* was the one who was always late on his Maths, and it was Jisette and Hadrin who had to bail *him* out of a slough of desperation. That was what friends were for, after all.

And for helping each other out when conflicts came up.

"What've you got?" Hadrin asked.

"Breakfast. Cook's Helper," Tafri told him, and Hadrin made a face, as he'd expected his friend would.

"Anything but *that*," Hadrin groaned, for Hadrin hated even the concept of "morning." "I've got scrubbing the bathing room, and I'd trade you, but not for a morning duty!"

"Well, *I* don't mind morning," Holly said—as Tafri had hoped she would, since she was a lark to her twin's owl. "But Tafri's got Orienteering right after lunch when I've got dish washing. Can we trade right around?"

That was quickly settled, much to Jisette and Borek's amusement—Jisette didn't *have* chores, as she lived in her parents' suite in the Palace itself, and Bardic didn't require anything of its Trainees that would interfere with the flexibility of their hands. So in place of things like scrubbing floors and heavy laundry, Bardic Trainees were required to put many hours in on cleaning, repairing and restoring musical instruments.

"What's this one like? Where's he from?" Borek wanted to know. Tafri quickly filled all of them in.

"Adelayan says that Rolan says that he's from one of the same horse trading clans as *his* first Herald," Tafri concluded, wondering at the coincidence.

"What—King's Own Talamir?" Holly asked. "Havens, I wonder if he's related?"

:Not really, except insofar as all of the people in the Giyano Clans are related,: Adelayan said, and Tafri relayed that as well. *:This youngling has been fostered on and off with a trading partner, though, so he hasn't the problem with being under a roof that Talamir had when he first arrived.:*

:What problem?: Tafri asked, baffled.

:Ask Myste; she was one of Talamir's pupils, she'll remember. Choose your moment wisely and you might dis-

tract her from handing out another headache of an assignment to your Bardic friend,: Adelayan said teasingly.

Well, Adelayan might think it was teasing, but Tafri thought it was an excellent idea and filed it away for future use.

Meanwhile he helped all of his friends with their assignment until Herald Myste herself came up to send them all to bed by the simple expedient of going around and blowing out all the lanterns in the Library. They weren't the only ones driven out of the study carrels, but they *were* the only ones who viewed Myste's arrival with displeasure rather than relief. When Holly made a feeble protest, the Herald tilted her head forward and looked sternly at them through the top half of the thick lenses of the divided "spectacles" she wore so she could see at all.

"Am I to assume that this plea for more time *past* your bedtime is because you failed to complete my assignment?" Myste asked with deceptive mildness.

Borek (who had *just* finished his work), clasped his hands and gazed at her out of big brown eyes he made to seem even larger, somehow. "Why—no, Herald Myste! It's just that we've gotten so fascinated by the way the negotiations with Duke Merano were handled that we wanted to see what else we could find!"

Myste's eyes narrowed behind the thick glass, but Tafri saw her mouth twitch a little. *"You,"* she told him, trying to sound stern, though Tafri could hear the laughter in her voice, "would probably find yourself hanged one day if it wasn't for Bardic immunity. As for the rest of you—the lights are going *out.* If you choose to short yourselves on sleep because you didn't get to the assignment when you should have, that's *your* choice, but you'll be doing it in your own rooms."

And with that, the plump Herald blew out the nearest lamp, forcing them to gather up their things and retreat to the staircase, trying not to giggle.

Well, at least the others were *mostly* done with their essays; it really wouldn't take more than some polishing, which could be done easily enough in their own rooms. So Tafri and Hadrin said good night to the other three on the landing; Borek and Jisette headed for Bardic and the Palace respectively, and Holly for the Girls' Side.

. All of Tafri's morning was spent in taking his charge through the same introduction to the Collegium that *he* had been through four years ago. Not that the lad was any trouble; by afternoon he'd managed to make a half-dozen new friends, and it looked as if he was going to fit right in with his year-mates as easily as a hand fitting a well-made glove.

By afternoon Tafri felt enough at ease with how the boy was doing to leave him to his own devices and do the scrubbing in the bathing room that he'd traded off his morning chore for. It wasn't his favorite thing to do, down on hands and knees, applying soap and pumice to the floor, but it was better than the other half of the job, which was applying the same substances to the bathtubs, basins, and privies.

Then, when he'd completed that job, it was time to collect his charge and take him to Herald-Captain Kerowyn for assessment in weaponry and riding. Given his background, Tafri guessed that the boy would be brilliant at the latter, and no better than anyone else his age at the former. He was right on both counts, but Herald Kerowyn, though she was fully as tough as her predecessor, Herald Alberich (who was now semi-retired), was nowhere near as frightening in appearance, and at least didn't intimidate newly Chosen into fumbling just by looking at them. She assigned the boy to Herald Jeri's section, deeming him neither so wretched that she would *have* to take him on herself, nor so good that she felt he could handle the extra attention. She and Jeri shared out the really good students in weapons, but she never let Jeri take students that were really abysmal. Tafri didn't know why—and *he* had been one of those who were really abysmal—but he was grateful.

By the time the day was over, the boy knew his way around the Collegia and had enough friends to see to it that he got to where he was supposed to be going until he knew the routine himself. At that point, unless he ran into trouble, Tafri's job as mentor was to let him be, and he did just that. After all, he had his *own* classes to attend to, and he was in his final year before his internship, so he didn't want to mess up at this late date.

This year, besides the usual weapons-class and History, he had a number of classes that were supposed to prepare him for duty in the Field. There was a complicated class in Law, one in Negotiation, a Strategy and Tactics class that (unlike the one given to officer-trainees in the Guard) concentrated on the use of *small* groups in combat. And, of course, Practical Maths; things like figuring out wall-making and bridge-building so that the walls didn't collapse at a look and the bridges didn't fall apart under the first heavy wagon. *Not* his favorite class, but he could see how it would help him out there.

Law and Negotiation were more to his liking. He didn't much care for the idea that he might actually have to *use* that Strategy and Tactics class.

But of all of them, his favorite was one held only every three days—with the intriguing title of "Magic, or Fakery?" Now that *real* magic was back in Valdemar, there were any number of folks who were playing on the fears and desires of ordinary folk by pretending to have powers they didn't. This class was supposed to help Heralds in the field figure out—and unmask—the fakers.

And it was taught by not one but a triad of teachers: the Hawkbrother Darkwind, the blind Karsite Sun-priest Ambassador Karal, and the White Winds Mage Shoshonna. Each session was about a particular power commonly claimed by mages or those pretending to be mages. Darkwind would show how it was done with *real* magic, and Shoshonna or Karal would show how it could be faked.

The fact that real magic was so much weaker since the Mage Storms actually aided the fakers, who didn't have to demonstrate any *great* powers, only small ones. Tafri had hoped he wouldn't have to skip this session to look after his charge, and it was with relief that he left the boy with his new friends and hurried over to Mages' Collegium to join the rest of his class in the late afternoon. It was a blustery early-spring day, and the wind cut through his cloak like a knife as he crossed the open ground between the two wings. He *could* have cut through the Palace, but he still felt rather diffident about doing that. And besides, it took longer that way.

He was glad he hadn't missed the class, for it was a fascinating demonstration of how a person could fake having either Mage-Gift *or* the Mind-Magic called Fetching. Karal deftly bent spoons "with his Gift," and Shoshonna made objects move on the surface of a table and appear to float in midair. All done by means other than magic, of course. Karal bent the spoon ahead of time while the class was momentarily distracted, then moved the bent portion into view so slowly that it *seemed* he was actually bending it before their eyes. And Shoshonna had taken one of her own fine hairs to make a loop she held between her thumbs—invisible at most distances, but strong enough to move small objects across the table or suspend them in the air.

Then all three of the teachers took turns in telling instances where these particular tricks had been used to intimidate or frighten others.

Frighten? Yes indeed. "I know of one case where the fake threatened to use his power to stop people's hearts if they didn't give him what he wanted," Shoshonna said, as Karal nodded.

"Indeed," the Karsite Ambassador agreed. "There were far more Sun-priests in the bad days before Solaris cleansed the Temples who faked their powers than there were those who actually *had* them. One demonstration of 'magic' and their congregations would do practically anything they wished."

The huge rust-and-white cat that never left the Ambassador's side nodded. *Now* Tafri knew that the Firecat was the equivalent of a Companion, and that Ambassador Karal literally saw through the Firecat's eyes, but when he had first seen them together it had seemed very odd that this "pet" went everywhere that Sun-priest Karal did.

After a bit more discussion, the class was dismissed, and Tafri made his way back through what was now an ice-edged wind to get to the Common Room in time for dinner. He made sure his young charge was happily ensconced at a corner table with his new friends, then sought out Hadrin and Holly.

"So what did you see this time?" asked Holly, as they all settled in together over bowls of stew that tasted very good after fighting the bitter wind.

He explained between bites. Holly couldn't wait to take this class herself; although she was no Mage, she had a fairly strong Gift of Fetching, and it fascinated her that similar effects could be produced both by real magic and trickery. Hadrin was not nearly as fascinated, perhaps because, unlike his twin, he had no really strong Gifts so the subject was still only of academic interest to him.

For that matter, Tafri didn't have a particularly strong Gift even of Mindspeech, except with Adelayan, but *he'd* been looking forward to the class since he first heard about it.

:Yes, and you are indifferent to Maths,: Adelayan pointed out later, when he discussed Hadrin's indifference to a class that was giving the Trainees a real handle on how to recognize something that Shoshonna said was a growing problem in Valdemar.

Tafri put his full weight behind the brush strokes he was giving to Adelayan's glossy flank. "Yes, but . . ." He sighed. "Look, what if someone tries to impersonate a Herald next?"

:What makes you think they haven't?: Adelayan countered. *:That's not the point, though. Your trouble is that Hadrin is indifferent to the subject, but that's because he isn't as inclined to think ahead as you are. Right?:*

Tafri thought it over and had to admit that this was the case.

:Look at his marks in Strategy and Tactics,: Adelayan pointed out. *:He's just not that good at thinking ahead. I think his sister got all the imagination that was intended for both of them!:*

Tafri had to laugh at that. "I guess that's true," he said, changing brushes to work on Adelayan's tail. "I've seen bricks with more imagination than Hadrin. But he is awfully good at Maths, and at figuring things out. . . ."

:And that's the point. Not even a Herald can be good at everything. *Right?:*

"Right." He mulled this over while he disentangled a minute knot. "So . . . the thing is that once he's had his

Internship Year—and he'll be put with a Herald who *does* have more imagination than a brick—he'll get assigned somewhere that a lack of that sort of forethought isn't a problem?"

:*Exactly. That's why we don't want any of you to hide your weaknesses. They have to be addressed, and if they can't be turned into strengths, then they have to be factored into what your assignments are.*: Adelayan nudged him affectionately. :*Which is another reason for having Companions, among many others. The primary one being, of course, that we are eminently superior beings whose place is to be worshipped and adored.*:

"Of course," replied Tafri, choking on laughter. "Of course!"

FIVE
Journey's End, and New Beginnings

For the past six months, Tafri had been riding circuit on his internship with a wily old fox of a Herald named Jonaton. Their circuit took them through farming country, rolling hills to the south and west of Haven that were dotted with small villages whose inhabitants seldom went further than the next village up or down the road during the course of their natural lives, and never saw any reason to want to. "Bucolic," was the term Jon used, with a twinkle in his eye.

Tafri had a certain amount of sympathy for their preferences; after all, if Adelayan hadn't Chosen him, he likely would never have left his own little hamlet.

Even the Mage-Storms had hardly made a mark here. The farmers and small-craftsmen were comfortable, prospering, and disinclined to stick their noses *out* of "local business." Whatever they wanted from the outside world generally arrived on their doorsteps anyway, with the advent of one of the four seasonal Faires. Spring was the first of the two Hiring Faires, bringing in an influx of new labor for house and field as laborers shook the dust of the property of one employer from their feet in hopes of finding a better one. Midsummer was a Faire more appreciated by the young—as was Midwinter, though Midwinter interfered less with a farmer's daily work. Both were nominally religious festivals, but the religious services that marked the Solstices were pretty much subsumed into celebration for all but the deeply pious. Midwinter was the Faire for children; Midsummer for the single. Autumn brought the biggest, the Harvest Faires, when livestock was bought and sold, surplus crops auctioned, and money was freer to be spent. Needless to say, these Faires did not all take place at the same time in every village—they tended to be spread out across the moon before and after the actual Solstice to enable merchants and entertainers to travel from village to village in order to fully profit.

Aside from those four seasonal punctuations, nothing much happened here. Squabbles were all petty ones. Tafri had ample opportunity to practice his skills in negotiation and to learn every nit-picking little variation on local law by heart.

For if there was one thing these people loved to do, it was argue and debate. Should a pair of farmers observe one boundary-marker that *might* have been moved by the root of a tree, it was off to the Law Courts with them, and if they couldn't settle there, then it was all saved up, savored and allowed to stew in its own juices until the Heralds came around on circuit. The smallest of changes to existing law or custom decreed by the Crown was the source of debate that went on for *days* before people grudgingly agreed to accept it.

Jon shared this burden equally with Tafri, although at first he had assigned his Internee the easiest and simplest of the cases. Mind, the easiest and simplest were not by any means the quickest to resolve; it seemed to Tafri that the more obvious the solution was, the more inclined these people were to draw out the argument as long as possible.

But they were generous in their hospitality, and cheerfully insular. They didn't go far from their home villages because they couldn't imagine anything *better* than their home villages, and didn't want to try.

If they were complacent, it was because they were protected from dangers they couldn't even guess at. And

that, Tafri had decided, was all right. There was no harm
in it if these little farmers and craftsmen, plump in their
embroidered feast-day tunics, considered themselves the
apex of civilization. They arguably produced the best
butter and cheese, the softest fleeces, the sweetest mutton, the most succulent beef, richest corn, the biggest
vegetables in the Kingdom—but they also produced
their share of brave young men and women who
marched off in the blue uniforms of the Guard to help
protect all of this pastoral richness—and even threw the
occasional Bard, Healer, and Herald.

They were in the middle of Midsummer Faire season,
at the moment, and although they seldom spent more
than a day or two in any single village, Tafri had the
feeling that they were probably going to sample every
Midsummer Faire on their circuit before they saw the
last of Midsummer Moon. He thought he knew why,
too—Faires attracted cheats and thieves as well as honest men, but the knowledge that a Herald was going to
show up at some time during the Faire could keep
crimes at the petty level.

They rode into Michelham, a peaceful little town nes-
tled in a green cup of a valley, hearing at a distance the
sounds of the Faire—the complaints of animals, for there
was always *some* buying and selling of livestock at all
four Faires, not just the Harvest Faire—distant bits of
music, mingled chatter, shouting, laughter, the screams
of excited children.

A slender but deep and swift-running stream was between them and Michelham. They crossed it on an
arched stone bridge, and on any day other than a Faire-
day, they would have been spotted long before this by
children, who would have brought word of their imminent arrival long before they made that crossing. But the
children had other concerns today than the arrival of a
couple of Heralds; it wasn't until they crossed the bridge
that someone actually saw them.

It was a curious sight—a shepherd, crook in hand,
without sheep. Easily explained of course, by the fact
that he'd brought lambs he intended to cull here, to sell
as meat on the hoof. But the look he gave them was
very peculiar.

"Eh, Heralds!" he saluted them. "Reckon ye'd best get onto the green, afore these fool townsmen get thesselves into a mort more trouble than they already bought thesselves."

And with that, he turned and walked rapidly away, as if he regretted having said anything at all.

Jon and Tafri exchanged a glance, and their Companions put their ears back and hastened their steps.

But they weren't quite quick enough to get to the village green without being intercepted.

"Herald Jonaton! Herald Tafri!" called a too hearty voice from Tafri's right. "Stop, would you?"

Both Companions halted, and the Mayor of Michelham came puffing up, out of breath and red-faced after making a sprint that was ill-suited to one of his bulk. "Well!" the Mayor said cheerfully. "Got a bit of a surprise for you. We've got no need of your services, and thank you kindly. So come and enjoy the Faire if you will, and take a holiday, or go on up the road to Fetheston."

It was plain, *very* plain, that it was the latter that the Mayor hoped they'd do. "Indeed!" Jonaton said with just as much hearty cheer as the Mayor—and just as false. "And how is it that you've managed your townsmen so well that the most wrangling lot of farmers in all the Kingdom have no need of our services? I must know! Such a revelation could ease things in every town and village from here to Lake Evendim!"

"Well—ah—" the Mayor broke out in a sweat. "You see, we've got a lad now as has a Truth Spell, but it's one as doesn't have to be *put* on anyone, if you'll take my meaning."

"Really?" Jonaton asked, eyebrows arching.

"Ah, it's always a bit off-putting, you know, to have that Spell put *on* you," the Mayor continued awkwardly. "And then to have your neighbors know you for a liar, if it shows you up—no, this is better. More *comfortable* like. Nobody gets showed up, the Spell just gives the Truth without any accusations, you understand. The lad that does it—he's quite a good Mage, and it's a wonder he isn't a Herald, he's that clever—"

"Indeed," Jonaton said dryly. "Well, let's *see* this paragon of yours! I am very eager to find out what it is he can do!"

"Um—" the Mayor prevaricated, but it was too late. The words were out of his mouth, and there was nothing for it but to take them where they asked, to a booth where a sharp-faced man was "holding court," quite as if he *was* a Herald.

They could hardly hope to remain unnoticed in their stark white uniforms and with the two Companions, so they didn't even try. And as soon as the crowd noticed they were there, people moved aside, some with guilty looks, some with curious, some clearly waiting gleefully to see what the Heralds made of their "replacement."

The man at the table gazed up at them—*not* getting to his feet—with brazen insolence. "Well, Heralds," he drawled. "You might as well go enjoy yourselves. *I* have matters well in hand here, where the law and disputation is concerned."

"So I hear!" Jonaton said, not a trace of his earlier skepticism showing. "If you've no objection, we'd like to watch! Neither of us have ever seen a different version of the Truth Spell before."

"And you won't, now," muttered a very quiet voice at Tafri's back—too low to be heard at the table.

The man waved his hand airily at them, dismissing them with a little flick of the wrist. "If it amuses you, be my guest," he said, and turned his attention pointedly and rudely back to the two people sitting in front of him.

"Now, you understand that the Spirits can't be fooled," he said sternly. "If *you*, Goodman Brell, are in the right, the pages of the Holy Book of Kernos will turn of themselves and stop at the page that your straw marks. If it is you, Herdsman, they will stop at *your* straw. Are you ready?"

Tafri didn't like the sly, smug look in the farmer's eyes, as if he already knew the verdict and was just marking time for the charade to be over. The Herdsman was nervous; *he* certainly didn't know what the result would be. . . .

The man made a few mystical passes and spoke something that sounded like (and probably was) gibberish. Then, with both hands flat on either side of the book, he gazed down at it—and the pages started to move, fluttering over, one at a time.

:I believe we've seen this before, Chosen,: noted Adelayan.

:I believe you're right,: Tafri replied. "Hold on a moment, friend!" Tafri boomed, startling everyone. "You know, this *might* just be Fetching Gift, and not a Truth Spell at all—"

"What?" gasped the Herdsman.

"So let's just make sure only the Spirits can *see* the Holy Book, for surely *they* know where to stop!"

And Tafri took an empty market basket from a startled housewife and clapped it over the top of the book.

"There now! The pages can turn freely enough in there—" he began, when the man who had been so very confident the moment before suddenly made a bolt for the back of the booth.

When it was all sorted out, the man's purse was found to be full of coin—every one of his "judgments" had been bought and paid for. And as for how the pages of the Holy Book had been turning by themselves—well, they hadn't. It had been one of the tricks Tafri had learned in that class on fakery. The man had learned how to blow hard enough on the pages of a book to turn them, but without any sign that he was doing so. A session under Truth Spell got all of that out of him, and it was very odd that no one *now* seemed to mind the Spell being "put on" anyone.

The Mayor had known, but none of the other town officials, and there was, very shortly, a new Mayor. The old Mayor and the cheat were placed in the town gaol to await the pleasure of the Town Council—it was, as Jon and Tafri both pointed out, a matter for the townsfolk themselves to decide, what was to be done with them. Then it was business as usual, with all of the grievances that the cheater had decided being heard all over again. And not surprisingly, most of his decisions were overturned.

They spent all day and most of the evening undoing what he'd done and setting right what he'd set wrong. They declined—as was proper—the hospitality of everyone, going on to the Waystation just outside of town to sleep, returning the next day and the next until all disputes were satisfied and all of the new laws expounded. For once, no one wrangled over those.

Curiously, Jonaton sat back during most of the disputes and only offered a word now and then on those he did have a hand in. And for the first time, Tafri found people looking entirely to him and not to Jon.

If he hadn't been working so hard, it would have been a heady experience. But he was so involved in disentangling every argument and getting to the heart of it that he didn't have the leisure to feel anything other than the weight of the responsibility. He knew *exactly* what Jon was about; unmasking the cheat had been exactly the thing needed to show that *he* wasn't playing second to Jonaton anymore. *He* had immediately dealt with the problem and solved it, without any intervention on the part of his Senior.

When they rode on again, after the last disputant declared himself satisfied, Tafri was too brain-tired to feel more than a weary sort of satisfaction.

"Well, lad," Jonaton said, when they were well down the road. "Disappointed?"

That was the last thing Tafri expected him to say. He turned in his saddle to stare at his Senior in surprise. "Disappointed? No, why?"

"You didn't get any thanks to speak of for unmasking the fraud," Jon pointed out. "All you got was work—"

"But—but—" Tafri gazed at him with his mouth open. "But that's what I'm *supposed* to do! If I wait around to get praised for every little thing I set right, I'd be a pretty sorry soul!"

"Sorry how?" Jon prodded.

"Because—well, when you're responsible for something, you just *do* it," Tafri spluttered. "It doesn't matter what anyone else thinks, and it *surely* doesn't matter if they make a fuss over it! As long as I'm doing a good job at it, as well as I can, that's what's important!"

He was about to go on, but Jonaton forestalled him with a kindly laugh and an upraised hand. "You'll do, youngster," was all he said. "You'll do."

And it was at that moment that Tafri realized it, what Jonaton had known for—probably—the last three days.

He *was*, well and truly, a Herald at last.

AN INTERVIEW WITH MERCEDES LACKEY

Denise Little

DL: Fans are always curious about where their favorite writers came from and how they became writers. Before we begin talking about Valdemar, can you tell us about yourself?

ML: (Laughing) I'm older than dirt. Older than you can imagine. Old enough not only to remember when Paul McCartney was in a group, not only to remember when he was in a group before Wings, not only to remember when he was in a group called "The Beatles," but to actually have seen that group in concert!

Yeah. *That* old. You can stop sniggering now.

(By the way, I was about a million feet away in the old Stockyards Arena in Chicago. I had to stand on the back of my chair to get little teeny glimpses of little teeny people on stage and you couldn't *hear* anything over the screaming, so we never knew just what they were singing. They could have been lip-syncing for all we knew. At least these days with the mega-amps you can actually hear the group you've come to see.)

Okay, maybe I'm not older than dirt; I'm fifty-one, born June 24, 1950, one day before the Korean War was declared, thereby saving my Dad from getting called back up. I'm not sure how pleased he was at my incipient arrival before then, but, boy, was he grateful the next day!

I started out as an infant and immediately set about rectifying the situation; it was no fun lying around in a crib all day, I wanted to *read,* dammit! There was a brief setback when it was discovered that I was nearsighted, but from then on it was a straight shot to books.

And the inside of a book was where I "lived" for most of my childhood and adolescence. I think I was about ten or eleven when I discovered my first science fiction book—my Dad read science fiction, and he'd left some lying around the house. Now, remember, this was back in the Dark Ages, when kids were often prevented from doing things that were good for them on the grounds that they "weren't old enough yet." I'd had to get special parental permission—actually bringing my Mom into the library *in person* (a note wouldn't do) to get a library card that allowed me to read in the "adult" sections rather than the "children's" library. (*Johnny Tremaine*, which is these days often assigned to kids in sixth or seventh grade, was considered to be "adult" material, if that gives you any idea of what it was like. And *all* science fiction was in the adult section, including Andre Norton's books). Even then I was only allowed five books at a time, and this was not enough to get me through the week during summer vacation. So I asked if I could read one of Dad's books and got permission.

The book was *Agent of Vega* by James H. Schmitz, and I was hooked. Psychic powers! Interstellar spies! Exotic worlds! The next time I got to the library I skipped right over all the biographies and historical novels and went straight for the science fiction section. I started with Andre Norton because her books had animals *and* psychic powers in them, so *Beast Master* and *Lord of Thunder* were my next two books, at which point I devoured all of Norton then went back to the beginning of the section with A for Anderson.

I wrote science fiction for myself, too, and illustrated it. I still have some of the drawings, though not the stories. I continued to write—mostly just for myself, although a couple of my things got published in the school "literary" magazine—right up through college (B.Sci., Purdue, 1972). Then real life kind of got in the way; I graduated from college right in the middle of the Nixon recession, got married, and trying to keep the bills paid was a teeny bit more important than amusing myself. I

still read science fiction and fantasy though, like crazy
(thank goodness for used book stores, which had only
just gotten started about then). I also joined the SCA,
or Society for Creative Anachronism, which I often refer
to (much to the wrath of the Authenticity Nazis) as "the
bunch of people that get dressed up like King Arthur
and hit each other with sticks on weekends." This was
back in the equally Dark Ages before there were Renaissance Faires all over the country, so people weren't
nearly as used to seeing folks in medieval garb in their
parks of a Saturday. At the same time, roughly, since
the two interests are very closely allied, I started going
to science fiction conventions in the Midwest. Meanwhile
I'd actually become Gainfully Employed as a computer
programmer. Trust me, this is relevant.

Then came the next moment that changed everything—
I got a job programming for American Airlines in Tulsa,
Oklahoma. Now, I didn't know anything about Tulsa. It
took me a while to find the SCA down here, and the
SCA events and SF Conventions were a lot farther apart
and fewer than they were up North. So I had time on
my hands and began to write again.

By this time I had discovered fanzines, and I had already started publishing costuming articles in them. So
I decided to start submitting stories to some of the ones
that were for fan fiction. Then I started writing original
stuff and submitting it, and that started to see print.

Then (next pivotal moment) I discovered filk. Filk is
science fiction folk music. There are entire websites devoted to filk, so I won't get into it here—but the point
is that I started writing lyrics and hooked up with Teri
Lee of the (then) Off Centaur Publications and started
getting my song lyrics published. And it occurred to me
that I might just be ready to try getting my stories professionally published. I had a book in the works—one
that later turned into the Arrows trilogy—but I knew
that it was in no way ready to be seen. My first submission, which was to Marion Zimmer Bradley's *Sword and
Sorceress* anthology, was rejected, but I got great advice
from her, rewrote half the story and sold it to *Fantasy
Book Magazine*. But not before I sold her my second

submission, for her *Friends of Darkover* anthology, which was my first sale (although it was not my first published story, since the magazine came out before the book did).

About this time, C.J. Cherryh discovered filk, which is how I met her. She became my mentor and helped me whip that book—"commit trilogy," she said—into shape. And the rest, as they say, is history. And at that point, I stopped having a life for a while. I would get up, go to work, come home, and write until midnight or later, then go to bed and start all over again. There are entire sections of popular culture from that period that I know nothing about. Didn't go to movies, stopped doing SCA stuff, didn't watch TV. The only time I went to science fiction conventions was to promote my own work. And the hard work started to pay off.

Along the way, Tony Lackey and I parted company, but it was an amicable divorce as such things go.

Meanwhile, I worked my butt off until I finally got to the point where I was able to make a living at writing. This is unusual; most writers—about ninety percent of them—have to keep their "day job" and write in their spare time, unless they are lucky enough to have a partner working full-time to support them. Writing is a precarious business, and there is no magic way to figure out what is going to be popular and what isn't. Sacrificing all your free time to getting the words on the page, though, will help.

About this time I met and eventually married Larry Dixon, who has been my writing partner, not only on the books where he is the credited co-author, but on many others besides.

Now we live outside of Tulsa, and I have a life outside of writing again. We have a collection of very vocal parrots, we rehabilitate injured birds of prey, I do cross-stitch, beadwork, sewing, and costume dolls, often sending my work to charity auctions, especially ones to benefit the Alex Foundation, Dr. Irene Pepperberg's nonprofit foundation to help support her research into parrot intelligence and learning, which has significant application in helping learning-disabled children. I must admit that it is very nice to be able to go see a movie or watch a TV show again! I still don't have a horse, odd as that might seem, but the birds do keep me busy, and it's seldom quiet around here.

I love what I'm doing; it's an extraordinary thing, to be able to do what you love for a living. I have absolutely no plans to stop, ever. I just hope that people continue wanting to read what I have to write for as long as I'm able to write it!

DL: Did you plan to become a writer when you were a child? And when and how did you make the transition from amateur to professional?

ML: I suppose when it comes down to it, I was a writer all along. Once I discovered science fiction I devoured everything I could find, but I quickly ran out of books to read—and, as I said before, this was in the days before the big chain bookstores, and most of my reading material came from the library or used book stores. So when I ran out of things to read, I wrote my own, mostly spin-offs of Andre Norton's books. Later I took some creative writing lessons one-on-one from one of my professors at Purdue (otherwise known as "English Literature Independent Studies," which I rated because I was an honors student) who was also a science fiction fan. I kept scribbling at odd moments, but the real impetus to write came when I discovered that there was such a thing as fan fiction—that there was a possible audience for what I was writing. Mind, I generally wrote "original" fan fiction—stuff not based on anything already published by a professional, rather than, say, Darkover fan fiction.

The next impetus for my writing, as I said, came when I began writing song lyrics—mostly about books. Through the songs I met C.J. Cherryh, who became my mentor and got me over the hump by putting me through seventeen rewrites of my first trilogy (which started out as a single book). Between C.J. Cherryh's coaching and Marion Zimmer Bradley's encouragement (not to mention her purchase of some of my first short stories for her anthologies) I finally got to the point where I sold my first three books to Elizabeth Wollheim at DAW.

DL: Was Valdemar something that existed in your mind before you became a writer, so that you became a writer to tell those tales? Or were you a writer first?

ML: I was definitely a writer first—I think I started writing when I was eleven or so. Valdemar just happened to be a big enough concept to become the basis for a lot of books—like Anne McCaffrey's Pern, or Marion Zimmer Bradley's Darkover.

DL: Is Valdemar a creation that grows as you write it? Does it take turns that surprise you? If so, what were they?

ML: Oh, it definitely grows as I go along, but I made sure I wasn't writing myself into any corners when I first started the series. I've always viewed it as being an entire world, with its own history, that I've just come into at some point in the middle. I can't say that it's actually surprised me, because I've always worked from the "what if" philosophy of plotting—if you ask that question enough times, you get a good plot. As I've written the books, it's as if the world has unfolded before me, sometimes in ways that I hadn't anticipated, but that were logical when they started to unfold . . . if that makes any sense.

DL: The Valdemar books span a fairly wide range of cultures and civilizations. Many of them have echoes in our own history. What kind of research do you do when you are shaping the various civilizations (or lack thereof) in Valdemar?

ML: I don't actually do research as such; when I'm coming up with a new culture or civilization I use things I've already read (and continuously ask that so-useful question "what if)." I'm a voracious reader, as you've probably already figured out, and there's no telling what is going to go into the mix.

DL: What sorts of things have you plucked from this world to place in Valdemar?

ML: Well, the Shin'a'in are a combination of Plains Indian and Mongols, the Haighlei are a combination of the great African empires and the Japanese, the Karsites are part medieval German and part Moslem, with a Babylonian religion.

DL: Where do you get the ideas for some of the more original and unusual aspects of your worlds?
ML: (Grinning) I belong to the idea-of-the-month club. Every month you get a packet offering the Idea, two Alternates, and a selection of previous ideas. But you have to remember to send that little card back with your preferences, or you could end up with the wrong genre, like all the ideas that romance writers have been using.

Seriously, it's that big question "what if?" that drives everything. I just keep asking it until I come up with an interesting answer.

DL: Do you have favorite time periods and characters that you like to concentrate on, or are your characters— like children—all beautiful in the eyes of their creator?
ML: Oh, I never write about anything I don't enjoy! The reason why I move around in the history and geography of this creation is so that I don't get stale, more than anything else.

DL: Valdemar has had both great heroes and heroines, and some remarkable villains. Which are more fun to write—the good guys or the bad guys? How do you balance these characters so that neither the forces of good nor evil overpower the world you've created?
ML: Well, that's the whole point, isn't it? Good and evil have to be kept in balance. Heroes are to a certain extent defined by their enemies. That's why a book is planned and plotted very carefully before the writing ever begins.

That said, although I do like my good guys, I find the villains very cathartic. They enable me to vicariously do a lot of socially unacceptable things—at least on paper!

DL: One thing that stands out in the series is the fact that almost every character has a recognizable voice and a strong and understandable motivation for his actions, even the villains. It's one of your great strengths as a writer. How do you go about creating characters to achieve this?

ML: Well, I sometimes start with the basic situation that the character is going to have to face; then I try and figure out what kind of a person would be most interesting in the situation. This, of course, often involves developing someone who gets mountains dumped on him on a regular basis. Sometimes I start with the character, and try to figure out what sort of situations would bring out the best and worst in that character. This also results in mountains being dumped on said character.

DL: The series has evolved over time, with the focal points of the books changing. How do you decide, when you start a new thread for the series, who to use as a focal character?
ML: Well, after all the books so far, part of the answer is "what kind of person haven't I written about yet?" I don't want to get repetitious, after all!

DL: In a related question, the timeline for Valdemar as we know it from information in the books runs for roughly fourteen hundred years, with a thousand year timeline of the world of Velgarth before that, since the Mage Wars decimated the planet. We've heard intriguing bits of myth and history from throughout Valdemar and Velgarth's past. With all that vast canvas to choose from, how do you pick where and when to start a book or a series, and how do you decide when to drop a particular thread for the time being and concentrate on something else?
ML: Long question, short answer. When I think I'm getting stale, it's time to do something else!

DL: Are we going to see stories from areas of the timeline that you haven't yet explored, like Valdemar's founding, or is there so much to tell in the times and places you're already involved in that it's hard to range through new ground?
ML: Right at the moment, I haven't thought past the next two books, both Arrows prequels, one about Skif, the other about Alberich. For all I know, I may go back to the Mage Wars.

DL: How do you keep all the times, mythologies, relationships, characters and so on that you've developed through so many books on Valdemar organized when you write? Is it hard to keep all the data straight, or have you got a system to make it easier?

ML: I reread the relevant books and take notes—but we do have a plan to eventually get most of the books on a CD with a search program! It's really quite hard to keep it all straight at this point, with so many books involved, and I do make mistakes!

DL: What was the easiest book you've written, what was the toughest, and why?

ML: The easiest are the Tarma and Kethry books—because they are just pure fun. The toughest were the Storms books—I don't handle huge casts of characters very comfortably, I'm afraid, and although I like reading about great epic battles and so forth, I'm not very apt with them.

DL: Magic use in the world of Valdemar has changed radically from the time of Vanyel to the time of Elspeth. In addition, it varies strongly from culture to culture, as in Karse and Rethwellen and Valdemar. Even closely related cultures, like the Shin'a'in, the Tayledras, and the Kaled'a'in, have strong differences in their approach to magic. And the world itself was nearly decimated by the Cataclysm at the end of the Mage Wars, and reverberations from that war are currently getting stronger, to the point of threatening the whole world once more. Given all the ways you've presented magic use, it clearly is something central to this universe, and the ability to manipulate it matters greatly to the basic story lines. Is magic something you use in an allegorical sense, or is all this variation strictly a storyteller's device? Was this something you had in mind from the beginning of writing the series, or was it something that evolved as you wrote the books?

ML: Magic is both a storyteller's device and an allegorical object—I try to make everything serve at least two purposes, and possibly more. It definitely evolved as I went along, though, I can tell you that!

DL: Did the idea of Companions really come to you in a dream?

ML: Argh! Much as I hate to say this, yes! Now, with that, here's the caveat; it was a dream-fragment, and there was a lot of work between that fragment and the finished product.

DL: Nonhuman characters play an important part in this world, and on an equal basis with the human characters. They've got their own societies, some of which interact with humans, some of which don't. I always enjoy that aspect of your work. What drives that for you—especially since it's done to a much greater extent than in classic fantasy? And where can I find a bunch of hertasi?

ML: I've always loved nonhumans, aliens of all kinds; my background is in biology, and to a certain extent biology is destiny. Things that wouldn't matter to a mammal are going to be very important to a reptile! That gives another twist to motivations. For what it's worth, I've been looking for *hertasi* myself! I'm a wretched housekeeper, and by and large an indifferent cook. I really need about six of the little guys to take the cleaning and cooking off my back.

DL: Do you have a message that you feel is central to your writing?

ML: Compassion and personal responsibility.

DL: The power of relationships to both heal and destroy those involved in them is a theme that recurs throughout your fiction. Is that simply a storyteller's choice, or is it something deeper and more personal?

ML: That comes from fifty years of pure observation. Do a little arithmetic and you'll see I was there for the worst and best of the 1960s and 1970s. If ever there was a time to see people trying everything possible in relationships, that was it.

DL: You've tackled a number of different issues in your work—everything from saving the environment to responsible pet ownership to overcoming prejudice to allowing people to make their own emotional and sexual choices without judging them. Does the story bring on the message, or does the message bring on the story? And how have your fans responded to these elements in your work?

ML: I don't think it's possible to separate story from message in really good fiction—if you try, you end up with no message at all (which is just candy-fluff writing, pure self-indulgence), or nothing but message (which is boring). I do think that readers respond positively when you aren't preaching at them, but giving them examples of why something does or doesn't work.

DL: You have a lot of outside interests that have found their way into the world of Valdemar—rehabilitating raptors, composing and singing original music and filking, and so on. Can you tell us a bit about the activities you pursue in the real world, and how they power your fiction?

ML: I don't think they power the fiction, but they do contribute to it, since they make the story and the world that much richer. The more "real" you can make the setting, the better! Right down to the bugs, if necessary—remember poor Frodo and Sam being swarmed by midges?

My big hobbies at the moment are raptor rehabilitation, my pet birds, beadwork, doll-costuming, and needlework.

DL: Several of these interests have sparked some fairly large scale "cottage industries," like your songs and the artwork from the books. Can you tell us a little bit about how that evolved?

ML: The songs actually started because I found it useful to write lyrics of my own about pivotal moments in the first books, and my good friend Teri Lee was kind enough to make albums out of them. Since then, the demand has been high enough that more people have been doing the songs, which I think is pretty nifty. As for the artwork, well, I think Larry Dixon is just brilliant, but I'm prejudiced.

DL: Is it odd, thinking about how your words can impact the lives of people you've never met, and sometimes even

*change them completely? Do you think about things like
that when you're writing, or do you tell your stories and
let the chips fall as they may?*
ML: I can't write about personal responsibility and not
try and live by it—I definitely do think about it and
make conscious decisions about what I write and how I
write it for that very reason.

*DL: I've been watching your career since your first book
was published, and have been pleased to see your rise
through the ranks to become one of the bestselling fantasy
writers working today. Is it still a shock and a delight to
see your name on a bestseller list?*
ML: Totally astonishing. Completely amazes me. I still
don't believe it, not deep down inside.

*DL: How has your success as a writer changed you and
your writing?*
ML: I hope it's made me very careful to try to come up
with the best possible book that I can, every time, and
to keep improving. I may not always succeed, but by
heaven, I do try.

*DL: How do you feel your writing has evolved through
time?*
ML: I hope it's improved, for one thing—I hope that
I'm learning how to handle complicated casts and plots
that I couldn't do years ago. One of these days I might
be able to manage an epic!

*DL: You've got some amazing fans, and a very organized
fandom, with several officially sanctioned fan clubs.
You've been remarkably involved with and accessible to
these fans. Can you tell us a little about how that evolved,
what the rules are, and what it looks like from your point
of view?*
ML: Well, I've tried to put the emphasis on the work
and not on the writer. The fan clubs have always been
for the fans to have fun in, not for me to get ego-boosts
from or set myself up as some sort of guru. That said,
if people wanted to play being Heralds, who are exceptionally self-sacrificing, I didn't feel as if they should just

put on a white outfit and say "I'm a Herald." I felt they needed to do some work to earn that status. Anne McCaffrey had set up a standard in her Weyrs where people had to earn points by writing and art to earn a dragon, and I just carried it a bit farther—after all, not everyone is a good writer or artist, but we can all go pick up trash on the highway. With that basic setup, it all just managed to proliferate by itself. Pretty amazing from where I sit.

DL: What's a typical day in your life like?
ML: A typical day is actually kind of boring—I start by feeding the birds; if I've got rehab babies, it's time for the first of four hand feedings, otherwise I make rice and veggies for the pets. Then I answer email, do some basic chores, run errands, then settle in for work. Around 8 P.M. I quit to give every bird an evening cuddle, watching TLC, Discovery Channel, History Channel, or something similar. Then it's back to work until bedtime.

Of course, the work itself is pretty exciting, and there's always the occasional wild bird crisis to enliven the week, especially in springtime—and I also do radar-reading in tornado season for the local Emergency Management office.

DL: I've always enjoyed hearing about your house—it's such a wonderful story. Can you share a bit of your odyssey in finding it and living in it with your fans?
ML: We needed a house, but what we need is not exactly what your ordinary family needs. We didn't need to be in a good school district, for instance. So we looked at a lot of odd buildings—old churches, a Moose lodge, an earth-sheltered house built into the top of a hill. Finally we found this thing—it's a two and a half story concrete dome with an octagonal wooden shell over it to make it look more like a normal house. There's a lot of living room, fairly small bedrooms, and of course it's round with curved outer walls, which makes placement of furniture kind of awkward. Larry went to see it first, then he brought me out to have a look at it just at the moment of a partial solar eclipse, which was pretty neat. When

we walked into the living room, there was a barred-owl feather right in the middle of the floor, and we rather took it as an omen.

It's not the easiest house to live in, but it's different! The acoustics in the living room are pretty weird; people in the loft sound as if they're right behind you. We've got a flock of geese and ducks, bantams and guinea fowl to take care of the ticks, and two peacocks outside, and of course our pet flock of parrots and cockatoos. We also have two big outside cages for rehab birds, all on six and a quarter acres with a small pond and a big garage.

DL: What's the best thing about being a writer? And the toughest thing?
ML: The best thing is being able to make a living doing something you love. The toughest thing is to stay focused and self-motivated.

DL: You've always done a great deal of collaborative work from the very beginning of your career. Can you tell us a little bit about that as it impacts Valdemar, and also about what makes sharing worlds interesting to you?
ML: The only person I share Valdemar with is Larry, and that's because I feel very possessive about this particular series. It helps a lot, though, because it's always good to have another opinion on things besides my own. It's very easy to get mono-focused on something and go overboard on it, or not give enough attention to something that really needs it.

DL: You've had some interesting mentors in your life as you've evolved as a writer. Could you talk a little about the people who've helped you professionally and personally?
ML: The big three writers are Marion Zimmer Bradley, C.J. Cherryh, and Andre Norton. Andre was my big inspiration and influence from the very beginning. Marion was the one who gave me my early sales and encouragement, and C.J. Cherryh was the one who gave me the critique I needed to get over the hump of amateur writing into professional-quality writing. And of course Elizabeth (Betsy) Wollheim is an ace editor! She's been the

editor on every Valdemar book. I don't think I could have gotten where I am without them all.

DL: What are you proudest of about your body of work? And do you have any scenes or stories you'd like to do over?

ML: I'm proudest of the fact that people have found something in the books that speaks to them. But as for doing things over—given a chance, I'd probably rewrite everything I've written but that's always the case. If you ever get satisfied with what you've done, you're dead.

DL: What are you working on now, and what can the fans look forward to in the future, to the best of your ability to predict it?

ML: After the two prequels to the Arrows books, one about Skif and the other about Alberich, I plan on doing another series, set in the "present" Valdemar, taking a youngster through the Collegium as it is now. I'd like to get back to the gryphons, and to Darian Firkin and the k'Valdemar Vale.

DL: Do you have any advice, based on your own experience, that you'd like to give to aspiring writers?

ML: The only way to become a writer is to write. Don't talk about it; glue your behind to the chair and write, at least four pages every day, even if you end up throwing them out. If you can't make the time, you aren't a writer. You have to motivate yourself; no one else can do that for you. If you can't do that, you are never going to be a writer. Write until you've finished a book, then send it out and write another one. And keep doing it until someone buys one. It's just that simple.

DL: You read a lot—what kinds of things do you read, both fiction and non-fiction? Can you share some of your favorite writers when you're reading for fun?

ML: Well, when I'm reading for research, obviously I read things about the culture and/or time period that my books are using. For instance, in the past I have read quite a bit about Native Americans, the Osage tribes in particular; Victorian medicine; Renaissance Venice;

Victorian and Edwardian domestic life; the Suffragist movement in the United Kingdom; medieval Germany; gypsies; serial killers and stalkers; Edwardian London; medieval Russia and Russian myth. Right now I have a backlog of books for current and future projects that include a great deal of Arthurian writings; more about the United Kingdom in the period of 1910-1920; World War I flying aces; Elizabeth I; Hypatia of Alexandria, John Chrysostom; Savannah, Georgia, in the 1950s; New York in the 1920s; pre-Columbian Indian culture around Ahokia; Germany in the 1930s and 1940s; Nazi occultists; the English countryside in the 1920s around Devon; English stately homes. . . .

Okay, that's research. Now for hobbies, of course, I read all manner of books on needlework and beadcraft, sewing and costuming.

For fun—well, I kind of go all over the map. Dorothy L. Sayers, Saki, P.O. James, Edith Wharton, Judith Tarr, Elizabeth Peters, Rudyard Kipling, Barbara Hambly, Roberta Gellis, Wilkie Collins, Katherine Kurtz, Arthur Conan Doyle, Robert Heinlein, Holly Lisle, Spider Robinson, F. Scott Fitzgerald, Patricia Wrede, Anne McCaffrey, Elizabeth Ann Scarborough, James H. Schmitz, C. S. Lewis, Maud Hart Lovelace, Joanna Rowling, Andre Norton. . . . I'm a dangerous person in a bookstore.

DL: Most writers were voracious readers before they became writers, and that's clearly the case with you. What writers do you feel formed your view of what fantasy and SF should be?
ML: Oh, right off the bat, James H. Schmitz and Andre Norton, the first two science fiction writers whose works I ever read. I think when it comes right down to cases, the roots to almost everything I write can be traced back to the influence of those two writers, with maybe some Arthur Conan Doyle and a few fairy tales thrown in.

DL: When you invented the Mage Wars, were you thinking of some of Earth's manmade disasters (global warming, nuclear weapons, pollution, the depletion of the ozone layer), and echoing them in Valdemar?

ML: Of course! Absolute power corrupts and makes selfish, and all that.

DL: The political sphere in Valdemar is a bit of an idealized one, thanks to the vetting of its rulers by Companions. But palace intrigues still find their way into the books, even in Valdemar, and especially in Valdemar's neighboring nations. In the Winds series, the Mage War crisis seems to be forcing politics to the fore, as all the various societies have to cooperate to deal with its repercussions. It's high drama and it sheds a lot of light on the world of Valdemar, but it's also extremely difficult to write—a big cast of characters, multiple viewpoint writing, lots of back story and varied settings, and an epic scale for some of the scenes. It's ambitious, to say the least. How did you decide to write this story, and did its scope scare you as you sat down to begin it?

ML: Oh, heavens—I have never felt comfortable with "Big Picture, Cast of Thousands" epics. The scope kind of crept up on me, and I am still not happy with my work in it. I don't feel that I did the job adequately, and I'm not sure I ever could, even if I took years to write the things. I am much more at home with a more intimate cast of characters—where there may well be a Big Epic Struggle involved, but the real story is how a couple of characters deal with it and their lives as they live through it. Mind, I suppose with practice I'll grow better and happier about writing that sort of thing, but it still is not the place where I'm the most comfortable.

DL: Family and friendship are the backbone of all of your Valdemar books, so I'd guess they are very important to you as well. Is that so? Could you tell us a little about your family life growing up? And do you mine that vein when you're writing Valdemar, or do you tend to work more with a composite of your own experiences along with everybody else's that you've ever read or heard about?

ML: I had a disgustingly normal childhood, with the sole exception that I was a plain, brainy nerd-chick and didn't fit in anywhere, especially with the popular crowd who of course thought I was hilarious to pick on. My big fantasy was that some day a UFO would land in the courtyard of the high school, the space aliens would pick ME to go with them, and everyone else would just have to watch in awe. Either that, or I'd become an astronaut or a famous scientist and the former jocks and princesses would see me on television. Or else I'd write a book that went to the top of the bestseller lists for a year, and I'd be rich and famous. Guess I'll have to settle for writing some decent books and having some of the greatest fans in the world—seems like a pretty fine life to me!

My parents are great, my little brother was no more of a pain in the rear than any other little brother. I hated high school, and what else is new for a plain, brainy nerd-chick? I did have a few good friends, a couple pen pals who were a lot like me, and when I got to college I had a darned good time (maybe a little too good for my grades' sake!).

I think, on the whole, I tend like any other writer to use everything that's around me, run it through my head, and turn it into stories.

DL: Vanyel's story is a favorite one of mine, because he cared so deeply for his country, because he sacrificed so much and so long to save it, and because he struggled so with his identity. In addition to its much-deserved commercial success and critical acclaim, this series was one of the first in the genre to feature a gay character whose sexuality was not the primary focus of the plot. The Magic books are important to the gay community for a lot of reasons, not least because they provide a strong, positive role model for people who've discovered that they are gay. Those books were written fairly early in your career, and you had to worry that they'd be controversial. How did you get the idea for the character of Vanyel? Did you set out to write a story with a gay character, and invent Vanyel; or did you discover, writing the outline for the story, that he was gay? Once you knew what you were getting into, did the thought of writing his story give you pause? And did you have any trouble when the time came to pitch the series to your publisher? In your opinion, how do Vanyel's sexual preferences and experiences fuel his development as a character?

ML: Okay, now first of all, I really need to point out that Samuel Delaney and Marion Zimmer Bradley among many others in the science fiction field had already established positive gay role models in their works. Gail Baudino and Elizabeth Lynn were taking things a lot further than I was, and of course there was Anne Rice's Vampire series, which was topping the charts. Now, actually the genesis of Vanyel was that Elizabeth Wollheim read the first submitted manuscript of the Arrows books (which was about the seventeenth rewrite) and wanted more magic in it, right at the beginning. I didn't want any magic in it, not "real" magic, I just wanted the psychic magic. So, to make her happy, I had Talia reading about some vague legend in the past that had "real" magic in it—that was Vanyel, and for some reason I made him gay.

I finished the Arrows books, and the next logical thing to do was to take my Tarma and Kethry stories, which I had written for an obscure magazine, and turn them into a book. Two books, actually. Then, well, I went back and looked at the Arrows books, I thought about what Katherine Kurtz was doing in her series, going back into the Deryni history, and it seemed logical to work with the character who'd lived at the time that "real" magic vanished from Valdemar and explain why it vanished. From that point, knowing that the character was gay, I decided that I wanted to work with him in such a way that he was a sympathetic character that just happened to be gay, rather than making being gay the focus of his character—because, when you come down to it, that's the way real people are. And being a subversive sort, I decided that I wanted to sneak his sexual orientation in on people—so what readers first got was a kid who is completely misunderstood by his father, who is picked on by his siblings, who is being forced into a life he is totally unsuited for, then sent off to a place where he's a total stranger. And then, nearly a third into the book, when readers are pretty well hooked and engrossed in his story and maybe beginning to identify with him, they find

out—along with him!—that he's gay. Surprise! And it has
come as a surprise to a lot of people to discover that gay
people are . . . people. That was the reason why I wrote
Vanyel the way I did—less for the sake of the gay readers
(although that was a factor), but for the sake of the ones
who weren't. I wanted people who didn't (consciously)
know anyone who was gay to realize that sexual preference
has very little to do with the worth of a person as a person.
By the way, it worked. I got a fair number of letters (and
still get them now and again) from people who opened
their minds and hearts because of those books. Best of all
were the ones who, because of Vanyel, reconciled with
brothers and sisters who'd come out of the closet.

Fortunately, my publisher already had a science fiction
series with a gay lead character in it (Marion Bradley's
Darkover series) and she didn't have any problem with
Vanyel. In fact, I left my Lambda Award with Betsy
Wollheim for her to display in her office for the first
couple of years after I won it because of her support for
the series. I figured she deserved it as much as I did.

Van's sexual orientation doesn't have as much to do
with what he is and becomes as some readers (and even
he) think. If you look at Lavan Firestorm, he's a similar
character in a similar situation. Both of their stories are
more about misfits who acquire great power and use it
responsibly than they are about sexual preference, which
is just one aspect of very complicated characters.

*DL: Most of the major heroic characters in the Valdemar
books come onstage as children, and grow up before our
eyes. Clearly, since you deal well with adult characters,
this is a choice on your part. Why do you do it, and what
do you think it adds to your fiction?*
ML: I like having characters develop and change, and
the most active time for development and change is from
the age of ten to around twenty. Fully adult characters
have to be forced into change; adolescents flow into it
naturally. And characters that change are a lot more
interesting for a reader.

*DL: In the character of Ma'ar, you've essentially followed
a single villain's rather strange path down through the*

*ages—his terrible actions and the destruction they leave
behind. Why did you choose to use a serial villain, so to
speak, and how did you decide what his incarnation
would be in each time period of your Valdemar books?*

ML: Larry helped me develop Ma'ar out of Falconsbane,
and it seemed to both of us that someone who was that
powerful and that evil was not going to settle for a single
lifetime, and would wrest some sort of serial incarnation
out of the universe—to the detriment of all concerned.
After that decision, the character followed logically. His
own logic, granted, but it was logical.

*DL: Speaking of villains, how did you come up with the
idea to reclaim the identity of one of the people subsumed
by the villain, and thereby develop a sort of spy in the
villain's mind? For what it's worth, I thought that was a
staggeringly original approach to the problem of understanding the villain's motivation.*

ML: At some point, given that Ma'ar was only following
a bloodline, it would have to happen that one of the
takeover victims would not only have the willpower to
resist, but would be worthy of "divine intervention." It
was Ma'ar's mistake to use, not a magic spell that could
only be selfish in intention as a trigger, but a simple
spell, that of calling fire. Granted, this would enable
Ma'ar to take a victim when the victim was relatively
young, but it also meant that sooner or later he'd claim
an innocent. Actually, Ma'ar probably claimed a lot of
innocents, but eventually he got one whose deity took a
rather more active part in the material world than
most—and at that point, Ma'ar was in big trouble, and
didn't even know it. (And there is nothing more satisfying to a writer than pulling off the downfall and destruction of a truly abominable villain in a clever and
logical fashion).

*DL: You've talked about what it took to become a full-
time writer. How tough was it, giving up five years of
your spare time to write?*

ML: Very tough. I wrote every waking moment I wasn't
working. I'd get up early and write before work, and on
my lunch break, then I'd come home and write while I

ate dinner, write until bed, and then I finally went to sleep. On weekends I wrote without a break. The only breaks I took were to go to science fiction conventions to promote my books, or visiting C.J. Cherryh to work on my books with her guidance. Even when I visited my parents over holidays I wrote. (I still do.) I wrote when I was sick, when I was recovering from a spinal operation, on holidays, on my birthday. If you want something badly enough, you make sacrifices for it, and I wanted to become a full-time writer that badly.

DL: Sometimes genre fiction is "ghettoized" by critics and academics. Although this has noticeably improved in recent years, it's still a problem. If you had a chance to explain and defend Valdemar to a bunch of these naysayers, what would you say to them?
ML: I wouldn't bother, frankly, because I'm in no position to make a judgment, and they have already made theirs and aren't going to change their minds. In the end, it all comes down to this: whether something outlives its maker (and quite frankly, I would rather that I had another century before anyone was in a position to find that out!). In their time, Rudyard Kipling, Arthur Conan Doyle, Jules Verne, H. G. Wells, Aldous Huxley, Mark Twain, the Brontës, Dorothy Sayers, Jane Austen, and countless others were dismissed as genre fiction writers, or as hacks. Their work has survived to be read and loved long past their own lifetimes. And countless more were dismissed as hacks whose works were forgotten. Meanwhile, writers who were lauded to the skies by critics have been utterly and completely forgotten. (If you want to prove this to yourself, go take a look at really old reviews from the turn of the century and try to find even a mention of some of those writers now.)

The best defense is survival. If I've got what it takes, the work will survive, and if it doesn't, well, hey, the critics will have been right! In either case, I won't be in a position to worry about it!

DL: You took writing courses in college. I did, too, and had to unlearn virtually everything I learned in college to write successful commercial prose. (Admittedly, I went to

*a pretty snotty college, so my experience may be atypical.)
Do you feel that your writing experience in college was
useful, and have you any words of wisdom for young
writers searching for a good writing program when
they're headed to college?*

ML: The "writing course" that I took was pretty unusual; it was a one-on-one with a professor in the English department at Purdue University (note: this was a
science/agriculture/engineering college—not a hotbed of
Literary Activity!) who was already a science fiction fan.
His sole advice and help was to show me how to analyze
the books I liked, take them apart and see what made
them work, and try to apply that to what I was trying
to write.

Writing courses at the college level have got to be
evaluated individually, but from what most people have
told me about their own experiences, I would say that
you would be better off to invest the money in a Clarion
workshop or something of the sort. Failing that, look for
books about writing fantasy, science fiction, and other
genre fiction by popular writers OF those genres. If you
are in a writing class taught by someone with utter con-
tempt for the genre in which you plan to write, you are
obviously going to be wasting your time at the best, and
may be setting yourself back, emotionally and in your
craft.

*DL: Do you have a favorite book or series among the
Valdemar books?*
ML: *By The Sword.* I love Kerowyn. She's got chutzpah.

*DL: For new fans, how would you recommend they ap-
proach the books—in the order they were written, or in
the order of Valdemar's chronology?*
ML: It's probably best to start with the Arrows books,
but after that, it doesn't matter until you get back to the
Winds books. Winds and Storms should be read in order,
I think.

*DL: You've hinted pretty strongly that most Companions
are reincarnated heralds in a spirit form. It's one of the
things that fans talk to death whenever and however they*

get together. Are we ever going to get deeper into who and what Companions are? A sort of creation myth and history, from the Companion's point of view? Or a Companion's Hall of Fame? Or will it all remain a bit of a mystery?

ML: Hinted? HINTED? Okay, folks, for the last time. Grove-born Companions are the equivalent of archangels— i.e., they never were human. Regular Companions are recycled Heralds. When a Herald dies, he's usually got four choices: come back as an ordinary person or Healer or Bard (no past-life memory), come back as a Herald (no past-life memory), come back as a Companion (past-life memory) or go on to the Havens (Bermuda) in which case you can always choose to come back as Herald or Companion after you get tired of sitting on the beach and drinking Piña Coladas. Companions have the same choices. Van, Stef, and Yfandes got another option, to come back as a bunch of trees, but that was an unusual case, and eventually they all went to Bermuda anyway. For the record, Stef prefers Mai Tais to Piña Coladas, and Yfandes goes for Bailey's Irish Cream.

Having totally destroyed my own mythos . . . I think it would be just too difficult to do the Companion point of view; I don't have a lot of experience in the angelic viewpoint. Haven't found any reputable sources, either (grinning).

DL: Do you have any tricks to help you deal with writer's block, or is that something that doesn't trouble you?

ML: I work on something entirely different until the reason for the block becomes clear. That's the reason why *Elvenblood* has taken so long. The book as outlined just wasn't working and wasn't going to work. Andre and I got together and changed it, and got it done.

DL: I'm glad to hear that we'll get a Collegium novel— the various guilds and divisions in Valdemar fascinate me. This was something you came up with very early on—it was present in the Arrows books. How did you decide what specialties to include when you set up the system back as a beginning writer?

ML: Well, all I can say is, they're in some part based on

real-world medieval history and in part on what seemed logical to me at the time.

DL: Do you ever struggle with rules or history or whatnot that you've put into early work, and that now limits you as you're working on a current book? If that's been the case, can you give an example, and tell us how you solved the problem?

ML: The biggest problem was finding a reason why there was no real magic in Talia's Valdemar, and then creating a way to get it back. Problems generally create books as long as you set your mind to asking questions instead of seeing blockages in the road.

DL: I've seen Valdemaran dream cast lists floating around the Web for years—do you have your own private mental casting list for some of your major characters? Or do you visualize your characters without the aid of Hollywood?

ML: I generally visualize them without actors in mind, but there are some fairly obvious choices. Lucy Lawless for Tarma, of course. Johnny Depp for Vanyel, though I don't know who I'd pick for "young" Vanyel. I'd like the boy from "Sixth Sense," Haley Joel Osment, for Lavan Firestorm. I think that David Bowie would make a fascinating Falconsbane, and Sting would be good for Firesong. I don't know how Cher would feel about going blonde, but she sure has the attitude for Kerowyn!

DL: Has there been interest that would result in seeing Valdemar on the big or small screens? If so, do you plan to encourage it or nip it in the bud?

ML: Not so much as a nibble, and I don't really think it would translate well, to tell you the truth. There's too much concentration on what's going on internally with the characters. Possibly the only books that would work would be the Tarma and Kethry books and *Silver Gryphon*. I would be very reluctant to discover what Hollywood would do with any of the others. For now, I find that it's more than satisfying enough know my books live in the minds of my fans.

A TRAVELER'S GUIDE TO VALDEMAR AND THE SURROUNDING KINGDOMS

Bard Jeriko

(as told to Kerrie Hughes)

BY the royal command of Her Majesty, Queen Selenay, I have been commissioned to write a practical travel book, one that will serve as a guide for those who wish to visit Valdemar and her allies. The Queen has seen that, with the wars against Karse and Hardorn finally over, traveling is not only popular but fashionable. She does not wish harm to come to her subjects because they are ill-prepared for their journeys or ill-informed of the hazards on the way. Nor does she wish worthy visitors to miss a pleasant interlude merely for lack of knowledge.

Therefore, she has asked me to compose a useful treatise on this subject. She feels that my fifty years of experience as a roving Bard will help to advise others of the joys and perils of travel in and around Valdemar.

Before I begin, I would like to point out that change is constant, and that the land of Valdemar is not immune to that powerful force of progress. Laws change, people change, and governments change. So do not despair if an inn or tavern I mention here is no longer in existence. Such surprises are part of the joy of travel, and the traveler who forgets this does so at the peril of spoiling his delight in journeying.

I wish to begin with a word about traveling in general. As the land of Valdemar and its environs open up to casual exploration, always remember that the best way to be welcomed anywhere is to have an educated mind, a joyous heart, a patient soul, and a grateful smile. These homely virtues will smooth your path as little else will. Though a healthy application of the coin of the realm never hurts.

Speaking of the coin of the realm, if your talents lead you to offer a song or musical accompaniment to those you meet along the way, it is customary to ask permission before performing, to make sure that you are not depriving local musicians of their livelihood. If you wish to perform in the inns you seek shelter in, you should share the money you earn with any resident minstrels or musicians that you displace from the stage. Also, I recommend asking for requests before launching into your newest song or original melody; the sound of well played old favorites will earn you more pocket change, and whet your audience's appetite for more adventurous fare.

If you tell a good story and know the latest news from wherever you have just passed, be sure you survey the room carefully before launching into a recitation for others. Travelers have found themselves in dire straits because they accidentally offended someone with a story or tale. I have personally witnessed a young man tell the tale of "The Bitter Wench" to an Earthwitch who felt it degraded the Goddess Agnira. The young man was lucky. He was asked to leave by the innkeeper, and so escaped the nasty fungus curse the Earthwitch was preparing to cast upon him. She may have mistaken the moral of the young man's tale, but it was still a foolish thing to tell it at an inn that sported the design of the Ladytrine. Agnira is the Crone aspect of this triple Goddess, and bears a strong resemblance to the Wench in the tale. It is always better and safer to ask the innkeeper if your story is appropriate when you are not sure of local customs.

Among the many travelers on Valdemar's roads, peddlers of goods or skills are welcome wherever they chose to go. The most successful wanderer I know is a man who sells his services as a knife sharpener and pot repairer. He carries everything he needs on one mule and has profitably and happily traveled Valdemar from the Forest of Sorrows to White Foal Pass.

* * *

At Selenay's request, I will start this travel guide with a brief history of the founding of my homeland.

Baron Valdemar founded the country of Valdemar with his followers long ago, when they fled from persecution in the Eastern Empire. The Baron was a good man and became a good king whose main concern was for his people. He knew that he had ruled wisely, and was certain that his son would rule equally well, but he worried that his descendants might not be fit rulers. The terrors of abusive government that had driven him to flee with his people and settle in Valdemar were clear in his mind as he prayed to all the benign Powers to find a solution to this dilemma. He was answered by a miracle—the appearance of the first Companions. These otherworldly Guardians, though they looked like white horses of the finest quality, were spirit beings who would ensure the continuation of a lineage of caring and competent rulers for Valdemar and justice and honor for Valdemar's people. By Choosing people willing to sacrifice themselves for the greater good of Valdemar, the Companions provided a class of incorruptible guardians for the country, from its rulers, who had to be Heralds to take the throne, to all the other Heralds who would serve the land as its dispensers of justice, its organizers of defenses in emergencies, and its messengers in times of peace as well as times of strife.

Heralds live and often die in the service of Valdemar, keeping it safe, honest, and well run. They are excellent company, and if you are offered the chance to join up with a traveling Herald, take it. Be sure to treat the Companions as the honorable and intelligent beings they are, rather than as the horses they resemble, or you will offend both Companion and Herald. Also remember that a Herald is in great demand and will often be called away from a planned trip in mid-journey to deal with emergencies.

Valdemar has always been hospitable to travelers, and the current peaceful relations with its neighbors and the ending of the Mage-storms have made travel more enjoyable and much safer than it has been in recent years.

As you journey, you will find the main roads well maintained, and the inns hospitable. Even in the areas where inns are not plentiful, it is generally safe to spend a night off-road, though Change-Creatures can be a problem in the wildest areas. There are places that should be avoided at all costs by casual tourists—among them, the Pelagiris Forest, which has never been fully tamed since the days of the first Mage wars. Before the Mage-Storms, the Tayledras people had the job of clearing out deadly creatures that were formed by the warped magic of the land. They were nearly at the end of their labors when the Mage-Storms and Change-Circles created new beasts, often with unfortunate results. The creatures distorted by the Change-Circles joined fearful beasts that have been there for a thousand years. Many of the creatures born or transported via Change-Circle have been killed or captured, but the forest is large and new sightings of monstrous animals are not uncommon. If you happen to come across one of these creatures, retreat if possible and seek help in eliminating it. I have seen the damage done by a Change-squirrel, and would never wish that fate upon anyone. Travelers would do well to learn archery, both to provide game for the cooking pot, and for their own protection. A hunting knife is also a necessity, useful for preparing dinner, and, should matters on the road take a dangerous turn, for protection.

Valdemar's capital city Haven is located in the center of the country. It would not be boasting to state that Haven has become a magnet for travelers, the city where all the guilds send their finest wares for sale, and where travelers may choose from a wide variety of excellent inns.

A favorite stopping place is *The Virgin and Stars* tavern, where third year Bardic students from the Collegium while away the hours. The public room serves a fine assortment of pies and roast meats, which you will enjoy while listening to the latest ballads the Bards have deemed ready to be tested on new ears. The regular crowd there welcomes those outside their circle, because any audience is still an audience.

The *Griffin's Egg* tavern is one of my favorites, if only because they serve an excellent red beer called the Red Griffin, a dark stout called the Black Griffin, and a marvelous golden ale called the Golden Griffin. It is a clean tavern that serves fine quality brews, and they make a spiced meat pie that is second to none.

Another tavern worth seeking out is the *Fivepenny*. The food is simple and cheap, so a frugal traveler can load his pack with the tavern specialty, sausage and cheese bread, a small hand-sized loaf filled with sausage, cheese, or both. If you ask, they will wrap it in wax paper for travel. It keeps well for a few days, and is delicious cold. They also sell wonderful small fruit pies.

Inns are plentiful in the town, with many choices available to suit any pocketbook. The ones nearest the palace are generally more expensive, while those closer to the city's edge are cheaper. This is because the streets of Haven are arranged in a spiral to prevent assault on the palace in times of war. Those with business at the palace but no royal lodging quickly grow wearied by the circular trek from their lodgings in the more distant inns, and the prices reflect this.

As you tour the city you might see the shield of Valdemar, a winged silver horse with broken chains rearing back on a blue field. The country's motto is "No One Way Is The True Way." Valdemar has been open to refugees and exiles from all over Velgarth since its founding. It is, of course, expected that visitors will follow all local laws, and keep any prejudices in check. If you need help, watch for Heralds and those wearing a uniform of dark blue and silver—the colors of the Royal Guard. Both can be counted on to direct or assist you. If you wish to tour the Palace, a guard at the Palace Gate can make the arrangements—though you should be aware that the Palace is not always open to visitors.

The Collegium, where the Heralds, Bards, and Healers are trained, is the pride of Haven. You can identify the students and those who have graduated by the color of their clothing. Herald Trainees wear gray, while full Heralds are dressed in brilliant white. I have often thought that any other hue would look shabby on the backs of the Companions, but I also hear many jokes about the

"Just shoot me" outfits. Bardic students wear russet red,
while full Bards wear scarlet. Healing students wear light
green, and full Healers wear deep green. I've seen several different shades of green on full Healers. It's a hard
color to look good in, and undoubtedly hard to clean
bloodstains from. I have noticed that the more experienced the Healer, the more mismatched and faded their
Greens are.

There are also Unaffiliated students at the Collegium,
who can be identified by their light blue uniforms. These
are the children of nobles or exceptional children. They
generally fall into two categories, Artificer and Scholar.

The Artificers are amazing inventors, and some of
them were instrumental in solving the Mage-Storm problem. They frequent a tavern called the *Compass Rose*,
located directly outside the palace gates. The tavern's
public area is divided into two rooms; in front is where
the students congregate, while the professors spend their
time in back. The students know they have graduated to
master status when they are invited into the back room
by their mentors.

The Scholars hang out in smaller groups at Haven's
bookshops. They read while sipping hot kav or chava,
and play games such as Hinds and Hounds. Kav is an
acquired taste, but chava is an addiction, albeit a minor
and pleasurable one. The scholars are the arbiters of arts
and literature throughout Valdemar.

Artisans flock to Haven to sell their wares when they
are not touring the Village Faires. Galleries in the city
display the best of an artist's current work for sale, and
can represent an artist while they travel, so if your creations merit such attention, you might wish to make an
arrangement with one of these fine establishments.

Lastly, I'd like to say a word about prostitution. Even
in the refined city of Haven, members of the gentle profession ply their craft. The city's laws do not forbid the
practice, and even serve to regulate it on some level.
This does not mean that the city's paid companions are
certain to be free from disease, but at least you can be
sure, if you choose to pursue your pleasures there, that
the company you pay for is a willing partner in the enter-
prise, not a slave forced into the trade. Some countries

still participate in pleasure slavery, but Valdemar is not among them.

If the town of Haven seems an overwhelming place to start your journey, there are many smaller cities in Valdemar to choose from. A novice traveler may find journeying stressful, or become homesick, or long for familiar territories. This is not uncommon, especially when coupled with an inability to speak the local language. Do not be ashamed if this happens to you. If you can, simply reroute your journey to maximize your level of comfort.

If you decide to travel beyond Haven, there are four roads conveniently headed North, West, South, or East from the city. I would suggest the following four journeys:

The North Trade Road to the Forest of Sorrows.

This journey will take you into colder climates, so pack warmly. I recommend this trip for the early summer months. You will pass through the towns of Westmark, Langenfield, Greenhaven, Hevenbeck, Waymeet, Berrybay, Kelmskeep, and Errold's Grove. The Forest of Sorrows and Crookback Pass are at the end of this road.

The entire journey from Haven to Crookback will take approximately three weeks by horse or seven by foot. It will take about eight to ten days to get to the first town of Westmark. Fortunately, there are a few inns along the way, so you will only have to camp every other day at the very most. Eating at the inns will save your trail rations for other days and provide you with a bit of camaraderie and possibly even income if you sing or tell a fine tale. Some establishments will allow you to sleep on the dining room floor or in the stable loft for a greatly reduced price, if you are willing to forgo the comfort of a private room. Farmers will sometimes, for a modest sum, allow a traveler to take shelter in their barns, but always ask permission, as it is illegal to trespass.

I have taken this trip many times now, and have stayed at every inn along the way. The innkeepers are

wonderful people and the food is always excellent. If
you are on horseback, the stables are all quite fine, with
a few specially equipped for Companions.

I once took a side trip in this area to the Temple of
the Cloistered Order of Kernos Sequestered. My father
was from a family that worshipped Kernos, and his eldest brother became a monk in the Order. The fighting
monks and their complete dedication to their art fascinate me. My father's sister went into the cloister to become a votary of the order, sealed voluntarily into a cell
and cared for by the cloister's helpers while pursuing a
life of prayer. This is not as bad as it seems, and I am
assured that any necessary comforts are provided, including medical assistance.

Westmark is a mid-sized town with several inns and
taverns. It is a pleasant place with a church and a town
hall. It is also the first place to resupply on the road, so
the prices are a bit high. If you can wait until the next
town to reprovision, do so, as the savings are considerable.

Over the next week, there are three villages off to the
west side of the trade road, each a half-day's travel off
the main road, but connected to each other by a dirt
track through the woods. The villagers do not wish to
waste time by traveling a half-day to the main route only
to go back again for another half-day after reaching the
next town access road. This dirt road is often used by
those with farm animals and equipment, though larger
caravans are expected to take the main road.

There is only one large inn in this area, the *North
Road Inn*, a very nice place to stay and eat, but it is
always busy, and its rooms generally go to well-heeled
patrons.

The next two towns are the sister towns of Waymeet
and Berrybay. They are fabulous places to visit during
the Harvest Festival, which takes place during Sovvan.
The two towns celebrate with decorations, feasts, and
parties. Merchants and carnival caravans stretch the span
between the two towns and it is easy to get caught up
in the excitement. The Temple of Kernos is nearby and
they stay open on Sovvan Eve for prayer. The prices at
the various town inns go up a bit at this time, so you

may wish to ask fellow campers to share a fire pit for economy and safety.

Another word of caution—you'll find pickpockets, thieves and fraudulent fortune-tellers at the Faires. Keep your wallet close to your chest, do not flash your coin, and don't pay a fortune-teller more than the advertised fee. It is a common and profitable ruse for an unscrupulous fortune-teller to scare a person into thinking they need to leave money for spirits somewhere, or pay off an old debt so a deceased loved one can rest. Pay no attention to such rantings, and keep your gold for better uses.

The next point of interest is Kelmskeep, where Lord Breon has a stronghold. There is no inn here, but he does not mind travelers camping outside his fortress. Lord Breon is a good man, but he will expect you to register with the gate guards if you plan on staying longer than a day. There are two taverns in town, and both allow overnighters to sleep on the floor, but troublemakers are not tolerated. I once saw a small party of young men escorted out of town when they were too boisterous.

The famous town of Errold's Grove, half a day away on the northernmost point of Valdemar, is host to several noteworthy dye and herb merchants.

Errold's Grove also has a settlement of Northerners from the Ghost Cat Clan nearby. These friendly newcomers are skilled leatherworkers who sell colorfully embroidered work. This town also has a healing temple nearby where the legendary Keisha Alder practices and teaches. The famous stories of Ghost Cat, Keisha Wisewoman, and Darian Owlknight can be heard at all three taverns and both inns on any given night.

A Herald station is a new addition to Errold's Grove, with a Herald and assistant permanently on duty. The Herald serves as justice, lawyer and ambassador for this part of the world. Northern peoples are emigrating to Valdemar on a regular basis, and sometimes the occasional peddler will set out for the territories to sell coveted dyes and herbs. It is highly recommended that anyone traveling to the Northern Territories register a travel plan with the Herald before leaving. This is vital, as the area is quite wild, and it is not unheard of for an inexperienced person or party to meet their death by accident or assault. If you do not return within a day of your registered arrival a search party will be sent out to find you.

Owl Inn is a wonderful place to stay. It has incredible venison and pheasant dishes and also brews excellent beer.

A word of caution about this area, as it has grown quite a bit in the last twenty years, and is very careful about preserving the land and environment. No hunting is allowed, as *dyheli* and other sentient creatures inhabit the woods. Travelers should never shoot at birds, as bondbirds fly nearby. Campfires are only permitted in certain areas and under certain conditions. These regulations are posted at every tavern and inn, and at the town hall, so ignorance of the laws will not be accepted as an excuse for any breach of them.

Hawkbrothers watch over these lands. If you thought they were merely legends, you'll quickly discover your mistake. The Tayledras people inhabit much of the Pelagiris and practice cleansing Magic to keep the land healthy and pure. They are the protectors of the forest, and if a Hawkbrother tells you to leave an area, then do so without question, as it is usually just as much for your safety as for the safety of the land.

K'Valdemar Vale is another few hours into the forest, and has an embassy and a meeting hall within its borders, the first of its kind. The Hawkbrothers patrol this area, their home, especially closely, watching for poachers and brigands. Those who wish to visit the Vale can get directions and escort to it by visiting the town hall in Errold's Grove.

The Vale is a marvel of *hertasi* ingenuity. Hot springs and multi-tier gardens make it seem like paradise. The gryphons, *hertasi, tervardi,* and *dyheli* roam here as equals with the human inhabitants. All four species are as intelligent as humans, and possess powers and talents of their own that make them invaluable allies. Treat them with tolerance and respect, should you have occasion to meet them.

Hertasi make themselves available as servants to the

Tayledras and their guests. Hospitality is one of their greatest talents, but should be met with proper appreciation and thanks.

Tervardi sing beautifully, and were once enslaved because of that talent. Concerts can be heard several nights a week at the Vale that will involve at least one *tervardi*, definitely an experience that shouldn't be missed.

Dyheli are less of a presence in the Vale, but have their own territory and can be found easily. They love good conversation and know many languages. They can even swiftly teach a new tongue to travelers who have need of it, though the experience can be an uncomfortable one for the traveler.

Gryphons are notorious for showing off. They don't need to do much to be impressive, though. I've never been more astounded by a creature in my entire life. Their voice is a purr, they smell like spice, and they laugh with vigor. The gryphons are the stars of the Vale.

The Hawkbrothers are a good deal like gryphons. The Vale mages dress in costumes that belong in art galleries, and wear almost as much decoration in their hair as they do on their backs. The scouts dress a bit more conservatively, but they still rival the birds in the forest in their finely crafted costumes. The *hertusi* often make these ornate costumes, and can sometimes be persuaded to outfit you if you impress them with your good manners.

I cannot stress enough the importance of listening to the Hawkbrothers, as they know the area and will escort you safely from Errold's Grove to the Vale and back again. Going alone can be dangerous.

Crookback Pass is about a day's journey from Errold's Grove. It is located right through the Forest of Sorrows, where the spirit of Vanyel was rumored to protect the Kingdom after his death. This is a tranquil area now, guarded by the Ghost Cat Clan. They will conduct you on a tour of the forest while providing protection for you for a small fee or trade item.

As wild and wonderful as the northern territory is, it can be dangerous. The Wolverine Clan is active here, and has killed travelers. The Wolf-Head Clan and outlaws do not follow the merchant/trader amnesty code, which states that merchants and traders will not be molested by any tribe. Captured women can end up as unwilling slaves to provide new sons for the tribe. Illness is a problem in the wilder areas, as the Change-Circles have caused mutations of various diseases. The Healers have traversed the area with cures and preventatives, but it is not unknown for a particularly virulent disease to adapt and thrive in the wilderness.

I do not wish to warn you away from such a journey, as I myself have traveled through the territories just one year ago. If you have an adventurous nature and do not mind rough camping, (there are no inns, taverns, or food carts), I recommend the trip. Some of my best memories were of the time I spent fishing with the Raven Clan and seeing the Great Bitter Waters.

I do caution that women will not want to travel through the lands of the Northern tribes alone. The men of the region do not address women directly and consider them to be subservient in status. The two exceptions are the Wisewomen, who are equal in status to a Shaman, or the woman warriors, commonly known as "Man-souled women," who are treated as neuters.

The tribes welcome traders and are always willing to purchase the dyes that Errold's Grove's tradesmen produce, as well as trade goods from all over Valdemar. It is said that they haven't seen a color they didn't like, so if you are willing to spend some money on dye cakes, you will be rewarded. The Northern Tribes also like to see a trader who brings glass beads. The friendly tribes can be found by following a trader's trail, which the Heralds will give you directions for not as a map, but in writing. A few tribes are in hidden locations, which they intend to keep that way. If a tribe does not want to trade, you will not find them, and you should not press the issue.

Along the way you will find that the climb through the mountain pass can cause extreme Mountain Sickness. If you have one of the breathing diseases, do not attempt it. If you are fortunate in your health, the view from the mountaintop will reward you. One sheer cliff on the other side of the mountain has a zigzag trail cutting into it from top to bottom. This path was carved by the Dark

Mage Leareth, who confronted Herald Mage Vanyel at Crookback Pass and met his match there. The exhilarating trek up that path is not for the faint-hearted.

West on Exile's Road to Lake Evendim

The second journey from Haven that I recommend runs west on Exile's Road to Lake Evendim. Once again, the first town is seven to ten days away, though there are a few decent places to spend the evening along the way. This stretch of road is heavily wooded, so there is some danger from wild animals. Fortunately, hunting is allowed here, and the local wildlife makes a fine dinner.

But be careful what you aim at. I met a *kyree* once along this road and shared my camp with him for an evening. He said a hunting party did not take the time to discern what he really was, and had actually shot at him that day. He held no grudge, but asked me to spread the word that caution would be appreciated. He told me several stories involving *kyree* and their brethren, which I passed on to the inn at Forst Reach and to a few others along the way.

Conveniently, *Prytheree Inn* is centrally located for travelers in the area. It's a long day's ride on a good dirt road, so you will want to leave early in the morning. It is a brave or foolish camper who attempts to sleep in Wyrfen Woods, as wild boars roam freely here. After the Mage-Storms, one was transformed into a grotesque beast that could hypnotize its prey. It took a party of six skilled hunters to kill it.

To get to Forst Reach, you need to detour north before Deercreek. The road is well marked and will also take you to the Ashkevron Manor, the ancestral home of Herald-Mage Vanyel Ashkevron.

The original manor, which was designed by Vanyel's great-great-grandfather Joserlin Ashkevron, still stands, but has been expanded through the years. The first design was a fortress with secret passages and a moat. Now the house resembles a minor palace with many rooms and halls to accommodate the large Ashkevron family, the fosterlings, and the servants. The stables are also impressive, with special stables for Companions. It seems there has nearly always been at least one Herald in the Ashkevron family since the days of Herald-Mage Savil.

The family provides horses for Valdemar's heavy cavalry. They began breeding these horses in Vanyel's time, under the direction of his brother Mekeal. The family is friendly to visitors and tolerant of admirers of their famous relative who wish to visit his home. The Bard at the Ashkevron court is always well-versed in the songs and deeds of Vanyel. This same Bard will entertain guests at the local inn on nights when the court does not require him.

Forst Reach and the manor was once the border of Valdemar. Two principalities, Baires and Lineas, existed just across this border, but a feud and Dark Magic wiped out all but one royal family member during the time of Vanyel. Their former capital cities of Highjorune and Qorthes still exist, but the countries became a permanent part of Valdemar once the last remaining heir to the thrones died. These cities are farming towns, with quaint inns and taverns, and worth visiting if only to hear tales of the feud and see the castles. Numerous signs in the inns proclaim, "Vanyel slept here." There is also a nightly ghost walk in the Linean Castle, detailing the famous slaughter of the royal family.

Deercreek is a lovely town with an inn that caters to hunters. The Ashkevrons sometimes stay there. Wild game makes up the majority of the house menu, including a variety of quail and pheasant dishes. If you need food or supplies, get them here, because the next town, Zoe, is a three-to-four-day journey west.

Zoe is one of the famous fisher towns of Lake Evendim. Many years ago slavery came to Lake Evendim, in the form of pirates and bandit gangs. The intervention of the Queen and her Heralds has cleared up this inhumane practice, and it is now safe to travel here.

The lake people are tolerant, down-to-earth folk who live simply and loudly. Consequently, the area has become a favored honeymoon spot for shaya'chern. Guided fishing trips are a prime local attraction, and the inns and taverns will happily make arrangements for you, should you wish to undertake one.

The fishing villages also sell a useful item, a cleansing stone found in the swim bladders of the giant Lake Evendim sturgeon, used for removing stains from white and light-colored leather. The sturgeons are also renowned for the good caviar they produce, a local delicacy.

After taking the circle tour of Lake Evendim, you may wish to travel the paths up the edge of the Pelagiris Forest to the Pelagir Hills and follow the Terilee River back down to Haven.

This is a trek that only the most experienced hunters and campers should try. There are no inns or taverns, and few farms along the river until it nears Haven. You will be watched by the Hawkbrothers, as you will be passing the k'Sheyna and k'Treva Vales. Be wary of everything around you. In some areas not all of the Change-Circles have been cleansed. If you find an odd circle of ground that does not match the surrounding landscape, do not pass through it. Usually they are harmless, but it's better to be safe than sorry. Also, remember that not all Change-Beasts have been captured. Even a harmless-looking rabbit may be a killer.

The south border of the forest from Lake Evendim consists of the Anduras River, and my warnings hold there, too. K'Vala and k'Sheyna Vales are near the forest edge, or you could continue following the river through Rethwellan and into Jkatha, an adventurous voyage indeed, but not one for the inexperienced traveler.

On one trip through the Rethwellan-Jkathan border in the company of several Tayledras, bandits attacked our caravan. We were outnumbered, and only prevailed when our mage used a swamp spell to sink our attackers three feet into the ground. While our assailants flopped about in muck, mire, and leeches, we hastily rode off. The mage also added a chigger spell, so I imagine the bandits were scratching for months. I highly recommend traveling with mages when possible.

We continued our trip by *dyheli* along the Dhorisha Plains to k'Sheyna. The forest seemed unusually quiet, as if even its animal residents had abandoned it. Since the trail we were on was generally heavily used, the

Hawkbrothers were concerned at the lack of travelers as well as by the unusual hush in the surrounding wilderness. We passed one abandoned camp that had piles of unused supplies left behind. A second showed traces of what appeared to be human blood. We were several hours past the second camp when we discovered the reason for the forest's eerie silence.

From the canopy above, we heard a snarl and saw a blur. One of our party was struck off her *dyheli* by a Change-lion. These deadly creatures are thankfully rare. They possess magic that enables them to remain invisible, even when you look directly at them. My fellow traveler took a direct hit from the beast and was dead before she hit the ground. The Hawkbrothers reacted instantly, letting loose several arrows into the lion, directed by the sound of its passing, which killed the creature.

We eventually made it to Kata'shin'a'in, a large seasonal trading town composed of colorful tents and colorful people. The phrase "they never saw a color they did not like" does not begin to cover the variety and visual intensity of the city—every citizen is a riot of shades and hues, every event a noisy chaos of clashing apparel. During the trading season as the traders and their clientele arrive, thousands of tents go up to shelter them and the goods for sale, then when winter comes they disappear like the drifting fallen leaves, leaving nothing behind but a few inns and permanent buildings to mark the city's passing.

The main commodity for sale in the tents is weaving of all kinds—carpets, blankets, textiles and embroidery are everywhere. The famed beast market where Shin'a'in-bred horses can be purchased is located on the outskirts of the city. The Shin'a'in keep their best horses for themselves, but despite that the animals they sell here have no equals in the world in stamina or intelligence. (They never sell stallions, so don't let anyone fool you into thinking they have a genuine Shin'a'in stallion for sale.) Companions can ride three times farther than a horse and much faster; the Shin horses fall somewhere in the middle in their abilities between ordinary mounts and Companions.

Beyond Kata'shin'a'in is the Dhorisha Plains, home of the Shin'a'in. For centuries this land was off limits to all except the tribes and their escorted friends. Before the recent Mage-Storms, Dhorisha was the home of Urtho's legendary tower, which was once thought to be a fable. This tower and its contents were instrumental in solving the Mage-storm problems. Magic was forbidden to the Shin'a'in by their Goddess for the tower's protection before the storms, but the ban was lately lifted to save all the lands, including the Plains. Stories of these great doings of our time can be heard at their best in Kata'shin'a'in, so I will not spoil the mystery for you.

I next made my way to Rethwellan, which is a marvelous place to travel. The country has been our ally for a long time, bound by custom and marriage, and their current ruler is closely related to Valdemar's royal family. This country hosts many Faires, both seasonal and town-oriented, just as Valdemar does.

The Rethwellan capital, Petras, is the site of an extensive archive that can be accessed by scholars with permission from the Royal Archivist. These archives are unique in that they are enchanted to prevent tampering. A king I know only as "The Honest" wished to prevent the destruction or rewriting of history, so he created a very intricate spell to protect the histories therein.

The capital is approached on a street called Carter's Lane, named for the extensive cart use on the road, which is wide enough to accommodate four wagons at the same time. The avenue sports a number of popular taverns, drinkshops, and inns, many of which were involved in the overthrow of Oathbreaker King Raschar, led by the Adept Kethry, Swordsworn Tarma, and the Royal Archivist of the time, Jadrek. Raschar, the Great-uncle of Rethwellan's current King Faram, killed his sister, the Princess Idra, and was found guilty of the murder at the Temple of Ursa just outside the city. Several inns, including the Pig and Potion, Fountain of Beer, Wheat Sheaf, and many other smaller taverns, housed the mercenary troops of Idra's Sunhawks for months to support the takeover. They still stand today, and are fiercely and justly proud of their heritage. The Temple of Ursa stands in memoriam to Princess Idra, and is open to visitors. The holy site where Idra exacted her revenge from beyond the grave has become a place of pilgrimage for victims of domestic violence and incest, who arrive here to pray for strength, guidance, and deliverance from their abusers.

Rethwellan is clearly a country of Magic. While Valdemar forgot Magic in the several centuries between Vanyel and Herald-Mage Princess Elspeth, Rethwellan magic prospered, and hosted various mage-schools such as White Winds, Blue Mountain, and Twin Suns. It was Rethwellan that welcomed fleeing mages from Karse during the Burning Times. It is also here that Adept Kethry was educated, and later founded her own school. I hesitate to specify their locations, as part of the protection of the schools is that "Those who seek to learn will find the way." The schools are not hard to find—in fact, many have spawned large surrounding towns—but it seems that those who wish to harm or who desire power for its own sake have a more difficult time seeking them out than most. By the time those inclined to evil reach their goal, they are expected and dealt with appropriately.

Rethwellan is also a country of mercenary companies, and a very powerful guild was formed to protect the mercenary members and the kingdom's population from abuse. Ruvan, and Jkatha also cooperate with the organization. It is only recently that Karse, Hardorn and Valdemar have been added to the guild. Entire towns are dependent on the existence of mercenary companies, which rent winter quarters and supply a clientele for the inns and taverns, along with a host of clever retirees to run them. Travelers should be warned about a rather insidious local drink known as Ehhris wine, which seems harmless at first, but creates an addiction so hard to shake that ruin can follow quickly. Sometimes these poor ravaged souls end up in discreet slave markets, even though slavery is illegal in Rethwellan, as it is in most civilized countries.

Despite this, do not think that Rethwellan is without morals. They worship the Goddess in all her aspects and have several temples throughout the land. The most popular version is the Ladytrine of Agnetha, Agnira, and

Agnoma. There are schools run by the Sisters of Agnetha to educate girls in what may be called the "womanly arts." She is the Goddess in her aspect of wife and mother, the caretakers of life. Her symbol is a sheaf of wheat and she is often depicted with twin babies, a boy and a girl.

Agnira is the wild horse-taming aspect of the Goddess as the defender of the land and tamer of energy; a horse is her symbol. I once saw a horse carved on the side of a green hill and outlined in white, chalky rock. The local village informed me that it was hundreds of years old, created long ago to honor Agnira.

Agnoma is the Goddess of wisdom, truth, and death; a snowflake represents her. I have not found evidence of her in the form of temple, school, or monument. On my next trip to Rethwellan, I plan to research this Lady-trine and put together a book about the worship of the Goddess.

The South Trade Road

My third trip recommendation from Haven is down the South Trade Road. The Terilee River flows from Haven and follows the trade road south to the border and into Karse. Travelers often fish the river or hunt for rabbit and small game, so pack a fishing pole and bow and arrows. This journey is wonderful on foot during the warm summer months.

The town of Kettlesmith is only four or five days away from Haven. Like the whole trip, the town is unremarkable but comfortable, with a standard inn and tavern. Five days further down the road and you reach Horn, then five more and you'll find Sweetsprings. The only real difference is that the towns get a little smaller as the border gets closer. Horn has a unique little inn called the *Bard's Cottage*, a slightly pricey romantic spot that newlyweds of the area seem to like.

There is a road outside Kettlesmith with a small bridge over the river that will take you to Three Rivers. It's a three-day journey, and quite literally ends at the point where the Terilee River branches off into three smaller rivers. It is a small bucolic jewel of a village, a bit rough-hewn but soothing for any traveler. This whole area did not fare well during the war with Hardorn and Karse. Two wars in a row have given the people a keen appreciation of the simple things in life.

I have noticed many retired mercenaries sitting in the corners of local inns. Buy them a drink, and you will be rewarded with stories that will make you laugh, cry, and appreciate life.

As you near the border near Sensholding and Cordor, the people are less friendly and more insular. The Holderkin live here and do not welcome strangers of any kind, even Heralds. It is said that the Holderkin actually started out as Karsites, but are now under the jurisdiction of Valdemar, the result of a border change in some distant war with Valdemar's ancient enemy. Do not ask to stay at farms in this area. You will not be welcome.

The women of the holds have a hard life. The legendary Queen's Own, Talia, is from this area and was the first Herald to come from it. Her Choosing changed the lives of the Holderkin, especially the girls, forever. Now a Herald must be permitted to speak among the children at reasonable intervals, and if a child is of age to serve the Queen and wishes to leave for the larger world, the family must allow it. This applies to boys as well, but because of their superior status to women at the tender age of ten, they do not often choose to leave. Many girls take advantage of the opportunity of the Herald's question, though, and I hear that the Queen's Own is most pleased by this.

White Foal Pass, where the famous battle took place in the time of Lavan Firestorm, is not far from here. From Sensholding, it is a four-day trek along the edge of the mountains. When you reach the battle site, the area still shows evidence of the conflict that raged here so many years ago. It has been more than three centuries since the fire that razed the entire pass. Vegetation that grows back after such a fire is a different color of green and not as dense as virgin growth. Trees like the firecone pine actually need fire to open the cones and release the seeds, which then sprout and grow. Though natural fires happen all the time, caused by lighting strikes and hot weather, a fire like the one Lavan Firestorm used to defeat the Karsites burns hotter, faster, and wider. You can tell the path of destruction still—the slopes of the pass have a lot more grass than the rest of the valley, the trees are shorter and less varied in kind, and there are more wildflowers. Up along one side is a firecone tree that is taller than the rest, a living memorial to Lavan Firestorm, nurtured by his friends who were saved by his valiant sacrifice. There is a path next to it, one originally made in his memory, now used and kept clear by local shepherds.

If it is a summer month, you may wish to travel on through the Combs into Rethwellan. Never attempt this in winter or early spring, because you will freeze to death. I have personally seen the dead bodies of the foolish or desperate who believed they could weather the treacherous Combs.

Rather than trying to traverse the Combs, another option is to go back east and follow the Terilee into Karse, or take the main road back to Valdemar.

Karse is now an ally of Valdemar and welcomes travelers and trade, thanks to the actions of the current Son of the Sun, Solaris. In the time of Vanyel, a coup in the Temple of Vkandis resulted in a reorganization of the hierarchy. The old ways were rewritten into a Writ and Rule that changed the power structure and allowed those with Magic to be burned as sacrifices. The next few hundred years became a time of terror in Karse, with magically gifted children taken from their parents and sometimes even burned alive. The God Vkandis finally intervened, choosing Solaris to be his Son of the Sun. In a country where women were second-class citizens at best, this caused an incredible upheaval, as did Solaris's efforts to root out corruption and restore the Holy Writ.

Karse's capital city of Sunhame is spectacular. The city is comparable in size to Haven, and is designed entirely around the Temple of the Sun God Vkandis, where the Sunthrone is located. It is easily accessible to pilgrims, as all the city's main roads go straight to the Temple. The corrupt priests of the old order profited from a thriving slave trade and the selling of deadly intoxicants. They also practiced Dark Magics that involved the summoning of demons. Solaris has eliminated these and other unlawful practices, and travel through Karse is once again possible.

What fear and fanaticism once destroyed, tolerance and education are now rebuilding. However, journeys in Karse can be difficult because inns are few and far between. I would recommend traveling in a small group and taking a cartful of trade goods. The welcome will be significantly warmer for a peddler than an ordinary traveler.

The country is fairly friendly, so you can often find lodging among the farms and taverns. The people are vibrant and pious, with a newfound renewal on life. Karsites cherish their children like no other culture I have visited. I assume this is a direct result of losing so many youngsters to the Burning Times. Do not bring up the topic, as they understandably do not like to discuss it.

The main road heading south to Ruvan from Sunhame passes by Lake Tiel and runs on to the town of Vondern—roughly a ten day journey. The trees and mountains are fewer over the border into Ruvan, a sparse land with no true winter. Instead, the region receives rain, and the earth turns to mud. Merchant guilds flourish here and sometimes war among one another. There is a thriving mercenary guild, and Hawk's Nest, the hometown of the Sunhawks, is located here.

The royalty of Ruvan, Prince Lothar, allows prostitution with taxation, as well as slavery. He has even allowed experimentation on criminals using Dark Magic. Faldis Juice and Lethe Wine, both narcotics, are used and abused throughout the land.

Women should not travel alone in this realm, and wary travelers can avoid trouble by following the laws and keeping their wits about them. It is my opinion that the slave trade here is not limited to criminals, so take care not to travel too far off of the Silver road. Stick to the towns of Delton, Brether's Crossroads, Hawk's Nest, and Oberdorn. Stay only in the well known inns that display a guild license for mercenaries. I recommend taking this journey mounted on a fast, reliable horse, one that isn't worth too much, as you do not want to invite a bandit attack.

The city of Delton, the first after the border, is the

site of Kethry and Tarma's defeat of the demon Thalk-arsh. Their tale is told well at the *Black Ewe Inn*, and properly enjoyed over a cup of fine Demon Slayer Wine. The town was once a den of pleasure, but prostitutes were sacrificed to the Dark God by the score. Now Delton has turned into a tourist trap—whether this is an improvement or a tragedy depends on your point of view. Little souvenir "Need" swords and Tarma and Kethry dolls of the very lewdest quality are for sale at the temple where the demon was destroyed.

Brether's Crossroads is another two-day ride away and has a little more dignity. A Temple of the Anathei Priests of the Purifying Flame is located just outside of town. They welcome visitors and provide good conversation.

Five days away is Hawk's Nest, and there are no inns along the way, so you will be camping on the journey. Get proper supplies in Brether's Crossroads. Hawk's Nest is a fortified town with a good reputation. The Sun-hawks are still active, so the law is well observed here. The *Falcon Inn* is the only place to stay in the town, but it has excellent rooms and a fine cook.

You can leave straight from Brether's Crossroads, cross the border on unpaved trails and head for Mournedealth. This is a long seven days ride and hunting is not reliable, so pack plenty of trail rations. Mournedealth is an old town with many inns, taverns, markets, and guilds.

The nobility there is comprised of fifty noble houses, a source of both pride and trouble for the town. The children of the fifty houses began a racing club, grouping themselves under the colors of red, yellow, green, blue, and black. These racing clubs turned into gangs and rivalries developed. I have not seen much of them during the last two trips I took there, and very few people speak of them. To me this means they are either abandoned or too well organized. I have heard rumors of an underground network of criminals, so it seems better not to speak of them while you are there.

Much of the wealth is not with the families, but held by the new merchants. Goldsmiths and silversmiths can be found throughout the city. Artisans in cloth, leather, silks, and all manner of finished clothing and jewelry also display their wares. Queen Sursha encourages fair trade and safe roads, so it is a good idea to look for bargains in the marketplace for future sale back in Valdemar, where such items are considered exotic.

Just outside the city is a school of White Winds mages founded, interestingly enough, by a *hertasi* Adept. Their mandate is self-knowledge and self-mastery. This is the school where the famous Adept Kethry became a journeyman. I had the opportunity to visit it once in the company of a journeyman from the Twin Suns school who wanted to visit a childhood friend. It was a tranquil place that welcomed visitors and questions, but it was not marked on the various maps, nor was it on the main road.

The Rethwellan Trade Road runs directly south to the Throne City, another ten days away. The city is large and fairly ornate, even a lot like Haven. It was the scene of a coup when the last King of Jkatha died and left the crown to his wife. The King's brother, Declin Lord Kelcrag, took the Throne City in an attempt to take the crown. His coup was not long-lived, as the city was taken back and Kelcrag defeated thanks to the talents of Idra's Sunhawks.

Further down the road are Northbend and Asire, but I have not been to either city yet. I have taken the High Spur Road west to the cities of Felwether, Fromish, and Lythecare. This route will then go directly to Kata'shin-'a'in. The Spur Road lower will go to Kadash and then Kata'shin'a'in. The entire circle can be traveled in one month of hard riding. I once traversed this circuit for a year, picking up goods in Kata'shin'a'in and selling them at the towns and farms along the way to supplement my performing. I made a bit of money, went back to Mournedealth to get silks, and sold them in Valdemar for a nice profit. Such a journey might still be profitable.

The East Trade Road from Haven to Hardorn.

The road to Hardorn only has one town on it, Trevale, nine days from Haven. There is an inn on the way, but once you pass Trevale there are no more. The war took a heavy toll on the area. Hardornians are not traveling much, preferring to concentrate on rebuilding their country. Right now, it is not profitable to run a sleeping inn on this route, but there are a few farmhouses along the way that are friendly.

Once you get closer to the border, you will see a difference in the landscape. The Dark King Ancar raped his country to power his war. The new King Tremane is doing his best to renew and cleanse the land. It is fortunate that our own consort to the Queen, Prince Daren, is earth sensitive, and was able to repair some of the damage, but there is much more to do before the land is fully restored.

My recent journey to Hardorn was mostly humanitarian, but partly business. I traveled with a caravan sent by Queen Selenay to deliver seeds for hardy wheat and a fast-growing squash that seems to take root anywhere. We were welcomed into every home and village by people eager for new stories and a new ear to hear their tales of woe.

One of the most noticeable differences in this trip was in the deserted lands near the border. Ancar stole the minds of all the able-bodied men there so he could force their bodies to battle the army of Valdemar. He killed their women and children, using blood magic to bind them to his horrific deeds. Sensitive souls tell me that unquiet spirits no longer walk there. It is to be hoped that King Tremaine's efforts to heal the land has released them.

The towns of Andersgate, Greenvale, Helecia, Pendran, Donnid, Shonar, and Tezukai still exist, as does the former capital city. Every city I went to was the same. Underpopulated, low on durable goods, but renewed with hope now that Ancar was dead. Women outnumbered men by three to one; still, children were plentiful. It has been years since the war ended, and the people are infectiously optimistic. I expect to see more farmsteads and a better economy when I go back again.

I hear the border of Iftel is now open to merchants and ambassadors as well as the odd traveler. I have a yearning to go up and see the Gryphon competitions and the various creatures from Urtho's reign who still survive in Iftel. New land beneath my feet, and a new and amazing destination . . . the trip beckons to my traveler's soul.

The world is open to those with a kind heart and an open mind. I wish you luck and good weather on all your journeys.

THE MUSIC OF VALDEMAR

THE novels of Valdemar had a very unusual genesis—Mercedes Lackey was a professional lyricist before she became a novelist, and some of her major characters began their lives in songs rather than in novels. Those early days have left their imprint on the kingdom of Valdemar—in the thread of music and song that is interwoven throughout the novels. But the music has continued to exist on its own, in a separate and complementary art form to the books. The next section of *The Valdemar Companion* explores that community, and its interdependence with and influence on the novels, in the words of some of the people who have brought the lyrics and songs of Valdemar to life, as well as providing a list of the available recordings of the songs of Valdemar.

BALLADEERS, BUSKERS, AND BARDS: THE MUSIC OF VALDEMAR

Michael Longcor

**"At least there was music.
There was always music."
—Magic's Pawn**

MERCEDES Lackey's Kingdom of Valdemar is filled
with color, romance, danger, adventure, and, as is always
the case where such a variety of cultures come together,
with music. Its inhabitants sing, perform, compose, and
listen to music of all sorts. Music is an essential part of
Valdemar's inhabitants' lives, as necessary to them as
eating and sleeping.

In our own world, music is too often a product of
mammoth corporate industries, who churn out prepro-
grammed hits like a burger chain cranks out french fries.
Food and music made for mass production too often
result in a product that is bland, over-processed, and
lacking that special human touch. In Mercedes Lackey's
books, the music of Valdemar is an art form that comes
from the heart.

Valdemar boasts professional musicians and performers at several different levels. At the top are the Bards,
who compose and perform music that blurs its border
with magic. Bards can set a mood powerful enough to
directly influence the thoughts and actions of the lis-
tener. Music is a Gift that is perilously easy to misuse,
but the Bardic Gift can also be invoked to soothe pain
and heal the hurts of the mind and the body, as is the
case in this passage from *Magic's Pawn* (p.272), when

Vanyel Ashkevron has his massive psychic wounds tended by a Tayledras Healer-Adept:

> "Cool, green-gold music threaded into the darkness; not dispelling it, but complementing it. It wound its way into his mind, and wherever it went, it left healing behind it; in all the raw, bleeding places, in all the burning channels. It flowed through him and he sank into it, drifting, drifting, and content to drift. It surrounded him, bathed him in balm, until there was nothing left of hurt in him . . ."

Bards are superb entertainers, but they are also agents of the King or Queen of Valdemar. Their Gifts are state assets, to be used for the welfare and protection of the kingdom and its subjects. To qualify for Bardic training, a candidate must have not only the Bardic Gift, but also one or both of the other two major requirements for a musician: the ability to perform brilliantly and the talent to compose and create.

The second class of musicians in Valdemar are the Minstrels, talented performers who perform popular music beautifully without sweeping away their listeners with projected emotion. They play a valuable part in Valdemaran society, even without having the Gift of the Bards. As Herald-Mage Trainee Tylendel says in *Magic's Pawn* (p. 158), "There are times when the Gift gets in the way of the music." The minstrels are the best of the popular music performers, for times when people just want to let down their hair and have a good time. Minstrels study their craft at the Collegium, alongside the Bards, Heralds, and Healers, and the best minstrels can match the Bards in their performing and composing skills. They lack only the Gift, the power to influence people with music at the deepest and most powerful levels. Minstrels are always portrayed as musicians making a living from their music, however grand or whimsical, passing both music and information from one place to another. In *Magic's Promise,* Herald-Mage Vanyel poses as a poor minstrel in order to scout out a dangerous situation outside Valdemar's borders. As he says (p.

196), "Nobody notices a minstrel asking questions; they're *supposed* to."

A little lower on the scale of musical performers are gleemen, itinerant performers with some talent, but presumably with less official training than the Minstrels and Bards. They are the least formally organized of Valdemar's musicians, and their singing skill is often combined with juggling, acting, sleight-of-hand, and sometimes other and less savory skills. If the Bards are Valdemar's mystical virtuosos, and the minstrels are its pop stars, the gleemen are its vaudeville acts and sideshow performers.

The fact that the Bardic Trainees, along with Herald and Healer Trainees, make up one of the three branches of Valdemar's elite training facility, the Collegium, shows just how important music is to the folk of Valdemar. In our world, a rough equivalent would be if West Point Military Academy got merged with Johns Hopkins University Medical School and the Julliard School of Music. There's another major difference between the music of our world and that of Valdemar: Valdemar offers the rather appealing picture of a world where musical composition and performance is a respected branch of public service, rather than a glitzy and often corrupt track to individual fame and fortune. When the opinion of an entire kingdom has to be changed to ensure its survival, the Bards of Valdemar are the ones who are called upon to make that happen. *In Magic's Price* (p. 332), the spirit of Vanyel the Herald-Mage speaks to Bard Stefan:

> "*:You have to use your Gift to convince the people of Valdemar that the Gifts of the Heralds are enough to keep them safe. You, and every Bard in the Circle. Which means that first you have to convince the other Bards, then the Circle has to convince the rest of the realm. . . . The Bards are the only ones that have a hope of pulling this off, Stef. And you are the only one that has a hope of convincing the Bards:*
> 'But that could take a lifetime!' Stefan cried involuntarily, dismayed by the magnitude of the task."

Aside from the Bards and their music being used as a powerful tool of the kingdom, the musicians of Valdemar love music for the same reasons that people everywhere do: because music can raise spirits, ease care, liven up gatherings, and because it's just plain fun. In *Magic's Price*, Vanyel, who by this point possesses the full Bardic Gift, takes part in a *bad* song contest. He and his love Stefan are challenged to "come up with the worst songs they know (p. 194). Trite, badly rhymed; badly-scanned—you name it." In Valdemar, at least, it seems people enjoy their music enough to occasionally poke fun at it.

Why is so much emphasis placed on the importance of music to the people of Valdemar? The best person to answer this is Mercedes Lackey herself (or "Misty," as she's known to friends and fans). I asked her that question recently and this was her reply:

"In the medieval period most of the news was spread by traveling musicians; that changed a little in the Renaissance, but only for the nobility who could afford messengers—the peasantry still got their news via traveling musicians, merchants, and entertainers. Bardic Collegium is an extension of that, with the traveling entertainers serving the same function in an official capacity. Interestingly enough, we're going back to that. A recent poll indicated that most Americans get their political opinions from comedians."

When I asked about her own early musical influences, she said:

"Classical and folk—Peter, Paul and Mary, Glenn Yarborough, The Chad Mitchell Trio, The Limelighters, The Weavers, all that bunch. I used to sit up at night with my transistor radio under the covers listening to an after 10 PM all-folk show out of Chicago."

Her own favorite styles of music?

"Truth to be told, I have two favorites. For writing to, it's instrumental—jazz, new age, and classical all

the way—lyrics interfere with my prose-brain cells.
For listening it's a mix of classical and folk, mostly
Celtic these days, though I have a significant Native
American collection as well."

Misty often uses lyrics and poetry as a way to facilitate
her fiction writing. That is, whenever she's stuck for dia-
log, description, or plot, she will hie herself off and write
a poem or a song about the character or story twist in
question, in order to crystallize what she wants to see
or say. As she put it:

"The songs help me to write the story, definitely,
nine times out of ten. The song 'Threes' came first—
I wrote it on a plane on the way to visit Teri Lee
and gave her my only copy, then decided to write
the story. A couple of other 'legend' songs have
come first as well—'Sun and Shadow' and 'Windrider Unchained,' both of which I have pretty well
decided will NOT have stories written about them,
as I think they work better as distant legends."

She has, as you might expect, clear ideas on the pre-
vailing musical styles of Valdemar, which are, she says:

"European (mostly medieval) folk, dance music and
vocal. No opera or anything like it, no groups of
instrumentalists playing music designed for formal
concerts. The instrumental music played as background at court functions is still dance music and
one- to three-person vocal. Sacred music is by choir,
though I haven't gotten into that, largely because I
haven't done much with religious life. It's entirely
possible that I'll do something appropriately different for some of the other countries outside Valdemar. I ought to have mentioned Shin'a'in drumming
by now, and somehow haven't."

Music and musical instruments fill the books. It's a
tribute to the depth and richness of detail in the Valdemar stories that musical instruments don't just appear,
like theater props hauled up from the storeroom. We get

to meet luthiers, the people who craft the instruments. A reader is as likely to encounter a harp or gittern as a sword or shield. There are also lutes, psaltries (another sort of stringed instrument), flutes, fiddles, horns, and drums. These are all instruments familiar to the cultures of our own Middle Ages and Renaissance. In at least one instance there's even an instrument bearing a close resemblance to our own world's modern steel-strung, twelve-string guitar. Vanyel Ashkevron, Herald-Mage of Valdemar, comes across one of these unorthodox instruments in *Magic's Promise* (p. 115):

> "Vanyel took it carefully, and struck a chord—
> It rang like a bell, sang like an angel in flight, and hung in the air forever, pulsing to the beat of his heart.
> He closed his eyes as it died away, lost in the sound. . ."

Before she was known as a writer and the creator of the land of Velgarth and the kingdom of Valdemar, Mercedes Lackey was known as a writer of song lyrics. There are the lyrics to literally dozens of songs scattered through the Valdemar books. Most of these have been set to music, some by Misty, others by various talented folks, including Heather Alexander, Meg Davis, Cecilia Eng, and Leslie Fish. Many of these songs have been recorded on an assortment of albums on both cassette tape and compact disk that contain at least some elements from or about the stories set in and around Valdemar. All are available in both cassette tape and CD, (except for *Owlflight,* which is on CD only) through Firebird Arts and Music. If you're interested in owning them, check the discography in this book. You can buy the various albums mentioned in it on Firebird's website, *http://www.firebirdarts.com.*

Music is a large part of the mortar that holds together Valdemar's life. It's entertainment, but it is never a thing to be sold short. When Stefan says in *Magic's Price,* "It's not in the nature of a Bard to do anything particularly constructive." Vanyel replies (p. 88), "I think you underestimate both yourself and the potential power of your office, Stefan."

Songs give life to the stories, and the stories inspire songs. They help us enter this shining kingdom called Valdemar, and let readers carry away a living piece of its heroes, villains, and people in their hearts.

BORN IN SONG: MAKING THE MUSIC OF VALDEMAR

Teri Lee

VALDEMAR was born in song, and it has been a delight for me to watch the world of Velgarth evolve from a handful of songs into, at my last count, a series of twenty-six books and ten albums with more of each on the way. I was there when that pivotal moment of birth happened—believe it or not. It all started from a chance encounter at a science fiction convention.

Back in 1982, I had a very small publishing company that specialized in science fiction and fantasy songbooks and recordings. This tiny company scraped up its meager resources and I traveled from California to the World Science Fiction Convention being held in Chicago.

There, sharing a small table with another small publisher and a gentleman selling original artwork created by his wife, we all sat packed in like sardines selling our assorted wares.

One afternoon, at the other end of the table, there was an animated conversation going on, and some sort of conference between the fellow on the end and the publisher in the middle. Moments later a piece of lined notebook paper with a handwritten piece of poetry was waved under my nose. It proved to be a very nice piece of space-related poetry. Not just rocket ships and bug-eyed monsters, but a song based on a real event in the United States space program. It was good, it was well written, and it was just what we needed to fill out a songbook we were working on called "Minus Ten and Counting."

Great, I thought, and looked up trying to figure out where these mysterious lyrics had come from. There stood the author, a shy red-haired woman, trying to retrieve her lyrics. When asked, she put her name and address on the bottom—Mercedes Lackey, Tulsa, Oklahoma. She never got her lyrics back. She eventually did get a contract, and then royalties when the song-book and cassette were published, and she even turned in another song for the collection. She became a professional lyricist, the beginning of a long and fruitful collaboration that resulted in many, many songs, among them those ten albums of music based on Valdemar I mentioned before.

In the world of fiction, if someone tried to sell a tale based on the chain of coincidence that led to a first encounter between Mercedes Lackey and me, I doubt it would be accepted by any editor. They'd all think it was too far-fetched.

As for the song, it turns out that Mercedes Lackey (known as Misty to her friends) had been standing in line behind two teenage boys who were marveling at their discovery that the early Apollo space program had suffered losses, and that several astronauts had even been killed. This ignorance so appalled her that she went back to her hotel room and wrote "Memorial," the story of the Block One Apollo spacecraft that caught fire in January of 1967, killing Virgil I. "Gus" Grissom, Edward White, and Roger Chaffee, and, being an old folk-music fan, set it to the haunting "Ballad of Springhill."

Then she showed the song to an old friend who just happened to be sitting at a dealer's table selling his wife's artwork, and the dealer showed it to the publisher sitting next to him, who showed it to the publisher sitting next to her, and the rest was history. Misty's professional songwriting career was born. (And this is the first chance to publicly thank both Mark Bailey and Margaret Middleton for being part of the chain that connected Misty with me.)

Misty quickly became a lyricist of great power, though she rarely wrote the music for her songs. In very short order she had written a number of songs for our anthologies, and even had enough material for an album of her own. The assorted singer/songwriter types floating through our recording studio figured out quickly what kind of treasure was arriving in the mail, and took to spiriting all of Misty's songs away. Misty began sending me multiple copies of each new set of lyrics, so that there was a chance that one copy would still be around after some chortling composer had made off with her latest work.

It was around this time that Misty, who by this time had become a good friend of mine, confessed that she also wrote fiction, and if it wouldn't be a bother would I mind looking at some of it? The first two short stories she produced grew out of songs that she had written earlier, "Threes" and "Kerowyn's Ride" (the stories later were expanded into the *By the Sword* novel). Both featured the team of Tarma the swordswoman and Kethry the sorceress. Misty's writing and her characters were good, and the early adventures of Tarma and Kethry eventually found a home in the pages of the *Sword and Sorceress* anthologies edited by Marion Zimmer Bradley.

So it wasn't a total surprise when Misty finally admitted she also had a novel in the works, and asked me if I could possibly take a look? The book was called *Arrows of the Queen*. It featured a girl called Talia and magical white horses set in the kingdom of Valdemar. I made some suggestions. She rewrote. And rewrote, and rewrote. She completely rewrote the novel three times at that early stage.

Then writer C.J. Cherryh heard some of the songs that Misty was writing about her characters and decided that anyone who could write lyrical poetry that well had the makings of becoming a prose storyteller. At that point I was able to let the fiction experts take over and keep my mind on the music, but Misty kept me posted on what was going on. C.J. guided Misty through a whopping seventeen more rewrites of what became the *Arrows of the Queen* trilogy: *Arrows of the Queen, Arrows Flight,* and *Arrows Fall.* That was before Misty even submitted the books to C.J.'s editor, Elizabeth

"Betsy" Wollheim at DAW Books, who put Misty through yet another grueling series of rewrites before finally accepting the manuscripts for publication. And with every rewrite, Misty learned something new and became a better writer.

To the outside world, it must have seemed as though Misty just exploded into the fantasy genre. But it wasn't as easy as it looked, even though Misty and Betsy had formed a solid partnership—the new author was determined to succeed at her craft, and her enthusiastic editor had faith in her work. Only Betsy—who has been the editor for all of the Valdemar novels from that very first book, and who has been instrumental in Misty's growth as a novelist—and a few of Misty's friends knew just how hard Misty was working. For three long years before her first novel was published, Misty worked full-time as a mainframe programmer for a major airline. When she wasn't programming, Misty wrote. She wrote before going to work, after work, on weekends, all during the holidays, and all through her vacations. And all of this writing was done with no guarantee of success or even, at least at first, of ever seeing it published at all. Once *Arrows of the Queen* was published, Misty continued this grueling schedule, and she kept it up for another five or six years before she was finally able to leave her programming job to write full time. The *Arrows* books were followed in short order by: the Tarma and Kethry books, *Oathbound* and *Oathreaker; Magic's Pawn, Magic's Promise* and *Magic's Price; By the Sword;* the *Wind* books; and then the *Gryphon* trilogy. By that time, Misty had become one of DAW's rising stars, just as she'd become a sought-after lyricist and writer.

It wasn't just Misty's talent and dedication that led to her success. Misty's ability to learn something from everyone she worked with undoubtedly had something to do with it. I know from working with her on her songs that she always listened, she took constructive criticism well, she rewrote endlessly until she and I agreed that a song was right. She showed the same determination and willingness to learn when she became an author as she had when she became a lyricist. She recrafted all her work—her songs, her stories, her novellas, and finally

her novels—as closely as she could to her editor's speci-
fications and until she was happy with the work herself,
and she did it all without complaint.

The books went on to become major successes with a
life of their own. And Misty continued to write lyrics,
many of which centered around Valdemar. Fortunately,
as was true with her books, she didn't have to make the
music of Valdemar come to life all alone. Just as Misty
had C.J. Cherryh and other writers to help her learn
while she was crafting the early novels of Valdemar, and
then Betsy Wollheim to edit her books and handle the
publishing of her fiction once she became a professional
writer, over the years a number of creative people have
helped Misty breathe life into the music of Valdemar.
Just like the world of fiction, many more people other
than the creator are involved in the final product. Singers,
songwriters, and instrumentalists have all collaborated to
make the recordings of Valdemar's songs. Though the
people involved in bringing Misty's music to life are far
too numerous to mention by name and project, a few
folks deserve special attention.

The Celtic folk group Golden Bough has been involved over the years in many of the Valdemar albums,
including the very first Valdemar album, *Heralds, Har-
pers & Havoc,* released in 1988. The creative core of
Golden Bough has always been Paul Espinoza and Margie Butler, who between them play just about every folk
instrument invented. Paul and Margie found time to
work Misty's music projects into their busy touring and
recording schedule.

It isn't just people who've had a hand in bringing
Valdemar's music to life. Recording technology changed
radically since we first started working with Misty's
music. The first albums we did were preserved on analog
tape using a very simple process. We set the microphones up, recorded a song, listened to it and if it wasn't
right, we moved the microphones, rewound the tape, and
tried again. Only when the first song was perfect could
the next song on the album be recorded. This painstak-
ing process was used to create a two-track stereo master.

Eventually we began using a four-track analog tape
recorder. The advantage of a four-track system was that

we could record a track of music—say a guitar—and
then go back and record a performer singing, and control
the relative volumes of the singer and the music in the
final mix. The songs could also be recorded in any order,
and we could have musicians come in and record at different times. This was a huge improvement over trying
to corral all the musicians, the engineer, and the location, which is what we had to do in the early days.

Then we moved up to eight-track analog. Many albums of Misty's music were recorded on our trusty old
Tascam eight-track tape deck, including *Heralds, Har-
pers & Havoc, Oathbound, Oathbreakers*, and *Magic,
Moondust & Melancholy*.

Along the way we started working in larger studios,
and graduated to sixteen-track and twenty-four-track
equipment on projects such as *By the Sword, Shadow
Stalker,* and *Lovers, Lore & Loss*.

Then computers and digital technology started to
make their presence felt in the studio. We began to link
computers, electronic instruments and recording equipment using MIDI, a special language that allows computers to talk to instruments and to recording equipment.
Using the new technology, a song could have a complete
complicated arrangement written on the computer in advance. Then, by hooking up a web of MIDI cables, a
whole collection of electronic instruments, computers
with sound cards and drum machines could generate the
entire song with only the vocal tracks to be added.

Owlflight took advantage of another leap of technology: digital editing. On this album we started by creating
basic chords and melodies on the computer, recorded
these onto digital tape, then we recorded all the instrumental tracks and vocals, then we took the digital tape
and fed all the audio recording to yet another computer,
to do on-screen graphical digital editing. To me, it felt
a lot like SF and fantasy coming to life in realty. They
say the best technology is indistinguishable from magic—
recording these days seems to bear that out.

Convincing singers to come in on a chorus at exactly
the same time has always been a challenge. With digital
editing, the problem can be corrected with a few mouse
clicks. Fixing the same problem on eight-track analog

tape involved locating the exact starting point of the chorus by moving the tape over the heads by hand, marking the start point with a grease pencil, then taking the reels off, reversing the reels—the entire tape is now playing backwards—lining up the grease pencil mark with the erase head, then hitting the play button for a second so that the erase head is activated, which got rid of the offending bits without hurting anything else. This is time-consuming and nerve-wracking too, because it was a permanent change on the tape. There was no way to correct a mistake if the editor goofed. These days, it only takes a couple clicks of the mouse. Add in the ability to undo any mistakes easily, and it seems like paradise in comparison to the old analog system of sound editing.

Back in those olden days of analog editing, all false starts, thumps, and odd noises had to be edited out with a splice block, tape, and a razor blade. More marking the tape with a grease pencil, running the tape slooooowly over the heads, then cutting out the offending bit and sticking the ends back together with the world's least sticky tape. At least if the edit was bad, the splice could be pasted back in, if it hadn't fallen on the carpet and become indistinguishable from all the other bits on the cutting room floor. Some people long for the good old days. Not people in the recording business. You can trust me on that.

It's been a pleasure to work with Misty on the songs that grow out of the novels she writes. I look at the line of books she's published and marvel at her achievement, then I play the albums of Valdemar, and simply enjoy.

I know that Misty would have made it on her own— she was too determined and too talented and too hard-working not to—but I was glad to have been a part of the musical pathway that Misty forged on her way to creating the world of Valdemar to share with us all. Misty's path to writing success has hardly been traditional, as most professional writers today don't generally start as lyricists, and most bestselling novelists don't come from the ranks of science fiction fandom. All in all, Misty has had an impressive journey—one that began at a chance encounter at a science fiction convention.

A DISCOGRAPHY
OF THE
SONGS OF VALDEMAR

John Helfers

In chronological order:

Heralds, Harpers and Havoc
(Firebird Arts & Music, 1988)

"Holderkin Sheep Song" by Mercedes Lackey
"Meeting" by Mercedes Lackey
"Threes" by Mercedes Lackey
"Philosophy" by Mercedes Lackey
"Her Father's Eyes" by Mercedes Lackey
"Dark and Stormy Night" by Mercedes Lackey
"Healer's Dilemma" by Mercedes Lackey
"Sun and Shadow" by Mercedes Lackey
"For Talia" by Mercedes Lackey
"The Face Within" by Mercedes Lackey
"Laws" by Mercedes Lackey
"Musings" by Mercedes Lackey
"First Love" by Mercedes Lackey
"Arrow's Flight" by Mercedes Lackey
"Fundamentals" by Mercedes Lackey
"Otherlove" by Mercedes Lackey

"After Midnight" by Mercedes Lackey
"Herald's Lament" by Mercedes Lackey

The songs on this album are all based on characters and events in *The Heralds of Valdemar* trilogy (otherwise known as the Arrows trilogy).

Magic, Moondust, and Melancholy
(Firebird Arts & Music, 1989)

"Wind's Four Quarters" by Mercedes Lackey
"Kerowyn's Ride" by Mercedes Lackey

These two songs are based on characters and events in the novel *By the Sword.*

The following additional songs also appear on this album, but are not related to Valdemar:
"Signy Mallory" by Mercedes Lackey
"Eumenides" by Mercedes Lackey
"Medic" by Mercedes Lackey
"Gil-Shallos" by Mercedes Lackey
"Lammas Night" by Mercedes Lackey
"F.A.P." by Mercedes Lackey
"Jirel of Jorey" by Mercedes Lackey
"Golden Eyes" by Mercedes Lackey
"Mis-Conceptions" by Mercedes Lackey
"Of Cabbages" by Mercedes Lackey

Oathbound
(Firebird Arts & Music, 1990)

"Lovers Untrue" by Mercedes Lackey
"Tale'sedrin" by Mercedes Lackey
"Lizard Dreams" by Mercedes Lackey
"Shin'a'in Song of the Seasons" by Mercedes Lackey
"Snow Beast" by Leslie Fish
"Shin'a'in Warsong" by Mercedes Lackey
"Gift of Amber" by D.F. Sanders

"Winds Four Quarters" by Mercedes Lackey
"Oathbound" by Mercedes Lackey
"Hindsight" by Leslie Fish
"Advice to Young Magicians" by Mercedes Lackey
"The Price of Command" by Mercedes Lackey
"Advice to Would-be Heroes" by Mercedes Lackey

These songs are all based on characters and events in the book *Oathbound*.

Oathbreakers
(Firebird Arts & Music, 1991)

"There's Always A Reason" by Mercedes Lackey
"The Swordlady, or 'That Song' " by Mercedes Lackey
"Need" by Leslie Fish
"Mirror Spell" by Mercedes Lackey
"The Leslac Version" by Mercedes Lackey
"The Archivist" by Mercedes Lackey
"The Sunhawks" by Cecilia Eng
"Oathbreakers" by Mercedes Lackey & Cecilia Eng
"Love Found" by Mercedes Lackey
"Suffer the Children" by Mercedes Lackey
"Contemplations" by Mercedes Lackey
"Surprised By Joy" by Mercedes Lackey
"Leslac's Last Lament" by Leslie Fish

These songs are all based on characters and events in the book *Oathbreakers*.

Shadow Stalker
(Firebird Arts & Music, 1994)

"Windrider Unchained" by Mercedes Lackey
"Demonbane" by Mercedes Lackey
"My Lady's Eyes" by Mercedes Lackey
"Web of Light" by D.F. Sanders
"The Colddrake" by D.F. Sanders
"The Shadow-Lover" by Mercedes Lackey

"Vrondi's Eyes" by D.F. Sanders
"Shadow Stalker" by Mercedes Lackey
"Earth Spirit" by D.F. Sanders
"Nightblades" by Mercedes Lackey
"Hawk Brother" by D.F. Sanders
"Magic's Price" by Mercedes Lackey
"The Herald's Creed" by D.F. Sanders

These songs are all based on characters and events in *The Last Herald Mage* trilogy.

By the Sword
(Firebird Arts & Music, 1994)

"Open" by Meg Davis
"Warrior" by Meg Davis
"Blade of Desire" by Meg Davis
"A Serious Business" by Meg Davis
"Thinking out Loud" by Meg Davis
"Draw the Circle" by Meg Davis
"On the Edge of the Forest" by Meg Davis
"Kyree" by Meg Davis
"Guardian of the Night" by Meg Davis
"Keep the Peace" by Meg Davis
"Women of Steel" by Meg Davis

These songs are all based on characters and events in the novel *By the Sword*.

Lovers, Lore, and Loss
(Firebird Arts & Music, 1995)

"Coming Home" by D.F. Sanders
"Confusions" by Mercedes Lackey
"Chosen One" by D.F. Sanders
"The Cost of the Crown" by Mercedes Lackey
"Trapped Between" by Mercedes Lackey
"Trio" by Mercedes Lackey
"Recall" by Mercedes Lackey

"Dark Ending" by Mercedes Lackey
"One Answer" by Mercedes Lackey
"Promise" by Mercedes Lackey
"Battle Dawn" by Mercedes Lackey
"My Lady" by D.F. Sanders
"Heart's Own" by D.F. Sanders
"Maiden's Hope" by D.F. Sanders

These songs are based on characters and events in *The Heralds of Valdemar* (otherwise known as the Arrows trilogy).

Dangerous Heroes
(Firebird Arts & Music, 1996)

"Monster in My Head" by Michael Longcor

This song is based on characters and events in *The Mage Winds* trilogy.

These additional songs also appear on the album, but are not related to Valdemar:
"Dangerous Heroes" by Michael Longcor
"Me and My Uncle" by John Phillips
"Building Fires" by Michael Longcor
"For the People" by Michael Longcor
"Eternity's Waltz" by Michael Longcor
"Hunter of the Damned" by Michael Longcor
"I Like to Watch You Walk" by Michael Longcor
"Here's to the Next to Die" by Benjamin Dowling
"The Wild Man From Borneo" by Kinky Friedman
"This Old Dog" by Michael Longcor
"Twilight of the Millennium" by Michael Longcor

From Kitchen Junk Drawer
(Firebird Arts & Music, 1998)

"Falconsbane" by Michael Longcor

This song is based on characters and events in *The Mage Winds* trilogy.

These additional songs also appear on the album, but are not related to Valdemar:
"Kitchen Junk Drawer" by Michael Longcor
"Silver Bullet Blues" by Michael Longcor
"Pillar of Hell" by Michael Longcor
"Ballad of James A. Moon" by Michael Longcor
"Privateer" by Michael Longcor
"Pennsic War IV" by Michael Longcor
"Tribes of the Draft" by Michael Longcor
"Badlands" by John Standefer
"Truck Drivin' Vampire" by Michael Longcor
"Pirates In England" by Rudyard Kipling
"Unicorn Song" by Michael Longcor
"Rhinotillexomania" by Michael Longcor
"Quest" by Martha Keller
"Imagination" by Michael Longcor

<u>Owlflight</u>
(Firebird Arts & Music, 2000)

"In the Pelagir" by Michael Longcor
"Errold's Grove" by Cecilia Eng
"People" by Michael Longcor
"They Don't Know" by Michael Longcor
"Bad Magic Day" by Michael Longcor
"Song of the Bear Clan" by Michael Longcor
"On the Bridge" by Michael Longcor
"Send in the Silver Gryphons" by Michael Longcor
"Snare and Deadfall" by Michael Longcor
"Song of the *Hertasi* Water Killers" by Michael Longcor
"Kuari's Song" by Michael Longcor
"Lilly" by Cecilia Eng
"Friends" by Michael Longcor
"Raucous, Rude and Rowdy" by Michael Longcor

These songs are all based on characters and events in the novel *Owlflight*.

A CONVERSATION WITH BETSY WOLLHEIM

Denise Little

ELIZABETH Wollheim, better known as Betsy to those of us lucky enough to number her among our friends, is (for the benefit of everyone who hasn't read the front matter in all the Valdemar books) the President and co-Publisher of DAW Books. She is also Mercedes Lackey's first editor, the person who bought her first book, and the person responsible for editing and publishing every Valdemar book. In the fifteen years since she bought *Arrows of the Queen*, Betsy and Misty have forged an editor/author relationship that is one of the most enduring in the publishing business. Naturally, Betsy's got a big stake in the world of Valdemar, and strong opinions on the events and characters within that world. She's also got some very fond memories of working with Mercedes Lackey through the years. I asked her to share some of these, and here's what she had to say:

DL: How did you first discover Mercedes Lackey's work?
BW: The author C. J. Cherryh, a seemingly unlikely source, first brought Mercedes Lackey to my attention. C. J. had been writing for DAW since the beginning of her career, and since she had published her first book with us, she knew we were interested in first novelists, so she would occasionally pitch young aspiring-author friends of hers to me. I say "seemingly unlikely" only

because C. J. was best known for her hard science fiction, and Mercedes Lackey was an aspiring fantasy writer. Both Carolyn (C.J.) and Misty were active in fan groups, specifically filk-singing groups, in the Oklahoma area, and Misty had written a song entitled "Signy Mallory" about one of Carolyn's most famous characters. The song impressed C. J. so much that she showed it to me. It impressed me, too.

DL: What caught your eye as you were reading it?
BW: it was clear to me from the lyrics of the song that Misty had professional writing talent. Signy Mallory is a very complex character; Misty's lyrics were extraordinarily perceptive, and her style was fluid, subtle, and clever. Naturally, I asked to see if Misty had written anything besides song lyrics, and she had. Pretty soon, I had an early draft of *Arrows of the Queen* in my hand.

DL: Did you know then how much potential that young author had?
BW: Obviously I thought that Misty had serious potential; but potential is a funny thing. I think most beginning professional writers have huge potential. The question is always whether or not they will fulfill their potential. I believe that genius is made up of a small amount of inspiration and a large amount of perspiration. Misty's potential is being fulfilled because of her serious hard work and intelligent planning. Of course, at the time, I had no idea whether Misty would fulfill her potential. How could I have known? But I'm very happy she did!

DL: When you made that first contact as an editor with Misty, what do you remember best about it?
BW: Misty's energy. Most new writers are wildly enthusiastic—ecstatic even—to have a publisher interested in their work for obvious reasons, and Misty was no exception, but she had a level of energy that was truly unique. I've never seen anyone turn around a draft or make a requested editorial change with as much speed and competence as Misty did. I was just amazed. She was a real firecracker!

DL: Did Misty have a clear idea of what she wanted to do with Valdemar, even in those early days? If so, what was that? Do you think she achieved her goals?

BW: Oh, yes. That's an understatement if I ever heard one. Misty knew exactly what she hoped to achieve with Valdemar. That was another thing that impressed me— that she knew so well even then what she hoped to do in her fiction. Misty said that she wanted to create a world that would be as real and vast as Marion Zimmer Bradley's Darkover, Anne McCaffrey's Pern, and Katherine Kurtz's Deryni, and have certain elements of each in it, along with many new elements. She wanted to give to her readers what these fantasy worlds had given her. Yes, I definitely think she achieved her initial goals, but she has new goals now. I imagine as long as she's writing she'll continue to work in every book to reach new heights as a writer.

DL: What kinds of advice—editorial and personal—did you give Misty then, and how do you think it changed her work?

BW: I'm sure I told her what I tell every new author: don't quit your day job until the income from your books equals or exceeds your regular yearly income! Misty has mentioned that I advised her to bring magic into the picture early on in the first book. I still feel that it's important for an author—especially a first novelist—to indicate to a reader that they will be getting what they want, and for fantasy readers what they want is magic. I can honestly say that I don't remember too many specific details from that first editing session—it was fifteen years and countless books ago! But I do remember that *Arrows of the Queen*, despite the helpful advice from friends (and in the case of C. J. Cherryh, a highly respected author), came in the way most first novels come in to a publisher—in a very rough state. Misty needed to do significant re-writing, fleshing-out, and polishing. Which, I might add, she did with extraordinary speed, willingness and ability.

DL: From the very first, you gave the Valdemar books a distinctive and cohesive look—what were your thoughts as you worked on those early covers?

BW: We had "discovered" an artist, Jody Lee, who had worked primarily on young adult books, including some quite famous ones. We loved her style. It incorporated more design elements than most fantasy artists do, and we were looking for an author to pair her up with. Misty's books seemed right for her style, and we were so happy with the resulting combination that we've used Jody for every DAW Lackey title since, even her non-Valdemar books. I think it's important to differentiate our DAW books by Mercedes Lackey from the books she publishes with other houses. Jody's covers do that for us.

DL: How did you make the decision to begin bringing out the Valdemar books in hardcover?
BW: Honestly, I wish we had published every book Misty's ever written in hardcover! The simple fact is that in 1986 when we started work on *Arrows of the Queen,* the DAW hardcover list was brand new—we had only published two hardcover books in the history of our company. It took several years for us to realize that our hardcover line was working—was successful—and by that time the Valdemar series was well underway. We decided to make *Winds of Fate* Misty's first Valdemar hardcover because it was an important book in the series: it tells the continuing story of Elspeth, who first appears in the *Arrows* series, and it brings back the Herald-Mages, who we hadn't seen since Vanyel. Readers can get very touchy when a book in a series that had previously been released only in mass-market format is brought out in hardcover format. A certain percentage of people don't like to, or can't, spend the money for a hardcover, and aren't happy about waiting another year or so to get the paperback. As a publisher, when you make a switch like that in a series, you have to do it with a "big" book. I wish we could have made the switch earlier, with *Magic's Pawn,* but our hardcover list wasn't as well established at the time that book was published.

DL: The hardcover books were beautiful inside and out— with illustrations, maps, and a lot of design elements— very different from most of what's on the shelves. Can you talk about how the decisions about laying out and putting those first hardcovers together were made?

BW: Many of our books have maps, and we try to add appropriate design elements to all of our hardcovers—we feel that when a reader is spending over $20.00 buying a book, that reader should get a deluxe product. But what really sets Misty's hardcovers apart is Larry Dixon's beautiful interior artwork. It was a very happy coincidence that Misty married Larry, who is not only capable, but also willing, to illustrate her books! And since Larry has worked with Misty on Valdemar since the *Magic* series, and has co-authored six Valdemar novels, who could possibly be a better choice to illustrate Valdemar?

DL: Do you think that the look of the books helped drive sales?

BW: That's an interesting question. There's no way we can possibly know if the beautiful packages increased Misty's sales. We love the look of the books, and we love Jody Lee's art, and the reception to them in combination has been excellent or we would have changed the look long ago. But would the books have sold fewer copies with a different cover look? I don't know—that's something we can't answer.

DL: What kinds of publishing decisions have you made through the years that have helped DAW and Misty build her career as the author of the Valdemar books so successfully?

BW: Well, I think the decision to put Valdemar in hardcover was an important one. The uniformity of cover art through all the books in the series was important as well, for identification purposes. Readers who see a new book in the series on the shelf can recognize it immediately. Also, we put Misty in a "lead book" position in our monthly list quite early on in her career—inspired in part by the phenomenal monthly paces her books were generating. Before we published the first Valdemar hardcovers, we used a beautiful special effect—printing the cover on silver foil stock—for the Magic books, which was quite effective and made the books really "pop" on the shelves. We're always trying something new to promote the books—we're about to launch a DAW-run Mercedes Lackey website. And, of course, promotion and advertising has always been heavy for Misty's books.

DL: how has Misty's writing changed over the years you've been working with her?
BW: Obviously Misty's craft has improved with each book. Experience is always the best teacher for a writer, and Misty's been getting plenty of that. Since Misty has published twenty-four Valdemar novels in fifteen years, to avoid burnout, we've been interspersing the Valdemar books on our list with non-Valdemar books in the last few years. The variety keeps everybody excited about the next Valdemar novel, so maybe it's healthy for Misty's Valdemar production to be limited to one book a year, with many other kinds of projects in the works between the Valdemar novels. The very last thing that I as a publisher and editor, and fans as readers, want is for Misty to get burned out on Valdemar! We have some very big and exciting non-Valdemar projects in the works here at DAW, including Misty's own version of the Arthurian legend. I can hardly wait to read them.

DL: What are your favorite Valdemar books, and why?
BW: I guess I'm very typical in this department—I have a soft spot for Vanyel. I suppose I have a history of editing book with gay male protagonists. I edited Marion Zimmer Bradley's *The Heritage Of Hastur,* which was among the very first novels in our genre with a gay male hero, which was inspired by Ursula K. LeGuin's *The Left Hand of Darkness.* I remember Marion telling me that she felt Ursula had set the stage for this development in our genre by publishing a book that featured a hermaphroditic alien race. I think the character of Vanyel is something very special, and I'm extremely proud that Misty won the Lambda Award for "Best Gay Male Fantasy Hero." I also am particularly partial to *By The Sword.* Kerowyn is so different from most female protagonists—she's a hard-core career mercenary who is disinclined to sentiment or romance. (In fact, when Kerowyn does fall in love, it disrupts her plans—I always

felt she was really annoyed by it!) I know that *By The Sword* is Misty's favorite among her books, and I could tell how much fun she was having while she was writing it, so I have nice memories of that time. When Misty finished writing *By The Sword*, it was the longest book she had written at that point in her career, and she called me up laughing, and said about the manuscript: "It's 666 pages long—the devil's number!"

DL: What are your favorite characters in the series, and why?
BW: I tend to like the scrappy, difficult types, like Tylendel, and Alberich. I love Kerowyn and Tarma for their toughness. I also particularly like Skandranon's (and many other gryphons') conceitedness. I think it's amusing and realistic to have characters with negative personality characteristics who manage to be likable despite them (or sometimes because of them). My newest favorite is Herald-Chronicler Myste, for obvious reasons.

DL: What do you think readers see in Valdemar that keeps bringing them back to the series?
BW: Many, many things. Valdemar is a very rich and rewarding place to be. And Misty brings her characters to life with unusual vividness, warts and all! I think the nature of mind-magic, as opposed to the wave-the-wand kind of magic, is that it's far more personal, and far more limited, and therefore more fraught with vulnerability. I think this makes it easier for readers to become immersed in a character's plight. I also feel that the bonds with magical creatures—the Companions and the bondbirds, are a potent draw. But I think it's the incredible breadth of the history and landscape of Valdemar, which keep readers coming back to the series. With two dozen Valdemar novels in print, Misty still hasn't excavated more than a fraction of the over two-thousand-year history of Velgarth/Valdemar!

DL: As a reader, what parts of Valdemar would you like to see explored in future volumes?
BW: This could be a very, very long answer! I love Valdemar, and I'd like to see every nook and cranny

explored, so I'll try to limit my response. One story I very much wanted Misty to write is the one that she'll be writing as her next Valdemar book: Alberich's story, *Exile's Honor,* is tentatively scheduled for publication in fall of 2002. *(It is now available.)* I would also love to read the story of the woman who became the sword Need. What was her life like before she became a sword? How did this happen to her? We've seen snippets of that story, just enough to whet my appetite, and it's a vast new area and time frame of Velgarth waiting to be explored. Naturally I'd like to know more about it. Talamir's story is another obvious subject for a book or a series: that story would bring us into a whole new era of Valdemar's history—the Tedrel wars, when King Sendar was slain and Talamir lost his original Companion Taver and was re-chosen by Rolan. That time period set up everything that has happened in Queen Selenay's rule, so I think it would add to the richness of the Valdemar we know to go exploring in that era. She probably isn't ready yet, but I hope that one day Misty will tell us about the story of King Valdemar and the founding of the kingdom named after him. Exactly what was going on in the Eastern Empire that could make an honorable noble and all his people abandon everything and flee together to the ends of the known world? On a more general note, I'd like to see Misty reincarnate a Herald her readers are familiar with as a Companion who is a central character in a book—I think that would put an interesting spin on the character of the particular Companion. I have my suspicions that Misty may have done that with Kerowyn's Sayvil, but it's been a side note, not the central part of a story. And how about the story of the very first Companions? I also think that fans would enjoy reading more about the students in Healer's and Bard's Collegium. We haven't read nearly as much about the nomadic, tribal, and militarily disciplined Shin'a'in as we have about their flamboyant cousins, the Hawkbrothers. . . . As I said, I love Valdemar. I could go on and on!

DL: How does it feel, knowing you've been part of bringing the world of Valdemar to life? What are you proudest of?

BW: It feels great! Obviously I'm very proud of Misty. It isn't everyone who goes from filksinging fan to best-selling author practically overnight. I'm also proud that Misty, in all of her books, works in elements of personal and social politics without lecturing or soap-boxing. The Valdemar books have subtle moral messages about all sorts of ethical issues. Since many of Misty's readers are young, I think that this is especially noteworthy. Misty has something important to say in each book she writes.

DL: Do you have any personal stories from years with Misty that you'd like to share with her fans?
BW: Yes, I most certainly do! I have many stories, but what I'd like to tell readers is what a profound effect Misty herself (I'm not talking about her books here) has had on my life. Since developing severe cat allergies after college (where I lived in an apartment with multiple felines) I had been a petless person until I got to know Misty. Misty, as her fans know, has a large menagerie of pet parrots, and is an expert in avian biology and psychology. Hearing Misty talk about her birds, and about her relationship with Dr. Irene Pepperberg, and Dr. Pepperberg's African Grey parrot, Alex, (who is undoubtedly the most famous parrot in the world) was so fascinating that I began to frequent bird stores in lower Manhattan, where I live. Quickly, I was hooked. I had never even considered a parrot as a pet, and, like most people, I was ignorant about the true nature of parrots. I knew parrots were smart . . . but affectionate, loving, even cuddly? I never imagined any such thing! Misty spent uncountable hours with me on the phone discussing the attributes of the many various types of parrots, and counseling me about what kind of parrot I might want to buy, and how to correctly care for my non-mammal pet. Now, nine years later, I am the happy owner of five parrots. I still call Misty for her expert advice. And Misty is extremely generous with her time, but that's not all. Three years ago, knowing my then eleven-year-old-daughter, Zoe, loved cockatoos, Misty flew from Oklahoma to New York carrying a baby cockatoo, a rare and expensive bird, as a present for my daughter. We were really overwhelmed. That brings up

another point—I could tell numerous stories about Misty's generosity of spirit. Over the years she has helped more friends in need than anyone I know, sometimes putting her own safety—even her own life—into jeopardy to do it. She and Larry are volunteer firefighters in her small town. In addition to that, Misty takes more people under her wing than anyone I have ever met. It's not difficult to see where her concept of selfless Heralds come from.

DL: What kinds of challenges have you faced as you brought this series from its first published book to today's success? Do any specific publishing problems and triumphs through the years come to mind that you'd feel comfortable sharing with the fans?

BW: The only thing that could even remotely be considered a problem involves Misty's incredibly prolific writing speed. Misty writes a lot, and loves to be involved in many projects at once, often working with collaborators. Obviously, one publisher cannot handle Misty's entire output. This can occasionally become problematic when two or more of her publishers schedule a book of hers in the same or consecutive months. It's in everyone's best interests not to have Misty competing for rack space against herself! Through the years I have developed relationships with certain of Misty's other editors and we have tried to avoid this particular situation. Though Misty publishes with other houses, I am very, very proud that DAW remains her main publisher. We are extremely happy that we have been the publisher of her Valdemar books, and now Misty is publishing a variety of other types of fantasy with us, including some absolutely terrific historical fantasy. We publish most of her solo work, and the only Misty-collaboration we publish is the one with her husband, Larry Dixon. Let me say in print that DAW has a greater commitment to her career than any other publisher. She is one of the brightest stars in the DAW firmament, and that is a triumph for us as well as for her!

DL: What kinds of goals and hopes do you have for future Valdemar books?

BW: *The New York Times* bestseller list would be good! The #1 spot on it would be better!

DL: As an editor, what do look for each time a new Valdemar novel arrives on your desk?
BW: In part, what any reader looks forward to: enjoying the story! But seriously, it's my job as the editor to make sure that Misty has given her readers the best book she possibly can, in every way. I try to make sure each story is well developed in every aspect, that the action is clear and easy to follow, that the atmosphere is well established, that the ending is satisfying, that the characters are well fleshed out. Those are the things that any professional editor gets to do with any book. I'm just lucky in that Misty's work is such a pleasure.

DL: Do you have any words of advice for fans who hope one day to follow in Misty's footsteps and become writers?
BW: The most basic advice of all: if you want to be a writer, you have to write. I mean that seriously. Most people who eventually become professional writers write because they are compelled to. I always say a real writer writes in all tenses: has always written, does always write, and will always write in the future. Just keep on doing it and don't let rejection stop you. Do it until you get it right, and don't give up!

THE REALM OF VALDEMAR

As legions of fans have discovered, Mercedes Lackey's Valdemar is a fascinating, beautifully imagined realm, and the novels set in it are compelling, engrossing narratives; in fact, they are as close to addictive as anything in fiction. The main problem with Valdemar—from a reader's point of view, anyway—is that the books just don't come out fast enough. Which means that, when a new installment in the series becomes available and it's time to sit down and start reading, for some of us, anyway, those once crisp and clear memories of Valdemar aren't as pristine as they were on the glorious day when we read the last volume. Another problem—and one that Lackey fans hope will increase steadily with time— is that with so many novels in the series available, it's getting trickier to keep all the players and events from the books straight, even without allowing for the lapse of time between their publication.

For all the readers who have suffered the effects of erosion of time on their memory, or who find that with twenty-six volumes' worth of Valdemaran history stuffed in their heads the fine details occasionally get patchy, and for those who have picked up the series in the middle or are still working their way through it, what follows are two very useful aids for these readers of the Valdemar novels: a short synopsis of every book, and a concordance of all the proper names, place names, invented words, and other uniquely Valdemaran terms. May your memories be so perfect that you never need them—but if that's not the case, enjoy!

THE NOVELS OF VALDEMAR

Kristin Schwengel
and Denise Little

FOR those looking for a quick refresher course in Valdemaran history, what follows is a summary of each of the
books in the series. These storylines are, of necessity,
abbreviated, being merely long enough to remind those
who have read the books of what happened when to
whom. By their very nature, there will be spoilers in
these story descriptions, so readers should be careful
when reading material about books that they have not
yet had a chance to enjoy. We've tried to minimize these
spoilers while still presenting enough of the story to
spark the memory of those who *have* read the books,
but the balance is a delicate and not always obvious one.
We have done our best here to encapsulate the genius
of Mercedes Lackey and Valdemar without in any way
destroying the reading pleasure of those new to the kingdom. May our efforts serve you well . . .

—THE EDITORS

THE HERALDS OF VALDEMAR
trilogy
(otherwise known as the Arrows books)

1987

Arrows of the Queen

Talia Sensdaughter is a misfit among her people, the stern Holderkin in the Borderlands of Valdemar. At thirteen, while running away from home to escape an unwanted marriage arranged by her family, she is Chosen by the Grove-Born Companion, Rolan, who has been on a months-long Search for her. She returns with him to the Valdemaran capitol of Haven, where she discovers that Rolan has selected her, despite her youth and inexperience, to be the Queen's Own Herald. She accepts the challenge, and vows to grow into the role. Although she enjoys her new life at the Heralds' Collegium, especially in contrast to her grim prior existence with the Holderkin, unexpected dangers lurk there. Rumors about the last Queen's Own indicate that his death occurred under suspicious circumstances, and Talia worries that her own life could be at risk as well. She's right—only the strength of Talia's bond with Rolan saves her when the hazing of the Unaffiliated students that has been making her life as a Heraldic trainee miserable turns murderous.

Talia's brush with death brings out her Herald's Gift of Empathy. It could not have manifested at a more crucial time—Queen Selenay desperately needs Talia's help raising Elspeth, the Heir, in order to save the spoiled, selfish child and turn her into someone whom a Companion could Choose. And the Queen needs Talia's advice on matters of the realm, in order to keep the forces threatening to destroy Valdemar from within and without at bay. Using only her Gift, Rolan's advice, and the help of the friends she's made at Haven, young Talia must unravel a sinister plot that threatens to topple the throne of Valdemar itself.

1987

Arrow's Flight

Now that Elspeth, the Heir to the throne, has been Chosen by the Grove-Born Companion Gwena, Talia is finally able to concentrate on her own future. Eighteen years old and a full-fledged Herald, Talia leaves Haven to serve her internship in the company of Herald Kris as they ride an eighteen-month circuit through northern Valdemar. Rumors that Talia is misusing her Gift of Empathy and accusing her of mind-control have spread throughout the land, even to these far-flung reaches of Valdemar. The rumors accuse Talia of influencing the Queen, the Heir, and even the entire Council, to do her will. Talia is horrified when she discovers, through Kris, just what people have been saying about her, and her concerns that she has misused her Gift, even unintentionally, push her to the edge of emotional collapse. Her fears and her self-doubt feed upon each other over time, leaving her shields so thin that she becomes a danger to herself and everyone around her. But Kris and the Companions are determined to help her. Isolated together far from civilization by a massive snowstorm, they work to properly train Talia to shield and ground, something she had always done instinctively until this crisis. The success of that training helps restore her confidence in her own talents and integrity, and events rapidly prove her fitness as a Herald. Kris and Talia finish the circuit in triumph.

1988

Arrow's Fall

Talia returns to Haven after her internship and takes her rightful place on the Council as Queen's Own, only to discover that she's arrived at a crisis point. King Alessandar of Hardorn has proposed marriage to Elspeth on behalf of his son, Ancar, and many members of the Council, particularly Kris's uncle and Talia's old enemy Lord Orthallin, are for the match. But Queen Selenay,

Elspeth, and Talia all have reservations. The decision is left open, pending more information. To get that information, Talia and Kris go to Hardorn as Selenay's official envoys in advance of the Queen. The more they hear of Ancar, the more convinced they are that the marriage should be avoided. The prince has an unsavory reputation among his people, and he's assembled what appears to be his own army, including wizards reputed to practice dark magic.

Their meeting with Ancar is decisive—the Heralds are determined to get back to Valdemar and stop the match at any cost. Then Talia learns that Ancar plans to kill his father and seize the thrones of Hardorn and Valdemar by force. When the two Heralds try to return to Valdemar with what they have learned, Kris and his Companion are killed and Talia is captured and tortured. Determined to save Valdemar, even if she can't save herself, Talia knows she must stop Elspeth and Selenay before they near the border with Hardorn. If her royal friends put themselves within Ancar's reach, they'll be doomed. Talia, with the help of a trader she rescued while riding her internship circuit, is able to smuggle a package out of her prison to Rolan: broken arrows marked with the secret Heraldic Arrow Code, to take to Queen Selenay. Talia takes comfort in knowing that if Rolan's mission succeeds, she'll have saved her country. But what she doesn't know is just how determined her country is to save her.

VOWS AND HONOR
duology

1988

Oathbound

Tarma shena Tale'sedrin is the last living member of her clan. With the aid of her oath-bound friend and blood-sister, Kethry, a nobly born White Winds Journeyman-level mage, she has delivered richly deserved deaths to every one of the lawless raiders who destroyed her people. Now finally free of that blood-debt, she and Kethry are at the end of their supplies, nearly penniless, and far from the Dhorisha Plains. They must seek their fortunes and make plans for a future that neither ever expected to live to see. Tarma is a sword-sworn Kal'enedral, a celibate warrior dedicated to the Shin'a'in Star-Eyed Goddess. Kethry is soul-bonded to a magical sword known as Need, who in exchange for giving her superb sword-fighting skills and healing her wounds requires her bearer to come to the aid of women in need. As they make their way back to Tarma's home, they journey through the city where Kethry was born—Mornedealth. Kethry's past catches up with her there, and she and Tarma must combine their talents to save her from the clutches of her evil former husband and the brother who betrayed her so long ago. After checking in with the Shin'a'in clan who is caring for Clan Tale'sedrin's assets, Tarma and Kethry go on the road as mercenaries to build a fortune and the kind of reputation that will enable them to found a school for mages and warriors. Their goal in doing so is simple. The two women will need orphans and children from other clans to join them as willing members to rebuild Clan Tale'sedrin. If they can make enough of a name for themselves, they can draw from the best of those volunteers, from their pupils, and from Kethry's as-yet-unborn children to put together their new clan. If they succeed, Clan Tale'sedrin will rise again, stronger than ever. In order to earn the money and reputation they need to have access to the best recruits, they become professional mercenaries, and seek adventures that Bards can sing about.

In the course of their travels, they defeat the demon Thalhkarsh by breaking his focus-bottle and sending him back to the Abyssal Planes. But an old act of mercy and justice undoes their good deed. A bandit raider they had once left alive, though bespelled to learn a lesson, unleashes the demon again. The bandit and the demon are both bent on terrible revenge, and will stop at nothing to destroy Tarma and Kethry.

1989

Oathbreakers

Tarma and Kethry join a respected mercenary company, Idra's Sunhawks, whose captain is third in line for the throne of Rethwellan. But when Captain Idra takes a short leave from her company after her father's death to resolve a dispute between her two royal brothers over the succession to the throne, she vanishes. When the captain stops sending messages, Idra's second-in-command sends Tarma and Kethry to Rethwellan's capital city, Petras, to try to find out what has happened to their leader.

In Petras, the women make contact with the Court Archivist, Jadrek, one of the few men in the court Idra trusted. After an assassination attempt on their new friend, the two flee the country with Jadrek, heading north to find the now-exiled Prince Stefansen. The new king, Raschar, has them pursued, but they escape nearly certain death and make it into Valdemar, where they discover Stefan. Sure now that Idra was murdered by Raschar, they make plans to return to Rethwellan. Tarma, Kethry, and Jadrek, with the help of the Sunhawks and the people of Rethwellan, will gamble their lives and their talents in a desperate attempt to overthrow Raschar and place the rightful heir Stefan on the throne.

1998

Oathblood

This collection brings together previously published short stories featuring Tarma and Kethry, along with a new novella.

1985

"Sword-Sworn"

Beginning with the destruction of Clan Tale'sedrin, this

story tells of the first meeting of Tarma and Kethry and how they came to be sworn blood-sisters.

1986

"Turnabout"

Tarma and Kethry are hired by a group of merchants to guard their packtrain after a series of ambushes. They join the train in disguise, hoping to learn who is working with the bandits. But they get more than they bargained for when the bandit responsible proves to be a master of disguise.

1990

"The Making of a Legend"

Occuring in the time span between *Oathbound* and *Oathbreakers*, this story tells of the bard Leslac, who seeks to make himself famous with tales of Tarma and Kethry, and wants an opportunity to see his idols at work. He gets it— but it isn't at all what he expected it to be.

1988

"Keys"

Need drives Kethry and Tarma into a small town just in time to stop an innocent young woman from being burned at the stake for killing her husband. While Tarma stalls, risking her life in a trial-by-combat to defend the girl, Kethry works desperately to solve the "locked-door" mystery of the murder and reveal the real killer.

1992

"A Woman's Weapon"

Tarma and Kethry pass a tannery that is polluting everything around it. When they inquire about the place at a nearby village, they discover that the Guildmaster of the competing tannery there is a good man, but ailing. The women suspect that he is being poisoned, and it's up to them to save him from the murderous attentions of his rival, a man who will stop at nothing to get what he wants.

1990

"The Talisman"

While Tarma and Kethry are traveling to the Dhorisha Plains, they stop in a small holding. There they find a former schoolmate of Kethry's, and a strange mystery that is on the verge of becoming a deadly threat. As they investigate, they discover that the power of belief is stronger than any force they can bring to bear on it.

1987

"A Tale of Heroes"

Tarma, Kethry, and Warrl come upon an area that is being terrorized by a strange mage-beast. When it is slain by a hero, they find out that killing the monster was not the only reason Need brought them there. Some monsters come in the guise of heroes . . .

1993

"Friendly Fire"

True to the Shin'a'in proverb, "friendly fire isn't," Tarma receives a cursed coin in her change when she purchases provisions for the road, and the coin brings bad luck down upon all of them until a band of unsuspecting brigands comes to their rescue.

1991

"Wings of Fire"

During summer on the plains with Clan Liha'irden, Kethry's oldest child, Jadrie, discovers a dying Shin'a'in shaman floating in the river. Tarma and Kethry ride into the Pelagiris Forest to find out what happened. They are trapped there by a mage whose gift is the ability to steal the magical powers of others. But even a clever mage is no match for Tarma and Kethry . . .

1998

"Spring Plowing at Forst Reach"

This story takes place in Valdemar, where the Ashkevrons are seeking a means to control the ornery descendants of their legendary Gray Stud. Tarma uses the Shin'a'in art of horsetalking on the animals, and is able to tame even the toughest beasts.

1998

"Oathblood"

Kethry's oldest child, Jadrie, is now twelve and has become fast friends with the ten-year-old twin daughters of King Stefansen's former Horsemaster. Jadrie, Meri, and Kira swear Shin'a'in hand-and-sword friendship to each other, a sacred vow binding them to aid one another. When the twins are kidnapped and their escort slaughtered on the way home from Tarma and Kethry's school, Jadrie insists on accompanying Tarma and Kethry when they go off in pursuit of the kidnappers. Their leader, a Jkathan fanatic who will do anything to prevent Meri from sullying the Blood Royal by marrying the prince of Jkatha, with whom she has lifebonded, is about to discover the hard way that it doesn't pay to upset a member of Clan Tale'sedrin.

THE LAST HERALD-MAGE
trilogy

1989

Magic's Pawn

Vanyel Ashkevron is everything his noble father doesn't want his oldest son to be—slight, fast, smart, far too attractive for his own good, and interested in fashion and music instead of horses and weapons. Vanyel longs to escape from his family home, where he is tormented by his father and his father's armsmaster Jervis, and go to Haven to become a Bard. Finally, after a practice bout with Jervis goes terribly wrong and leaves Vanyel with a broken arm, his frustrated father sends Vanyel to foster at the Collegium in Haven with his aunt, the powerful Herald-Mage Savil. While there, Vanyel discovers that he does not have the Bardic Gift. But his disappointment is balanced with joy when he becomes lifebonded with one of Savil's protégés, the talented and Gifted Herald-Trainee Tylendel Frelennye. When Tylendel's identical twin Staven is assassinated in an ongoing blood-feud between the Felennye family and the Leshara clan, Tylendel becomes obsessed with revenge. He asks Vanyel to help him. Because of their lifebond, Tylendel can pull power from Vanyel to build a magical Gate to the Leshara homestead, then use his own powers to summon a pack of deadly *wyrsa* to destroy the Leshara family. The disastrous plan works, until Tylendel's Companion Gala repudiates him and throws herself in front of the magically summoned killers, sacrificing her life to buy time for Savil and the rest of the Heralds to get to the boys and stop the *wyrsa* before a bloodbath can take place.

Savil and another Herald-Mage take down the Gate after they've got the *wyrsa* under control, and the released energy surges through Vanyel, nearly killing him. Driven insane by the terrible consequences of his actions, Tylendel commits suicide. The lost and despairing Vanyel is Chosen by the Companion Yfandes, even though his very survival is in question. The backlash of Gate-energy has opened up all of Vanyel's many potential Mage, Heraldic, and Bardic Gifts, leaving the channels of his mind raw and the boy in torment. None of the Healers or Mages in the Collegium can help him, so Savil takes him to her friends, the exotic and elusive Tayledras in the wild Pelagir Hills. Only their Mind-Healers and Adept-Mages can help the grieving, suicidal youth, and only they can control him if he refuses to be helped. The frightened boy is torn between reaching out to his new friends or refusing to feel at all so that he can never be hurt again, when a clutch of deadly cold-drakes makes his decision clear for him. Vanyel discovers that he must learn to live and perhaps even to love again, and open himself to the feelings of others, but—most importantly—he must learn to use his formidable powers to help save those who cannot save themselves, even at the risk of his own life.

1990

Magic's Promise

At the age of twenty-eight, Vanyel is the most powerful Herald-Mage in the embattled Heraldic Circle. After an exhausting stint doing the work of four on the Karsite border, Vanyel goes home to Forst Reach to relax, accompanied by his Aunt Savil. Once there, while balancing his family obligations with his desperate need for rest, he learns of tensions across their border in the neighboring lands of Lineas and Baires. Baires is ruled by the Mavelans, a family of mages, while the Lineans are opposed to magic in all its forms.

The trouble between the two lands comes to a head when Vanyel and Yfandes sense a distant mind-cry for help coming from Highjorune, the throne-seat of Lineas. Riding pell-mell through the night, they arrive at the palace in Highjorune the next morning to discover an appalling and amazing sight: an older Herald beating a young Companion bloody, trying to get a newly Chosen boy off the Companion's back. The boy, Tashir Remoerdis, is the young heir to the Linean throne, and the only survivor of the previous night's slaughter by an unknown force of every person in the palace from the highest noble to the lowest servant. The older Herald, Lores, believes that the boy, in a panic, used his new and uncontrolled Gift for Fetching to destroy all of the palace's occupants. Vanyel offers young Tashir sanctuary at Forst Reach while he and Savil try to find out what really happened in the Highjorune palace. Tashir's life and the fate of two nations hang in the balance as Vanyel seeks the truth behind the massacre.

1991

Magic's Price

King Randale is finally dying after a long illness, painfully withering away beyond even the ability of his lifebonded partner, Healer and King's Own Herald Shavri, to help him. Randale's heir, his cousin Treven, is being rushed through Heraldic training as a result. Treven has lifebonded with Shavri's child Jisa, who, though it is not widely known in the court, is actually Vanyel's daughter—a boon given to Shavri and Randale by the Herald-Mage when it became apparent to them that Randale's illness had left him sterile. Jisa's need for a child and Valdemar's need to have an apparently fertile monarch should a dynastic marriage become necessary had led to Vanyel's decision to honor their request for his help sixteen long years ago. Now, though Randale's body is failing him, he is determined to endure as long as he can for the good of Valdemar. Even in the face of unbearable pain, he's hanging on to life until Treven can be made ready to rule.

Vanyel's nephew Medren, a Bardic Trainee, tells Vanyel that his roommate at the Collegium, Stefen, has the ability to sing away pain. A test of Stefen's Gift proves that Medren is right, and Stefen is made a Full Bard and stationed at court to attend the King and keep Randale's agony at bay for as long as possible. Before too long, Bard Stefen's determined romantic pursuit of Vanyel is making the Herald-Mage's life very interesting.

While doing what he can to ease Randale's royal burdens and avoiding the urge to give in to the almost irresistible temptation provided by the young Bard's advances, Vanyel throws himself into spell-castings to augment the magical protections of Valdemar and to reduce his country's dependence on the embattled Herald-Mages, who are being killed much faster than they can be replaced, especially since no children with the Mage-Gift have been Chosen in years. Vanyel, Savil, and two other Herald-Mages alter the magical Web protection-spell that covers all of Valdemar so that it will be a link between all Heralds, and function indefinitely without their direct supervision.

When two Herald-Mages die under suspicious circumstances, Savil becomes convinced that someone outside Valdemar is targeting them, and that she will be the next victim. Vanyel doesn't believe her until Savil, too, is slain. Grief-stricken and desperate to defeat the powerful enemy he now knows is responsible for these deaths and many others, Vanyel insists on going north to carry the fight to the unknown mage, even though visions that have haunted him his whole life lead him to believe he is marching toward his own death. But he knows that the evil he is trying to stop is so unspeakable that it is worth any price, even the ultimate one, if that's what it takes to destroy this enemy. In the company of Stefen, now lifebonded to him, and his companion Yfandes, Vanyel rides out to meet his destiny—the most dangerous and deadly battle of his life.

KEROWYN'S TALE

1991

By the Sword

With her brother's marriage taking place the next day, young Kerowyn has her hands full preparing and supervising every detail of the bridal feast. Since her mother's death, she's been in charge of the domestic affairs of the family keep, despite her youth and her longing for adventure. The granddaughter of the famous sorceress

Kethry, she knows that her destiny has to be for deeds more interesting than saving the bread sculpture meant to accompany the meal from falling to the floor. Then, in the middle of the feast, she gets her wish for adventure. The keep is attacked by well-armed and organized brigands. The casualties are appalling—her father is slain, her brother is wounded, and the bride-to-be, Deirna, the sheltered niece of a nearby baron, is abducted, stolen along with all of her wedding gifts. Kerowyn, barricaded in the kitchen with her staff, manages to survive the attack.

It's clear that there was a plan behind the violence. This was no random crime, and if someone doesn't avenge it, Kero's family will lose everything to the bride's avaricious uncle. As the only family member still standing, Kero goes to her grandmother, seeking help to rescue Dierna. Kethry gives Kerowyn the mage-sword Need, which grants the young girl fighting abilities and protection from magical attack in exchange for avenging crimes against women. With the sword's aid, and with a little help from Kethry's partner Tarma and the *kyree* Warrl, Kero is able to free Dierna from the mage who abducted her.

But her success leaves her an outcast at home. Her brother and his new wife are uncomfortable with, rather than grateful to, their rescuer. Undaunted, Kero leaves with Tarma and Kethry after the wedding, seeking training to be a mercenary soldier.

After years of training side-by-side with Daren, a prince of Rethwellan, Kero joins the Skybolts, a well-respected unit founded by a former member of Idra's Sunhawks, the company that Tarma and Kethry had once belonged to. Kerowyn proves herself to be a superb soldier. After the company is nearly decimated fighting against Karse and is left in the hands of someone less than capable of doing the job, Kerowyn is voted Captain. Under her leadership, the company more than doubles its size, and becomes the best in the world at their business.

Their reputation leads them to bigger and deadlier wars. As part of an unwritten aid agreement between Rethwellan and Valdemar dating back to the days of

King Stefen, Kero and her company are hired by Rethwellan to aid Valdemar in fighting against Ancar of Hardorn. Ancar is destroying his country to rebuild his armies, using blood-magic to bind peasant conscripts to his officers, then sending the resulting mindless troops in large-scale waves against his enemy. Facing nearly certain death at the hands of these unending assaults, Kero and her Skybolts volunteer for a suicidal charge against the enemy, a desperate attack that might allow Queen Selenay to escape alive from the battlefield. A last-second cascade of earth-magic and the timely arrival of Prince Daren and the Rethwellan army combine with the Skybolts' courage to save the day. During the course of the battle, both Kerowyn and Daren are Chosen, and Daren finds himself life-bonded to Valdemar's Queen. Now Kerowyn has to find a way to balance her conflicting responsibilities—as Captain of the Skybolts, as Companion Sayvel's Herald, and as a woman in love with Herald Eldan, who met her on a distant battlefield more than a decade ago, and has loved her ever since.

THE MAGE WINDS
trilogy

1991

Winds of Fate

After Ancar's failed invasion, Valdemar works during the resulting uneasy peace to prepare for the next attack. Herald and Heir Elspeth leaves Haven to find and negotiate with honorable mages willing to work for Valdemar. Kero gives Elspeth the sword Need before she leaves, telling her that the sword has chosen her to be its next bearer. Elspeth and Skif head out, finally ending up at Kata'shin'a'in, where they ask Kero's relatives for help. The Shin'a'in give her a map of the Dhorisha Plains, with a ring of red ink marking a spot on the northwestern edge, clearly the place the Shin'a'in want them to go. As Elspeth and Skif near that destination, they are attacked by a pack of magic-made beasts. At a ruin at the edge of the Plains, they make a stand against the lethal creatures. Arrows from unknown allies kill some of the beasts, and a pair of gryphons help drive off the rest. Elspeth and her friends survive the battle, and go to meet the strangers who aided them in the fight.

The archer is Darkwind k'Sheyna, a scout and former Mage of the Tayledras who stopped using magic after an accident fractured the Heartstone of k'Sheyna Vale and left the Clan crippled and divided, half in this Vale and half in a new location. Darkwind's mother died in that disaster, and he fears that he, as the youngest Adept, did something that triggered the Heartstone's meltdown. Torn by guilt and uncertainty, he now refuses to use his mage powers. Before the accident, k'Sheyna Vale's leaders thought that their area was cleansed of wild magic, but now they've discovered that the area to the south is still blighted. What they don't know is that it is home to a blood-path Adept named Mornelithe Falconsbane, who lusts after the immense magical power contained in the Heartstone, and who has mentally enslaved Darkwind's father, Starblade, in order to seize that power. But Darkwind discovers his father's enslavement when he saves Nyara, the catlike changeling daughter of the evil Adept. Nyara's information lets Darkwind free his father of the spell that binds him to Falconsbane. The Vale can begin to heal again. Released from his burden of guilt and fear, Darkwind once again takes up the use of his Mage powers.

He and Elspeth make a pact. He will train her Mage-Gift, if Elspeth will help Darkwind protect his Clan. They work together with the gryphons, Treyvan and Hydona, as well as with Elspeth and Skif's Companions and the sword Need, to foil an attempt by Falconsbane to steal the gryphons' children. They are even joined by Nyara, who desires nothing more than to fight against the evil that is her father. Together with the help of the Shin'a'in Swordsworn and their Star-Eyed Goddess, they drive Falconsbane out of their lands and back to his lair.

Winds of Change

With Falconsbane out of the way for the moment, it's time for the troubled k'Sheyna clan to begin to heal. Darkwind's father Starblade embarks on the slow process of recovering from Falconsbane's compulsions upon his mind, aided by his new bond-bird, the wounded hawk-eagle Hyllarr. Skif and Elspeth are welcomed into Clan k'Sheyna, and Elspeth begins her training as a Mage with Darkwind, Treyvan, and Hydona as her first teachers. While Treyvan hones Darkwind's long-unused skills, Hydona guides Elspeth in the basics of mage-craft.

But not everything is going well—k'Sheyna's mages are able to weaken their unstable Heartstone, but they are unable to repair it. Finally, they end their long isolation from other clans and send a message to the nearest Vale, k'Treva, asking for help. That aid arrives in the person of Firesong, a powerful Healing Adept. His plan to solve the problem of the flawed Heartstone is bold and dangerous: he intends to shatter the stone entirely, after removing all of its energy and anchoring it in the Void, the space between Gates, then move it to the new Vale. But an early test of his strength against the stone goes horribly wrong, as an attack by Mornelithe at that crucial juncture kills the Shin'a'in shaman, Tre'valen. Though Firesong could shield the Heartstone, he could not spare the energy to shield anything else. The Healing Mage is tormented by guilt over the young shaman's death. Mornelithe bides his time before the next attack, determined to take terrible vengeance on Nyara, k'Sheyna, and the gryphons in retaliation for his defeat. And when Firesong has anchored the Heartstone's energy in the Void, he strikes. But before he can destroy those who have opposed him, his daughter Nyara penetrates his stronghold and attacks him. Unprotected against a physical attack, Falconsbane is destroyed— sucked into the Void—but the move of the Heartstone's power to the new Vale is still not complete. Something powerful from the Forest of Shadows grabs Firesong's energy construct in the Void and pulls it away from k'Sheyna Vale to ground it in Valdemar's palace in Haven. Elspeth and Darkwind will have discover who was responsible—against all reason, they believe that it might be the spirit of the Last Herald-Mage Vanyel, who died nearly six hundred years before.

1993

Winds of Fury

Ancar of Hardorn is furious at being unable to conquer either Karse or Valdemar, who have ceased their old enmity and allied against him. He is even more upset that he is only a Master mage, when he yearns to become an Adept. While seeking a path to greater powers, he tries to reconstruct a Gate-spell from an old manuscript, but in his ignorance and inexperience he loses control and brings Mornelithe Falconsbane to him from out of the Void. Ancar puts coercion spells on his new treasure, and has the evil mage carted out of sight and held for later use. Mornelithe's mind has been weakened by the months he spent in the Void, and this enables the spirit of the young Shin'a'in An'desha shena Jor'ethan, whose body Falconsbane stole long ago, to emerge. Unlike any other person taken over by the ancient spirit of the mage Ma'ar in his quest for immortality, and there have been many through the thousands of years since Ma'ar's death, including Falconsbane, An'desha's spirit had survived intact by hiding in a concealed corner of his own mind rather than fighting the takeover. Aided by two Avatars of the Star-Eyed Goddess, An'desha shields himself from Mornelithe and learns from the Adept's memories. He realizes that Falconsbane/Ma'ar is evil and must be destroyed, even if he loses any chance to regain his own life in the process.

When Darkwind, Elspeth, Skif, Nyara, Firesong, Treyvan, and Hydona try to Gate from k'Sheyna to k'Treva, their Gate-spell is twisted and they end up in the Forest of Sorrows, brought there by the spirit of Elspeth and Firesong's ancestor, Vanyel Ashkevron. He warns them that he must take down his ancient protections around

Valdemar. He wants them to warn the Queen and prepare for what will come. Elspeth and her party proceed to Haven, where she electrifies the assembled Court by abdicating her position as Heir in favor of her younger twin siblings. She prefers to concentrate her energies on her Mage-Gift—training it and using it in Valdemar's protection, for she believes that Ancar will not wait long to attack once the Border protections are down. Her instincts are right—Ancar, under Mornelithe's influence, decides to spend his troops in an all-out effort to conquer Valdemar. His attacks roll right over Valdemar's defenses, and Kero and Elspeth suggest a complete evacuation of the country in Ancar's path while a small counterattack group slips in disguise into Hardorn, with instructions to destroy Ancar, his teacher Hulda, and Mornclithe Falconsbane, even if it costs them their own lives.

THE MAGE WARS
trilogy

Taking place a thousand years before Valdemar was founded, this trilogy is the history of Urtho, the Mage of Silence, and of his creations, the gryphons, and his people, the Kaled'a'in clan k'Leshya.

1994

The Black Gryphon

Urtho, the Mage of Silence, is fighting for the lives of his people against the Mage Kiyamvir Ma'ar, a bloodpath Adept who wants Urtho's lands, power, and knowledge, and is willing to destroy everything in his path to get them. Every day brings new casualties and the pain of loss, though it seems, for the present at least, that though they give up a little more ground every day, defeat is not inevitable. Urtho's delight is in creation, not destruction, so the war is a great sadness for him, but it must be waged if everything he believes in is to survive. Urtho's most beloved creations are the gryphons, and the brash and brave Skandranon Rashkae, the Black Gryphon, is the greatest of gryphons.

Ma'ar's forces continue to advance through Urtho's territories, despite their army's unceasing efforts to stop them. Even the great Skan himself can't win the war single-handed. Though they have many victories to celebrate, the defeats keep piling up. Ma'ar's forces are willing to stoop to tactics that would never even occur to the life-loving Urtho and his forces. Giving way to the inevitable, Urtho begins to plan the evacuation and eventual destruction of his Tower, not wanting any of his power or weapons to fall into Ma'ar's hands where they would be subverted and abused. But before he can put his plan into action, a traitor in the midst of Urtho's own troops brings slow death to Urtho and the Tower. Struggling to survive long enough to see his people saved, Urtho gives his most potent weapon to Skan, hoping his beloved gryphon can find one last chance to destroy Ma'ar before Ma'ar can bring pain and death to everyone they love. Skan makes it to the center of Ma'ar's territory and, against all hope, brings down their enemy. Now Skan must survive to enjoy his victory and to lead the people Urtho fought so hard to save as they face a world shattered by the destruction of the Mage of Silence.

1995

The White Gryphon

Ten years after the joint destruction of the fortresses of Ma'ar and Urtho, the Kaled'a'in Clan k'Leshya has settled in the distant west, carving out a city in the wilderness from cliffs overlooking the sea. Envoys of the Haighlei Empire far to the south arrive, claiming the land as theirs, and demand that the settlers leave or be removed. Knowing that their new home, the city of White Gryphon, could not be easily defeated, the leaders of the city offer alliance with King Shalaman in exchange for the territory. Skan and the kestra'chern Amberdrake, along with their families, return with the Haighlei envoys to negotiate for their right to stay.

The Haighlei are a people bound by custom, forbidding change except when it is mandated by the king once every twenty years during an eclipse—an event which is soon approaching, and which could be used to make the alliance Skan hopes for official. The tentative agreement between White Gryphon and the Empire is jeopardized when a number of murders occur in the palace, each staged to appear as though either Amberdrake or Skandranon had committed them. With their lives and the well-being of their people at stake, Skan and Amberdrake must prove their innocence before the true killer strikes at the heart of the Haighlei Court, and destroys their hopes of building a permanent home in this distant land.

1996

The Silver Gryphon

Skandranon's son, Tadrith, and Amberdrake's daughter, Silverblade, are partners in the Silver Gryphons, the policing force of White Gryphon. Their first assignment takes them to a far outpost, something both youngsters are excited about, perhaps because they feel smothered by the concerns and reputations of their famous parents when they are at home. They fly out, Tad guiding a carry-basket to hold Blade and their supplies, all made weightless by magic. The first few days of travel are uneventful, but on the third morning of their journey disaster strikes. All the magic drains out of the basket and, despite Tad's best efforts, the two fall to earth, breaking Tad's wing and Blade's collarbone in the resulting crash. All of the magic has been drained from their equipment, as well, including their communication gear. They make camp where they landed, but soon realize that predators are watching them, and possibly even stalking them. Though injured and in pain, they are not about to give up. They pack up everything useful that they can carry and make a run for the cliffs of a nearby river, struggling to evade their pursuers.

Though they can't call for help, the absence of Tad and Blade has been noted. White Gryphon sends out search and rescue parties, and the rescuers soon realize that Tad and Blade must be lost in the area where all magic seems to have vanished. Their frantic parents join two of the rescue parties, and the group Skan and Drake are in soon finds the wrecked basket and begins to trail the youngsters: The unknown predators, however, locate the would-be rescuers, and Skan and Drake must struggle to stay alive long enough to save themselves and find their missing children. Fighting side-by-side, Tad, Blade, Skan, and Drake discover truths about their relationships that would have taken years to learn in civilized society. And before they are done, they teach the beasts who thought to trap them a deadly lesson.

THE MAGE-STORMS
trilogy

1994

Storm Warning

Emperor Charliss, ruler of the vast and powerful Eastern Empire, is choosing his Heir. To test his current favorite, Grand Duke Tremane, he places Tremane in command of a major operation of the Imperial army, currently stalemated after its initial successes in the invasion of Hardorn. If Tremane succeeds in conquering Hardorn, he will be first in the line of succession in the Empire and will be trained to take over the Iron Throne upon Charliss's death. If Tremane fails, his chief rival, the ruthless assassin Adept Baron Melles, will be named Heir. The situation is clear to Tremane—success will make him Emperor, but failure is a death sentence.

Back in Valdemar, unaware of events in the far East, Firesong and An'desha now live together in an indoor Vale in Haven. But, though he knows that his life these days should be without care, An'desha is haunted by terrifying nightmares of something gone horribly wrong, and he fears that they are prophetic, warnings of dire events to come.

Under the respective leadership of Queen Selenay and the Son of the Sun Solaris, Valdemar and Karse continue to strengthen their alliance, despite centuries of hereditary enmity between the two countries. Solaris has sent has a diplomatic team to Valdemar—Sun-priest Ulrich and his secretary and Priest-in-training, Karal. Like An'desha, Karal feels lonely and out of place in Haven, so Queen's Own Herald and Empath Talia introduces the two boys, beginning a fast friendship.

In Hardorn, Grand Duke Tremane has consolidated his position and is about to improve upon it when a vast wave of mage-energy rushes through, disrupting all of the army's permanent magics. Although the Mage-Storm traveled from east to west, Tremane believes that it is an attack sent by Valdemar. He is already concerned by Valdemar's actions, particularly by the newly-formed Alliance between Valdemar, Karse, the Shin'a'in, the Tayledras, and the Kaled'a'in. In a desperate act of retaliation, he sends an order to his agent in the Valdemaran court to kill as many of the foreign envoys as possible in a bid to destroy that Alliance.

But the Valdemarans had nothing to do with the Mage-Storm. They only know that an assassin, most likely one from the Eastern Empire, has attacked them—and successfully. Karal's master Ulrich is among the dead, as is the Shin'a'in ambassador. The Alliance remains firm, and Karal takes his master's place in the Valdemaran Court. Investigations reveal that the Mage-Storms, which were predicted by An'desha's dream, are an echo of the original Cataclysm resulting from the death of Urtho and Ma'ar, with the echo taking place in reverse, starting slowly and building over time.

As the storms' effects increase, all of Valdemar, from the Artificers and the Mages to the Heralds and the envoys from foreign lands, struggle together to find a way to shield the peoples of the Alliance, as well as to deal with the continued threat from the Eastern Empire, and from Tremane and his forces.

1995

Storm Rising

The world of Velgarth is being battered by steadily increasing mage-storms, echoes from the Ancient Cataclysm that resulted from the deaths of Urtho and Ma'ar. Tremane and the Imperial forces in Hardorn are suffering terribly under their increasing onslaughts. Having heard nothing from the Emperor, Tremane must assume that Charliss has abandoned them in the face of the current disaster. It is left to him, then, to find a solution that will save his troops. After raiding an Imperial supply depot using forged Imperial Orders, Tremane has enough goods and gold coin for his men to survive the winter, though he has cut his last ties to the Emperor to get it. Tremane withdraws his army from Hardorn's frontiers to the town of Shonar, and when his men are all accounted for, he sets up a permanent encampment, driving his troops to prepare for the worst winter weather imaginable. By the time the icy storms close in on them, Tremane and his men have prepared well enough to survive.

In Valdemar, the temporary shield they erected to absorb the worst of the storms is working for now, but a more permanent solution is desperately needed. Karal is convinced that the next step in defeating the mage-storms must involve the Imperials to be effective, and he and An'desha scry the Imperial camp, looking for someone they can approach on behalf of Valdemar. They discover Tremane, and find him to be more open-minded and reasonable than they had anticipated. Though Karal knows that Tremane is responsible for Ulrich's death, he knows he must get past his hatred of the man for the good of Karse, Valdemar, and all of the Alliance. Despite shock and dismay from Selenay and Solaris when they discover what he has done, both rulers come to see that Karal is right. The Alliance adds a new member—Tremane's Hardorn.

The Valdemaran artificers discover by sheer accident that a powerful magical force generated from the center of the concentric circle of the mage-storms would temporarily cancel the worst of their effects. The Shin'a'in envoy tells of the weapons of Urtho still buried beneath the remains of his Tower, which the Shin'a'in have guarded for centuries. Sejanes, one of Tremane's Mages, uses his expertise with Portals to Gate a group to the ruins near k'Leshya Vale, and a hand-picked task force including Firesong, Karel, An'desha, the gryphons Treyvan and Hydona, the Companion Florian, and the Firecat Altra travel to the Tower, hoping to find a way to use Urtho's own tools to create the counter-storm they need to buy them time to truly stop the Mage-storms. Working together, this unlikely group from different races, different cultures, and different lands has the fate of the world balanced in their hands.

1996

Storm Breaking

Still encamped at Urtho's Tower after generating their counter-storm, the Allies from all over Velgarth are determined to come up with a permanent solution to the mage-storms, for they know that the deadly cycle will continue to build until it triggers a second Cataclysm unless someone can find a way to stop it. They feel that they, of all possible groups, have the best chance to do so, especially with the things they've found among the ruins of Urtho's Tower.

While their friends are working on a way to stop the mage-storms permanently, Darkwind and Elspeth travel to Hardorn as the official representatives of the Alliance to Tremane's encampment at the town of Shonar. After getting to know and trust Tremane, they convince him to participate in an earth-binding ceremony that ties him to the land of Hardorn. When it becomes clear that Tremane has earth-sense to a profound degree and so would never be able to abuse the land or its citizens, the people of Hardorn declare him their king.

The secretive northern country of Iftel also sends a delegation to Tremane and the Alliance. To the shock of nearly everyone, it seems that Iftel is protected and closely watched by Vkandis, the same god that reigns over Karse. Equally interesting is the fact that the delegation from Iftel is a troop of gryphon-fighters, descended from a lost wing of the ancient Mage Urtho's armies. Tashiketh, the leader of the troop, works with Elspeth, Darkwind, Tremane, and Solaris to try to shield important mage-nodes and Heartstones from the building mage-storms.

Back in the Eastern Empire, Emperor Charliss has learned of what has gone on in Hardorn, and has disowned Tremane. Now he names Tremane's greatest enemy as Heir. The Emperor blames both Tremane and Valdemar for the collapse of the Empire during the mage-storms, and plans to use the last of his mage-power to destroy them both. And if he does so, adding the power he can release to the power of the mage-storms at their height might just destroy a good chunk of the world along with Valdemar. Strangely, it is Baron Melles's character flaws—his ruthless self-interest and his superb assassin skills—rather than his strengths that enable him to avert that disaster.

Just as the storms reach their crest, the group at the Tower, in concert with the Artificers back in Haven, a number of Spirit Avatars, the ghosts of Herald-Mage Vanyel and Stefen and Yfandes, and even the sword Need, discover a possible solution to the mage-storms—but the price of using that solution might be the lives (or the closest equivalent, in the cases of several of the more unusual beings present) of everyone gathered at Urtho's Tower.

THE OWL TRILOGY
(otherwise known as Darian's Tale)

This series begins about a year after the end of the mage-storms, and takes place in the far northwestern corner of Valdemar, on the country's border where a number of very different cultures meet.

1997

Owlflight

Darian Firkin is an orphan in the village of Errold's Grove, fostered against his will to the small town's somewhat ineffective mage, Justyn. Darian's parents disappeared in the Pelagiris Forest during a mage-storm, and the villagers decided what to do with Darian without ever consulting him. After hearing the villagers repeat every day that his much beloved parents were crazed to go into the forest, and that they brought danger to the village every time they did so, not to mention what a useless and troublesome boy he was, Darian is turning into a resentful teenager.

But before Darian can make his mind up to run away or rebel, disaster strikes the village. A well organized group of brigands destroys the volunteer militia, and is heading straight for the town bent on mayhem. Darian hears the alarms and comes back from the forest just in time to see Justyn call a Final Strike upon himself, destroying both the lizardlike monster at the head of the army and the only bridge into the town, but not halting the brigands' advance permanently. All Justyn's sacrifice can do is buy enough time to allow the villagers to escape. Darian flees back into the forest, where he eludes his pursuers with the help the Tayledras scout Snowfire k'Vala and his bond-bird, the eagle-owl Hweel.

The Tayledras are in the area to reshape the reforming magical ley-lines and nodes into a matrix that will be beneficial to themselves and the Valdemaran Herald-Mages, and to prevent rival Dark mages from locking the gathering power to themselves. They offer to adopt Darian into their Clan, on the condition that he learn to use his Mage-Gift. Darian agrees. The Hawkbrothers assume that the villagers have escaped to Lord Breon and Kelmskeep and have no need of them, but they feel a real liking and sympathy for this upset boy that leads them to offer him their protection.

When the clan learns that the villagers did not escape, but instead have been captured and are being used as slave labor by the invaders, the Tayledras realize that they must do something to save Darien's people. Though greatly outnumbered, they make a bold night strike to free the villagers and break the brigand's hold on the village before the shaman-mage leading the brigands can steal the magical power building there and use it for his own dark devices. And Darian, who came along only as their guide to the village, finds himself facing that very mage, with the fate of all the people he loves dependent upon his ability to face down and destroy this powerful foe.

1998

Owlsight

Some four years after *Owlflight*, Keisha Alder is the Healer at Errold's Grove, and the small town is now a thriving village. Having cleansed the forests north of Valdemar, Darian and the Hawkbrothers return to k'Vala Vale. They are unable to remain there for long, however, for gryphons on a far northern patrol have seen another group of barbarians coming south. Unlike the brigands that nearly destroyed Errold's Grove, this is an entire Clan rather than an invading army, and they are obviously planning to settle in the area.

Darian and a group of volunteers take occupancy of the Vale near Errold's Grove that Mage Starfall had begun years ago, and call it k'Valdemar. When the northern Clan shows no signs of stopping before they reach Valdemar's border, Haven sends a force led by Herald-Captain Kerowyn to offer settlement agreements to the tribe. The Valdemarans learn that the Clan has been stricken by a plague and believes that they have been led to this place by their totem animal, a Ghost Cat, to find a cure. Darian and Keisha realize that the Clan has a point—a cure must be found, or the disease could spread to Valdemar. The two work together in a desperate attempt to find a cure for the illness, as well as the means to deliver it the Ghost Cat Clan and have them accept it, before they and the people of the Clan and of Valdemar are decimated by disease and war.

1998

Owlknight

K'Valdemar Vale near Errold's Grove has become a neutral ground where the disparate peoples of the area can come together to settle their differences. Darian Firkin k'Vala k'Valdemar is in the unusual position of having a tie to each of the communities that make up this unique vale—the Tayledras, the villagers, Lord Breon's people, and the Ghost Cat Clan—and he has a position of authority in each of them, but despite his responsibilities to these disparate groups, he has personal issues he wants to attend to. He is very much in love with Healer Keisha, and he still wants to learn what happened to his parents. Prophetic dreams seem to indicate to him that his father and mother are still alive, and that he should locate them. Following old trapping trails, he finds the bones of a human foot at the very edge of a Change-Circle, sheared off in a boot that he recognizes as his father's. Using Darian's find and magic, Firesong is able to determine that Darian's father is still alive and lives somewhere far to the north and west.

Darian forms a search party to help him look for his parents. His friends and he will travel under the guise of traders, taking Keisha's dyes and spices as trade goods. As they work their way north, Keisha also teaches her Healing skills to the Wisewomen and Shaman of the clans they stay with. The Wolverine tribe, led by a shaman-mage, has taken the place of the vicious Blood Bear Clan that was destroyed years ago in Errold's Grove, and now are attacking and destroying all the tribes in their path. In order to find Darian's parents, the searchers must pass through the Wolverine Clan's territory. Darian is faced with a choice—whether to put everyone that he loves at risk in the harsh lands and hostile tribes of the distant North, or to give up on the dream of finding his parents. Or there might be a third choice—if he can only find a way to defeat the enemies threatening them all, with a tiny force of allies and a great deal of cleverness.

THE EXILE
duology

2002

Exile's Honor

Alberich had spent most of his youth in the Karsite military schools training to be an officer. As the bastard son of a tavern wench, he knew that he was lucky to have been selected for training although he had had to leave his mother at thirteen. Pushing himself ruthlessly, he rose in the ranks with almost unnatural speed, and in battle, he had an uncanny way of knowing what the enemy's next move would be, and when and from where an attack would come. Instinctively, he attempted to hide this ability, almost a "sixth sense," from the Sunpriests of Karse who kept careful watch for anyone exhibiting the "demon powers" of Valdemar. Those they caught were "cleansed" in the fires of Vkandis Sunlord.

When Alberich became one of Karse's youngest captains, he received a special gift—a handsome white stallion "liberated from the enemy." But his commission and his gift were merely a ruse, for the Sunpriests suspected Alberich's special ability and set him up for capture. Rescued from the fires by his strange white horse and carried over the border into Valdemar, Alberich's life was saved by the Healers of the Collegium. Living among those he had always considered his direst enemies, he learned a truth he would never have dreamed existed: that he had been Chosen to be a Herald, and that his white horse was not a horse at all, but a magical, telepathic being who had sought him out. But unlike most newly Chosen Heralds, Alberich was filled with confusion and mixed feelings. He was a Karsite, and could never truly be anything else, although he was forever banned from his homeland. Uneasy in his new home, nonetheless he is pleased to be singled out for his outstanding military expertise by the aging Weaponsmaster Dethor, who is looking for a Herald to train as his eventual replacement. Excused from the usual student Collegium responsibilities, he goes to live with Dethor in the salle and becomes his Second. Training students satisfies Alberich like nothing else, but he accepts another unique duty from King's Own Herald Talamir: that of a very special kind of spy. Alberich already works undercover in the slums of Haven, but agrees to allow his Karsite memories to be "transplanted" into the minds of Heralds who would then be able to infiltrate into Karse. Alberich only agrees to this because the Karsites have hired the deadly and ruthless Tedrel Mercenaries to wage war against Valdemar—a war that Alberich realizes could destroy both Karse and Valdemar. Meanwhile, young Princess Selenay has taken a liking to the taciturn Karsite and has made him her personal bodyguard and Champion. After years of devastating skirmishes with the Tedrels, the forces of Valdemar eventually must confront them on the battlefield. In battle King Sendar is killed, Talamir nearly dies from the loss of his Companion, but is saved by Rolan, another Grove-Born Companion, Alberich wins the support of Valdemaran troops by his extreme valor, bravery and loyalty, and the new Queen Selenay names Alberich as temporary Queen's Own Herald until Talamir is able to resume his duties. Alberich returns to Valdemar in a position of honor and respect and he realizes that he can be loyal to his newfound nation without betraying Karse or his values.

2003

Exiles' Valor

Alberich has come to accept that his life is now rooted in Valdemar, and has fully given his loyalty to the country's new queen. Queen Selenay assumed the throne after the death of her father in the Tedrel Wars. Alberich played an important part in securing Valdemar's victory in those terrible wars, but even with victory, the country is still facing all kinds of threats—from neighboring countries, and from fractioning factions in the Valdemaran Council Chamber.

Selenay is young, attractive, and intelligent, but in many ways she is not yet fully ready for the responsibilities that have been thrust into her hands. She relies on Alberich for protection, for a cool head, and for an understanding of the nasty infighting that already threatens her rule.

The Council wants nothing more than for Selenay to get married and provide an heir to the throne. On that they are all agreed. But the council's list of prospective grooms is a disaster—with one of them merely ten years of age, others as old as ninety, and all of them wrong for Selenay for one reason or another. Most of all, they are anathema to Selenay because she knows that the Council wants a King, not a Queen, and would prefer a King that they can control. And every prospect on the Council's list would owe loyalty to the Council, not to her. With the help of Herald-Chronicler-Second Myste, Selenay manages to strike off every candidate the Council can agree on. But even though she's got the Council stalled, somebody is making trouble for her reign behind the scenes.

Alberich has been searching the city under cover, keeping track of the people fomenting rebellion. He can find the low level plotters, but he has not been able to find the identity of the powerful and shadowy presence behind them, stirring up unrest and paying people to cause trouble. When Queen Selenay stages an Ice Festival in the city to brighten spirits and get the minds of her people off the memories of the Wars, it provides opportunity to everyone who wants a chance to intrigue against the palace. And Alberich notices one particular young man—young aristocrat Devlin Gereton—receive a secret message from actor Norris Lettyn during one of the dramatic performances at the Festival. Alberich decides to keep a close eye on both the young men.

Myste infiltrates Lettyn's dramatic company. Soon enough she is able to get hold of enciphered communications that may hold the key to conspiracy, if she and Alberich can crack their code and determine their meaning.

As Alberich and Myste close in on the intrigue that is playing out before them, they discover that it is a plot to bind Selenay to a very eligible foreign prince from Rethwellan—handsome young Prince Karathanelan. Someone who knows Selenay far too well has been feeding information about her deepest desires to the plotters. By the time Myste and Alberich have discovered the plot and decoded the messages, it is too late. Selenay has chosen the Prince for her Consort. On the surface, it seems to be a love match. But Alberich doesn't trust the Prince. And none of the Companions can stand to be around him. It's clear to Alberich that Selenay doesn't know nearly enough about her handsome new husband.

The more that Alberich and the Heralds find out, the less they like the situation. The new Consort is sneaky, underhanded, and arrogant. He surrounds himself with dangerous sycophants. He's not welcome back in his own land—even his own brother, the King of Rethwellan, doesn't trust him.

But the Heralds can't act upon their doubts. The marriage has taken place. Selenay is pregnant.

What Alberich *can* do is to carefully train a bunch of new and unobtrusive guards for his Queen. Under the guise of training them to play a new game, he shows a bunch of young Herald-trainees how to counter every move he can think of that the Prince might use to try to end Selenay's life. Alberich suspects, though he can't prove it, that the ambitious Prince is plotting to get rid of his wife once their child is born.

And Alberich is right. Shortly after Elspeth is born, when Selenay is taking a relaxing ride around the Home Farms, the Prince makes his move. Selenay is nearly overpowered, but manages to fight off her assailants for a crucial few seconds. Alberich and his Herald-trainees arrive in the very nick of time. They save Selenay, and kill the Prince and most of his co-conspirators.

But, to Alberich's dismay, he is not able to confirm

his deepest suspicions that, pushing all of them around like pieces on a chessboard, Lord Orthallen is somehow behind all of these troubles.

Without the evidence to prove it, all Alberich can do is keep his eyes open and be prepared for the next attack.

INDIVIDUAL NOVELS

2000

Brightly Burning

Lavan Chitward is a misfit in his own family. His parents are important in the Needleworkers' and Cloth Merchants' Guilds, but he has absolutely no urge to follow in their footsteps. When the whole family moves to Haven because of his parents' work, he loses even the comfort and familiarity of the home he has known his whole life. When they are unable to interest him in apprenticing, his family sends Lavan to the Merchants' School in Haven, hoping he'll learn a great deal and find a trade that calls to him. But Lavan's hopes for the future are dashed by his discovery that the school is dominated by student bullies who torment and abuse the younger children. When the bullies attack Lavan, he feels ill, and his skin glows red with fever. He tries to avoid the older boys, but one terrible day they find him, trap him in an unused classroom where no one can come to his aid, and flog him nearly to the point of unconsciousness. Rage builds within Lavan, and that ill feeling comes over him again, this time overwhelming him. Lavan has the Gift of FireStarting, and in this awful moment, it comes to life in an uncontrolled surge of power that makes room burst into flame and kills the four boys who tormented him.

Badly burned, Lavan is taken to the Healers' Collegium for treatment. When he awakens, he is Chosen by Companion Kalira, who says she will be able to control his Gift for FireStarting even when he cannot. Despite the accusations of murder lodged by one of the dead boys' family, the Heralds stand by Lavan. Valdemar is now openly at war with Karse, and Lavan, with his extraordinary abilities, has become one of the most important Heralds in the land. However, the Heralds fear that one day, even with Kalira's help, Lavan will not be able to control his rage and will destroy everything near, be it friend or foe.

But events prove that fear to be unjustified. Even when the crazed mother of one of the boys who died puts him at terrible risk and confronts him in front of the King and most of the city of Haven, he is able to control his Gift. And as the war with Karse intensifies, his talent saves the day in battle after battle—until an overwhelming force gathers at Valdimar's border, and the enemy makes the mistake of targeting Lavan's Companion Kalira. From that moment, the enemy's fate is assured, and Lavan Firestarter's name will go down in Valdemar's history books.

2001

Take a Thief

Herald Skif is the first thief to be Chosen in the history of the Collegium. But he would never have guessed his fate back when he was a poor orphan left in the care of his uncle, Londer Galko, who owns the run-down *Hollybush* tavern in the poorest part of Haven. Skif's life is an endless series of chores, hunger, and ducked blows.

Skif spends his afternoons roaming the city taking what he can from the wealthier families in Haven, including the food that keeps him from starvation. His favorite source of sustenance is the home of Lord Orthallen, since that nobleman's household is so large that no one notices Skif slipping in and out. One day, as he's hiding there in a washroom loft, Skif surprises a young thief in the act. In exchange for his silence, Skif asks the thief, Deek, to teach him what he knows.

Deek brings Skif to meet Bazie, his teacher in thievery. Bazie makes his living by taking in foundling boys and teaching them the art of thieving. His motto is to never take more than what is needed, because to do so invites trouble. Bazie and his boys accept Skif into their lives after trouble at the Hollybush leaves Skif without a home.

Bazie proves to be a fine teacher and a caring mentor, a man who takes the boys he trains into his heart. It's the first time since his mother died that Skif has felt like he was part of a family. He spends a satisfying few years with Bazie, steadily becoming more skilled in all the thieving trades. Then Skif returns home to find his building in flames and Bazie and his friends dead in the wreckage. Wild with grief, Skif would have gone to his own death trying to save them if not for Herald Alberich, who pulls the boy back from the fire and knocks him unconscious.

Homeless and grief-stricken, Skif makes it his mission to find and get revenge. In the course of his quest, he realizes that the ultimate orders came from someone very powerful. After finding the arsonist, Skif spies upon him day and night, hoping to discover who ordered the fire. In the course of his surveillance he again meets Herald Alberich, and is Chosen by the Companion Cymry. When the arsonist is killed, Skif fears his last link to Bazie's killer has been severed, but finds a new set of clues by threatening his Uncle Londer, who has a finger in most of the unsavory activities in the city. That information links the man responsible for the fire with a crime ring that kidnaps and enslaves children. Skif offers himself as bait and, with Alberich as his backup, lets himself be kidnapped. The plan works, and reveals that Guildmaster Vatean, a friend of Lord Orthallen's, is behind the slavery ring in Haven as well as the arson that killed Bazie and the boys. The reformed thief begins his new life at the Collegium with the largest family he could imagine, the Heralds and Companions, and with a vow to help and defend the helpless of Valdemar as his way of fighting back against those who would do evil.

1997

Sword of Ice and Other Tales of Valdemar

A collection of short stories set in and around Valdemar, three of which are co-authored by Mercedes Lackey.

"Sunlancer" by Philip M. Austin and Mercedes Lackey

A young Karsite captain is troubled by the actions of Vkandis' priests. The questions of a scholar, a guest of his grandfather's who is actually a Herald in disguise, make Clarrin realize that the priests counterfeit their miracles.

"The Demon's Den" by Tanya Huff

Herald Jors is inside an old mine when a rockfall buries his legs. His Companion goes to the nearby mining village for aid, but only blind and legless Ari, the former chief engineer of the mine, is willing to go back to help save him.

"Ironrose" by Larry Dixon and Mel White

In a Hawkbrother Vale, Ironrose the smith and Sunrunner the hunter each long for the other, but both are too shy to act. Two *hertasi* conspire to join the two.

"Babysitter" by Josepha Sherman

Leryn, a gem-merchant whose caravan has been destroyed by bandits, finds a dead gryphon in the wilds north of Lake Evendim. Knowing he can't leave her gryphlet to die, he cares for it.

"The Salamander" by Richard Lee Byers

A former mercenary, now a sword-teacher, is hired by a minor leader of the Blue faction in Mornedealth to find out who among the Greens is torching her properties.

"A Child's Adventures" by Janni Lee Simner

A Companion comes to the small village of River's Bend, Choosing Inya. Inya refuses to go with the Companion, saying that she is too old to be a Herald and that the Companion should have chosen her granddaughter.

"Blood Ties" by Stephanie D. Shaver

Rivin is a twelve-year-old boy whose mother died five years ago. After he takes his two younger sisters to their aunt for care, his older sister Sattar acts strangely but refuses to answer his questions.

". . . Another Successful Experiment" by Lawrence Schimel

A Herald-Trainee named Chavi invents a team game for Heralds and Companions, which can be used for equitation practice and combat training.

"Choice" by Michelle West

Kelsey, a tavern barmaid, insists on helping a wounded Herald get his urgent messages to Haven. They hire onto a caravan, for his Companion is too badly injured to bear him, but the caravan is pursued, for others do not want the Herald to tell his story.

"Song of Valdemar" by Kristin Schwengel

Revyn, a young Healer-trainee, resists his own interest in Healing. When he learns that his beloved younger sister has died of a fever, he blames himself. Finally she appears to him in a dream and helps him accept his calling.

"The School Up the Hill" by Elisabeth Waters

Leesa, the new scullery maid at an inn in Bolthaven, is Mage-Gifted. Her MindSpeech is so strong that she "hears" the instructions the teachers at Quenten's school give their students.

"Chance" by Mark Shepherd

Guardsman Jonne saves Vanyel's life on the Karsite Border after a mage-attack slaughters the rest of the camp. They hide in Jonne's family's quartz mine, where their relationship grows closer.

"Sword of Ice" by Mercedes Lackey and John Yezeguielian

Herald-Mage Savil is drawn by a MindSpeaking falcon to save a Hawkbrother, Starwind k'Treva, who has been struck by lightning. When he is sufficiently healed, he tries to convince the Elders of his Vale that Savil must be made a Wingsister.

"In the Forest of Sorrows" by John Heifers

The spirit of Vanyel saves a boy named Treyon, who

is Gifted with Foresight and MindSpeech. He is fleeing a group of bandits, led by a mage named Ke'noran, who plans to sacrifice the boy so she can steal his untrained Gifts.

"Vkandis' Own" by Ben Ohlander

Ancar is invading Karse after his first defeat at Selenay's hands, and a regiment of infantry moves across the desert to meet him. One of the priests of Vkandis in their company is Solaris, a powerful provincial who argues often with the other two priests.

"A Herald's Honor" by Mickey Zucker Reichert

Heralds Judaia and Martin are lifebonded, but Martin avoids Judaia, having made a promise to a former lover that he would never be with another woman. On their circuit together, Judaia tries to show Martin that what is right is most important.

"A Song for No One's Mourning" by Gary A. Braunbeck

A young thief named Olias meets a strange boy who has a powerful untrained Mage-Gift. The boy, L'lewythi, uses music to take Olias to an alternate world he has created, but the peaceful realm is shattered by Gash, a destructive force that is part of the boy's magic.

"Blue Heart" by Philip M. Austin and Mercedes Lackey

Selenay's "shadow," a Herald-spy and assassin, tells her of a legend of the mountains near White Foal Pass. His Companion, Pilane, is a historian, and the two have researched the Blue Heart butterfly and the girl Pilane who may have been turned into the butterfly.

2003

Sun in Glory and Other Tales of Valdemar

A collection of short stories set in and around Valdemar, one of which is written by Mercedes Lackey.

"Errold's Journey," by Catherine S. McMullen

Set during the Urtho-Ma'ar War, it chronicles the destruction of Urtho's tower and the journey of Errold, who is still an apprentice mage, to lead a group of refugees displaced by the recent war and find a suitable location to found the village that will be Errold's Grove.

"The Cat Who Came to Dinner," by Nancy Asire

Reulan, a Sun-priest of Vkandis in a small town in Karse, adopts a stray cat, and later learns that it is a Firecat named Khar. In return for it saving his life one day, he travels to Sunhame both to fulfill his pilgrimage requirement for his position and to get Khar a fish. But when he arrives, an avatar of the Sunlord chooses him to be the next Son of the Sun, the supreme ruler of Karse.

"Winter Death," by Michelle West

Kayla lives in Riverend, near the northern mountains of Valdemar. One day, Heralds come looking for her, seeking her help, but she doesn't go with them until a Companion Chooses her. The King's son, Gregori, a powerful Empath, has been broadcasting terrible waves of emotion that puts anyone who feels them into a catatonic trance. Only Kayla, a powerful but untrained Empath, has the ability—and the experience of losing her own family—to stop his maddened rampage of magical grief.

"A Herald's Rescue," by Mickey Zucker Reichert

Santar works as a stableboy in his father's stalls, until one day, when a Companion comes and selects him to rescue his injured Herald. Santar conquers his fears and goes on the ride of his life, but when he arrives at the site where the Herald is supposed to be, he finds nothing but the Companion that chose him for the mission—who then Chooses him as a Herald as well. Santar has passed the Companion's test, and sets out for Haven.

"In the Eye of the Beholder," by Josepha Sherman

Marra, the only survivor of her village, is traveling through the forest trying to find someone, anyone who will hear her tale. Thinking she is being followed, she stumbles across a man, Albain Tanderek, who had been changed into a combination of man and animal. When they find Lord Derick, the pillager of her village, in his fury Albain mortally wounds Derick. As he is dying, Marra weaves a spell to transfer Derick into the monstrous body that Albain had, and transforms Albain back into a human again.

"Trance Tower Garrison," by Fiona Patton

Ander Harrow is a young guardsman in the besieged Trance Tower, on the edge of the Ice Wall Mountains. One night, Andy glimpses a Companion in the foothills. After seeing it for the next four evenings, Andy suggests that the garrison attack the enemy to let a small force reach the Companion to see who it will Choose. His friend Garet is Chosen, and a second Companion Chooses Andy, then the two young men ride for Haven, and help.

"Starhaven," by Stephanie Shaver

Vess is a Herald-Mage on a mission to evaluate a purported Healer at a village near the Pelagir Forest. On the way, he stops at the site of a sister town, Starhaven, where he was raised, and where all of the inhabitants were mysteriously killed many years ago. During his investigation, he learns that the Healer is being used by a blood-mage to draw power from the townspeople. He teams up with the spirit of a mage from Starhaven to destroy the blood-mage once and for all.

"Rebirth," by Judith Tarr

Herald-Mage Mathias, fighting for Princess Vera against her brother Lord Dashant, sacrifices himself in a spell that wins the battle. He passes to the next world, but also receives a vision that Vera still isn't safe. Drinking from a magical fountain, he transformed into a Companion back in Valdemar. Mathias finds Vera, and sees Dashant summoning a creature to destroy her. Mathias kills Dashant and himself. The Companions sentence him to be eternally reborn—as Vera's child, so he will be close to Valdemar for the rest of his days.

"Brock," by Tanya Huff

Herald Jors is stationed in a town as a substitute for

the sick Herald Isobel. Living in town is a seemingly slow-witted boy named Brock, who thinks he is a Herald. A flooded river strands Brock and Jors with the hide tanners, a tight-knit clan led by a cruel woman. While waiting for the river to recede, Jors watches Brock interact with the children of the woman, teaching them kindness and consideration in his own way as well as the value of standing up for themselves.

"True Colors," by Michael Longcor

Rincent rides from town to town in Herald's Whites, only Rincent isn't a Herald. He's a con man who found a suit of Herald's uniform. When two children ask for help against bandits, Rincent holds them at bay them until help arrives—in the form of two real Heralds. Rincent is given a choice—face trial for impersonating a Herald, or go to Haven, and work for Valdemar in an official capacity. Rincent accepts this chance to start a true new life for himself.

"Touches the Earth," by Brenda Cooper

Anya is an apprentice Healer with plenty of ability, but lacking confidence in herself. When bandits kidnap children from their village, Anya and her mentor Tim go after them. They find the bandits, and Tim is injured while battling them. Anya finds Justine, a girl from the village, who is badly wounded as well. Anya releases her doubts and saves the girl's life, tapping into her inner power at last.

"Icebreaker," by Rosemary Edghill

In the town of Talastyre, Elidor is a journeyman scribe who dreams of being Chosen. But his lot is to be an scribe, reading about the adventures of the Heralds and their Companions. One cold winter's day, a Companion does come for him, but it leads him to a Herald trapped under a coach. While rescuing the man, Elidor learns the difference between stories and reality, and is thankful for his quiet life as a scribe.

"Sun in Glory" by Mercedes Lackey

After the ascension of Solaris to the position of Son

of the Sun in Karse, a Priest-Mage envoy visits Valdemar with an offer of alliance. However, Vkandis has requested that a Herald become a Karsite priest—and that the candidate be escorted by Alberich. Alberich, Talia, and Dirk travel to Karse and meet Solaris. At the ceremony, Talia is named the first of the White Robe Priests of Vkandis. Talia, Alberich, and Dirk ride back to Valdemar, with Alberich reflecting on the changes in his adopted nation and his homeland.

2005

Crossroads and Other Tales of Valdemar

A collection of short stories set in and around Valdemar, one of which is written by Mercedes Lackey.

"Transmutation" by Larry Dixon
The sequel to "A Perfect Day In Valdemar," in which the gryphon Kelvren used almost all of his power to heal cavalry officer Hallock Stavern's injuries. Stavern has recovered, but now Kelvren is dying. While waiting for help to arrive, Kelvren rallies the Valdemar soldiers and gives hope to a young boy. The proud griffin also gains what he wanted the most—to become a legend by playing an instrumental part in defeating the rebellion.

"The Feast of the Children" by Nancy Asire
Pytor is a priest of Vkandis. In the days before the Feast of the Children, girls and boys that show magical talent are either conscripted into the priesthood or burned alive. Pytor has sent six special children to Valdemar. But the priest who will inspect the village is an old friend, Chardon, and Pytor doesn't know if Chardon will force him to reveal what he has done. However, Pytor has a Firecat ally who helps him block the black-robed priest's mental scan, saving both the children and the priest.

"Death in Keenspur House" by Richard Lee Byers
A sequel to "The Salamander," this new tale has fenc-

ing master Selden investigating a murder in the Keenspur mansion, one of the top noble houses in Mornedealth, right before a wedding that would join the Greens and the Blues together by marriage. Seldon discovers that an ancestor, Yshan, has become undead and has been manipulating events to bring back the Blue-Green rivalry. Selden destroys Yshan's body, and stops the Keenspur groom from killing his bride with a cursed sword.

"Dawn of Sorrows" by Brenda Cooper

Bard Jocelyn is traveling with Bard Silver on her Circuit. Jocelyn wrote a legendary song, "Dawn of Sorrows," and Silver asks about the story behind it. Jocelyn tells how the mother, Dawn, gave her child to Valdemar to become a Herald, then accompanied Jocelyn to convince people to leave the area, which was being threatened by Ancar. The two came to a destroyed town, where Dawn was killed by a spell trap. Jocelyn has been guilt-ridden ever since, but Silver helps her come to terms with Dawn's choices as they sing "Dawn of Sorrows" together.

"Horse of Air" by Rosemary Edghill

Paynim was a Herald until a terrible accident killed his Companion. He now travels the land, mending pots, and helping people in his own way. In the Armor Hills, he finds a young albino girl with such a strong Bardic Gift that she can make anyone believe anything. Assisted by the spirit of his Companion, Paynim breaks the girl's spell over the villagers. Paynim takes her back to Haven for training, and also knows peace himself, now that he had one last chance to feel his Companion's presence again.

"A Change of Heart" by Sarah A. Hoyt and Kate Paulk

Ree is a street rat—literally. Caught in a Change-Circle during the mage storms, he has become a mixture of human and rat, containing the worst characteristics of both races. One evening, he stumbles upon a hurt human boy. Ree takes the boy, Jem, back to his lair, until he is healed, then tells him he never wants to see him again.

But when Ree runs into trouble in the sewers beneath the city, it is Jem that saves him, and Ree realizes that they do belong together.

"All the Ages of Man" by Tanya Huff

Herald Jors has been on Circuit alone for months, until an emergency lands him with Alyise, a cute Intern. Jors fights his attraction to her, even though Alyise is more than willing. Alyise's and his Companions get him intoxicated so he is able to relax, and they end up in bed. The next day, Jors realizes that despite the events of the previous evening, nothing has changed—they will complete their Circuit, he will teach, she will learn—but neither one has to sleep alone from now on.

"War Cry" by Michael Longcor

Rury is a Valdemaran soldier during the Tedrel Wars, with a strong gift of Empathy that hinders him in his duty. A Herald helps him train his gift enough to shield himself from the emotions all around him. During the final battle, when King Sendar is killed and the Companions Mindsend the message that the King is dead, their grief and rage pours into Rury, and he broadcasts it everyone around him, turning the tide of the battle. After Valdemar has won, Rury's gift is burned out, and he is just an ordinary man again.

"Strength and Honor" by Ben Ohlander

Colonel Tregaris is a commander in the Karsite army who learns of a plot to overthrow the current government and install a new Son of the Sun. He joins the rebels, and pays for it with his life as he tries to stop the black-robed priests from summoning a fire demon. In the end, he meets an avatar of his god, and dies knowing that he has done the right thing.

"The Blue Coat" by Fiona Patton

Treyill, Bayne, and Kellisen are the last of the Goshon clan, travelling south into a young kingdom—Valdemar. Treyill is a shaman, and has been unwilling to use his gift of dream prophecy. They sign on with a river boat caravan carrying stone to Haven and help fight off river bandits, thanks to Trey's accurate interpretation of his dreams. When they reach a village, the three Goshon accept an offer to join the Valdemar Guard in Haven.

"Safe and Sound" by Stephanie Shaver

Lelia is a Bard-trainee trying to compose an original song idea for her test before the Council. Finding the journal of Herald Daryann, she realizes that the deceased Herald's brother, Wil, is at Haven, and tries to learn about Daryann from him. Her questions infuriate Wil, who has mourned the loss of his sister for years. When he finally tells the story, he realizes that his mortally wounded sister returned to Haven not only to deliver valuable intelligence, she also wanted to say good-bye to him. Lelia composes her song, and Wil accepts his sister's passing.

"A Song for Two Voices" by Janni Lee Simner

Garen and Nara are Holderkin, the peasants that live in stern obedience to their patriarchal traditions. When a Herald on patrol helps fight off bandits intent on killing Garen, Nara heals his wound with a song, and then tells the Herald of their way of life and how they met, and how she became his fourth wife. A touching story of love not only for another person, but also for a way of life.

"Finding Elvida" by Mickey Zucker Reichert

Herald-Trainee Elvida is ambushed along with two other Heralds. While trying to save the surviving Herald, who is wounded, her Companion is injured. They barely make it to a cave, with the bandits waiting for sunrise to finish them off. Elvida sends out a distress call, and seems to summon an army of Heralds to their aid. However, once the bandits flee, the army vanishes, and Elvida realizes that she has the Gift of Illusion. Her self-doubt also disappears, and she goes on to finish rescuing the other Herald and Raynor.

"Darkwall's Lady" by Judith Tarr

Merris was traded as an heir to the mysterious Lady of Darkwall Keep before she was born. A Herald-Intern, Coryn, warns her about the rumors surrounding Darkwall. Merris, accompanied by Coryn, goes to the Keep earlier than expected, and finds it empty except for the catacombs where the real lady of the Keep resides, a magical serpent-like creature, who plans to take over Merris's body like she has done to other girls for centuries. Coryn and his Companion arrive and destroy the creature. Merris assumes leadership of Darkwall, with Coryn posted as the Herald in residence.

"Naught but Duty" by Michael Z. Williamson

Arden leads his mercenaries, the Toughs, in the service of so-called King Miklimar, a craven conqueror who kills innocents and destroys villages. Arden is not happy with the work, but follows orders. He wants to free himself from the contract, even though he would have to lose a fight to do so. When the order comes to put a town "to the sword," he does so, ordering his soldiers to tear down buildings, but not hurt anyone. The opposing lord captures them, and offers his own contract, which Arden accepts.

"Landscape of the Imagination" by Mercedes Lackey

Tanna, Kethry and Warrl are broke and stuck in the law-abiding Duchy of Silverthorn. They head for the Pelagir Forest, pulled there by Need, who senses a woman in danger. They find Nanca Jente, a sorceress who hires them to escort her to a Gate. Once through the Gate, they begin playing a simulated game, practice for real combat. Tanna and Kethry excel at defeating the various enemies they come up against, and, together with Nanca's magic, the three women and Warrl win the entire campaign, and make plans to play again.

Short stories from other anthologies

1991

"Stolen Silver"

In *Horse Fantastic,* **edited by Martin H. Greenberg and Rosalind M. Greenberg**

A young Karsite captain named Alberich has a bright future, always seeming to know where his forces are needed. When he is accused of unholy witchcraft, only his strange new horse can save him.

1995

"A Dragon in Distress"

Co-authored with Elisabeth Waters, in *Sword and Sorceress XII*, edited by Marion Zimmer Bradley

Tarma and Kethry are pulled by Need through a portal in the Pelagirs that takes them to another world. The portal was built by a female dragon seeking aid for the young princess in her care, who has been abducted by a prince.

VIRTUAL VALDEMAR

Russell Davis

THE world of Valdemar is a familiar one to millions of Mercedes Lackey's fans. In a shared journey of the imagination, they've wielded swords and magic, ridden Companions, met Hawkbrothers, marveled at bondbirds, and watched gryphons soar. They have cheered on Vanyel and Talia and Elspeth in their victories and despaired at their defeats. But apparently the nearly thirty books available so far on Valdemar haven't been enough to keep them satisfied—the fans want more.

In fact, if the World Wide Web is any indication, they want *a lot more*. A quick tally on the Yahoo! search engine using the term "Valdemar" generates only one official website—but it turns up nearly thirty thousand web page matches. The fans, it seems, have been busy, and they've done more than take this world to heart. They've put it online and started a worldwide conversation. While few of these sites are blessed and authorized by Mercedes Lackey, there's no doubt that a patient web surfer can find many worth looking at. But be aware that when you're heading off to find the virtual Valdemar, you're going to find a *very* large place.

To start your journey, here a few of the authorized and official Waystations:

First and foremost is the official Mercedes Lackey Fan Club (called Queen's Own) website, located at: <u>http://www.dragonlordsnet.com/qo.htm</u>

This is a great place to begin looking for virtual information about Valdemar. Among its other features, it boasts an email-based chat subscription, a non-fiction journal, a list of approved fanzines for fan-written fiction, and numerous other resources, including information on taking on a Valdemar "persona."

This process allows the serious fan of Valdemar to "become" a Herald, Herald-Mage, Bard, Healer, Mercenary, Shin'a'in, Kal'enedral, Tayledras, or a White Winds mage by following a specific series of steps and criteria developed by Mercedes Lackey. While the details for each persona are different, here's a brief outline of the steps involved in attaining a Herald persona within the Queen's Own fan club:

1. Basic Requirements:
   a. Develop a character and write about him/her—the finished biography must be a minimum of three double-spaced pages, and should detail the person's physical characteristics, likes, dislikes, and so on. (Worth ten points.)
   b. Develop the character's friends and relatives—again, this should be a minimum of three double-spaced pages, though it doesn't necessarily have to be as detailed. (Worth ten points.)
2. Extra Point Requirements:
   a. Choose two or more activities that interest you (from a list of eighteen on the website) and complete them. Possibilities include writing a short story, designing a costume, attending a martial arts class, or learning about the care and feeding of horses. (All are valued at five points each.)
3. Becoming Chosen:
   a. After you have accrued a total of twenty-five points, you may be chosen and will randomly select your Gifts (there's a table on the website) by rolling a six-sided die.
4. Get Recognized by the Queen's Own:
   a. After fulfilling all of the requirements and sending the Queen's Own fan club the details, you will be formally recognized in the fan club newsletter.

This all sounds like a lot of work; however, it can be done—hundreds of people have completed the requirements to become a Herald. Becoming a Herald-Mage, (and not everyone can do this) is an even more arduous process, and includes learning four magic tricks (to become a Hedge Wizard), writing a twenty-page paper and learning four more magic tricks (Journeyman Herald), writing two additional twenty-page papers and learning four more magic tricks (Master). Finally, to become an Adept Class Herald Mage, the site requires writing three more twenty-page papers, and learning another four magic tricks. Needless to say, the list of those who have completed these demanding requirements is much shorter. At this writing, only eight people have become Adept Class Herald-Mages since the club began.

The best place to check out the books is the publisher's website, located at http://www.dawbooks.com, where all the novels of Valdemar are listed, as well as news of forthcoming titles, and an author bio, and other goodies. The site also has a link to a special place just for Mercedes Lackey fans, http://www.penguinputnam.com/lackey. The site is still being built at press time, but it promises to be the comprehensive site about Valdemar.

The another official site is Firebird Arts & Music, located at: http://www.firebirdarts.com. While this is not a Valdemar site per se, it does contain a huge amount of information on Valdemar, and—more importantly—it's a commercial site that sells Valdemar-influenced music, poetry, art, and a variety of Valdemar-related collectibles. It's also the location of an excellent forum where fans can e-mail in questions that may be answered online by Misty herself. Not only are all of the Valdemar novels available here, but fans can also get cover art prints from the novels by artist Jody Lee, CDs and cassettes featuring the music of Valdemar, Hawkbrother jewelry, and even clothing patches showing the crest of Valdemar.

Perhaps one of the best features of this site is the silent online auction of items made by Mercedes Lackey or her husband Larry Dixon for the purpose of raising money for their favorite charity, the Alex Foundation. The Alex Foundation supports the research of Dr. Irene Pepperberg of the University of Arizona, who researches the intelligence, cognitive, and speaking abilities of African Grey Parrots. This research has made amazing contributions to the treatment of and therapy for learning-disabled children. Some of the items that have been auctioned off here through the years include original, signed manuscripts by Mercedes Lackey, a Hawkbrother Courtship Feather, and a variety of handmade pouches, necklaces, and other jewelry.

If you want to look a little farther on the Web, you might want to try some of the Valdemar WebRings, sites that are linked together and share a common interest in the works of Mercedes Lackey. A few of the better ones include:

1. The Queen's Own Official WebRing, located at: http://q.webring.com/hub?ring=qsown. This links to several websites related to the writing and work of Mercedes Lackey.
2. The Heraldic Collegium WebRing, located at: http://dragonlordsnet.com/ufcindex.htm. This links to a fair number of websites that have to do with Valdemar, the Herald Mage Vanyel, and more.
3. The Official Vanyel Fan Club, located at: http://h.webring.com/hub?ring=vanyel. This chapter of the Queen's Own Official Fan Club is dedicated to the hero of The Last Herald-Mage Series, and maintains a mailing list via email as well as a newsletter for its members.

This is just a small sampling of the treasures that are out there, changing and developing every day on the World Wide Web. The virtual world of Valdemar is a rich one, bounded only by the skill and imagination of the fans, and the legalities of copyright law. Grab your search engine and go exploring—the reward will be a chance to surf the thousands and thousands of Valdemar web pages and chat rooms, containing everything from book reviews to discussion groups to role-playing games to fan fiction, all awaiting the arrival of an intrepid Internet adventurer to find and enjoy them. To all you explorers—wind beneath your virtual wings, and speed to your search engines.

MAPS OF VALDEMAR

**Larry Dixon
with Daniel Green**

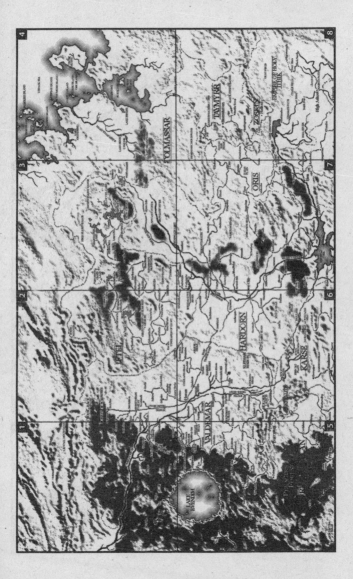

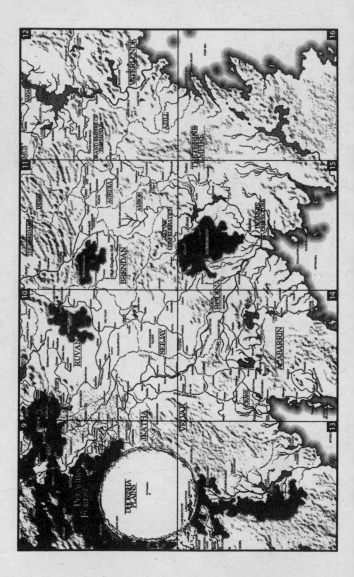

ICE WALL MOUNTAINS

HIGH HILLS

Heverix

Greanhav

TERILES RIVER

Langer

K'Saunii

Knowles

Riverlord

K'Chona

K'Treva

Errold's Grove

K'Valdemar

Kelmskeep

K'Shira

Deerlun

K'Sheya

Gravhall

Oorthes

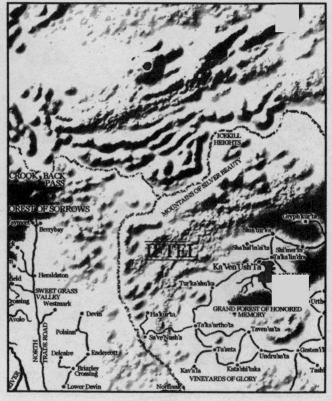

2

HIGH FLIGHT RANGE

DARING FLIGHT RANGE

GLACIER P

GRYPHON
GLORY
LAKE

CLEARWATER
LAKE

BLUE VEIL LAKE

Sav'ind'ra

Ta'pen'ta

Toс'in'ta

Ra'shin'ta'ra

Ku'ta'shi'kur'ta

Amus'ta'shai'ta

Lenem'lca

Icekeep

Kon'sen'lin'a

Medru'shin'ta

RAMPANT
GRYPHON
LAKE

COLD
DEATH
PASS

O'Sha'ha'iin'a

FAITH FOREST

Wolf's Summit

Kas'kur'sata

Ka'ven'ushta
'ka'ta
Zhan'tkas

Siran'drashkae

Hero's Gate

Amb'i'dra

WINDSWEPT
MOUNTAINS

DESOLATE ROAD

NOVANN WOODS

a

HERO RANGE

BRAYBANT RIVER

ki'ta

Yu'shin'ta

BENBROOK LAKE

3

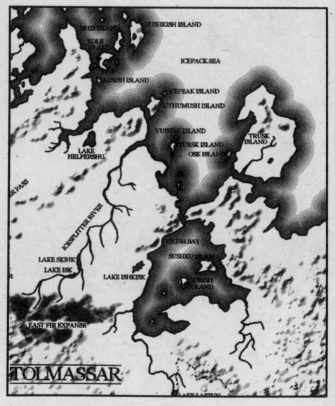

5

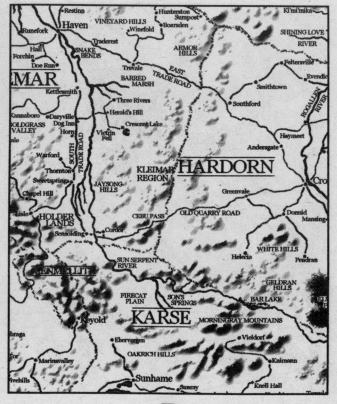

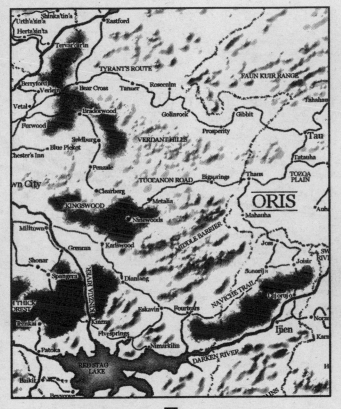

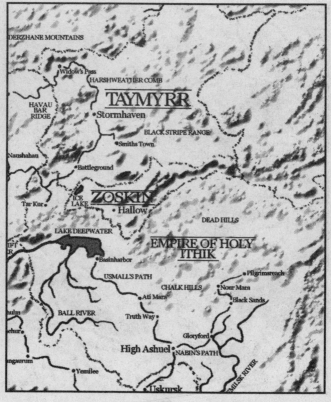

Hielmarsh
Kaliska
K'Veyas
Bolthaven
Forest C
Darken Dale
Brandenburne Hollow
K'Riza
Rowatan
Avaa
Mourne
K'Onsova
K'Lissa
TERMIG HILLS
Ta'Gik'kin
PELAGIRS FOREST
Lumbok
Azobin
Atabar
Kachah
K'Shayna
Lythec
BERTASI SWAMP
My'inta
DHORISHA PLAINS
SHIN'A'IN TRADE ROAD
Kata'shin'a'in
JKAT
Ka'Venusho
HA

9

12

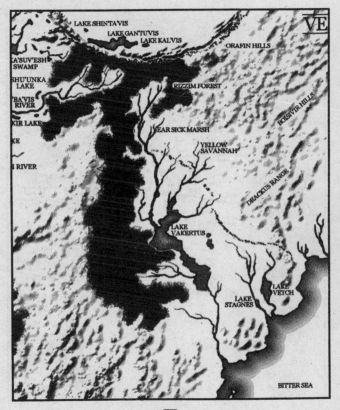

LAKE SHIN'TA'VIS
LAKE GAN'TU'VIS
LAKE KAL'VIS

ORAFIN HILLS

A'SUV'ESH
SWAMP

SHU'UNKA
LAKE

RIZZIM FOREST

'BA'VIS
RIVER

KIR LAKE

EAR SICK MARSH

BOISVIR HILLS

KE

YELLOW
SAVANNAH

I RIVER

DRACKUS RANGE

LAKE
VAKERTUS

LAKE
VETCH

LAKE
STAGNES

BITTER SEA

13

14

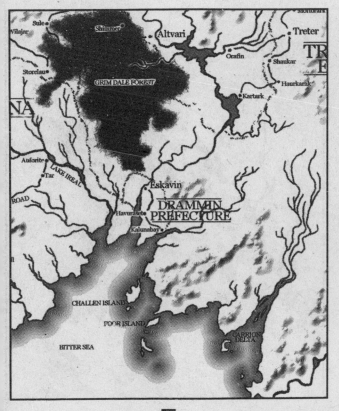

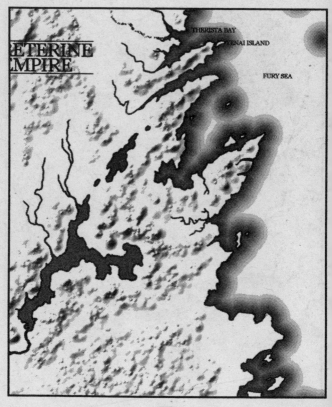

THERISTA BAY

YENAI ISLAND

FURY SEA

RETERINE
EMPIRE

16

THE VALDEMAR
CONCORDANCE

Teri Lee, Juanita Coulson, Kerrie Hughes, and Denise Little

THE following abbreviations are used to denote where the defined term appeared in the Valdemar books:

ARROWS: The *Heralds of Valdemar* Trilogy (Talia's trilogy)
BB: *Brightly Burning* (Lavan's book)
BV: Some terms are used throughout the Valdemar series, and are basic vocabulary for that world.
EXILE: Exile's Honor and Exile's Valor (Alberich's books)
GRYPHON: The *Mage Wars* Trilogy
LHM: The *Last Herald-Mage* Trilogy (Vanyel's trilogy)
OATH: The *Vows and Honor* Duology/*Oathblood* (Kethry and Tarma books)
OWL: The *Owl* Trilogy (Darian's trilogy)
STORM: The *Mage-Storms* trilogy
SWORD: *By the Sword* (Kerowyn's book)
TT: *Take a Thief* (Skif's book)
WINDS: The *Mage Winds* Trilogy

Terms and foreign words are listed alphabetically, without regard to punctuation.

Although this is contrary to standard dictionary practice, to make the concordance easier to use, we have listed characters by their first name with their last name following (if known), and their title (if any) in parentheses (King, Herald, etc.). When a first name is not available, characters are listed by last name only. We have made one exception to this—characters from large families (Alders, Ashkevrons, etc.) are listed under their last names, with important characters cross-referenced by their first name as well, so that they can found in a central grouping for ease of keeping track of them while reading.

Although we have tried to make this concordance as complete as possible, please note that Mercedes Lackey's novels cover more than two thousand years in the Valdemar/Velgarth timeline, and the descriptions of people, events, and places may not remain the same from book to book, depending on how things have been recorded in the canon. Also, as Mercedes Lackey has mentioned, certain kingdoms, events, and cultures have purposely been left vague, so that she will be able to explore and write about them in later novels without being restricted by what she might have written earlier.

The writers and editors are all too aware of the fact that mistakes are inevitable in such a mammoth work. Comments, questions, and suggested additions or corrections may be sent to the following address:

John Helfers
c/o DAW Books
375 Hudson St.
New York, NY 10014

Abel (Duchess)
A court lady in Haven who waged a fashion war with Lady Isend. *(BB)*

Aberdene's Eye
The astronomical body that Herald-Mage Kilchas was observing on the night he was pushed from his tower and killed. *(LHM)*

Abevell
A Rethwellan town carved into the side of a mountain where the Skybolts were ordered to take prisoners. *(Sword)*

Absel (Brother)
An elderly priest at the Temple and Priory of Thenoth, the Lord of Beasts. *(TT)*

Abyssal Plane
One of the otherworldly planes of existence inhabited by creatures—some good, some evil—that can be summoned by a mage. *(LHM, Oath)*

Abyssal Plane Elementals
Semi-intelligent creatures that inhabit the Abyssal Planes. White Winds mages gain the cooperation of these entities with favors, as do Herald-Mages, but they can be called and commanded by any Master or Adept mage. Disturbances in the normal flows of magical energy can also at-tract them. *(Oath)*

Adain (Bard)
His youthful bout with Mical shattered one of the Collegium's expensive mirrors in the training salle. *(Exile)*

Adan (Companion)
The Companion of Lord Marshal's Herald, Turag. *(BB)*

Adem (Guardsman)
A highborn guard at the Palace in Haven, friend of Rubrik's. *(Storm)*

Adept
The highest classification of mage, able to tap into both ley-line and node energy. *(BV)*

Aderin
A viscount at the Imperial Court who brought his six daughters to Valdemar to look for husbands. *(Storm)*

Ado Larsh
The only member of the Errold's Grove's militia who survived the Blood Bear Clan raid. He was so traumatized that he was barely able to tell the villagers what had happened. *(Owl)*

Agnetha
The wheat crowned Goddess of the LadyTrine. A school in Rethwellan teaches the womanly arts in her name. *(Sword)*

Agnira
The horse-taming Goddess of the LadyTrine, naturally Kerowyn's favorite Goddess. *(Sword)*

Agnoma
The Crone Goddess of the LadyTrine who is symbolized by snowflakes. *(Sword)*

Ahela
K'Leshyan term of endearment. *(Storm)*

Ah'kela shen Liha'irden
A young Shin'a'in apprentice in training with the Liha'irden Clan's Chief Shaman. *(Oath)*

Ahrodie (Companion)
Herald Dirk's Companion, she Chose him when he was eleven in a marketplace on Fair Day. *(Arrows)*

Air elemental
See *vrondi*

Ajela
One of Tuck Chester's sisters. *(BB)*

Aksel Tarselein
One of Alberich's early teachers, a Weaponsmaster in Karse, one of the few people in Karse who maintained good relationships with the Mercenaries' Guild. He provided information to Valdemar that helped them win the Tedrel Wars. *(Exile)*

Albayah (Prince)
The eldest son of Jkatha's Queen Sursha, soon to be betrothed to Merili. *(Oath)*

Alberich (Herald)
A Captain in Karse's army, Chosen deep in Karse by Companion Kantor, who saved him from being burned alive by his troops for having Mind-magic. Rescued by his Companion from certain death and taken back to Valdemar, Alberich became one of the finest Herald weaponsmasters of all time. Despite a lack of trust from the Queen's councilors because he was from Karse, he worked undercover for Queen Selenay, gathering information and carrying out special missions. He was highly respected for his military and fighting skills and was also a superb teacher of those arts. He was instrumental in saving Queen Selenay's life many times, but especially during the last battle of the Tedrel Wars, and during the assassination attempt upon her life staged by her first husband, Prince Karathanelan. *(Arrows, Exile)*

Alchemy (Master)
One of Master Levy's teachers. *(Storms)*

Alder, Ayver
Keisha's father. *(Owl)*

Alder, Garry
One of Keisha's five brothers. *(Owl)*

Alder, Keisha
Healer of Errold's Grove. In addition to her Healing Gift, she also has the Gift of Empathy. She discovered cures for the diseases afflicting the Northern Tribes, and eventually become famous as a Wisewoman among them. Married to Darian, and sister to Herald Shandi. *(Owl)*

Alder, Rafe
One of Keisha's five brothers. *(Owl)*

Alder, Rondey
One of Keisha's five brothers. *(Owl)*

Alder, Shandi (Herald)
Keisha's younger sister, Chosen by Companion Karles as a teenager. Her Gifts are Empathy and Foresight, and she has a talent for dyeing and spinning, embroidery, and making friends. Romantically involved with the Tayledras plant specialist Steelmind. *(Owl)*

Alder, Sidonie
The wife of Ayver and over-protective mother of Keisha, Shandi, and five strapping sons. *(Owl)*

Alder, Tell
The middlemost of Keisha's five brothers. *(Owl)*

Alder, Trey/Torey
One of Keisha's brothers. *(Owl)*

Alderscroft
A village a hundred leagues from Haven and the original home of the Chitward family. *(BB)*

Aldon (Father)
The patriarch of Valdemar's largest religious sect and a member of Queen Selenay's Council. *(Arrows)*

Alessandar (King of Hardorn)
The much-loved ruler of Hardorn and friend to Valdemar who was assassinated by his son, Prince Ancar. *(Arrows)*

Alistair (Lord)
One of Ancar's mages bound into service by coercion

spells. He was ordered to care for the captured Falconsbane. *(Winds)*

Alliance, The
Treaty-bound nations—initially Valdemar and Rethwellan, later expanding to include the Tayledras, the Shin'a'in, Karse, Hardorn, and eventually Iftel. United in finding a solution to the Mage-Storms, and in resisting the armed incursions of other nations. *(Owl)*

Altra
The Firecat appointed by Vkandis to assist Karal. *(Storm)*

Alys
A female member of the Fellowship of Errold's Grove, in charge of the herds. *(Owl)*

Amaly
The elder daughter of Herald Pol and Healer Ilea, she is a Healer and married to Ranolf. *(BB)*

Amarites
An incident involving this group created tension between Valdemar and Queen Lythiaren of Rethwellan, and was a potential source of mistrust when King Randale warned her about the anti-mage crusade launched in Karse. *(LHM)*

Amba-resin
Ingredient in perfume. *(Owl)*

Amber
A gemstone formed from fossilized plant resin, it is Herald-Mage Vanyel's preferred focus for magic. *(LHM)*

Amber-of-Scent
A trade good brought to Valdemar by the Ghost Cat Clan that has a gray-white, greasy appearance, and a heavy, musky-sweet fragrance. *(Owl)*

Amber-of-the-Sun
A yellow, golden-brown, or red gemstone traded by the Ghost Cat Clan that is often used for jewelry. *(Owl)*

Amberdrake k'Leshya
A kestra'chern of the k'Leshya Clan, he was the most skilled at his profession among the Kaled'a'in. He allied himself to Urtho at the beginning of the Great War and placed his services at the command of Urtho's Army. Spectacularly dressed and immaculately groomed when possible, he eased the pain and tensions of those who fought, but had no one to ease his pain as the war dragged on. A particular friend of gryphon Skandranon and *hertasi* Gesten during the Great War and afterward, he was an Empath with the Gift of Healing. He became the mate of Winterhart, the father of Silverblade, and a member of the White Gryphon Council. *(Gryphon)*

Amberwing
A Tayledras scout. *(Winds)*

Ames
One of Bazie's former boys who left to join a circus as a pickpocket. *(TT)*

Ami
A dishwasher at Rathgar's Keep during the wedding banquet. *(Sword)*

Ananda Pellard
An Errold's Grove resident, she was the owner of a bad-tempered rooster killed by an owl. Everyone was secretly grateful to the owl, but Ananda carried on at great length, as though she had suffered a terrible loss. *(Owl)*

Anastesi
The name of Keisha's favorite lady-doll from childhood. *(Owl)*

Anathei of the Purifying Flame
A religious order that believes Evil does not know it is wrong and can be convinced to do Good. Their main temple is located in Oberdorn. They took Thalkarsh into their care after the battle at his temple. *(Oath)*

Anberg
A captain in the army of the kingdom of Karse and Alberich's superior during that country's border fights against bandits. *(Arrows)*

Ancar (Prince/King)
The King of Hardorn after he assassinated his father,
Ancar plotted to overthrow Valdemar by killing Queen
Selenay and forcing Elspeth to marry him. A Master-
level Blood-Mage, his reign was characterized by atroci-
ties and murder, including the torture of Talia and the
murder of Herald Kris and his Companion, carried out
while they were invited guests of his country and diplomatic envoys from an allied state. He subjugated his people, murdering any who opposed him and binding them
as mind-enslaved troops to be slaughtered during his
wars of attempted conquest against his neighboring
states, all of which failed. The Companion Gwena tram-
pled him to death during one of Hardorn's wars with
Valdemar after Ancar went mad and attempted to kill
Adepts Elspeth and Darkwind in a duel of magic. During that fight, Vree distracted him, and Gwena destroyed
him. *(Arrows, Storm, Winds)*

Anda (Herald-Mage)
A Herald-Mage assigned as Crown representative to
Lord Breon's territory, partner of Companion Eran, residing in k'Valdemar Vale. He was taught his mage-skills
by Treyvan and Hydona. *(Owl)*

Anderlin's Freehold
A neighboring home base for some of the numerous
Ashkevron cousins and cousins-in-law. *(LHM)*

Anders
A Skybolt that Kerowyn considered throwing at Elspeth
to distract the Princess if she hindered her war preparations. *(Sword)*

An'desha shena Jor'ethan
Shin'a'in of Bear Clan, offshoot of Wolf Clan. His
mother was an outClan Kata'shin'a'in woman; as a result
his hair was golden brown and he was often taunted as
a half-breed. In his early teens he developed mage gifts.
Some in his clan felt this was further evidence that he
was unclean and should take a vow of celibacy. Refusing
the only other option available to Shin'a'in, becoming a
shaman, An'desha fled north to the Hawk-brother lands.
When he cast a small Fire-Calling spell, his body was

usurped by Ma'ar. The boy was a descendent of Zendak, one of Ma'ar's previous incarnations, and Fire-Calling was a trap enabling the Adept to return as Mornelithe Falconsbane. But An'desha held onto his identity, hiding within the monster's mind, waiting for an opportunity to reassert himself and reclaim his stolen body. The Avatars of the Shin'a'in Goddess, along with Firesong and Need, helped free An'desha and he rebuilt his life. His hair is now white from dealing with magic and his once greenish-yellow eyes are now a pale silver color with slit, catlike pupils, a memento of Falconsbane's experiments with Changing. *(Storm, Wind)*

Andi
A young woman from Errold's Grove, almost as skilled as Shandi at spinning thread. *(Owl)*

Andrean Senson
Talia's brother, he was a second son and kind to his sister. When Talia was nine, Andrean was killed during a brigand raid, removing support and affection from her life. *(Arrows)*

Andrel (Healer)
The Healer to the Heralds and Herald-Mage Savil's former lover. He treated both Savil and Vanyel after the terrible events at the Grove's Bell Tower. *(LHM)*

Andros (Herald)
The Herald that escorted the aged Bard Stefen to the Forest of Sorrows, where Stefen disappeared to join Vanyel in his afterlife. His Companion, Toril, made Andros forget that he had accompanied Bard Stefen to the forest. *(LHM)*

Anduras Fair
A Jkathan fair made famous by the Shin'a'in horse traders. *(Oath, Sword)*

Animal Mindspeech
The Gift that allows one to communicate with animals. *(BV)*

Anjeyla
A Sixth Form student and Tyron's girlfriend at the Merchants' School. *(BB)*

Apponel
A god honored by some of the Skybolts. *(Sword)*

Arawell (Guildmistress)
The guildmistress of the Weavers and a member of the Queen's Council. *(Arrows)*

Arboli
Archduke Tilden's scholarly eldest daughter. *(Oath)*

Arborn Hunting Cat
Tilden brought some kittens of this breed to Tarma and Kethry's school as Midwinter gifts for the children. *(Oath)*

Ardana Flinteyes
The only surviving officer after the Skybolts' rout during the Karsite "bandit" incursion, she became the Skybolts' leader by default when both Lerryn Twoblades and Icolan Ar Perdin were killed. In Kerowyn's opinion, the woman was a terrible officer with no head for strategy, a quick temper, and questionable or non-existent ethics. She led the Skybolts to near-total destruction before they mutinied in favor of Kerowyn. *(Sword)*

Ardatha (Companion)
The Grove-Born First Companion who Chose King Valdemar in the early days of the realm. *(Arrows)*

Aren (Herald)
The Herald who brought a Healer to tend to Alberich after his escape from Karse. *(Arrows)*

Argonel
A powerful sedative and muscle relaxant fatal in large doses. *(Arrows; LHM)*

Arissa (Bard)
Dean of the Bardic Collegium. *(Exile)*

Aristo
A slang term for a member of the nobility. *(Oath)*

Arms of Valdemar
The symbol of the monarch and kingdom, the emblem shows a winged white horse wearing broken hobbles. Sometimes, the animal is depicted with a broken chain around its neck. Underneath is the motto "There is no 'One True Way'." *(Arrows)*

Arnod (Herald-trainee)
Assigned to attend Master Ulrich and Karal in Haven. *(Storm)*

Arnod
One of Quenten's assistant mages. *(Sword)*

Aroon
A *kyree* of the Hot Springs Clan who came to help Herald-Mage Vanyel, his Companion Yfandes, and Bard Stefen. *(LHM)*

Arrkeyla
A Silver Gryphon of Kel's acquaintance. *(Owl)*

Arrow Code
The secret code used by Heralds in an emergency, unique patterns notched into the fletchings on arrows and shot, delivered or left to be found by other Heralds. In addition, broken and beheaded arrows indicate death and disaster, and colors banded on the shafts have meanings as well—white for "nothing wrong," green to send a Healer, purple to send a priest, gray to call another Herald, brown to watch for a message, blue for treachery, yellow for military aid, red for great danger, black for death or catastrophe. *(Arrows)*

Artero (Herald)
Lavan's Field Investigations instructor at the Collegium during King Theran's reign. *(BB)*

Artificers
The engineers, inventors, and technicians of Valdemar. They train in Haven, but their unofficial headquarters is the Compass Rose tavern. They were instrumental in discovering how to stop the Mage-Storms. *(Storm)*

Artis Camlodon
Chief Healer among Urtho's forces. *(Gryphon)*

Arton
Tarma's magical disguise created by Kethry—it made Tarma look like a male mercenary. In this disguise, Tarma got a job in King Raschar's guard, got him to trust her, and finally got him to confess that he'd tortured and murdered his sister, Idra. *(Oath)*

Arvale annexation
A troubling postwar problem in the time of Valdemar's King Tavist, it was a crucial point in the Arvale-Zalmon negotiations. *(LHM)*

Arved (Herald)
Valdemar's Seneschal during the time of King Randale. *(LHM)*

Arven
Vanyel's daughter by one of Guard-Captain Lissa Ashkevron's shaych guards. *(LHM)*

Ashaka
A k'Leshyan endearment. *(Storm)*

Asheena
The Mage Starwind k'Treva's bondbird, a white gyrfalcon. *(LHM)*

Ashke
A Tayledras word meaning "beloved." It was Tylendel's special name for Vanyel, one he explained as a play on the younger boy's family name of "Ashkevron." Years later (Bard) Stefen used the same term of endearment. *(LHM)*

Ashkevron
The surname of Herald-Mage Vanyel, the Ashkevrons are a large family of hard-working low nobility. The Ashkevron holdings lie west of Haven, and for a while formed the western border of Valdemar. The family gained renown as horse breeders—their hunters and later their sturdy warhorses were among the best in Valdemar. Ashkevron heavy horses were routinely used for Valdemar's heavy cavalry. *(LHM, Winds)*

Ashkevron, Ariel (Herald)
The daughter of Vanyel's brother Mekeal. Her Companion is Darvena. *(LHM)*

Ashkevron, Charis
Vanyel's youngest sister. *(LHM)*

Ashkevron, Deleran
One of Vanyel's numerous siblings. *(LHM)*

Ashkevron, Diera
A volunteer scout with the Guards at the Karsite front. *(BB)*

Ashkevron, Heforth
One of Vanyel's younger brothers. *(LHM)*

Ashkevron, Jehan (Lord)
The master of the Ashkevron manor when the travelers from k'Sheyna came through the Gate. *(Winds)*

Ashkevron, Joserlin
Vanyel's great-great Grandfather who designed the original manor-keep at Forst Reach. *(LHM)*

Ashkevron, Joserlyn
Herald Andros was assigned to deliver a palfrey wearing a saddle as a present from Joserlyn Ashkevron to his sister. *(LHM)*

Ashkevron, Kaster
One of Vanyel's brothers, appointed Second Councilor and Seneschal of the March of Lineas-Baires. *(LHM)*

Ashkevron, Kemoc (Lord)
Lord of Forst Reach during King Roald's reign. *(Oath)*

Ashkevron, Lissa
Vanyel's older sister who signed on to join Trevor Corey's training school for young swordswomen. After graduating from Corey's school she joined the Guard and was eventually promoted to captain. *(LHM)*

Ashkevron Manor
The longstanding Ashkevron family household west of Haven. *(LHM)*

Ashkevron, Mekeal
The second son of Withen Ashkevron, he became heir to the Holding after Vanyel was Chosen. As a young man he bedded Lady Treesa's maid Melenna and fathered Medren. As an adult he married Roshya and fathered six children. He gradually grew into competence in his management of Forst Reach. *(LHM)*

Ashkevron, Ria
Wife of Vanyel's brother Kaster. *(LHM)*

Ashkevron, Roshya
Mekeal Ashkevron's wife and the mother of his six legitimate children, she became Forst Reach's Castelaine when Lady Treesa moved to court. *(LHM)*

Ashkevron, Savil (Herald-Mage)
Vanyel's beloved aunt and his teacher in Haven. Savil ran off to the capitol city when she was fourteen and was Chosen by her Companion, Kellan, the moment she passed the main gates. One of the best Herald-Mages in Valdemar, she was also an excellent teacher, and was given many of the most promising students among the Heralds as her special responsibility, among them Tylendel and later Vanyel. She held an anchoring position in the Guardian Web protecting Valdemar. She died fighting a mage-construct raven sent by the Dark Mage Leareth to assassinate her. Note: Herald Kerowyn's Companion is named Sayvel, and has a strong interest in teaching. *(LHM)*

Ashkevron, Treesa (Lady)
Vanyel's mother and the wife of Withen Ashkevron. *(LHM)*

Ashkevron, Vanyel (Herald-Mage)
See Vanyel Ashkevron

Ashkevron, Withen
Vanyel's father, Treesa's husband, and the Lord of Forst Reach in the reign of King Randale. *(LHM)*

Asra (Guardsman)
A Guard posted at the West Gate of Highjorune in Lin-

eas who was bribed by Vanyel to look the other way when he left the city. *(LHM)*

Assassin Mage
Sent by Dark Mage Leareth to assassinate Lady Treesa, he infiltrated the Ashkevron Manor under the guise of an insane man, and wounded Father Beren, Lady Treesa, and Vanyel before he was killed. *(LHM)*

Assembly of Peoples, The
The governing body of Iftel that is composed of humans, gryphons, *kyree, dyheli, ratha,* and *tyrill. (Storm)*

Astera
A major goddess in Valdemar. After Father Leren's mage-directed attack and the discovery that an entire temple school had been "purchased" and its priests tempted to serve evil, the priests of Astera sent "finders" into every Temple along the Border to uncover any other traitors to the faith. *(LHM)*

Atus
One of the mages Falconsbane sacrificed to build up a store of magical energy to steal the power-locus. *(Winds)*

Aubri
A rufous broadwing gryphon, he is one of Skan's oldest friends who eventually became the training advisor to young Silvers at White Gryphon. *(Gryphon)*

Audria's Teeth
An oath employed by Wendar, Rathgar's seneschal. *(Sword)*

Aurinalean Empire
The united principalities east of Hardorn. Also known as the Eastern Empire. *(Storm, Winds)*

Autumnwing
The leader of a group of Hawkbrothers who asked to borrow Elspeth's bathing pool. *(Winds)*

Avatars
Otherworldly creatures that serve deities as messengers and/or agents of divine orders. *(Winds, Storm)*

Awhani
The wisewoman of Gray Wolf tribe. *(Owl)*

Aya
Firesong's bondbird, a white firebird, part of a new bondbird strain that the young mage created. *(Winds)*

Ayshen
The *hertasi* baker for a k'Vala scout team, he became chief of *hertasi* at k'Valdemar Vale. *(Winds)*

Azurehart
A Tayledras noted for his abilities as a dyer. *(Owl)*

Azurestar
The shaman of Cat Clan when the Kaled'a'in split into the Shin'a'in and Tayledras Clans after the Cataclysm. *(Winds)*

Bachelor's hall

The quarters at Forst Reach allotted to unmarried young men. *(LHM)*

Backet, "Old Man"

A villager of Errold's Grove. *(Owl)*

Baern

Herald-trainee Nerissa added his name to her extensive list of amorous conquests. *(Arrows)*

Baires

A western border country north of Lineas once ruled by the Mavelans. When they tried to usurp the Lineas throne through assassination, the plot backfired and killed every member of the Mavelan family. As a result, Baires and Lineas became vassal-states of Valdemar. *(LHM)*

Bard

A Bard is much more than a talented musician. To qualify as a Bard, a musician must have the Bardic Gift—the ability to influence listeners through Mind-magic while singing. In addition, a Bard must have at least one of two additional gifts: Creativity—the ability to compose and/or arrange music, and Talent—the ability to perform vocal and/or instrumental music at a high level. Bards are trained at the Collegium in Haven. Full Bards wear scarlet uniforms, while Bard-trainees wear red-brown. *(BV)*

Bard Cottage
A pricey lodging where Herald Rubrik found quarters for the Karsite ambassador and his secretary. *(Storm)*

Barda
A member of Errold's Grove's Fellowship community and the selected representative of the village to the Council at k'Valdemar Vale. *(Owl)*

Bardic Chronicles
The records of songs and the stories behind them stored in the Collegium's archives. After Vanyel's death, any song dealing with magic could not be kept in the repertory of Valdemar's bards, who mysteriously "forgot" them. *(Winds)*

Bardic Collegium
The Bardic portion of the Collegium where students learn all aspects of music including the use and control of the Bardic Gift. Vanyel was enrolled there on his Aunt Savil's orders, taking courses in History, Literature, and the Religions of Valdemar. A Bardic student wears rust-brown robes, while a master wears scarlet red. *(LHM)*

Bardic Council
The seven members appointed by the Bardic Collegium to meet and consider the status and dispositions of Bardic trainees and candidates. *(LHM)*

Bardic Gifts
These Gifts separate true Bards from ordinary minstrels and are related to the Gift of Healing. The true Bardic Gift can be best described as Projective Empathy, or the ability to manipulate an audience's mood through music. The Creative Gift is the ability to create and compose original music. The Musicianship Gift is sometimes referred to as a Talent or the ability to perform. To be granted Bard status, the individual needs two of the three Gifts. *(BV)*

Bardic Immunity
The right to adopt Gifted apprentices if they are legally free. It is a protective law sanctioned by the Council to ensure such Gifts are not lost or carelessly ruined. It

also protects a bard from retaliation if his songs offend the audience. *(Oath, LHM)*

Barlen
Dealer in dyes at Errold's Grove's market. *(Owl)*

Barnebin
Horsemaster for the Ashkevrons. successor to Ben Dotes. *(BB)*

Baryl Longarm
A mercenary living in semi-retirement at the White Winds school where Kethry studied. Before Kethry left to take up her nomadic life, Baryl gave her Need. *(Oath)*

Basilisk
A large and ugly reptilian created during the war between Urtho and Ma'ar. Basilisks have poisonous bites and can hypnotize their prey with a difficult-to-resist mental compulsion. *(Gryphon, Storm, Winds)*

Basket-spell
The spell that makes it possible for a carry-basket to float. *(Gryphons)*

Battlesteeds
Also called warsteeds, they are the product of Shin'a'in breeding. Intelligent, agile, strong, with great endurance, able to survive on poor forage, these mottled gray horses with thick necks and huge, ugly heads can travel from sunrise to sunset at a ground-devouring lope. They have had their herd behavior modified to pack behavior. To prevent control of the breed from leaving Shin'a'in hands, only culls are sold out of the clan, and the stallions never leave the Dhorisha Plains. *(Oath, Sword)*

Bazie
A former mercenary who lost both his legs during the Tedrel Wars, he became the benefactor of a gang of young thieves in Haven, including the boy Skif. He died in a fire that was set on his landlord's orders to avoid paying fines on an unsafe building. *(TT)*

Beak
A term for Valdemar's city watchmen who patrolled for thieves, robbers, and drunks. *(TT)*

Beaker Bowman
Formerly one of the Sunhawk scouts but now partnered with Jodi n'Aiker, another retired Sunhawk, he is a horse-talker and trainer of messenger birds. *(Oath)*

Beast-Healers
Sometimes called horse leeches, their healing Gifts are generally employed to cure animals. During the war they help out at the front lines as combat medics. *(Owl, LHM)*

Bedbox
A simple box used for sleeping in at Waystations, it is lined with a Herald's bedroll or fresh grass for easy cleaning. *(Arrows)*

Beel Galko
Middle son of Londer Galko, and Skif's cousin. He became a priest in the Temple of Belden, a charitable order that taught poor children how to read, write and do sums, and learned to be a good man there, despite his lawless and difficult father. Beel was responsible for turning Londer in to the authorities for his most terrible wrongdoings. Beel also made sure that Skif was not at the inn when the resulting raid took place. *(TT)*

Beglamorment
A spell to make the object of one's desire see what he or she most wants to see. *(Gryphon)*

Bel
Drunk, abusive, cross-dressing owner of the *Inn of the Green Man* in Highjorune. *(LHM)*

Bel
Scout lieutenant with the Skybolts. *(Sword)*

Belinda
Bride of Val, Lord Breon's son and heir. *(Owl)*

Bells (Companion)
Part of the formal tack for Companions worn for ceremonial or special occasions. The chiming bells announce that a Companion is on the road. *(BV)*

Belton
One of Tarma's students who sought her out for advice on revenge. *(Oath)*

Beltran (Herald)
King Valdemar's Herald, he was Chosen by the Grove-Born Companion Kyrith, and became one of the first three Heralds. *(Arrows)*

Beltren (Herald)
A first-year mate of Herald Keren's who died during Talia's first term at the Collegium. He and his companion were ambushed and pushed over a cliff. *(Arrows)*

Ben Dotes
A retired Horsemaster who had worked at Ashkevron manor. He was a superb volunteer scout at the southeastern battlefield during the war with Karse. *(BB)*

Bendan
A hunter of the Snow Fox tribe. *(Owl)*

Benjan (Father)
The priest of Errold's Grove. *(Owl)*

Berd
The groom at the Palace stables at Haven, he told Stefen about chirras when the Bard first encountered the creatures. *(LHM)*

Berda Lunge
A member of the Haven City Guard, she was recruited to be one of Princess Selenay's Personal Guards during the Tedrel Wars. *(Exile)*

"Berden's Ride"
Song about a legendary message-rider Herald. A romantic account of Berden was included in a book Lavan read to the Chester family at Midwinter Festival time. *(BB)*

Bern
A human scout with the Silvers, he joined Regin's search party and spotted the place where Tad and Blade crashed. *(Gryphon)*

Berrybay
One of the northern towns near the Forest of Sorrows, and the site of a Herald Resupply Station. *(Arrows)*

Berta
The barbarian persona that Elspeth adopted as part of her disguise when she and Skif journeyed through Rethwellan. *(Winds)*

Berte
The old woman who cared for Stefen before he was snatched up by Bard Lynnell and carried off to Haven. Berte was using him to beg, and had already sold her own children to support her drinking and drug habits. *(LHM)*

Berthold
One of Alberich's early teachers, a Weaponsmaster in Karse. *(Exile)*

Beryl (Herald)
A Herald who died during Talia's second year at Court. Her death caused Queen Selenay profound guilt, because she believed she had sent an inexperienced Herald on a fatal mission. *(Arrows)*

Bessa, Underwife
Talia's mother who died in childbirth, leaving her upbringing to the care of Keldar Firstwife and the other women of Sensholding. *(Arrows)*

Bestet
An ancient Battle-Goddess. The sword Need survived the Cataclysm because she was triple-shielded in the heart of Bestet's Temple, in a casket within a shrine. *(Storms)*

Bet Micherone (General)
One of Urtho's officers, she took Laury's people under her command in the reshuffling necessary before the final battle. *(Gryphons)*

Beth
Keisha's beloved rag doll. *(Owl)*

Bethtia
One of Hadanelith's victims in White Gryphon. *(Gryphons)*

Betrothal necklace
A piece of Royal Haighlei jewelry made of ancient amber, gold, and bronze. If the King presents this to a woman, together with a dozen Lion Lilies, it is a proposal of marriage. *(Gryphon)*

Bevis
One of Sewen's men, wounded in the concluding battle of the Jkathan civil war. *(Oath)*

Biijal Tribes
They live on the Empire's Eastern Islands and are known for crafting valuable plush rugs. *(Storm)*

Binn
Prince Daren's orderly, a grizzled veteran of a dozen wars. *(Oath)*

Bird-lords
Colloquial name for the Hawkbrothers used by the peasant land holders in Tayledras territories. *(LHM)*

Birdkin
A common name for the Hawkbrothers. *(Winds)*

Bitter Sea
A body of water far south of the known realms. *(Sword)*

Black Angel Mushroom
This fungus kills by a combination of convulsions, liver failure, and terrifying hallucinations. Tylendel's mother died after eating Black Angel. *(LHM)*

Black Bear Clan
Northern tribe-folk from far beyond Valdemar's northern border. Darian's expedition to find his parents met with them. *(Owl)*

Black Kings
Rulers of the Haighlei Empire. *(Gryphon, Owl, Storm)*

Black Riders
A group of Kal'enedral who, with Vanyel's help, gave

Falconsbane mysterious and magical gifts that puzzled and distracted him while k'Sheyna and their allies prepared to attack. The Dark Adept did not know who they were, but An'desha, trapped inside Falconsbane's mind, recognized the Riders as Sword-Sworn servants of the Goddess. *(Winds)*

Black ring
One of the gifts left for Falconsbane by the Black Riders. Made of a shiny, black, unbreakable substance, it resembled a wedding ring carved with harvest symbols. Widows sometimes wore similar rings in place of their wedding ring as a symbol of mourning. *(Winds)*

Blacke Ewe
An inn known for its spiced sausage that Tarma and Kethry stayed at in Delton. *(Oath)*

Black-robes
The feared demon summoners and heretic burners of Karse, until Solaris made the black robe simply a ranking above ordinary priests but below the red robes. *(Storm)*

Blackfoot
Sturdy bay mare hunter with a touchy mouth kept by Vanyel's father. When Vanyel rode her to Wyrfen Woods, he used a bitless halter to avoid agitating her. *(LHM)*

Blessing
Among the Shin'a'in, the survivor(s) of an almost extinct clan blessed the youngest child of her hosts (Clan Liha'irden, in Tarma's case). The hosts tended the slain clan's herds and properties while the survivor waged blood-feud against the murderers. This arrangement lasted until the avenger died or returned. If the survivor hadn't returned by the time the child blessed was old enough to take up their own sword, all the entrusted property belonged to its caretakers. *(Oath)*

Blood Bear Clan
An outcast clan of northern barbarians whose shaman used Change-circles to create warriors who were more bear than human. They invaded Errold's Grove, but

were repelled by Darian and the Hawkbrothers. After that the remnants of Blood Bear joined the Wolverine Clans, but disgraced themselves by breaking the rules of battle. *(Owl)*

"Blood Bound"
An ancient song traditionally ascribed to the same Bard who wrote the Tandere Cycle. *(LHM)*

Blood-debt
A Rethwellan law that states a murderer's family must pay the family of the slain. *(Oath)*

Blood-feud
An ancient Shin'a'in tradition that allows a person to seek revenge on those who have committed great harm. The petitioner asks the Goddess to become Swordsworn and, if accepted, may go on Blood-feud. The price to pursue such revenge includes service to the Warrior aspect of the Goddess, life as a neuter, and sword service to the Clans. Swordsworn Shin'a'in dress in black until the blood-feud ends. *(Oath)*

Blood-magic
A form of Dark magic that draws upon the released energy from the torture or death of a living thing to enhance the powers of the magician. Ma'ar, Ancar, Hulda, and Noyoki were all Blood-magic users. *(BV)*

Blood-path
Blood-path mages use the energy from the torture and/ or death of something living to create power. Humans give the most energy but animals or land can also be used. *(BV)*

"Bloody Carthar's Fourteen Wives"
A cautionary fable that Tarma and Kethry used to frighten the flirtatious new bride they escorted during their mercenary days. *(Oath)*

Blue Mountain Mages
A group of mages similar to those from the White Winds school who use magic responsibly. *(Oath, Winds)*

Blue Mountain Mage-School
A mage-teaching establishment established by a Blue Mountain Mage. *(Oath, Storm)*

Blues
Unaffiliated students at Haven training to be scholars or artificers. Many are the children of nobles, but some are talented youngsters there on scholarship. The Unaffiliates' uniforms are light-blue. *(Arrows, Storm)*

Boar spear
A weapon used by Raven Clan defenders and hunters, it is a long spear with a short sword-sized blade and an iron crossbar to stop the body of a skewered boar from continuing up the shaft of the spear toward its wielder. *(Owl)*

Bogles/Boggles
Generic term used to describe unclassified dangerous entities. Used in Karse and Valdemar to describe the howling monsters that the Dark Servants sent during the night to harass the border defenders in the Karsite war; also used in Valdemar and Hardorn to describe the change-beasts created by the Mage-Storms. *(BV)*

Bolthaven
Skybolts' winter quarters on the southwestern border of Rethwellan, close to the Pelagir Hills. During Kerowyn's years as Captain of the company, it more than doubled in size and became home to a fine annual horse faire, featuring Shin'a'in-bred animals provided by Kerowyn's cousins. After the Skybolts moved to Valdemar, Quenten took over the land and founded a White Winds Mage-school. *(Storm, Sword, Winds)*

Bolton
The Skybolts' deeded border town in eastern Valdemar. Queen Selenay gave it to Kerowyn and the Skybolts when they helped win the war against Ancar. *(Sword, Winds)*

Bondbirds
The magically and genetically altered avian species that choose to be mindlinked to the Hawkbrothers. Very intelligent, they are usually, though not always, raptors

and live much longer than their normal counterparts. Eagles, falcons, owls, crows, firebirds, and several other species have been bred to be bondbirds. *(BV)*

Book of the One
The *Book of the One* is the holy book of a monotheistic religious group from the Three Rivers area of Valdemar. Mero frequently quotes from it. *(Arrows)*

Book, The
The dreaded log of Herald-trainees' demerits and misdeeds kept in the Provost-Marshal's office. *(Arrows)*

Bors Porthas
A former assassin/agent, he is now Melles' valet. *(Storm)*

Bornam's Bastards
A mercenary infantry company, one of four hired by the Menmellith Council to capture Karsite bandits. *(Sword)*

Bottomless Barrel Inn
An inn in Oberdorn owned by a genial host named Oskar. *(Oath)*

Boys' Raids
A rite of passage for Ghost Cat Clan youths. The boys sneak into neighbors' houses and steal small items, which are later returned. After numerous protests from Errold's Grove, the ritual was changed to a form of counting coup—trying to sneak up on *dyheli* herds and mark an animal's side with a painted palm. *(Owl)*

Bram
A General with the Imperial forces and spy for the Emperor in Tremane's army, he was the spokesman for the delegation of spies for various masters who approached Tremane about converting to his side permanently. *(Storm)*

Bran Kerst
The town of Shonar's Master Goldsmith, one of the delegation of citizen leaders who came to Tremane with suggestions for combining labor forces to serve both the townsfolk and the soldiers. *(Storm)*

Brancher
Term for a young gryphon, beyond the age of a nestling, but not yet a fledgling. *(Gryphon)*

Breakneedle Street
A culvert vented down this lane from the Tailor's Court's Lady Fountain until it was diverted by the Blues in a prank designed to flood a secret gathering room in the Virgin and Stars Tavern. *(Arrows)*

Breda (Bard)
The senior Bard with the Collegium during Vanyel's time, she possessed all three of the Bardic Gifts. *(LHM)*

Brendan
Otherwise known as the High Kingdom of Brendan, a land far to the east in the known world of Velgarth. *(Oath)*

Brenden Keep
The manor of Lord Trevor Corey, where Lissa Ashkevron trained in sword work before joining the Valdemar Royal Guard. *(LHM)*

Breon (Lord)
Overlord of the area that includes Errold's Grove and lord of the manor at Kelmskeep, a heavily fortified and garrisoned outpost in northwestern Valdemar. *(Owl)*

Bret
The Artificer who was asked to carry the report to Queen Selenay informing her about the Change-animals and worsening waves of Mage-Storms. *(Storms)*

Brether's Crossroads
The town where Tarma and Kethry killed the bandit gang that murdered Tarma's Clan, and the site of Tarma and Kethry's first meeting. *(Oath)*

Briar burl
At the Collegium, Mero teased Talia by asking her how she would prepare this huge, inedible root into a meal. *(Arrows)*

Briarley Crossing
Tuck's home village in north Haven. Briarley Crossing

lies between Lower Devin and Endercott, just off the Nodding Hill road. *(BB)*

Briary Holding
Managed by Lady Cedrys, near where Joserlin Corveau was fostered when he was thirteen, before he was sent to Forst Reach Holding. *(LHM)*

Brightbird
One of Amberdrake's family, lost to him in the chaos that erupted while he was away at College in Predain. *(Gryphon)*

Brightmoon
A Tayledras scout. *(Winds)*

Brightsib
Tarma's nickname for Herald Roald, after a shared meeting with the Star-Eyed. *(Oath)*

Brightstar k'Treva
Vanyel's son by Snowlight k'Treva, who was willing to have twins, one child for herself and one for the shay'-a'chern pair Starwind and Moondance to raise. Brightstar's bondbird is a huge white owl. *(LHM)*

Brightwind k'Treva
Tayledras Adept too old to help Starwind and Moondance deal with an invading swarm of colddrakes moving toward k'Treva vale. *(LHM)*

Brindle Mastiff
Tilden brought puppies of this breed as Midwinter gifts for the children at Kethry's keep. *(Oath)*

Brinle-bushes
A bushy shrub. Kethry hid the Sunhawks from Lord Kelcrag's sentries by creating an illusion the mercenaries were simply part of the landscape, like a thicket of brinle-bushes. *(Oath)*

Brion (Herald)
Herald being trained in Mage-Gift of weather control. *(Winds)*

Brodie (Old Man)
A failed Healer, he fled north out of Valdemar and be-

came a veterinarian to the local peasants' animals. Master Dark forced Brodie to treat his bandit hirelings when they were wounded. Brodie saved Vanyel after the bandits nearly killed him, and he released the bonds placed upon Vanyel by the Dark Adept. Vanyel killed Brodie in his insane rage after being released from his bonds. *(LHM)*

Broken Arms
A tavern in Haven named for its sign displaying broken arms—a warning to anyone who breaks the peace in that establishment. If they do so, they will possess broken arms just like the ones on the tavern's sign. *(TT)*

Broken Sword Inn
A Mornedealth inn catering to mercenaries run by Hadell and his family. *(Oath)*

Brothers of Perpetual Indulgence
People who participate in drunken revelry and hedonistic adventure are sometimes teased with accusations that they are joining this fictitious order. *(LHM)*

Brownie
A gentle milch cow at the Chesters' farm where Pa Chester taught Lavan how to milk. *(BB)*

Bryerly (Countess)
Distantly related to the Lady Treesa's relatives, the Brendewhins. The kindness of Countess Bryerly eased Treesa's way into the Palace social scene. *(LHM)*

Bryon
One of Ancar's mages, he was ordered to accompany and control Hardornen troops sent to invade Valdemar. *(Winds)*

Brytha
The white *dyheli* mage stag Darkwind rode to Hardorn. Brytha was Firesong's usual mount, and carried him from k'Treva Vale to k'Sheyna Vale and then to Valdemar. *(Winds)*

Bumblefoot
Bondbird foot infection which can permanently cripple the bird if not properly cared for. *(Owl)*

Burning Pines

Site of the last battle of Lavan Firestorm. During the invasion of the Dark Servants of Karse, Lavan called down an all-consuming fire that destroyed the enemy and himself. To this day nothing will grow there except grass and firecone pines. *(Arrows, BB)*

By the Names and the Powers

A pledge made by the priest of Felwether when he accepted Tarma as Lady Myria's champion and Kethry as the potential solver of Lord Corbie's murder. *(Oath)*

Cafri
The *hertasi* who was Kechara's best friend, playmate, and caretaker in White Gryphon. *(Gryphon)*

Calla
One of the *hertasi* assisting the Healers in Ka'venusho. *(Gryphon)*

Calum
A scout and career fighter with the Guard, he led Lavan's scout party to a good defensive position on the battlefield at White Foal Pass. *(BB)*

Cariodoc (Lord)
One of Queen Selenay's counselors. *(Arrows)*

Cartage Guild
Operated in Jacona, capital of Charliss' Empire, the guild for professional drivers of carts for hire. *(Storms)*

Carter's Lane
A street in the Rethwellan capitol of Petras wide enough for four wagons to travel abreast. It is where several popular inns and taverns, including the Pig and Potion, are located. *(Oath)*

Caryo (Companion)
Queen Selenay's Companion, she once kicked Prince Karathanelan, Queen Selenay's devious first husband. *(Exile, Arrows)*

Cascade shields
A layering technique for constructing protective shields. The only shield actually using power is the outermost one, until something contacts it. *(Winds)*

Cat-child
Justin's friend and a former victim of Wethes Goldmarchant's sadism, she helped Tarma rescue Kethry from his clutches. She eventually became a weapons merchant. *(Oath)*

Cataclysm
The term describing the aftermath of the Mage-Storms caused when Urtho and Ma'ar's headquarters were destroyed. *(Gryphon)*

Cathan (Lady)
A councilwoman and speaker for the Guilds during the reign of Queen Selenay. *(Arrows, Storm, Winds)*

Cave of the Winds
The Tayledras end of the Gate through which Herald-Mage Savil brought the dying Vanyel. *(LHM)*

Cavil (Herald)
The Herald pulled off Circuit duty to escort the k'Sheyna Gaters who arrived at Ashkevron manor. *(Winds)*

Cedrys (Lady)
Mistress of Briary Holding. *(LHM)*

Ceejay/Seejay
The land southeast of Karse, where Mind-magic and slavery are practiced. *(Storm, Winds)*

Celandine (Master)
An artist, painter of portraits, designer of furnishings, and maker of palace decorations, he was the Eastern Empire's spy at Haven. Tremane ordered him to release assassination weapons known as "little birds" in an effort to break Valdemar's foreign alliances. He murdered Ulrich and Querna, envoy of the Shin'a'in. *(Storm)*

Celin
He was the shaman of Ghost Cat Clan, and performed

the sweat lodge ritual that made Darian Firkin an official part of the clan. *(Owl)*

Cendal-wood
A sweet-scented, vermin-proof wood native to Valdemar used to build food storage bins at the supply posts along the Herald circuit routes. It is also used to build chests and wardrobes. *(Arrows)*

Chadran (Bard)
A champion swordsman and full Bard, he taught history at the Collegium in Vanyel's time. *(LHM)*

Chagren shena Liha'irden
A Swordsworn Shin'a'in Healer who aided Karal in the aftermath of the mage weapon channeling at Urtho's Tower. *(Storm)*

Chana
A *hertasi* and Gesten's daughter, she was in charge of packing the carry-basket for Tad and Blade's trip to Outpost Five. *(Gryphon)*

Change-beasts
Created by the Mage-Storms, they were the result of the twisted magic associated with Change-circles. Change-beasts were also created by magical scars left on the lands by the great Mage-Wars. Some Dark Adepts created Change-beasts intentionally. Sometimes the parents are normal, but their offspring have new attributes, frequently dangerous ones. There are assorted species, including Change-bears, Change-boars, and Change-lions. *(Owl, Storm, Winds)*

Change-children
Humans or creatures modified from their original form by magic, sometimes intentionally by Adept Mages, sometimes by accident, as in the change-circles and in the untamed areas of the Pelagiris Forest. Nyara was a Change-child. *(Winds)*

Change-circles
Caused by the Mage-Storms, they are circles of land where matter is transposed or exchanged from other places or other states of being in the wild mage-energy

of the storms. Unwary beasts and humans caught in them during the storms are altered, sometimes fatally. Northern barbarian Blood Bear Clan members entered such circles voluntarily and emerged as Change-beasts. Animals and plants weren't the only things altered within the circles. A new paralytic disease created in the circles afflicted Blood Bear Clan and all the people they encountered during their raids and battles. *(Owl, Storm)*

Change-lions
A form of change-beast with huge canines extending far beyond the jaws, capable of working primitive invisibility magic. As long as they do not move while a human is looking directly at them, they cannot be seen. *(Winds)*

Channel
Someone with the ability to channel magical energy, who can work with a mage to store power or to funnel or filter power too strong for the mage to handle directly. Channels cannot control, see, or sense the power themselves. *(LHM, Storm)*

Charis (Herald)
She rode circuit near Valdemar's southeastern border, and brought the bad news about the Karsite Invasion. *(BB)*

Charliss (Emperor)
The nineteenth Emperor of the East, he was known as "The Immortal." An Adept, his mage powers prolonged his life to nearly two centuries. One of the many sons of Emperor Lioth, Charliss ascended to the throne at age thirty, and held power ruthlessly until his death. *(Storm)*

Charm-makers
Slang term for a hedge-wizard or mage of little talent. Ancar referred to weather-wizard mage applicants as mere charm-makers, until Falconsbane told him weather-wizardry was a genuine craft. *(Winds)*

Chasern
A fruit grown in k'Sheyna Vale. *(Winds)*

Chass
A Herald trainee with the Gift of weather-working. *(Winds)*

Chava
A hot, sweet drink, sometimes topped with beaten cream, popular with the Hawkbrothers. The *hertasi* also make a cookie with chava. *(Winds)*

Cherin
Tremane's chief aide. *(Storm)*

Che'sera
A blue-clad Kal'enedral and scholar from Kata'shin'a'in who is a shaman and Swordsworn to the Old One. *(Storm)*

Chester, Cassie
One of Tuck Chester's sisters. *(BB)*

Chester (Granny)
Tuck's grandmother, a spry, blue-eyed old lady with flossy, snow-white, curly hair. She was called Curious Kit in her youth, because she always wanted to know, "What else happened?" when hearing stories or news accounts. *(BB)*

Chester, Guy
One of Tuck's brothers. *(BB)*

Chester, Hal
One of Tuck's brothers. *(BB)*

Chester, Jan
One of Tuck's younger brothers. *(BB)*

Chester, Ma
Tuck's mother. *(BB)*

Chester, Merry
One of Tuck's sisters, a boy-crazy blonde. *(BB)*

Chester, Pa
Tuck's father. *(BB)*

Chester, Sheela
One of Tuck's sisters. *(BB)*

Chester, Stane
One of Tuck's brothers. *(BB)*

Chester, Trinny
One of Tuck's sisters. *(BB)*

Chester, Tuck (Herald)
Lavan's best friend, partnered by Companion Dacerie.
He is from a very large and noisy farm family in Briarly
Crossing. *(BB)*

Child-bane
An herbal abortifacient. Moon-flower powder was much
kinder; rather than eliminate an early pregnancy, daily
use prevented pregnancy altogether. *(Sword)*

Children of My Other Self
The name the Star-Eyed Goddess gave Herald Roald
and his Companion. *(Oath)*

Children of the Hawk
The Tale'sedrin Clan of the Shin'a'in, originally called
the Taylesederas or Brothers of the Hawks. *(Winds)*

Children's Cloister
A Karsite center where youngsters taken by the Black
Robe Priests live and study until they are accepted as
novice priests or servants, or are given to the fires as
unusable or intractable. *(Storms)*

Chirras
A northern pack animal with triple-layered fur to endure
cold weather. They are tall as a horse but with a longer
neck. Their clawed feet are doglike, enabling them to
scratch away snow drifts or walk atop them. Chirras
have large, floppy ears and rabbitlike faces. Curious and
intelligent, they are fond of music, and can hum in coun-
terpoint to it. *(Arrows, LHM)*

Chitward, Archer
Lavan's father, a cloth merchant, married to Nelda Hardcrider, a needle-worker. *(BB)*

Chitward, Feodor
Lavan's brother. *(BB)*

Chitward, Lavan
See Lavan Chitward

Chitward, Lerris
Lavan's Uncle. *(BB)*

Chitward, Macy
Lavan's sister and later one of the Queen's embroiderers, she was the only member of his family that Lavan felt close to. Lavan's best friend, Tuck, had a crush on her. *(BB)*

Chitward, Nelda *(née Hardcrider)*
Lavan's mother and the Needleworker's Guild Representative for five counties. *(BB)*

Chitward, Samael
Lavan's older brother, apprenticed to one of their father's colleagues in the Cloth Merchants Guild. *(BB)*

Choose/Choosing
The process of selecting Heralds, carried out by the Companions, who make those choices by their own unfathomable but unerring criteria. They Choose irrespective of age or gender, but tend to select youngsters just entering adolescence and boys more often than girls. Once Chosen, a Herald enters into a lifelong bond between herself or himself and the Companion. A Herald's death usually means the death of the Companion as well. *(Arrows)*

Chorran (Lieutenant)
A young Valdemarran officer in the Tedrel Wars. *(Exile)*

Christa (Herald)
Trained by Dirk, her Gift was Fetching. On her internship assignment, she died saving children from raider fires in a village near Gyrefalcon's Marches. Dirk felt guilty because he had never fully trained her on how to use the Fetching Gift to transport people, and those instructions would have saved her life. *(Arrows)*

Chroniclers
They are the keepers of the Archives. Many of Valdemar's Guilds and important estates employ Chroniclers to maintain their historical records, as does the Heraldic

Collegium.. Herald-Chronicler Myste's records form a major part of the history of Valdemar as we know it. *(BB)*

Chulka
Chief hunter of the northern Gray Wolf Clan. *(Owl)*

Cinnabar (Lady)
Urtho's kinswoman, a Healer of noble birth, a gracious lady and Tamsin's lifebonded mate. *(Gryphon)*

Cinsley
The White Winds Adept who was rescued by the *hertasi* Gervase of the Pelagir Hills. In gratitude, Cinsley made the lizardman a Mage and adopted him as his apprentice. *(Oath)*

Circuit
A regular route assigned to Heralds, with each Circuit covering specific sectors of Valdemar. The Heralds provide justice, communication from Haven, and stability for the kingdom's outlying districts. At any given time, most of the Heralds will be out riding these circuits, gathering information for the Queen, and explaining the latest laws of Valdemar to the people. *(Arrows)*

Citizens for Rights Group
Jacona's Underground Resistance movement against Baron Melles' undeclared martial law and his other repressive new measures. *(Storm)*

Clan banner
The symbol of a Shin'a'in clan. After the bandit raid, Tarma retrieved her clan's banner and took it to the Liha'irden camp. *(Oath)*

Clan Elders
The ruling Council of each Tayledras Vale. The members do not have to be elderly, but they are appointed by the other Clan Elders or are elected by the group they are representing (scouts, Mages, etc). *(Winds)*

Clan Keep Voorthayshen
A Tayledras community with structures that make use of natural elements, including trees, ferns, hot springs for bathing, and sky lights for illumination. The furnish-

ings and decorations mimic leaves or bent branches, blending in with the Keep's theme. The Keep sits in a tear-drop shaped vale guarded by a magical barrier. *(LHM)*

Clan Mother Kethryveris
Kethry's title when she became the matriarch of Tale'sedrin Clan. *(Sword)*

Clan of the Racing Deer
Also known as the Liha'irden Clan. Racing Deer Clan watched over Clan Tale'sedrin's assets until Tarma had completed her revenge and rebuilt her clan. *(Oath)*

Clan of the Stooping Hawk
Also known as the Tale'sedrin clan—Tarma's people who were attacked by bandits and massacred. Tarma was the only survivor. She and Kethry rebuilt the clan with fosterlings, adoptees and Kethry's children. *(Oath)*

Clans of the Folk
Kyree communities. They have a treaty with the Tayledras. Aroon, the far ranger of the Hot Springs *Kyree* Clan, acknowledged that since Vanyel was Wingbrother to the k'Treva, his clan was honor-bound to give aid and shelter to him and his friends. *(LHM)*

Clave
One of Bazie's fences for stolen textiles. *(TT)*

Clay (Widow)
A resident of Errold's Grove, she had a bad leg and therefore couldn't be expected to do field work so she did the town's basketwork, knitting, and sewing. *(Owl)*

Cleaning stone
See sturgeon stone.

Cleansing Fires
Before Solaris, groups of people selected by Karse's priests were burned at the stake as heretics. These mass burnings were known as Cleansing Fires. *(Storm)*

Clerence (Duke)
One of the Empire's less admirable members of the nobility. *(Storm)*

"Cletius and the Bathtub"
A fable cited by Natoli as an example of inspiration which may occur when someone quits trying to think too hard of a solution to a knotty problem. *(Storm)*

Clevis (Prince)
The oldest son of King Theran and Queen Fyllis. *(BB)*

Climbing tool
Used by Tayledras scouts to aid their movement through trees, it has a hooked end and can be used as a deadly weapon as well as a tool. *(Owl, Winds)*

Cloister
A temple dedicated to the Goddess but used in a restrictive form by the Holderkin. The Cloister is served by women called to the vocation and they spend their entire lives in prayer for the souls of their people. Garbed head to toe in all-concealing robes, they vow never to leave the Cloister and observe an oath of perpetual silence. *(Arrows)*

Cloistered Order of Kernes Sequestered
An order where the nuns voluntarily have themselves sealed into small solitary cells where they spend the rest of their lives worshiping and praying. The cells are comfortable and anything that the inhabitant needs is attended to by cloister workers and overseen by the Priestess. *(BB)*

Clover tea
A favorite with Lady Treesa and the women of her bower, clover tea is reputed to prevent aging and keep the complexion young. Red clover is preferred, but white clover is also used. *(LHM)*

Cold Blades
Followers of the Cold God, they are identified by a spider-web brand on one palm. They become assassins to provide a legacy for their families or to do penance for a terrible sin. If they are not killed while fulfilling their assignments, they commit suicide, leaving no trail back to whoever hired them. *(Winds)*

Cold God
A deity worshipped far to the south of Valdemar. Some of his worshippers hire themselves out as assassins. *(Winds)*

Colddrake
One of Ma'ar's evil constructs, also known as ice dragons. They resemble huge snakes with stubby legs. They are slow-moving, but can hypnotize their prey into submission. They inhabit the Pelagir Hills and Northern Territory. *(BV)*

College of Chirurgeons
A university in Predain where Amberdrake was sent when he was thirteen to study modern medicine. *(Gryphon)*

Comb, The
A range of hills along the Rethwellan-Valdemaran border. Sheer rock faces and narrow goat tracks hold barely enough scrub vegetation for grazing. Many travelers die attempting to cross in winter. *(Oath, Sword)*

Commander Sterm
He carried out Melles and General Thayer's martial law orders for Jacona, the Empire's throne city. *(Storms)*

Companions
These are otherworldly creatures that resemble magnificent snow-white horses with brilliant blue eyes. As intelligent as a human, they search out those who will be Chosen as Heralds. The process of Choosing forms a mind-to-mind link that may only be broken by the Companion. Communication between Companions and their Chosen is through Mindspeech or more subtle channels, if a Herald is not Gifted in that respect. A severing of the bond by the death of the Herald often means the Companion's death as well.

Initially, all Companions were Grove-Born, magically materializing as adults, just as the first three companions did. Eventually, enough took up residence in Haven that natural reproductive processes began. One Companion is always Grove-Born, and is the one that Chooses the Monarch's Own. "Ordinary" Companions are the reincarnated spirits of former Heralds, though they keep this knowledge from the Heralds. Without the Companions, Valdemar's independence would not have been possible, nor would its long and enviable history of just rule and domestic stability. *(BV)*

Companion's Field

A rolling pasture in the palace grounds dotted by trees and dells containing a parklike area watered by sparkling streams. It is the home for the Companions, their foals, and for unbonded Companions. The facilities include an elaborate open, building, heated stable, and the Grove from which the first Companions emerged. *(BV)*

Companion's tack

The colors of a Companion's tack are silver and royal blue. The bridle is a hackamore; no bit could control a Companion, and the use of one would be an insult. The saddle is very comfortable for both Companion and Herald, with a high cantle, stirrups and a prominent pommel. Skirting is well-equipped with snaffles and leathers to fasten objects or a wounded or unconscious Herald securely during a long and arduous ride. Each Companion's sigil, a vowelless representation of the Companion's name, is carved into the saddle. Formal tack includes silver bells strung along the reins to announce in advance the arrival of the Companion and Herald, and blue silk ribbons to braid into the Companion's mane and tail. *(BV)*

Compass Rose, The

The tavern where the Artificers gather to socialize and study. The front room is where students gather and the back room is for the Masters. A student is considered to have graduated to Master status when invited to the back room by a Master mentor. *(Storm)*

Conclave

The Karsite term for Solaris' court in Sunhame. *(Storm)*

Conn Levas

A mercenary mage attached to the Sixth Wing of Urtho's forces, and one of Amberdrake's clients. A greedy, self-absorbed man who was totally focused on increasing his personal wealth and prestige, he eventually turned traitor and assassinated Urtho. *(Gryphons)*

Constructors
Eastern Empire mages who built edifices and machines with their spells and magic. *(Storm)*

Cor
The leader of a trio of invading Northern barbarians who chased young Darian into the Forest, where he was killed by Snowfire's arrow. *(Owl)*

Corani
One of Urtho's Generals. *(Gryphon)*

Corbie (Lord)
Lady Myria's miserly husband who was murdered under mysterious circumstances. She was accused of his death until Kethry, Tarma, and Need defended and exonerated her. *(Oath)*

Cordor
The closest village to the east of Sensholding in Valdemar's southern border lands. *(Arrows)*

Coroc (Herald)
A Herald-trainee whose father was the Lord Marshal. *(Arrows, TT)*

Corthu
A Shin'a'in word meaning "one being." *(Oath)*

Corvi
The *hertasi* who accompanied Amberdrake on a diplomatic mission to the Haighlei. *(Gryphon)*

Corwith
A snow-winged owl, one of Wintermoon's two bondbirds. *(Winds)*

Cory (Lord)
He escaped the fear spell at King Leodhan's Court because he had retired to his estates. Later, Lord Cory commanded a levy for Urtho. *(Gryphon)*

Courier's Road
The route usually taken by Mages when travelling through Jkatha. *(Oath)*

Covia
A village of approximately seventy in population, it is situated on the edge of Tayledras lands. *(LHM)*

"Crafty Maid, The"
A popular song. Vanyel played it at the inn where he stopped along Exile's Road. *(LHM)*

Crag Castle
The personal residence of the Eastern Emperor, located in the capital city, Jacona. *(Storm)*

Crathach (Healer)
A powerful mind healer, he worked with Alberich to transfer Karsite memories into Herald volunteers' minds so that they could survive as spies in Karse during the Tedrel Wars. He also served in King Sendar's Personal Guards during the Tedrel Wars. *(Exile)*

Crescent Lake
A settlement area of The People of the One, a rare monotheistic group among Valdemar's various polytheistic religions. Their teachings are written down in the Book of the One. *(Storm)*

Cress
One of the flock of young females at Haven's Court in Vanyel's time. She knew the term shay'a'chern, and that it could be applied to Tylendel. *(LHM)*

Crone
A facet of the Goddess worshipped by the Shin'a'in. Her symbol is a smooth black stone and her element the snow-scented, bitterly cold North wind, which numbs memory and makes loneliness bearable. *(Oath)*

Crone's Oathbound
They are to the Crone aspect of the Goddess what the Swordsworn are to the Warrior aspect of the Goddess, Shin'a'in bound to her service, often as the Shamans, Healers, and Elders in each Shin'a'in Clan. Elders may or may not also be Healers or Shamans. The Oathbound are bound, like the Swordsworn, to all the Clans, and serve the Goddess with their minds and talents. *(Oath)*

Crookback Pass
Where Vanyel confronted Leareth and killed the Dark Mage with his Final Strike. The Pass is the southern terminus of the only route through the mountains, and lies very close to the home caves of the Hot Springs Clan of the *kyree*. Leareth's magic altered the Pass with a knife-clean cut straight through the rocky barrier, making an easy attack route for invaders. Vanyel marveled at both the amount of power necessary to carve the pass, and the power required to mask the sorcery being used. *(LHM)*

Crown and Candle
The inn in Hardorn where Talia and Kris met Trader Evan, who told them the truth about Prince Ancar. *(Arrows)*

Crown of Prophecy
The symbol of office worn by the Sun of the Son. The original crown was lost during the battle between the "the Prophet of Vkandis" and Menmellith. The large gold statue of Vkandis-In-Glory in his Temple wore a replica of it molded in one piece of solid gold with the statue, to discourage possible theft. During the miracle of Solaris' ascension as Son of the Sun, the god's statue came to life and walked to Solaris, removed the crown from his head, shrank it to human size in his hands, then placed the crown on Solaris' head. *(Storm)*

Crystal paperweight
Sent to Falconsbane as a gift by the Black Riders to distract Ma'ar. The large, clear crystal should have been a perfect scrying tool, but would only show a strange castle halfway up a remote mountain peak. *(Winds)*

Cube-maze
A magical device left in the ruins of Urtho's Tower. The object resembled a pile of hollow cast-metal cubes stacked randomly atop one another. The Adepts activated the cube-maze to counter the Mage-Storms. *(Storm)*

Cuelin (Master)
Head of one of Haven's glassmaker studios that specializes in religious glass. *(Exile)*

Cymry (Companion)
Skif's Companion. *(Storm, Arrows, Winds, TT)*

Dacerie (Companion)
Companion of Herald-trainee Tuck Chester. *(BB)*

Daelon
One of Falconsbane's servants, killed by a backlash of mage power when Darkwind and Vree destroyed the crow simulacrum. *(Winds)*

Da'gretha
See Kal'enel.

Dakola District
The run-down area in the city of Kimbata in the Haighlei Empire where Kanshin's house was located. *(Gryphon)*

Damen
A boy who unwillingly served Lord Rendan's bandit gang and the Dark Mage Leareth. He was killed when Vanyel escaped from his spell-bonds after being tortured and nearly killed. *(LHM)*

Damina (Herald)
A teacher at the Heralds' Collegium and one of Pol's card-playing friends. *(BB)*

Dancer (Companion)
One of Yfandes' two foals. *(LHM)*

Dancers
The group of two hundred entertainers in Khimbata that perform only for the King and his Court. *(Gryphon)*

Dane (Guardsman)
A guard and bully in the town of Selina who attacked Kerowyn and had her thrown in jail. She was freed on the word of many witnesses, and he had to pay her medical bills. *(Sword)*

Dantris (Companion)
Herald Keren's stallion Companion, and an active participant in Herald-Trainee Talia's rescue from the icy river. The bond between Herald Keren and Dantris is exceptionally powerful, and he is strongly tied to the other Companions with Mindspeech. *(Arrows)*

Dara
The sword Need told the story of the two sets of twin gods and goddesses, Kerenal and Dina, Karanel and Dara. *(Winds)*

Darenthallis Jadrevalyn
Informally known as Prince Daren, the youngest son of King Megrarthon Jadrevalyn of Rethwellan. Picked on by the spoiled middle son of the royal family, Daren was sent off to Tarma for training and to forestall fraternal feuding before it got out of hand. The lanky boy with dark blond hair and grayish hazel eyes was Kerowyn's first lover. When his eldest brother Faramentha ascended the throne, Daren became his Lord Martial, and proved worthy of the position. His mother was an earth-priestesses, which gave him earth-sense. During the war with Hardorn, Daren was able to see beneath the seemingly ordinary surface of the invader's realm and detect a sick land ravaged by ruthless blood-mages. He was Chosen as a Herald during the heat of battle, and became lifebonded to Queen Selenay very soon after. He is now Royal consort of Queen Selenay, father of Lyra and Kris. *(Storm, Sword, Winds)*

Daria (Herald-Trainee)
A tall and pretty young woman, one of the most competent people Lavan Firestorm had ever known. *(BB)*

Darian Firkin k'Vala k'Valdemar
An orphan adopted as a boy by Errold's Grove, he was apprenticed to the village wizard, Justyn, when Darian's

fur trapper parents disappeared in the Pelagiris Forest. The villagers thought him ungrateful and lazy, and he returned the favor by thinking they were dull cowards unworthy of respect. When the Blood Bear Clan attacked, Justyn died in a Final Strike defending the town and Darian was chased into the woods, where he was saved by Snowfire, a Hawkbrother from k'Vala Vale. Together, Darian and the Hawkbrothers saved Errold's Grove. The Hawkbrothers adopted Darian into the k'Vala clan and began training him to use his Mage Gifts. When a second northern tribe came to Errold's Grove, the Ghost Cat Clan, its members were afflicted by a illness spreading throughout the north. Darian helped Keisha Alder come up with a cure, and they formed a bond that led Keisha to eventually become Darian's wife. Darian grew up to lead the new k'Valdemar Vale, which served as an embassy between the Hawkbrothers, northern immigrants crossing into the country, and Valdemar. Darian's bondbird was the eagle-owl Kuari, and the teacher who brought him to Adept status was Firesong k'Treva. *(Owl)*

Dark Adept
A skilled mage who follows the evil paths of magic, including blood-magic. *(BV)*

Dark Servants (Leareth's army)
The term the Valdemar army used for the troops of the Dark Mage Leareth. The soldiers wear dull black metal armor and helms and carry unornamented round shields and long broadswords. *(Arrows, LHM)*

Dark Servants (Karsites)
The term the Valdemaran army used for the Karsite Sun-priests who sent monsters to harass and kill soldiers while they slept. *(BB)*

Dark Wing Road
The road that runs through Rethwellan and Jkatha from a crossroads past the Pelagiris Forest to the Dhorisha Plains. *(Winds)*

Darkfell Peak
A mountain near where Guardsmen cornered the brig-

ands that were raiding Gyrefalcon's Marches. During a parley there, the bandits killed the Guards' envoy and the Guards declared "no quarter." The outlaws were slaughtered to the last man, but the kidnapped children the guards had hoped to rescue were murdered by the bandits before they died when it became clear the Guards were showing no mercy. *(Arrows)*

Darksib
The pet name Herald Roald gave Tarma after their shared encounter with the Star-Eyed Goddess. *(Oath)*

Darkstone
A Tayledras Adept who helped teach Darian mage skills. An emotionless man, he'd chosen his use-name young and grown down to it—he wasn't necessarily the best instructor for a youngster. *(Owl)*

Darkwind k'Sheyna
Son of Starblade, he was the Council Elder representing the Scouts. His bondbird was Vree, a forestgyre. A strong Adept by age nineteen, he anchored the West when k'Sheyna tried to drain the Vale Heartstone before a move. The stone fractured, killing his mother. Darkwind had been called Songwind, but was so traumatized by the disaster he chose the new use-name Darkwind, swore not to employ magic again, and became a scout. When he met Elspeth, Darkwind was estranged from his father and confused by the problems affecting the Vale. When it became apparent that Mornelithe was responsible for all the problems, he promised to train Elspeth's mage abilities in exchange for her help. Darkwind and Elspeth became life mates and, after defeating Mornelithe, they went to Valdemar, where Darkwind served as an envoy from the Tayledras. Later, he was instrumental in the defeat of Ancar and helped to create the shields that enabled the Valdemar Heartstone to survive when the Mage-Storm solution was employed. *(Storm, Winds)*

Daro (Innmaster)
The kindly host who supplied Talia at her first town stop on her journey to Haven as Chosen, giving her food, a

waterskin, and utensils which had been left behind at his Inn. *(Arrows)*

Darowife
The wife of the friendly tavern owner Daro. *(Arrows)*

Darthela
The new bride of Sir Skolte, a middle-aged hereditary knight who hired Tarma and Kethry to escort her to Fromish before winter set in. Darthela was disappointed in her bridegroom, but as Sir Skolte pointed out, she was sixth of seven daughters, and her father was happy to marry her to anyone. *(Oath)*

Darvena (Companion)
Companion to Herald Ariel Ashkevron. *(LHM)*

Darvi (Herald-Mage)
The son of Queen Elspeth the Peacemaker, he was a Herald-Mage and Heir of Valdemar. Darvi died in a fall on a slippery staircase, which advanced his son Randale unexpectedly to the position of Heir. *(LHM)*

Darzie
A gryphon athlete, Darzie was one of White Gryphon's fastest couriers and racers. He was assigned to carry a Mage into the rainforest to set up a Gate for the rescue and search parties looking for Tad and Blade to use. *(Gryphon)*

Davan (Herald)
One of Talia's year-mates at the Collegium, he used his gift of Farseeing in the critical opening battle in the Valdemaran-Hardorn war. *(Arrows)*

David
An engineering student injured in the boiler explosion. *(Storm)*

Dawnfire k'Sheyna
A Tayledras scout, seventeen years old, and Darkwind's lover. Her bondbird was Kyrr, a female red-shouldered hawk. While spying on the gryphons through her bondbird, she encountered a mage trying to harm them, and was killed while fighting him. Though her mortal form

was slain, Dawnfire's spirit form merged with that of her bondbird. She became an avatar of the Star-Eyed, where she appeared either as a great shining vorcel-hawk or as a woman made of glowing liquid glass, with a suggestion of great wings behind her head. Later, she and Tre'valen helped An'desha escape from Falconsbane, and worked with the team at Urtho's tower to stop the Mage-Storms. *(Winds, Storm)*

Dawnmist
Snowfire's mother. *(Owl)*

Daystar
A Tayledras scout. *(Winds)*

Daystorm
A fox-faced female Tayledras scout with two crows as bondbirds. *(Owl)*

Dazzle-headache
A migraine characterized by sudden, fierce onslaught and extreme sensitivity to light. *(BV)*

Death-bell
During the reign of King Valdemar, a temple was built in the Grove at Companion's Field and a bell installed, except for the clapper and bell rope. Before the bell could be completed, the King died and the bell magically rang. The temple vanished long ago, but the tower remains. Now, whenever a Herald dies, the bell tolls, and every Companion in Haven gathers before the tower to mourn. *(BV)*

Deban
A large city in the Eastern Empire taken over by a new cult after the Mage-Storms began. *(Storm)*

Dedren
One of the widows of the Red Fox Clan's shaman. Neta the *dyheli* instructed Dedren how to guide her tribe's survivors to safety in Snow Fox territory. *(Owl)*

Dee
One of two apprentices that assist Rethaire, the Sun-hawks' Healer-Herbalist. *(Oath)*

Deedre (Herald-Mage)
A Herald-Mage whose prime focus was topaz. *(LHM)*

Deek
A fifteen-year-old boy Skif met while hiding in Lord Orthallen's house. Deek brought Skif into Bazie's family and helped him learn thievery. Deek would eventually leave his criminal life to become a guard for a traveling gem-merchant. *(TT)*

Defender of the Faithful
One of the sub-titles of the Karsite Son of the Sun. *(Storm)*

Delian (Companion)
Companion to Herald Tantras. When the suddenly sensitized Vanyel was overwhelmed by a deluge of voices in his mind, Yfandes commanded Delian to tell his Chosen to shield Vanyel. *(LHM)*

Dellar (Bard)
Chief Councilor of the Bardic Circle in Haven. *(LHM)*

Dellcrag
A northern landmark in Valdemar. The path between Dellcrag and Mount Thurlos was the legendary route used by the Dark Servants for their invasion. *(Arrows)*

Delphor (Lord)
A courtier posted to the palace at Haven. Princess Elspeth longed to play with his children, but Hulda persuaded her that the Heir to the throne was above associating with ordinary nobility. *(Arrows)*

Delton
A city in Ruvan, and Thalhkarsh's first center of operations. The geasblade Need sensed terrible danger there and diverted Tarma and Kethry to deal with it. *(Oath)*

Demon
Creature summoned from the Abyssal Plane by Karsite Black-Robe Sun-priests using the blood sacrifice of their fire victims. Demons are semi-intelligent and extremely dangerous, and usually attack at night. After Solaris as-

cended, the practice of calling demons was outlawed. *(BV)*

Demon-horse
Karsite term for a Companion. *(BV)*

Demon-Riders
Karsite term for Valdemar's Heralds. *(Exile)*

Demon Warriors
Living weapons conjured up by Prince Ancar's mages, the deadly seven-foot creatures appeared from a sulfurous, yellow-green fog and had dark pits in their skulls that contained dim red lights instead of eyes, fangs, and leathery yellow hides. Each was armed with a double ax and a sword. *(Arrows)*

Demon-Wolf of Hastandell, The
A legend cited by the plump priest of Anathei during his philosophical debate with Tarma. Ourra, the Demon-Wolf, didn't know the sheep he preyed upon were someone's property. When finally caught at his crime and enlightened by a priest, Ourra, who was actually a *kyree,* was terribly embarrassed and did his best to atone. To worshippers of Anathei, this tale is a prime example of the nature of good, evil, and conversion to the Light. *(Oath)*

Demonic focus
This magical item enables a demon to keep himself in the human plane of his own free will. The sorcerer Leland tried to imprison an imp in such a bottle. He summoned Thalhkarsh by mistake, who killed him. The bottle then became Thalhkarsh's demon focus. *(Oath)*

Demonsbane
Vanyel Demonsbane was one of the heroic epithets Bards bestowed on the Herald-Mage in their songs written after the battles along the Karsite border. Vanyel took the place of several Herald-Mages and repelled a major Karsite invasion of an area in Valdemar known as "the disputed territories." *(LHM)*

Dende
A Skybolt who fell victim to fever, and who was sent

with other victims from the unhealthy lowlands to the mountains to recover. *(Sword)*

Dent (Armsmaster)
Employed at Rathgar's Keep, he taught young Kerowyn archery and the basics of knife righting. Dent was killed by bandits at the wedding feast massacre. *(Sword)*

Derk
The scullion at Rathgar's Keep who almost dropped an enormous edible sculpture intended for the wedding feast. Only Kerowyn's quick action saved it. *(Sword)*

Derrel Lutter (Mayor)
A shopkeeper and the most prosperous resident of Errold's Grove, he and his wife regarded themselves as the village's most prominent citizens. After the barbarian invasion, Derrel became a very self-important Mayor. The Council had to develop ways to circumvent his tendency to take over so they could get certain projects accomplished. *(Owl)*

Derrian (Derry) (Herald-Trainee)
Assigned to one of Herald Pol's archery classes, Derry kept his bowstring and those of his fellow students' dry, earning approval from their instructor. *(BB)*

Derthenwood
A popular silver-colored wood used for carving. *(Oath)*

Derwit
One of the Sixth Formers at the Merchant School and an accomplice of the bully Tyron. Lavan gave Derwit the nickname "Dimwit," in retaliation for the humiliating nicknames Tyron used to insult his victims. *(BB)*

Desi Farane
A prostitute in Haven and sister to Trana. *(TT)*

Dester'edre
A Shin'a'in word meaning wind(born) sibling. *(Oath)*

Destillion (King)
Deceased King of Rethwellan. Father of Raschar, Idra and Stefansen. *(Oath)*

Destria (Herald)
Two year-groups ahead of Talia in training, she broke both her legs while rescuing half a dozen children from a flood. Her Companion Sofi got Destria and the children to safety. Later Destria rode circuit with Herald-trainee Christa, and was badly burned in the bandit raid that caused Christa's death. Talia was able to assuage Herald Destria's suicidal guilt and put her in contact with Herald Vostel, who had suffered similar burns, yet overcame them. Her amorous adventures were many and enthusiastic. *(Arrows)*

Dethor (Herald)
Weaponsmaster under King Sendar. *(Exile)*

Devan (Master Healer)
Devan treated Talia after the near-fatal attempt on her life by the Unaffiliated students and after her imprisonment and torture in Hardorn. His special Gift was healing trauma. *(Arrows)*

Devaril (Captain)
Ranking officer of the Demons, he never saw the need to employ Healers and Mages until his defeat while in the employ of Lord Kelcrag. He offered Kethry a job after the Sunhawks' Mages decimated his force and Idra's Healers saved his leg. *(Oath)*

Devaril's Demons
A respected mercenary company that fought for Declin Lord Kelcrag. After the battle, a mercenary's truce was declared, and Captain Idra's Healers treated many of Devaril's wounded. *(Oath)*

Deveran Remoerdis
He was the head of the House of Remoerdis of Lineas, killed in the massacre at his palace by the Mavelan clan. *(LHM)*

Devid (Cook)
The cook at Tarma and Kethry's school. *(Oath)*

Devid Stoen
Chief Husbandman of Shonar. With the Mayor and

Chief Guildsman, he came to talk to Tremane about the problems of the mage weather. *(Storms)*

Devlin Gereton
A young Valdemarran nobleman who involved himself as a go-between in the plot to marry Queen Selenay to a devious and dangerous Rethwellan prince. *(Exile)*

Dharin
A member of the Clan of the Stooping Hawk, and Tarma's betrothed. They planned to be bonded after both finished their sword-training, but Dharin was killed in the bandit attack. *(Oath)*

Dharra
A gryphon Mage. *(Gryphon)*

Dhashel
One of Falconsbane's servants, he was sent to collect information about Ancar. *(Winds)*

Dhon
A Shin'a'in word meaning "very much." *(Oath)*

Dhorisha Plains
The Dhorisha Plains are the Shin'a'in's home. A vast grassland situated in an enormous, circular crater, with its rim a hundred man-lengths below the surrounding cliffs that divide it from the Pelagiris Forest and the high desert country, the Plains held in their center the remains of Urtho's tower, which was destroyed in the Cataclysm after the final battle of the ancient Mage-Wars. The explosion left a glassy, barren ruin in a massive crater, but the Star-Eyed Goddess answered the prayers and sacrifices of her people, covering the wasteland with rolling grasslands strewn with blooming plants. In the Shin'a'in tongue, the Plains are called Dhorisha Shin'a, or The Plains of Sacrifice. The Shin'a'in are stewards of the vast grasslands, guardians against intruders who would seek to penetrate to the Plains' center and steal the buried arcane weapons left from the Mage Wars. *(BV)*

Dianelle
One of Hadanelith's victims in White Gryphon.
(Gryphons)

Dib Dawkin
A small boy, one of Keisha's patients in Errold's Grove.
After a fight, he had a nosebleed, a black eye, and a
tooth knocked out. *(Owl)*

Dierna Brodey
Daughter of Lord Orsen Brodey and the bride of Kerowyn's brother, Lordan. *(Sword)*

Dierne
A *hertasi* with Urtho's forces, he helped the exhausted
mage Viktcren back to his tent. *(Gryphon)*

Dina
The sword Need told the story of the two sets of twin
gods and goddesses, Kerenal and Dina, Karanel and
Dara. *(Winds)*

Diona
Tilden's wife. *(Oath)*

Dira Crimson
A rug seller whose son was adopted into Clan Tale'sedrin by marriage. *(Winds)*

Dirak, Councilor & Baron
An ally of Tremane in the Eastern Court and in charge
of the Imperial Civil Servants. *(Storm)*

Dirk (Herald)
The first Herald Talia ever met—she saw him on the
South Trade Road leading into Haven after she was
Chosen, and he reassured the frightened girl that she
was heading in the right direction. The Companions believe that the two life-bonded at that moment. Dirk's
special Gift is Fetching, a talent he combined with Herald Kris' FarSeeing ability to pinpoint objects at a distance and transport them. Talia and Dirk denied their
feelings for each other at first because neither was ready
for a serious relationship. They were married shortly

after Dirk and Elspeth Fetched Talia from Ancar's prison in Hardorn. *(Arrows, Sword, Winds, Storm)*

Disciplines
The various divisions of k'Leshya: Artisans, Administrators, Scholars, Husbandry, Mages, Shamans (who never go abroad with k'Leshya's delegations) Silvers (gryphons and humans) and Kestra'chern (this last group also includes the trondi'irn). *(Gryphon, Storm)*

Distance-viewer
Velgarth name for a spyglass. *(Winds)*

Dolly
One of Skif's young friends at the temple where he went to school. A small girl, he considered himself her protector. *(TT)*

Domery
Sunhawk Kyra's distant kin. When the scouts were going around Lord Kelcrag's stronghold, Kyra recognized Domery's lands and found the party a place to hole up for a while. *(Oath)*

Domesday Book
The official records kept in towns and villages all across Valdemar. Mayors and headmen throughout the kingdom write down their accounts of local conditions and send the reports to the capital. Since their versions may not always include full and true descriptions of situations, the Heralds check on their accuracy during their circuit rides through the sectors. *(Arrows)*

Dominick (Herald)
A Herald whose old room at the Palace complex featured a door leading to the garden. It was assigned to Vanyel when he arrived at his Aunt Savil's school for Heraldic trainees. *(LHM)*

Donni (Herald)
The protege of Herald-Mage Savil, she was lifebonded to Herald-Mage Mardic Dark. An apprentice thief when she was Chosen, Donni helped save Vanyel's life on the night he tried to commit suicide. Years later, when Vanyel was a Herald-Mage, Donni and Mardic were killed

in a battle with a Karsite necromancer, defeating his attack on a town by calling his flames onto themselves. *(LHM)*

Doolie
One of Geyr's messenger hounds, Doolie delivered crucial information to Kero during the battle with Hardorn. *(Swords)*

Dooly
One of Bazie's fences for stolen textiles. *(TT)*

Doomslayers
A mercenary Company that fought for Valdemar during the Karsite invasion. Six Doomslayer prisoners of war were tortured by Karsite priests, leaving them mindless shells. *(Oath)*

Dorilyn (Herald)
A Herald mourned by Vanyel on his return from the Karsite border. Herald Dorilyn was one of many Heralds who died or were killed in the line of duty since Vanyel acquired the rank of Herald-Mage. *(LHM)*

Dosent roots
Tubers with the texture and taste of cheese when served raw. *Hertasi* at k'Sheyna Vale kept them stocked in the common area of the kitchen. *(Winds)*

Double-sight
An ability used by both Healers and kestra'chern, it is the ability to simultaneously observe outward physical distress and see pain inside the patient. *(BV)*

Dragon
A Haighlei legend depicted at Court functions by the Royal dancers, who imitate the serpentine creature, which in Haighlei belief embodies Water and Earth combined. *(Gryphon)*

Dragon Solution
Lord Havirn's attempt to appease the monster killing his people by feeding it criminals, hoping it would leave "honest folk" alone. *(Oath)*

Drakan
Falconsbane's captain of the troops, in charge of administering punishments Falconsbane didn't have time to bother with. *(Winds)*

Drake (Herald)
One of Talia's year-mates at the Collegium, twin to Edric. The boys both possessed the powerful Gift of Thought-sensing, and were particularly attuned to each other. *(Arrows)*

Drake
See Amberdrake k'Leshya

Dreamerie
A narcotic indulged in by Old Berte, Stefen's caretaker. Stefen feared the woman's addiction would eventually force her to sell him as she had her own children in order to buy more. *(LHM)*

Dreamseeker k'Treva
The Tayledras scout detailed by Firesong to fetch Starwind and Moondance when Herald-Mage Savil Gated to k'Treva Vale to ask for help for Vanyel, who was dying from a leech-blade wound. *(LHM)*

Drusi
k'Vala *hertasi*. Ayshen's mate. *(Owl)*

Du'dera
A Shin'a'in phrase meaning "(I) give (you) comfort." *(Oath)*

Dudlyn (Lord Baron)
An elderly Rethwellan nobleman who rode a fat palfrey. *(Sword)*

Dunwythie
Family name of a clan attending Lordan's and Dierna's wedding. Their stern and competent matriarch encouraged Kerowyn and helped the wounded after the raiders' attack. *(Sword)*

Duross
The god of Rains, whose old temple in Oberdorn was

taken over by the female Lastel Longknife to resurrect the worship of Thalhkarsh. *(Oath)*

Dust
A gentle dapple gelding Tarma and Kethry took to Petras in their disguise as Shin'a'in traders. *(Oath)*

Dyheli
One of the five sentient non-human races allied with the Tayledras. *Dyheli* look like deer, but they are strong enough to carry a human on their back. They have huge, human-sized heads and enormous brown eyes that provide better forward vision than that of ordinary cervines. They are powerful Mind-Speakers; a *dyheli* king stag can control the minds of his entire herd if necessary. *Dyheli* can also teach a human a foreign language (or several) in moments by implanting the language directly into the subject's mind, though the process is painful for the human. *(Owl, Winds)*

Dyheli **tack**
The equipment used to make human riders comfortable on *dyheli*-back, comprised of a light saddle with belly, chest, and rump girths, looped leather stirrups, a thick saddle pad to protect the rider from the ridges of the *dyheli's* backbone, and a hand grip located where the horn would be on a horse's saddle to help the rider maintain balance. Some groups of *dyheli* will tolerate a loose hackamore-style headgear to help stabilize and balance the rider, others won't. Other *dyheli* tack has been designed to accommodate larger bond-birds, and consists of a belly band and padded platform supporting a perch. Smaller bond-birds roost on any convenient set of *dyheli* horns. *(BV)*

Dyrstaf
An enchanted item containing a potent fearspell. Ma'ar planted one in the Court of High King Leodhan of Predain. *(Gryphon)*

Eagle-owl

A nocturnal predatory bird with the silent flight and habits of an owl, but the general build of an eagle. The Tayledras use them as bondbirds. *(Owl)*

Earth-binding

A ritual that spiritually connects someone to his land. Used traditionally to bind the monarchs of Hardorn and Rethwellan to their kingdoms, and enable them to sense trouble or strife within their boundaries. The ruler must have the innate Gift of earth-sense for the ritual to be successfully performed. *(Storm)*

Earth-father

A Hardornen deity, partner to the Sky-mother. The couple is represented symbolically by the colors blue and green, or by a half white and half black circle. *(Storm)*

Earth-mages

The term for Mages who use the natural world's energies to work their relatively minor spells—though minor spells, well-used, can have a major effect. *(Storm)*

Earth-magic

A form of magic related to earth-sense and used by hedge wizards and earth-witches. The ability to perform earth-magic is connected to the natural condition of the land, and the restoration of abused land to its wild state. This magic is not related to either true-magic or high magic, although it can be linked to Mind-magic. *(Sword, Storms)*

Earth-witchery
A form of very low-level magic, simple spells a shepherd wise-woman might know and use. *(Oath)*

Earthsong k'Sheyna
A Tayledras scout who tried to breed a vulture as a bondbird. *(Winds)*

Eastern Empire, The
A collection of conquered countries east of Hardorn ruled by 200-year old Emperor Charliss. *(Storms, Winds)*

Eclipse amulet
An amulet worn by the leader of the barbarians that attacked Errold's Grove. When the Ghost Cat Clan approached the village years later, Darian was relieved to see that no one among the newcomers wore such an amulet. *(Owl)*

Eclipse Ceremony
A combination of natural phenomenon and ritual observed in the Haighlei Kingdoms once every twenty years. When the eclipse occurs, a certain amount of cultural change is permitted by Haighlei custom, depending on how full the eclipse is. This is the only time any sort of change is allowed in their rigid society. Any change to be enacted for the next twenty years is decreed by the Emperor and his Chief Priest during the Eclipse Ceremony, and new interpretations of holy writings are announced during this time as well. *(Gryphon)*

Edric (Herald-trainee)
The twin brother of Drake, and one of Talia's Yearmates. *(Arrows)*

Eere
Skyshadow's bondbird, a suntail hawk-eagle. *(Owl)*

Egon Potter
An elderly Guildmaster potter who gave hearthroom to Tarma and Kethry when they rode into his small settlement. He also warned them about danger in the vicinity, a bear that turned out to be a shape-shifter. *(Oath)*

Ehrris-wine
A very sweet and somewhat narcotic wine. *(Winds)*

Ekele
A Tayledras tree dwelling used for meditation, sleeping, teaching, and recreation. Each *ekele* has clear windows made of tough, flexible, transparent membranes and is accessed by a hatchway in the floor. The lowest room is usually a weather-buffer and cloakroom. The second story is often a gathering chamber, with a ceramic stove. The top floor is a sleeping area and a storeroom or study. Individual dwellings are furnished with a table and chairs, all fixed to the floor, and a sleeping pad. *Ekeles* are warded against fire by set-spells and a transparent resin painted on the trunks. They are approached from the ground either by permanent staircases affixed to the treetrunk, or, if the *ekele* is not in a protected Vale, via a rope ladder that can be pulled up when not in use. *(BV)*

Elcarth (Dean)
The diminutive and scholarly Dean of the Herald's Collegium during Selenay's reign. When he decided to retire after Hardorn was defeated, he chose to stay on as the Collegium's Historian. *(Exile, Arrows, Winds, TT)*

Eldan (Herald)
Kerowyn's love. Eldan's Gifts were animal and human Mindspeech. Kerowyn met Eldan and his Companion Ratha when she rescued them from the fires of a Karsite Priestess. The mercenary and the Herald were lifebonded, but Kerowyn feared marriage and denied her feelings for years, determined to remain independent. Eldan used long-distance Mindspeech while Kerowyn slept to maintain contact with her. During the war with Hardorn, Kerowyn came to Valdemar and was Chosen, enabling them to share life as a couple. *(Owls, Sword, Winds)*

Elders (Holderkin)
A group of older, married males who govern the Holderkin. Their word is law among their people, and can only

be overturned by the Heralds with great difficulty. *(Arrows)*

Elders (Shin'a'in)
Advisors and councilors to the various Shin'a'in Clans. Each group consists of a Shaman, a Clan Chief, a War-leader, and a Healer. *(Oath)*

Elenor
The youngest daughter of Herald Pol and Healer Ilea, she is training to be a Mind-Healer. *(BB)*

Elibet (Lady)
The Valdemaren Councilor who objected to Elspeth's battle plan against Hardorn. *(Winds)*

Elise
A palace chambermaid and one of Talia's confidants, Elise helped identify the Blues who tried to drown Talia. *(Arrows)*

Elite Guard
The unit of Hardornian Guards stationed outside the capital of Crown City; in Ancar's time they supported his reign and consisted of malicious men who bullied townspeople and travelers alike. *(Winds)*

Elivan
The *dyheli* Wintermoon rode while he and Skif searched for Nyara. *(Winds)*

Elkin
A skilled glassblower in Haven. *(Exile)*

Ell
An Imperial or Hardornen measurement, approximately the length of a forearm. *(BV)*

Eloran (Companion)
Partnered with Herald Mical. *(Exile)*

Elrodie (Herbalist-Healer, Earth-witch)
A teacher at Quenten's school delegated to welcome Elspeth and Skif. *(Winds)*

Elspeth (Queen)
A monarch of Valdemar, also known as Elspeth the Peace-maker. Her reign was characterized by self-sacrifice and tragedy. She bought peace for Valdemar with a love-less alliance marriage to avoid conflict with the neigh-boring kingdom of Iftel. After her husband died, she wished to follow her heart and marry Bard Kyran, but for the sake of the realm she denied herself that joy, using her potential remarriage as a powerful political bargaining tool. Her son Darvi died young, forcing her unwilling grandson Randale to become Heir. When El-speth died, the fragile peace she built fell apart, leav-ing a Valdemar filled with petty barons trying to carve out their own kingdoms. *(LHM)*

Elspeth (Princess, Herald)
The daughter of Queen Selenay and her consort, the traitorous Prince Karathanelan of Rethwellan, Elspeth was almost removed from the line of succession when still a child. Elspeth's problems were caused by a for-eign nurse, Hulda, who taught her to be a brat, hoping to destabilize the royal line. Queen's Own Herald Talia transformed the Heir into a proper young lady. At fif-teen, Elspeth was chosen by the Grove-Born Compan-ion Gwena, and was formally designated as Heir. At Kerowyn's first meeting with Elspeth, the sword Need woke and sang, indicating to Kerowyn that Elspeth should be Need's next bearer. Carrying Need, Elspeth served as her country's envoy on a mission to find hon-orable mages willing to work in Valdemar to counter Ancar's deadly magic. On the journey, she discovered that she had incredible mage potential. She trained with the Tayledras and met Hawkbrother Darkwind k'Sheyna, who later became her husband. Elspeth dis-covered she was a descendant of Herald-Mage Vanyel when she met another of Vanyel's descendants, Heal-ing Adept Firesong k'Treva, who taught both Elspeth and Darkwind. After achieving Adept status, Elspeth felt she could serve Valdemar better in the field, so she abdicated her claim to the crown in favor of her young twin half-siblings. *(Exile, Arrows, Storm, Sword, Winds)*

Empathy
The Gift of Empathy is possessed in some degree by most Healers. Empaths feel emotion the way a Farspeaker can hear words. An Empath can also "see" if certain emotions are strongly connected to a person or event. *(BV)*

Empire Mages
The term for the Adepts of the Emperor Charliss, their ranks are distinguished by the color robes they wear: purple, blue, or red. *(Storm)*

Empyreal Plane
The sixth plane of otherworldly existence. Even the most powerful Mages cannot coerce the services of beings from this plane, but can only hope the creatures are curious or feel like responding to their call. *(Oath)*

Enderby (Lord)
A councilman for the Forst Reach area who resigned in favor of Withen Ashkevron when Vanyel moved his parents to Haven. *(LHM)*

Enelve'astre
See Kal'enel.

Erdane (Bard)
One Vanyel's very few old acquaintances still alive when the Herald-Mage returned from his tour of duty on the Karsite border. *(LHM)*

Erek
One of Vanyel's guard-escorts on his exile's journey to Haven. *(LHM)*

Eren
A Skybolt Healer, he sent Shallan for Need when Kerowyn was wounded. *(Sword)*

Eren (Companion)
Companion to Valdemar's Heir Presumptive (Herald) Treven, Eren helped Treven and Jisa find a priest willing to marry them and ensure that the marriage was legally binding. *(LHM)*

Erna Dele
A resident of Errold's Grove who never thanked anyone for their help, yet always scolded Darian for his ungratefulness. *(Owl)*

Errold's Grove
A village of about fifty buildings on the forested side of a bridged ford over the River Londell, located near Lake Evendim on the far northwestern edge of Valdemar, and part of Lord Breon's holding. Once an important border town, the village was largely forgotten when war with Hardorn broke out, seeing a Herald only about once a year. Errold's Grove changed after it was attacked by the Blood Bear Clan. In the years after the town was saved, a Tayledras Vale was founded nearby, trade resumed with dye-merchants and fur trappers, troops were sent from Valdemar, a permanent Herald was assigned to the village, and the leaders of the village and the Vale worked together to manage the influx of refugees from the North. *(Owl)*

Ersala
The Sunhawks' horse buyer, whose purchase of extra Shin'a'in horses gave Tarma and Kethry stock for their horse trader cover story as horse-dealers while searching for Captain Idra. *(Oath)*

Estan (Companion)
Partner to Herald Mirilin. *(Exile)*

Esten (Companion)
Companion of King Randale. *(LHM)*

Estrel
The wife of Justin Twoblade and mother of Kethren, a former shepherdess with a vast knowledge of herb-healing and midwifery, she was placed in charge of Tarma and Kethry's nursery at their school. *(Oath)*

Etaven
The Shin'a'in word for water. *(Oath)*

Ethen
The Commander of Emperor Charliss' personal guard, he replaced Commander Peleun. *(Storm)*

Ethereal Varirs
Creatures of the Elemental planes who can be bargained with for favors or for something they want from the earthly plane. *(Oath)*

Evalie
The name Talia gave the imaginary Companion she wished would Choose her. *(Arrows)*

Evan (Herald)
Herald and instructor at the Collegium, his specialty is teaching trainees in the use of Foresight. His Companion is Jolene. *(BB)*

Evan (Trader)
A trader accused of murder in Westmark who was exonerated by Talia's Truth Spell, Evan later repaid his debt to her in Hardorn, confirming her suspicions about Prince Ancar and later smuggling items Talia had requested into her prison cell. *(Arrows)*

Evendim, Lake
The circular lake that lies on the westernmost border of Valdemar and is actually a great inland sea. The perfectly circular impact crater is the last remaining evidence of the great power released by the destruction of Dark Adept Ma'ar's fortress at the end of the Mage Wars. Lake Evendim is the home of fisherfolk, hardy humans that harvest the giant sturgeon in the lake. *(Arrows, Owl)*

Evening Court
A Haighlei Royal Custom that the King is obliged to attend, although he does not necessarily stay for all the events and entertainments. *(Gryphon)*

Everet (Archpriest)
The Archpriest of Valdemar during Vanyel's time, he was deeply concerned over the growing anti-mage crusade in Karse. *(LHM)*

Exile's Road
This road leads west from Haven to Lake Evendim, and passes through the villages of Hall, Deercreek, and Zoe. *(LHM)*

Exorcism
A religious rite performed by Karsite priests that can take one of two forms. In the first form, the priest casts the ghost out of the possessed victim or object and bars it from being able to return. In the second form, the priest blesses the ghost and helps the spirit see where it is supposed to go, then the priest helps break any bonds holding it to this plane and send it on its way, if it is ready. *(Storm)*

"Fair Maid of Bredemere, The"
A classic tragic romantic song of Valdemar. *(LHM)*

Faires
Celebrations held all over Valdemar, gathering merchants, entertainers, and townsfolk together for revelry and fun. Four major seasonal Faires were held every year, during the Spring Equinox, in Midsummer, at the Harvest, and at Midwinter. *(BV)*

Falcon of Light
One of the Son of the Sun's titles. *(Storm)*

Falconsbanc, Mornelithe
See Mornelithe Falconsbane

Faldis-juice
A delicious but addictive liquid narcotic derived from the Faldis fruit. *(Sword)*

Fallan
An innocent chambermaid sent to "entertain" the "hero" who slew the dragon terrorizing Lord Havrin's lands. She didn't please him, so he beat her and complained to the innkeeper, who promptly fired her. Tarma and Kethry saved the poor girl by introducing her to a good man who needed her. *(Oath)*

"Falling of the Sky and the Stars"
A phrase the *kyree* historian Rris used to describe the time of the ancient Cataclysm. *(Storm)*

False One, The
Solaris' predecessor as Son of the Sun, who was inciner-
ated by lightning during a Midwinter Fire-Kindling Ceremony for his corruption of Vkandis' sacred Rules and
Writ. *(Storm)*

Falthern (Lord)
A border lord who made his keep available to Queen
Selenay and her party during the crises with Hardorn.
(Arrows)

Fanshane (Lady)
A noble at Shalaman's Court, she was a thoroughly de-
tested harridan blamed for ruining Lady Sherisse, among
others. She was one of Hadanelith's victims. *(Gryphon)*

Faramentha Jadrevalyn
Rethwellan's King, Megrarthon's heir, and Daren's oldest sibling. Known as Faram, he was also brother to the
late and unlamented Karathanelan, Queen Selenay's first
husband and father of Princess Elspeth of Valdemar.
During her training days at the Collegium, Elspeth
began corresponding with him, learning a great deal
about her relatives. She also discovered that the Hulda
sent from there to become her nursemaid was not the
same Hulda who actually arrived in Valdemar. Though
Faramentha is the half-brother of Elspeth's treacherous
father, he is far more sensible and likable than his dead
sibling, and is loved by his people. *(Arrows, Oath,
Sword, Winds)*

Faras
A *hertasi* massage specialist. *(Winds)*

Farist
Nickname for Herald Griffon's Companion, Harevis.
(Arrows)

Farnherdt (Healer)
A retired Healer who was summoned along with many
other Healers to help the seriously injured Talia after
her rescue from Hardorn. *(Arrows)*

FarSeeing/FarSight
Also known as Looking or Seeing, it is a Heraldic Gift

enabling the possessor to see people or events at a distance far beyond normal vision. Heralds who are not Mindspeakers are likely to be Farseers. Farseeing can be linked with Fetching to transport people or objects from a distance. *(BV)*

Father's Mother
Title for the ruling matron of a Holderkin family, often the mother of the senior male in the Holding. *(Arrows)*

Fayshan
A priestess of the Cloistered Order of Kernos Sequestered. Fayshan was given charge of Jisette Jelnack after the King's Judgment condemned the insane woman to permanent confinement in the Cloister. *(BB)*

Feast of the Children
A holy ritual in Karse. Parents were ordered to bring their children to the Temple to be inspected by the Sunpriests. Until Solaris banned the practice, those suspected of having "witch-powers" were burned alive or taken for the Temple. *(Storm)*

Featherfire k'Treva
Daughter of Herald-Mage Vanyel and the Tayledras woman Snowlight. Featherfire is Mage-Gifted, a twin to Brightstar, who was adopted by the Mages Starwind and Moondance of k'Treva Clan. *(LHM)*

Featherless Son
A fond nickname the gryphons Treyvan and Hydona gave Darkwind. *(Winds)*

Fedor (Herald)
A Herald, his Gift is Foresight. He was assigned to assist Lord Marshal Weldon at the Karsite front, speaking for the ForeSeers among the Heralds. *(BB)*

Fedris
One of Ancar's mages, he accompanied the first contingent of troops attacking Valdemar and controlled them with coercion spells. *(Winds)*

Feeling
A Heraldic Gift related to Empathy. *(LHM)*

Feka
A bitter stimulant herb brewed as a powerful tea.
(Sword)

Felar (Companion)
Companion to Seneschal's Herald Jaysen Kondre.
(LHM)

Felara (Companion)
Herald Ylsa's Companion. He and Ylsa helped save
Talia after she was thrown into the frozen river by
Blues. *(Arrows)*

Feldar's Teeth
A mercenary company that surrendered to a Karsite
mercenary group and were murdered. *(Oath)*

Feliss
An injured gryphon among Urtho's forces treated by
Winterhart. *(Gryphon)*

Fellis-oil
A moderately effective insect repellent made from the
fellis plant. When Valdemaran army waited in the
swamps for Prince Ancar's army to attack, the oil did
not keep the midges and mosquitoes that infested the
area away. *(Arrows)*

Fellowship, The
An Errold's Grove sub-community of a dozen families
united by their religious beliefs in peace and non-
violence. They are noted for their diligence, hard work,
and skill in handcrafts, particularly textiles. *(Owl)*

Felwether
The town where Lady Myria was to be executed for the
alleged murder of her husband. *(Oath)*

Ferd
One of the Artificer students injured in the boiler explosion. *(Storm)*

Ferla Dawkin
Dib Dawkin's mother, who brought the injured boy to
Keisha for treatment. *(Owl)*

Fern Holl
One of the Fellowship farmers, she protested (with Kilmer) at an Errold's Grove Village Council meeting. *(Owl)*

Ferris-oil
An oil with a distinctive odor used for many purposes, including polishing woodwork. The Companions like the thick oil, since it not only fends off biting insects, but is good for their hooves and coats. *(Arrows, Oath)*

Fess
An aged, wizened palace guard posted at the suites of Queen Selenay and her Court, well past due for retirement, but too proud of his position to let go just yet. *(Arrows)*

Festival days
Annual holidays. These are celebrated across Valdemar even among the puritanical Holderkin; their horses wear bridle bells on Festival Days. When young Talia heard bridle bells on the day Rolan Chose her, she realized they must be those of a Herald, because no local horse would be wearing them on a non-Festival day. *(Arrows)*

Fetchers
The term for those rare Gifted who can transport objects, or, with great effort and risk, living beings. Herald Dirk is one of the few who possess this Gift during Selenay's reign. *(Arrows)*

Fetch/Fetching
Those with the Fetching Gift can retrieve objects or people from a distance. Generally the target needs to be within sight of the Herald doing the Fetching, but the Gift can, in rare occasions, be combined with Farsight to Fetch people and things from long distances, with the FarSeeing Herald zooming in on the target and giving the focus to the Fetching Herald, as Dirk and Elspeth did with Talia when she was imprisoned in Hardorn. *(Arrows)*

Field Uniform
The standard Heralds' outfit for Circuit riding, hard use,

or fighting, constructed of leather, raime, wool and linen. Field Uniforms are made for comfort and ease of movement, and may be added to in layers depending on the weather conditions. *(BV)*

Fifty Noble Houses
The collective term for the hereditary high-born of Mornedealth. *(Oath)*

Filix
The Master Mage of the Silvers of White Gryphon. While accompanying Regin's search team to look for Tadrith and Silverblade, he was killed by the magic-absorbing *wyrsa* they encountered. *(Gryphon)*

Final Strike
The unstoppable and self-sacrificing magic of last resort for a Mage, releasing all his personal energy and any power he can grab from his surroundings in a massive explosion, killing the Mage and any opponents nearby. Herald-Mage Vanyel Ashkevron used a Final Strike to stop the Dark Mage Leareth and his army at Crookback Pass, and the Mage Justyn used one to buy time for the villagers of Errold's Grove to escape when they were attacked. *(LHM, Owl)*

Fiona (Lady)
Partner to Lady Arawell in a sheep importation project which promised to boost the widowed Fiona's family fortunes and those of Arawell's Weaver's Guild. *(Arrows)*

Firecat
The Karsite equivalent to Companions, they are reincarnated former Sons of the Suns who advise those who need guidance in ruling the country. About the size of a bobcat, they are catlike in appearance with cream-colored coats with red points on the ears and tail. Firecats have the ability to Gate themselves and objects they carry in a method they call Jumping. *(Storm)*

Fire elemental
See Sandaar

Fire Kindling Ceremony
One of the holiest days in Vkandis' annual calender, it

occurs in Midwinter in Karse. All fires across the land are extinguished, then relit from fires ignited at each of Vkandis' temples, fires that are lit when a beam of light from the midwinter sun hits the temple altar. *(Storm)*

Firebird
Once considered to be a fable, these colorful birds inhabit some Valdemaran woodlands and the Pelagiris Forest. They ignite flames around themselves when they are alarmed, or during display behaviour. Firesong k'Treva developed a brand new bondbird strain from the breed, and bonded with the Firebird Aya. Aya's displays are controlled showers of sparkling fake fire. *(Oath, Owl, Storm, Winds)*

Firedance
A Tayledras scout. *(Winds)*

Fireflight k'Treva
A Tayledras Adept of Vanyel's time. *(LHM)*

Fireflower Retreat
A study center for Kyllian Mages. This particular School produces graduates equally versed in mage-craft and Healing. *(Owl)*

Firefrost k'Vala
An elderly and cheerful Healer-Mage, one of Darian's Tayledras teachers. Her bondbird is a snow white peregrine. Firefrost earned her name by Healing many cases of severe frostbite, including an entire family of *tervardi* during a blizzard when she was a teenager. *(Owl)*

Firelance
The k'Leshya clan's chief trondi'irn. *(Owl)*

Firelord
One of the many heroic epithets the Bards gave Vanyel in their songs. *(LHM)*

Firemare
A member of Amberdrake's family lost in the chaos triggered when Ma'ar's armies swept through the land. *(Gryphons)*

Firemare Valavyskya
He was an Elder for the Owl Clan of the Kaled'a'in after the Mage Wars. *(Winds)*

Firesong k'Treva
A Healing Adept, son of Starfall k'Treva, the descendant of Vanyel Ashkevron, and one of the most powerful Tayledras Mages ever. Intelligent, charismatic, confident, almost unbelievably handsome, vain, theatrical, highly Gifted in his craft, Firesong is a man and a Mage who loves an audience. In his youth, he created a new breed of bondbird from firebirds. With his bondbird Aya flaming above his head and riding a white Mage *dyheli*, he made quite an entrance when he was called to k'Sheyna Vale to help repair its damaged Heartstone. He trained Princess Herald-Mage Elspeth and helped Darkwind become an Adept. When Mornelithe was attacked and An-'desha freed, Firesong followed Mornelithe's soul to the nether planes and ripped it apart, then burned the remains, thus destroying the reincarnation of Ma'ar forever. Later, as the Tayledras envoy to Valdemar, Firesong was central to the effort to stop the Mage-Storms. His face was permanently scarred when the sword Need exploded in his hands while directing the power from one of Urtho's devices in the last battle to prevent a second Cataclysm. He used beautifully decorated masks to cover the damage to his face. He was one of Darian Firkin's teachers. *(Storm, Winds, Owl)*

Firesong k'Treva
A Tayledras Gate guard in Vanyel's time, she recognized Herald-Mage Savil when she arrived unannounced at k'Treva vale from Forst Reach seeking help for the wounded Vanyel. *(LHM)*

FireStarters
The Gift to start fires at will. It is one of the few Gifts that has little use to the Heraldic Circle except as an offensive weapon. Herald Lavan "Firestorm" Chitward had the strongest recorded Gift of FireStarting in Valdemar's history, and while it may have saved Valdemar, it certainly killed him. It is Herald Griffon's Gift as well,

and a burden to him because it is very easy for him to lose control of the fire. *(Arrows, BB)*

Firestarter/Firestorm, Lavan
See Chitward, Lavan

Firestorm
A Tayledras scout, his bondbird is Kreel. *(Winds)*

Firkin, Daralie (Dar)
Darian's mother. Her husband's trapping partner, she was caught with him when a Change-circle engulfed their camp in the forest outside of Errold's Grove and transported them far away to the northwest. *(Owl)*

Firkin, Darian
See Darian Firkin k'Vala k'Valdemar

Firkin, Ravin
Kelsie's twin and Darian's younger brother, unknown to him until he finally found his parents in Raven Clan territory. *(Owl)*

Firkin, Kelsie
Darian's little sister, and Kavin's twin, she was the first to see Darian when he arrived in Raven Clan village. *(Owl)*

Firkin, Kullen
Darian's father. He lost a foot when he and his wife Daralie were caught in a Change-circle and suddenly transported from the forest near Errold's Grove to Raven territory far northwest of Valdemar. Daralie and he became welcome members of Raven tribe and made a new home with them. *(Owl)*

Firkin, Ranie
Darian's youngest sister, born after his parents were transported from the forest near Errold's Grove to Raven territory far northwest of Valdemar. *(Owl)*

Firkin, Tel
Darian's youngest brother, age two, born after his parents were transported from the forest near Errold's Grove to Raven territory far northwest of Valdemar. *(Owl)*

First Council of Elders
A loosely organized organizational body among the Tayledras. *(Owl)*

First Level Judgment
A basic law course taught at the Collegium. Tuck Chester used what he learned in that course to allay Lavan's concerns about his role in the bullies' deaths. *(BB)*

Firstwife
The highest possible status for a female in the Holderkin culture. A firstwife supervises all other wives of a Holder male, and organizes the household and all its children. *(Arrows)*

Fisherfolk
The people who inhabit the shores of Lake Evendim and earn their living by harvesting its waters. The men hunt giant sturgeon with spear and harpoon, and use line and nets to harvest smaller freshwater fish. During the warm summer months, the women dive for sponges. The Fisherfolk are a tough bunch who must routinely deal with natural threats such as disastrous weather, uncertain seas, freezing winters, and also face human threats like pirates and slave raiders. *(Arrows)*

Fivepenny Street
A broad street in Haven with a number of taverns and drinking establishments. An alley off this street gave access to the back door of the Griffin's Egg, a tavern favored by the Unaffiliated students. After a prank in which the Blues flooded the third-year Bardic students' gathering place, the Bardic Trainees retaliated by starting a trash fire near Fivepenny Street to smoke out their tormentors. Eventually Dean Elcarth had to straighten out the resulting uproar. *(Arrows)*

Fivetree
One of the towns on the northern Circuit ridden by Herald Kris and Herald Intern Talia. *(Arrows)*

Flea-wort
A kind of shelf-fungus which grows on fallen, winter-

killed trees, harvested by Healers for medicinal uses. *(Owl)*

Flecker
One of Falconsbane's underlings sent to gather information about Ancar. *(Winds)*

Fledgling Healers
The term for students at Healer's Collegium in Haven. They wear pale green robes. *(Storm)*

Fletcher
An elderly Holderkin landowner who married Talia's sister Vrisa as one of his Underwives in an arranged match. *(Arrows)*

Floating barges
After the Cataclysm, the k'Leshya retained the knowledge to make these transport devices. The covered barges are made near weightless by magic, independent of how much mass is heaped in them, and can hover with a height range from treetop level to a finger's length off the ground. Though usually drawn by beasts, they can also be moved by magic. Having no intrinsic weight of their own, they make it possible to haul large cargoes with virtually no strain to the beast pulling them. *(Gryphon, Storm)*

Florian (Companion)
An unattached Companion who worked with Karal, answering his questions about Valdemar, including the ones about the Companions. Eventually he became the young priest's staunch friend and protector, willing to sacrifice himself to save Karal and all the lands and peoples threatened by the Mage-Storms. *(Storm)*

Focus Stone
A semi-precious or precious gemstone which helps a mage concentrate his or her powers. Each mage has a prime focus stone, which will harness their energies best, and a secondary stone, which is less effective. A prime focus stone is required to set a Mage-Web, particularly when a Herald-Mage is Guardian. *(LHM)*

Forbidden Places
What the Northern barbarians called Change-circles.
The Ghost Cat tribe's shaman warned his Blood Bear
Clan counterpart to shun such dangerous locations, but
to no avail. *(Owl)*

Forest of Sorrows
A large forest on the far northern border of Valdemar,
the Sorrows are said to protect the kingdom from invasion. Legend holds that with his dying breath Herald-
Mage Vanyel cursed the forest, saying "nothing which
intends evil to the realm or its people will live more
than five minutes within the vast woods." In fact, the
spirits of Vanyel and Stefen and Yfandes took root in
Sorrows and manifested to deal with any threat to Valdemar. After the Mage-Storm solution, Vanyel and his
friends crossed into the Havens. They no longer protect
the Forest of Sorrows. That job now falls to the Ghost
Cat Clan. *(Arrows, LHM, Storm, Winds)*

Forest of Wendwinter
A vast wilderness far to the north of Valdemar. The Ice
Wall Mountains and Crookback Pass lie beyond it.
(LHM)

Forest spirits
A superstition that spirits stalk the people who wander
into the Pelagiris Forest. In reality, the spirits are the
Hawkbrothers, and the stalking is quite real. *(Oath)*

Forestgyres
Largest of the bondbirds other than eagles. *(Winds)*

Formal Tack
The tack a Companion wears at Court Parades and formal occasions. It consists of a light leather saddle dyed
deep blue, tooled and worked with silver. The chest and
rump bands are adorned with silver bells, as are the
hackamore's reins. Formal tack is marked with the sigil
of the Companion, a vowelless representation of the
Companion's name. *(LHM)*

For'shava
A Shin'a'in word meaning "very, very good." *(Oath)*

Forst Reach
The ancestral land of the Ashkevron Family. The Forst Reach Holdings lie almost directly west of Haven, off Exile's Road. Until the Baires-Lineas annexation, Forst Reach was on the border of territory claimed by Valdemar. *(LHM, Oath, Sword, Winds)*

Fortellan
The site of an Imperial Depot looted by Tremane. *(Storm)*

Forten (Companion)
Herald-Mage Mardic's Companion. *(LHM)*

Fortunea (Companion)
Companion to Herald-Bard Jadus. Jadus was admitted to the Bardic Collegium in his youth. In his third year, something drew him to Companion's Field. Fortunea Chose him and turned his life upside down. Though resentful at the time, he later confessed to Talia he wouldn't have traded a moment of his subsequent life for the Laureate Bard's coronet, and he owed it all to Fortunea. *(Arrows)*

For'a'hier
Shin'a'in name for the Firefalcon clan. The dying shaman found near Tarma and Kethry's camp was from that clan, which was regarded as "different," producing the most shamans among the various peoples, and even an occasional mage. *(Oath)*

Fountain of Beer Inn
The inn in Petras where Justin Twoblades and Kyra sought out their contact. *(Oath)*

Free-lancers
Sometimes termed "freeswords," they're fighters for hire and not affiliated with any Company. Cheaper because they haven't posted bond with the Guild, they are also considered less reliable than bonded mercenaries. *(Oath, Sword)*

Frelennye
Herald Tylendel's family surname. The Frelennyes engaged in a bitter feud with the Leshara Holding, one

that threatened to drag the entire surrounding region into their conflict. *(LHM)*

Froggy
Sixth Form bullies' nickname for a girl in Third Form at the Merchants' School. *(BB)*

Fromish
A Jkathan town east of Lythecare, and Sir Skolte's home. Tarma and Kethry safely delivered his new bride there, and hired on as guards for an outbound jewel merchants' caravan. *(Oath)*

Frostfire
A reclusive Tayledras Adept. When he was burned in a fire, Starblade mistook the mysterious white-haired figure who rescued him as Frostfire. *(Winds)*

Fry
What Cook Tel's helper calls Minstrel Renfry. *(LHM)*

Full-bond
A complete mental melding of a Tayledras with her or his bondbird. If the human can't come out of the full-bond, the human's body will eventually die and his or her spirit will be completely absorbed into the bondbird, diminishing as a result. *(Winds)*

Fyllia
A Herald-trainee who hailed from Forby on Lake Evendim, a village at the end of Hollyton Road. *(BB)*

Fyllis (Queen)
The wife of King Theran and Queen of Valdemar during Lavan Firestorm's time, her Gift was Empathy. She was the third daughter of the Duke of Brendan, located on Valdemar's far southeastern border. Fyllis and Theran were both Chosen as Heralds while he was still the Heir. It was a love match as well as being a very good political marriage. *(BB)*

Gacher
One of the young *dyheli* stags who volunteered for the dangerous expedition to the northwest. He was killed by a colddrake. *(Owl)*

Gaerazena
One of Hadanelith's victims in White Gryphon. *(Gryphon)*

Gala (Companion)
Herald-trainee Tylendel Frelennye's Companion. Gala provided the only known instance of a Companion repudiating her Chosen. She gave her life to amend a wrong Tylendel had committed in his madness after his twin brother Lord Staven Frelennye was murdered. *(LHM)*

Gallen
Headman of Covia, a western village under siege on the fringe of Tayledras territory in the Pelagirs. Gallen was rough-hewn, but a strong leader. He informed Starwind and the other Tayledras mages of the vicious encroachments of the Blood-Mage Krebain. *(LHM)*

Gandels
Pelageris Forest predators, they run in packs and can be influenced magically—Falconsbane often herded them into k'Treva's territory to provide a distraction. *(Winds)*

Garber (Commander)
General Shaiknam's second. Among those serving Urtho, both officers were poorly regarded, in particular

for their unthinking and wasteful treatment of non-human combatants. *(Gryphon)*

Garland of Death, The

A litany dating from Urtho's time that all mages of k'Leshya, including the gryphons, were required to learn. It detailed an inventory and set of descriptions of the weapons hidden in Urtho's Tower on Dhorisha Plains. *(Storm)*

Garth

One of Vanyel's escort-guards on his exile's journey to Haven. Tall and dark, Garth was a common swordsman. Employed by Lord Withen Ashkevron, Vanyel sarcastically referred to his escort as the shadow of "Sun and Shadow". *(LHM)*

Garth

A Sunhawk scout, he was a dark, tiny man, who rode a tall Shin'a'in gelding. An excellent tracker but a lousy archer, helped find a back way into the Jkathan rebels' stronghold. *(Oath)*

Gartheser (Lord)

Royal Counselor who spoke for the North, and Lord Orthallen's closest ally. Thin, nervous, and balding, he made a poor impression on Herald Talia at her first Council meeting, right after Elspeth's Choosing. Talia read Gartheser's feelings, picking up strong displeasure. She also felt a faint note of disappointment and wondered if that was because Gartheser had hoped his kinsman, not Elspeth, would be named Heir. Gartheser was Orthallen's "yes man" on the Council. *(Exile, Arrows)*

Garthhold

Settlement area in the Pelagir Hills held by the Tayledras, who gave immigrant farmers permission to work the land. When a colddrake queen attacked the settlement and killed several people, the Tayledras sent help, including young Vanyel Ashkevron, who destroyed the beast. The courage of the farm folk in putting their lives back together after sudden tragedy gave Vanyel the insight that enabled him to become a good Herald. *(LHM)*

Gate

A magical means of instantaneous long-distance transportation. A Gate is erected by a spell that can only be cast by an Adept, and can only connect to a point the Adept knows thoroughly. Its fabric is spun from the Mage's own energy resources. These are connected to the Gate by a scintillating cord of energy-like spider silk. The energy comes to rest in a continuously shifting pattern laid over the Gate arch, spinning out and reaching into the Void where more spider threads seek the anchor at the other end, the destination in the mind of the Adept. The gate can be used by anyone or anything while it is open, but except in unusual circumstances, the Adept building the Gate must stand where the Gate originates and maintain the energy flow to hold the Gate open while others go through. *(BV)*

Gate guards

Tayledras sentinels armed with spears and bows and arrows. Not mages themselves, they are still sensitive to the signs of a Gate being activated in their territory. When Herald-Mage Savil came through a Gate from Forst Reach, Gate-guards were waiting for her. These Tayledras are clan members who, if they have a Mage-Gift, prefer not to use it. They serve as Healers, scouts, border-guards, and craftsmen, and guard the few places within the Vale's shield that need both tangible and intangible protection. *(LHM)*

Gate of Judgment

It stands beyond the Pillars of Wisdom in the evocation of the death-curse against an Oathbreaker. *(Oath)*

Gate-invocation

The spellcasting of the selected portal's right and left sides, threshold, and lintel, before the actual work of spell weaving the Gate can take place. It helps if the Gate-invocation is cast over an appropriate structure, like a door, archway, or gate. It is also easier if the portal is cast on sanctified ground like a temple, or the entrance to a temple. *(LHM)*

Gate-spell

A spell that enables a mage to cross great distances instantly. It is the most personal of spells, and requires great power and great skill from the Mage who attempts it. Only one mage can build a particular Gate, because only one mind can direct the energy needed to a precise location. A mage may use energy from another person or persons in the creation of the Gate. The spell-wielder must have a firm and intimate knowledge of the location of where the Gate is to exit, and be able to visualize the scene exactly. First the anchoring Portal must be erected with a Gate-invocation spell, then the actual Spell Weaving of the Gate is done. Gating warps space back upon itself. As the threads of energy seek the far end of the Gate under the mage's direction, the Gate pulls power from the mage. That is the moment of greatest danger for the mage, as the Gate can drain the Mage to unconsciousness if the mage is careless. When contact is made with the exit portal, the power threads lock on and the Gate achieves a stable, though temporary, solidity. Taking down the Gate enables the mage to regain some of the expended energy, replenishing enough lost energy to keep the mage from collapsing. Using sanctified ground, or repeatedly using the same terminal portal eases the difficult task of Weaving a Gate. The six permanent Gates which existed in Urtho's time were enormous fused-stone arches, each one tied to its own magic node from which it drew power. For years after the Cataclysm, Gates could no longer be erected; and when it became possible to build them again, everyone was wary of sending living beings through them until it was certified that procedure was really safe. *(BV)*

Gathering

A Holderkin trade fair, an infrequent opportunity for isolated communities to see and buy outsiders' goods. *(Arrows)*

Gathering tent

A Shin'a'in communal structure. Tarma's people were celebrating in their gathering tent when they were attacked and killed by bandits. *(Oath)*

Gavis (Companion)
Companion to Herald Courier Sofya. Yfandes learned Companion Gavis and his Chosen were stopping at an inn on Exile's Road and suggested that she and Vanyel stop there for the night as well. Vanyel twitted her about having a thing for the young stallion's over-muscled charms. *(LHM)*

Gaytha
The housekeeper at Heralds' Collegium during Queen Selenay's reign. She was originally Governess to House Ravenscroft, and was thus well equipped to teach courtly graces to students. Matronly and middle-aged, she was well-liked by the Herald-trainees. Gaytha was appalled to learn from Talia of the Holderkin custom of marrying off girls at age thirteen. *(Arrows)*

Geas
A powerful, almost unbreakable magical compulsion. Kethry explained to Tarma that she was under a geas embodied in the magic sword Need, one which compelled her to help women in trouble. *(Oath, Sword)*

Gellwin (Lady)
Seeing that Vanyel's mother felt left out of things when Lord and Lady Ashkevron moved to Haven's Court, Stefen introduced Lady Treesa to Lady Gellwin and Countess Bryerly, two of the queen bees of the Court's social set. Lady Gellwin took Treesa under her wing. *(LHM)*

Gelmar
Rendan's older brother and former leader of the bandit gang, Gelmar had become disabled from a head injury. Finally, Rendan ordered his sibling taken outside and abandoned as worthless, an object lesson to other members of the band. *(LHM)*

Geof Larimar
A farmer living in the northern reaches beyond Valdemar's border who hired Old Man Brodie. Like everyone Brodie had worked for, Larimar did not realize the failed Healer was using magic to heal the animals he treated. A roan colt of Larimar's had broken its leg, but

Brodie convinced him the injury was only a treatable dislocation. Grateful that he would not have to put down a valuable beast, Larimar paid the aged Healer with a smoke-cured ham. *(LHM)*

Gem
One of Quenten's apprentice Mages assigned to find a weapon that could hit the enemy's Mage. *(Sword)*

Gentian Arbelo (Healer)
A senior Healer, he served with Kerowyn's Skybolts. *(Owl)*

Geoffrey
One of Sewen's officers, he sat on the storage chest in Captain Idra's tent after the battle, guarding their mustering-out pay. *(Oath)*

Geoffery of Helmscarp
A nobleman secretly involved in the alliance of pirates and slavers who were harassing Lake Evendim's fisherfolk. *(Arrows)*

Gercattle
Grazing animals generally pastured with sheep in the hills of Jkatha. During the siege of Lord Kelcrag's stronghold, most gercattle herds disappeared, taken to feed various warring armies. *(Oath)*

Gerdo
A contortionist performing with a traveling carnival. He and his wife Sara took Liam under their protection after the boy was assaulted, because they had suffered the same kind of violence. *(Winds)*

Gerichen (Father)
Priest at Haven's Temple of the Lord of Light (Karse's Vkandis) during the reign of Selenay. *(Exile)*

Gerick (Herald)
One of the Heralds who died during Talia's education at the Collegium during *Arrows of the Queen*. Somewhat absentminded, he is remembered during *Arrow's Flight* as the Herald who left a valuable ring at a Circuit Waystation. Since it was the Queen's gift to a Guildmaster,

it had to be recovered. His interns Dirk and Kris worked together to retrieve it. Kris Saw where the ring was and Dirk Fetched it in their first attempt at teamwork. After that, the two young Heralds were recruited to find and retrieve items for Selenay—they referred to themselves as the Queen's Thieves. (*Arrows*)

Gerond (Herald-trainee)
One of Elspeth's year-mates. Herald Talia sounded him out when she was trying to figure out why Elspeth was being so secretive. (*Arrows*)

Gerrold
A Sunhawk. Kethry traded a *jesto-vath* spell to keep his tent warm and dry in exchange for an expensive silk waterproof cloak Tarma could wear on patrol. Later, during the trek to get behind Lord Kelcrag's position, Gerrold and his horse Vetch fell through a collapsed section of the mountain path. Kethry hastily formed a magic net to save them and help Gerrold back to the narrow trail. (*Oath*)

Gerrolt
An Eastern Army officer. After the Mage-Storms began, he reported that strange new insects and higher life forms had appeared around troops' camps. (*Storm*)

Gerth the Axe
One of Lord Rendan's ambushers, killed by Vanyel. (*LHM*)

Gervase (Wizard Lizard)
A White Winds order Adept, Gervase was a truly unique sorcerer. He was a *hertasi*, one of the race that still live in the Pelagir Hills and were once tree-lizards until magic altered them. Gervase saved Adept Cinsley of the White Winds from relentless pursuers, and as a reward was granted his wish to become a mage. He become Cinsley's apprentice. The talented Pelagir changeling lived three times as long as a human sorcerer and attained legendary status, eventually rising to become the High Adept of his entire order, and guiding it to the eminent position it held in Kethry's time. (*Oath*)

Geslaken
A name Ma'ar used in one of his incarnations. *(Winds)*

Gesta
A Mornedealth Guard (and one of the ugliest men Tarma had ever seen), he was willing to take over Catchild's watch while she helped rescue Kethry from Wethes Goldmarchant. *(Oath)*

Gesta
Hertasi Healer who treated wounded gryphons. *(Winds)*

Gesten
Hertasi. Skan and Amberdrake's servant/companion since the start of Ma'ar's War. *(Gryphon)*

Gesten
A *hertasi* term of friendly respect. *(Storm)*

Gestena
Shin'a'in word meaning "thank you." *(Oath)*

Get'ke
Shin'a'in term meaning "(could you) explain." *(Oath)*

Geyr
A Skybolt, a black man who came from a land so far to the south of Rethwellan that Kerowyn had never heard of it before she met him. Geyr's specialty was working with trained messenger dogs, which were a tremendous asset to the mercenary company. After Bel retired, Geyr became Co-Lieutenant with Shallan. *(Sword)*

Ghost
Name given by Yfandes to the Companion who Chose Tashir Remoerdis. The young stallion was so traumatized by the events that occurred when he arrived in Highjorune that he couldn't remember his name. He was a Mindhealer, a gift rarely found among Heralds, and unheard of in a Companion until then. *(LHM)*

Ghost Cat Clan
This Northern barbarian tribe migrated from their traditional lands toward Valdemar and Errold's Grove. Scouts quickly decided they were not invaders because they brought their whole tribe, including the sick, feeble,

elderly, and children, including infants. The tribe's totem is the Ghost Cat, and it led them to Valdemar in hopes of finding a cure for the terrible Summer Fever afflicting them. *(Owl)*

Ghosts
Restless spirits of the deceased. According to the Writ of Vkandis, no one who is of the Faith could become a ghost. There is also a Karsite tradition that the unblessed dead are hungry, vengeful night roamers. *(Storm)*

Gielle
One of the mages Judeth summoned to the planning session when the White Gryphon Council learned Tad and Blade were missing. Gielle was formerly a mercenary mage with Urtho's forces. At that time he was a Journeyman, but the Cataclysm transformed him into an Adept. *(Gryphon)*

Gies
A swarthy Skybolt scout, he was Tre's twin, and distinguishable from his brother only by his deeper voice. *(Sword)*

Gifts
Paranormal abilities possessed in greater or lesser amounts by members of the Collegia. Some Gifted have very little talent. A few command quite powerful Gifts. These Gifts are Valdemar's answer to the Old Magic still used in neighboring kingdoms. Mindspeaking and ThoughtSensing are among the more basic ones, used regularly in contacts with the Companions. Other talents include Empathy, FarSeeing, FarSpeaking, Fetching, FireStarting, and MindHearing, with a number of variants on these and other talents. In general, the strongest Gifts seem to be associated with Healers rather than Heralds. The Gifts of Communication are somewhat similar to those Healers employ, and in an emergency Heralds with those Gifts can be called upon by the Healers to assist in treatment, as Talia often was. Contact with a Companion and powerful emotion enhances the development of the Chosen's latent abilities. In Valdemar's history, the development and training of these

Gifts gradually displaced any knowledge of "true magic" in the realm until no record was left that such magic ever existed, or how it had been used. Unusual or unique Gifts, such as FireStarting, often appeared during eras when there would be a desperate need for such talents. *(BV)*

Gil Jarad (Healer)

Lord Breon's Healer. Gil was a withered looking little man, very deliberate, though he could move quickly when needed. He had iron gray hair, small black eyes, and bowed legs. He tried to instruct Keisha in medical arts but had too little of the Gift himself to help her develop Shields and Sight. He had once been a horsetamer at Lord Ashkevron's Forst Reach. *(Owl)*

Gildas (Lord)

Councilman, and speaker for the South and its rich grainlands. *(Arrows)*

Gillyflar tea

A stimulating tea that Skif often drank before going out on a night job so he would be alert. *(TT)*

Gisell

A Karsite Sun-priestess from a noble family, she volunteered to help Valdemar with magic. A proud woman, she resented being coached by her assigned partner Rashi, a pigkeeper's son. But as she had alienated everyone else in magery class, he was the only one who would work with her. *(Storm)*

Gittern

A guitarlike instrument, related to the lute. Craftsman Rolf Dawson had been experimenting with making a new sort of gittern, which he demonstrated to Vanyel at Forst Reach's Harvest Fair. The innovations involved twelve rather than six strings, all made of metal instead of traditional gut. Bard Stefen became adept at playing the new instrument; his favorite was one of the twelve-stringed variety. *(LHM)*

Gleemen

Travelling minstrels and entertainers, under the name

they were known by the common farm and village folk. Tallo, the young man who became the Tayledras Mage Moondance, fell in love with a young gleeman and ran away with a traveling troupe. *(LHM)*

Goatsfoot mushroom
A mushroom which affected Healers and certain Heraldic Gifts when eaten. In particular it distorted Thoughtsensing and Empathy for several days afterward, depriving the Healer or Herald of those abilities and causing dizziness and disorientation. Herald Talia was affected by this fungus during her mission with Herald Kris to Hardorn. She and Kris weren't sure if being given the drug was accidental or deliberate, but it strongly affected Herald Talia's power to detect possible treachery. *(Arrows)*

Goddess
Worshipped in many forms and under many names, not only in Valdemar but throughout the realms of Velgarth. Most often, the Goddess was prayed to in one of her guises as Maiden, Wife, or Crone. In Rethwellan she was recognized as all three forms and known as the LadyTrine. *(BV)*

Goddess of the Four Winds
The nomadic Shin'a'in worshiped a four-fold version of the Goddess: Maiden, Mother, Warrior, and Crone. *(BV)*

Goddess's Servants
Holderkin menials assigned to particular corridors within Temple cloisters. They serve the Temple their entire life and have even less freedom than the Temple's Handmaidens. *(Arrows)*

Golden Beauty
Highly prized fall apples. At the Merchant School, Tyron demanded that one of his young victims keep him supplied with the fruit, and punished him when the boy didn't. *(BB)*

Goldenoak
A coarse grained yellow-brown wood popular for con-

struction, cabinetry and housing. The acorns of the tree are used to fatten pigs for the winter, and many farmers claim that the best meat comes from hogs fed on goldenoak acorns. The ground acorns are mixed with nuts and baked into a hearty bread in the North of Valdemar. In regions where the goldenoak is abundant, it is claimed that the gold in goldenoak refers to the wealth the tree brings, not just to the color. *(Arrows)*

Gordun
Tremane's Chief Artificer and Mage, a homely, square-faced man with thick, clever fingers. *(Storm)*

Gorley (Lady)
The sensible and long-suffering widow of Viden's late and unlamented bully, Lord Kendrick Gorley. *(Oath]*

Goshon
A member of the weasel family, prized for its rich, dark brown fur that lived in the northern lands. Clan Chief Vordon of Ghost Cat Clan said Valdemarans had no name for it, though he expected that once traders started bringing in its soft pelts, they would become highly prized. *(Owl)*

Graceless
One of the big mares trained by Beaker and Jodi. Teamed with Hopeless, she was an expert at taming recalcitrant male horses. *(Oath)*

Grand Common
A grazing ground outside the walls of Shonar. Several of the town's children were lost herding livestock there when a mage-blizzard hit the area. *(Storm)*

Grant's Hold
A town near Viden. Together with the adjacent town of Lyavor, it took in the majority of the area's transient trade, leaving Viden's inn to serve mostly local customers. *(Oath)*

Gray
Captain Idra's palfrey, the gelding she rode on her last trip to Petras. As soon as Tarma and Kethry were invited to the palace, Tarma created an excuse to search

the Royal Stables for Gray, but couldn't find him, confirming their fears about Idra's disappearance. *(Oath)*

Gray stud
A big, bad-tempered stallion sold to Vanyel Ashkevron's brother Meke under the false claim that he was a part-bred Shin'a'in warsteed, and used by Meke to found a line of heavy horses that eventually became the standard war mounts for the Valdemaran Guard. *(LHM, Oath)*

Gray Wolf Clan
A friendly tribe inhabiting the mountains far to the north of Valdemar. *(Owl)*

Grays
Slang name for Herald-trainees' uniforms. *(BV)*

Grayse (Sergeant)
A sergeant with Captain Lissa Ashkevron's Guard company, he was the son of one of Forst Reach's holder families. *(LHM)*

Great Battle Magic
Offensive and defensive major magic used in wartime, including magically summoned weaponry, like lightning and fire bolts, calling down demons on the enemy troops, and so on, and the shielding of troops against such attacks. These magics were limited in use because they rapidly drained the mages responsible for them and the ley-line and node energy around the battlefield, depleting them for the time it took to regenerate the energy to power magic of that potency. *(Oath)*

Great Beast
An'desha's name for Mornelithe Falconsbane. *(Storm)*

Great Crater Sea
Name used by the Tayledras for the immense depression formed when Ma'ar's fortress was destroyed during the Great Mage Wars, which soon filled with water. Outlanders called the vast circular crater-lake Lake Evendim. *(Winds)*

Great Garden
A carefully cultivated garden in the Haighlei Palace at

Khimbata shaded by enormous trees. In its center is a bowl-shaped amphitheater floored with grass where entertainers perform during Evening Court. The only break in the amphitheater's circle is the door providing access to the Palace. *(Gryphon)*

Great Hall of Hardorn
The largest room in the Hardornian palace, where Court was held. The walls were paneled in birch, the floor was polished gray granite, and the overhead beams were varnished maple. There were gilt and gold fittings and crystal ornaments everywhere and battle flags hanging from the rafters. A map of Velgarth with Hardorn at its center was inlaid in stone in the floor in front of the throne. *(Winds)*

Great Hall of Justice
Located in Highjorune, capital of Lineas, it was the repository for the kingdom's important documents. Herald-Mage Savil and Tashir read the treaty between Baires and Lineas kept on display at the Great Hall and discovered a possible motive for the massacre of the Remoerdis royal household: according to the treaty, if either reigning House died out and assassination could not be proven, the surviving House inherited both thrones. *(LHM)*

Great Hall of Rethwellan
A large hall in the palace at Petras, built of buttercolored marble and lit at night by massed tapers that made the walls seem to glow. *(Oath)*

Great Hall of Valdemar
The largest room in the Palace, it has a high vaulted ceiling supported by slender ironoak pillars. Battle banners and Heraldic pennons, many dating from Valdemar's Founding, hang from the rafters. Tall, narrow windows fill the west wall. In the evening, lamps and candlelight gleam on the highly polished woodwork. This is where Valdemar's court dines formally, and where major assemblies take place. *(Arrows)*

Great Harsey
A town in Rethwellan, where Kethry's son Jendar moved

the White Winds school she founded to in order to be closer to the capital, Petras. *(Oath)*

Great Pass, The
Created by Leareth, the northern mage who fought Herald-Mage Vanyel. The Great Pass cut smoothly through the Ice Wall Mountains, and emerged just north of the Forest of Sorrows. Wide enough for an army to pass through, it provided an easy path for Northern invaders to march to the border of Valdemar, though Vanyel blocked one end of it in his Final Strike against Leareth. *(LHM, Owl)*

Great War
Sometimes referred to as the Great Wars or the Mage Wars, the conflict between Urtho and Ma'ar and their attendant forces. *(Gryphon)*

Greater Gates
Rare permanent Gates. Urtho made six of them, and tied them to nodes to keep them open. Falconsbane intended to make a Greater Gate out of the proto-Gate Firesong created. *(Gryphon, Winds)*

Greden
Falconsbane's underling who failed to fulfill the orders to bring Need back to his master. *(Winds)*

Greeley
Valdemar's Seneschal under King Theran, previously the Seneschal of the king's country estates. *(BB)*

Green-bands
Zhaneel's term for squires and sergeants in Urtho's forces who wore green armbands and acted as field-Healers during combat. *(Gryphon)*

Greeneyes
Tarma's pet name for Kethry. *(Oath)*

Greenhaven
A small town off the North Trade Road in Valdemar's northern sector, Greenhaven is on the Heralds' regular circuit. *(Arrows)*

Gregoth
Leader of the bandits who attacked and killed Tarma's people. *(Oath)*

Grek'ka'shen
Shin'a'in term for a carrion-eating creature. It eats things even vultures won't touch, and occasionally its own young. Calling someone a *grek'ka'shen* is a profound insult. Tarma reserved the word for King Megrarthon's middle son, Karathanelan. *(Sword)*

Grenthan Miles (Healer)
One of the middle rank of Healers serving with Kerowyn's troops. *(Owl)*

Grenvis
Mage and Lord of the lands west of the Pelagir Hills. Some of the peasants had held their settlements from Grenvis. Phellip, citizen of a village located near k'Treva Vale, had seen cold-drakes in action in the old days, when Lord Grenvis was under attack from enemy mages. *(LHM)*

Gretshke
Semi-demonic creatures, they are mostly head, teeth, and appetite. Though not immune to cold iron, *gretshke* can be overwhelming in swarms of hundreds or thousands. Vanyel had encountered a swarm and the Adept Mage commanding them on the Karsite border. Circumstances he found after the massacre at the Lineas palace forcibly reminded him of the damage inflicted by *gretshke*. *(LHM)*

Grevas
General Thayer's secretary. *(Storms)*

Greyhame, Duke
His levies fought alongside the Sunhawks in the Jkathan civil war. His officious sentry challenged Tarma's scouting party and received a lesson in manners from Ironheart. *(Oath)*

Griffin's Egg
A tavern used as a watering hole by the Unaffiliated students at the Collegium. After flooding the Bardic stu-

dent's lair, the Blues fled for cover to the Griffin's Egg, which didn't protect them from being smoked out by the vengeful Bardic students. Herald-trainee Skif's contribution was to snatch every Blue purse that he could get his fingers on and leave them hanging in an embarrassing place. *(Arrows)*

Griffon (Herald)
One of Talia's year-mates. His Companion is Harevis. A tall, somber young man, his Gift was FireStarting. In the battle with Hardorn, he used his Gift to turn some of the demon warriors into walking pyres. Then he joined forces with Farseer Davan, Rolan, Talia, and Dirk to locate and destroy Prince Ancar's primary mage. He eventually became Herald to the Lord Marshall of Valdemar. *(Arrows, Storm)*

Grimkin
An unidentifiable blob in the very bad painting Justyn displayed of Wizard Kyllian, probably meant to be the wizard's cat familiar. *(Owl)*

Grindel
Author of *Discourses On Unnatural History,* a book Archivist Jadrek and Herald Roald had studied. They agreed the only translation worth reading was the Orwind edition, not the Ouenta. *(Oath)*

Ground and Center
The basic technique for controlling paranormal talents. To one with Sight, unGifted and untrained Gifted persons radiate auras of energy that don't mesh, and flux erratically. Once a Gifted person learns to Center, those multiple flaring energy fields fuse into one. Grounding stops the flaring. The Gifted are trained to find a stable place within the body to Center. Finding a similar place outside the body, in the earth itself, provides the connection and the stability needed for Grounding, which essentially shunts excess Gift energy into the ground, and provides a solid platform from which to use and control the Gift. *(BV)*

Grove
A wooded area in the Companion's Field noted for its

aura of peacefulness. A holy place, it is the site where the first Companions appeared in answer to King Valdemar's prayer, and it is the place where all new Grove-Born Companions appear. However, the Companions tend to avoid it except when a Herald dies and the Bell Tower of the Temple rings a death knell, or when a new Grove-Born Companion arrives. *(BV)*

Grove Temple
A very ancient marble structure in the middle of the Grove, barely larger than the common room of the Heralds' suite, the Temple has a porch flanked by pillars, solid bronze doors, and the Bell Tower holding the bell rung for the death of a Herald. Two benches and an altar are its only furnishings. Behind the altar there is a bas-relief depicting the moon, sun, stars, and swirling clouds containing suggestions of male and female faces. *(BV)*

Grove-Born
The term for the original Companions and for any Companions who were not conceived by natural means, but appeared, fully adult, within the Grove of Companion's Field. The Monarch's Own Companion is always Grove-Born. Grove-Born Companions also appear in times of need, as did Gwena, Elspeth's Companion. Knowledge of her Grove-Born origin, however, has been hidden from the Heralds. *(BV)*

Grumio
A silk merchant whose packtrains were being plundered. On one raid Lena, his niece and only heir, was kidnapped. He had little hope she was still alive, but hired Tarma and Kethry to avenge her and make certain the raids were stopped. *(Oath)*

Gryfalcon
A term Amberdrake coined to describe Zhaneel's unique physical traits. She had a longer wing-span than typical gryphons and hands instead of claws. *(Gryphon)*

Gryphlets
Baby gryphons, like Jervan and Lytha, the young of Treyvan and Hydona. Gryphlets are very sensitive to

power flows in their birth area. They also have Mind-speech, and are as active and mischievous as any highly intelligent younglings. *(BV)*

Gryphon
A majestic creature with the head and forelegs of an eagle, the body of a lion, and powerful hawk wings. Gryphons are bold, intelligent, and crafty, with magical Gifts and the ability to speak and Mind-Speak. Their laughter is a high-pitched whistling and their language is tonal. They have a pleasant spicy smell, like cinnamon. Created by the Mage Urtho, he considered them to be his children. The gryphons Treyvan and Hydona arrived in Valdemar and took up residence in the ruins near k'Sheyna Vale when Darkwind was seven or eight years old. They chose that site because it contained old magic, which was beneficial for their nestlings. Gryphons are instinctual earth-mages and they have the innate ability to detect truth. Treyvan and Hydona were the advance guard for the group from White Gryphon, known as the Spirit Clan or Lost Clan, k'Leysha, who were seeking unoccupied land to found a Vale for settlers from there. *(Gryphon, Winds, Storms, Owl)*

Gryphon-guards
Two gryphons who attend the Haighlei Emperor, serving alongside the younger sons of other Black Kings. *(Gryphon)*

Guard, The
The military and peacekeeping forces of Valdemar, with detachments posted throughout the kingdom, particularly along the border, around the Palace, and in major cities. Lissa Ashkevron became Captain of a Guard unit, which impressed her relatives at Forst Reach. *(BV)*

Guard uniforms
Worn by Valdemar's military, they are bright blue for regular guards, while Palace Guards wear midnight blue. *(BV)*

Guardian Spirits
What the Shin'a'in call the Companions, deeming them

superior to Ethereal Spirits and the equals of Spirit-Kalenedral. *(Winds)*

Guardian beasts

A creation of Mornelithe Falconsbane, they are bat-winged creatures taller than a man, half-wolf and half something unnamable. *(Winds)*

Guardians

Herald-Mages who kept watch on the four quarters of Valdemar through their Mage-Web. Using that network, they could Sense any threat crossing the border and sound the alert. An Adept Mage participating in the Web needed to focus about a fourth of her or his mind on the Web's tuning, and the contact was effective whether awake or sleeping. The position of Guardian was one of great honor and responsibility, and could be very draining to the Adept Mages keeping watch. When the number of Herald-Mages began to dwindle, Herald-Mage Vanyel created a spell to tie all of the existing Heralds into the net and dispense with the need for Guardians. In effect, the Heralds became a living warning system against invasion or threat to Valdemar. *(LHM)*

Guild

Guilds are cooperatives of workers in the same or similar trades. They regulate and protect workers and their craft. In some trades, apprenticeship is limited to those able to buy into the Guild, unless they find masters willing to waive the fee. For mercenary soldiers, the process is this: They place a bond with the Guildhall. Those mercenaries in good standing wear their Guild tags on a thong about their necks to prove they paid their dues. These dues support Guildhalls, where hiring is done and disputes are settled by a board of Arbitrators. Kerowyn went to such a Guildhall in the town of Selina to tell her side of the quarrel with Ardana and receive justice. Other guilds include Woodworkers, Needleworkers, Potters, Leatherworkers, Traders, and so on. *(Oath, Sword)*

Gulian

Known as Old Man Gulian, he was the rudest man in Errold's Grove. *(Owl)*

Gwena (Companion)

When Elspeth was fifteen, Gwena was born from the Grove. Elspeth was called to the Grove and watched as Gwena materialized, then was Chosen, but Elspeth does not remember the experience. In fact, all the Heralds were mildly hypnotized to remember Gwena as a shy, normal companion who had not yet Chosen. Gwena was brought to Valdemar to be Companion to the first Herald-Mage since Vanyel, and it was essential to keep both of their capabilities secret until Elspeth was ready to take her place in history. Gwena, like Roland, could Mindspeak over long distances. Gwena and the Companions guided Elspeth to her destiny, even though she often resisted them. Gwena killed Ancar, trampling him to death while cursing him for all the pain he had caused. (*Arrows, Storm, Winds, Sword*)

Gwynver

One of three widows of the murdered Red Fox shaman. With the other two, she agreed to help lead their clan's survivors to Snow Fox territory. (*Owl*)

Gyrefalcon's Marches

One of Valdemar's Great Courts lying outside the capital city of Haven, it was the site of a series of brutal bandit raids which terrorized villagers during Talia's first months as Queen's Own. One attack nearly destroyed an entire village and its people. Herald-Intern Christa lost her life there, saving children from a fire. Queen Selenay and the Council tried to organize defenses with the Guards and Heralds. Lord Orthallen argued that the situation demanded a larger army, causing Talia to abhor his political manipulation of a terrible human tragedy. (*Arrows, LHM*)

Hackamore
A reined, bitless halter, often used for riding Companions. *(BV)*

Hadanelith
A false kestra'chern in White Gryphon. He had forged Amberdrake's name on his credentials and passed as legitimate for some time before he was caught. Manipulative and cruel, with a sadistic hatred of women, he tortured many of his clients and was exiled from White Gryphon for his crimes. Noyoki found him in the forest and took the madman into his employ, hiding him in Kanshin's house and using him in a scheme to assassinate Shalaman. *(Gryphon)*

Hadell
Landlord of Mornedealth's *Broken Sword Inn.* He served with Jervac, the friendly Gate Guard who recommended Hadell's establishment to Tarma and Kethry. Hadell had to quit the service when he got a tendon cut in a brawl. He used his mustering-out pay to buy the inn. *(Oath)*

Hadli
One of Quenten's eleven apprentice mages. A dark-haired, plump girl, she had the ability to touch Prince Daren's temples and feed information he had directly into Quenten's mind and those of other mages. *(Sword)*

Hagen
A Skybolt scout. Shallan's lover, Relli, was off with Ha-

gen's unit on patrol when Captain Twoblades gave orders to quit camp in a hurry. Hagen's group barely got back in time to pull out with the rest before the Karsites attacked. *(Sword)*

Hai
Shin'a'in term meaning "yes." *(Oath)*

Hai shala
Shin'a'in term meaning "do you understand?" *(Oath)*

Haighlei
Six nations lying far to the south of Valdemar. Their leaders are known as the Black Kings, and among them is King Shalaman. His kingdom and another lie between the Salten Sea and the Western Sea; four more realms lie further south, dividing a continent between them, which is joined to the northern two by an isthmus. The k'Leshya lived among these people after the Cataclysm and became their allies. *(Gryphons, Owl, Storm)*

Haighlei music
Performed by uniformed Royal Musicians who have been trained in their art since childhood. Some use plucked or bowed stringed instruments, others flutes; the other half of the orchestra is made up of gongs, drums, and various percussion instruments. Listeners in White Gryphon found the resultant music infectious but overwhelmingly loud. *(Gryphon)*

hai'she'li
Shin'a'in term meaning "yes," literally, "yes, I swear!" *(Oath)*

hai'vetha
Shin'a'in term meaning "yes, (be) running." *(Oath)*

Hakan
Steelmind's bondbird, a buzzard. *(Owl)*

Halcom (Brother)
A priest at the Temple and Priory of Thenoth, Lord of the Beasts. He had a club foot and came from a noble family. *(TT)*

Halfway Inn
A hostelry that sits in the middle of the forest that divides Forst Reach from the rest of Valdemar. The name is a conscious pun. *(LHM)*

Hall of Fragrant Joy
Tower-topped building in Khimbata where Skandranon and Amberdrake were held prisoner. It was a part of town where prostitution was a business, and the hall was well known but private. *(Gryphon)*

Halloway
A town in Hardorn. Reports from Halloway after a Mage-Storm indicated that some rocks had melted into puddles and then resolidified in a heartbeat, occasionally trapping living things within the hardened stone. *(Storm)*

Hammer Lung
(Tuberculosis) A new disease that afflicted some members of Snow Fox tribe. The symptoms were a racking cough and extreme difficulty in breathing, especially after any exertion. The victims were unable to endure altitude sickness, and thus couldn't journey over the Great Pass and south to Ghost Cat Clan's newfound home and the "holy *dyheli*'s" Sanctuary, where Healers might help them. *(Owl)*

Hammer-jays
Birds in the Pelagiris with a bell-like cry. *(Owl)*

Hanbil Brason
Owner of the village inn in Errold's Grove. *(Owl)*

Handmaidens of the Goddess
Term for the repressively cloistered Temple women among the Holderkin. Forbidden to speak or ever leave the Temple precincts, they effectively became the institution's living chattels. *(Arrows)*

Hanging Goose Tavern
A tavern in the city of Shonar in Hardorn, it was a hotbed of resistance against Ancar, and a place where the surviving royalist faction met after his father's death. Gwena told Darkwind to go there alone after sundown. He was to say to the beer pourer, "I drink my beer very

cold"—a key phrase that would let the local network of royalists know he was the man they were expecting and not a spy. *(Storm)*

Hansa
Firecat who attends Solaris. Hansa advised Solaris to make Herald Talia an honorary Sun-priest as a means of cementing the alliance between Valdemar and Karse. *(Storm)*

Hardaxe (Goodwife)
Generous citizen of the first town Talia reached on her flight from Sensholding. The Goodwife had a daughter a bit older than Talia, and supplied some castoff clothes for her to use during the rest of her journey to Haven. *(Arrows)*

Harde
General of Imperial forces assigned to Hardorn. He told Grand Duke Tremane that they had to do something about the increasing Mage-Storms. *(Storm)*

Hardorn
A kingdom which borders Karse and Valdemar to the east, and the Eastern Empire on its western border. King Alessandar of Hardorn made a proposal for Elspeth's hand in marriage to his son, Prince Ancar. Hardorn possessed a large standing army, a fact that made it a useful nation for a marriage-alliance. When Talia and Kris went to Hardorn to investigate the proposal, they discovered that Ancar was disliked and mistrusted by Hardorn's people. While they were there, Ancar assassinated his father and plotted to use Elspeth to take over Valdemar as well. Ancar killed Kris and his Companion and captured and tortured Talia in pursuit of this goal. Talia was able to get word to Valdemar in time to stop Queen Selenay and Elspeth before they crossed into Hardorn. Ancar then declared war on Valdemar. He used Blood magic to drain his lands and persecuted his own people, killing anyone with a claim to the throne. He began a series of failed wars of conquest on all his neighbors, including multiple attacks on Valdemar. After Companion Gwena killed Ancar, the Eastern Empire invaded

Hardorn. But the Mage-Storms disrupted the invasion. Hardorn went without a king until Duke Tremane was crowned. Tremane began the process of restoring Hardorn, and made alliances with Valdemar, Karse, and Iftel. *(Arrows, LHM, Storm, Winds)*

Harevis (Companion)
Herald Griffon's Companion. Griffon called her Fairist, as in fairest of all rhyming with Harevis. *(Arrows)*

Harris Neshem
An Errold's Grove farmer, his only livestock consisted of a few chickens. He had to borrow his brother's oxen to plow his field. He and his brother were related to Kyle Osterham, whom they helped to Wizard Justyn's cottage when Kyle cut himself woodchopping. *(Owl)*

Harrod Dobbs
A glassmaker and member of Errold's Grove's Village Council. *(Owl)*

Harthen (Herald)
A Herald who agreed with Dirk that chirras "sing," which was later proved to Talia and Kris while they waited out a blizzard in a Forest of Sorrows Waystation. *(Arrows)*

Harvest Fair
A common annual festival throughout Valdemar celebrating the results of the growing season and the bounty of the land. Usually accompanied by dancing, music, and a trade fair, though these celebrations are much quieter among the Holderkin. *(BV)*

Harvestfest
Another name for Sovvan, the celebration of the season's turning and a time of year when the barrier between the real world and the spirit world is thinnest. *(LHM)*

Hashi
Neuter *kyree,* he was his clan's representative in k'Valdemar Vale, and accompanied Darian on his journey north. *(Owl)*

Hathkel (Viscount)
One of Tarma's and Kethry's early employers. The job ended with them isolated at Hathkel's estate, far from any city and other employment. *(Oath)*

Haven
Valdemar's capital, it lies in a river valley. Originally a small walled city, it now spreads far and wide beyond those original walls, with the greatest growth extensions clustered along the four main Trade Roads. Within the city's first wall lies the Palace, the Collegium, and a green belt of land which includes Companion's Field. Outside the gates of the Palace Wall are the nobility's residences. Further out sit the homes of wealthy merchants, craftspeople, and Guild officials, and then the homes of average citizens, then the mercantile district, and last of all the city's slums and manufacturing areas. The Palace and the nobility's buildings are made of granite; lesser structures are of wood. Haven's main streets spiral outward away from the Palace grounds and its enclosing beige brick walls. At their widest, the streets can accommodate three carriages. At the city's lower levels are shops, offices, and the better inns, which have lodgings on the upper stories. Outside of the wealthy areas of Haven, and away from the main roads, the city is composed of narrow lanes so closely crowded together that opposing eaves touch. *(BV)*

Haven Heartstone
After Vanyel hijacked the power of the K'Sheyna Vale heartstone during Firesong's attempt to move it, Elspeth and the other Adepts found the Haven Heartstone centered in a large globe of crystal on a stone table in a long-unused Palace room on its lowest floor. That room was a replica of a room directly above it, which served as a decoy. The crystal globe was fused to the table and the stone pillar beneath, which was in turn fused to the floor and down into the bedrock. The globe was the physical link to the Web of power that bound all Heralds and Companions together. *(Winds, Storm)*

Havens, The
A phrase used to describe the realm beyond this life. *(BV)*

Havirn (Lord)
Farmer Landric's nobleman. Lord Havirn's attempts to deal with the monster killing his people failed; no hunter could catch it. So Havirn resorted to a "dragon solution": Since the beast wouldn't eat animals, criminals were tied up and left as prey in hopes the monster would leave taxpaying citizens alone. Havirn also offered a reward of half his holdings and his daughter's hand to any hero who could slay the beast. *(Oath)*

Hawk Dance
A traditional Shin'a'in dance. The Shin'a'in shaman Tre'valen performed this dance for the Tayledras at k'Sheyna Vale, after much coaxing by the scouts. *(Winds)*

Hawkbrothers
See Tayledras. *(BV)*

Hawkflight
A Tayledras Gate-Guard. Firesong sent him to fetch Brightstar to assist Herald-Mage Savil when the Mage arrived unannounced at the Vale. *(LHM)*

Hawkmen of the Deep Woods
The phrase Damen, serving boy of Lord Rendan's gang, used to describe the Tayledras. He thought of them in the same way the cutthroats did the Heralds of Valdemar, as unseen and dangerous figures to be feared for their powerful magic. *(LHM)*

Hawk's Children, The
The Tale'sedrin clan, Tarma's people. *(Oath)*

Hawksnest
The Sunhawks' winter quarters, a tiny hill town which owed its existence solely to the mercenary company. Their dependents lived in the sheltered mountain valley year-round. A fortified barracks complex stood between the town and the valley's entrance. When the company was away on business, a solid garrison and all mercenaries-in-training remained to guard Hawksnest. That freed the fighters to concentrate on the campaign at hand. Tarma's and Kethry's quarters there were mod-

est, a plain double room on the first floor of the granite-walled barracks. Wood walls were paneled over the stone. There were pegs to hold weapons, stands for armor, a single wardrobe, two beds, three chairs, and a table. The only luxury was a wood-fired stove. *(Oath)*

Hawkwind
An alias Amberdrake adopted in Khimbata when disguised as Skandranon's bodyguard. *(Gryphon)*

Ha'shin
Shin'a'in honorific for "teacher." *(Oath)*

Haydee Dallas
A member of the Haven City Guard, she was recruited to be one of Princess Selenay's Personal Guards during the Tedral Wars. *(Exile)*

Hayka (Companion)
Companion of Malken, a very young Herald-trainee with an unwelcome Gift of powerful Foresight. Hayka and the boy's mentor agreed it was best to close off the Gift for the time being, to save the child's sanity. *(BB)*

He Who Made The Barrier
A cryptic reference to Vkandis uttered by Tashiketh, the gryphon wing leader from Iftel. The gryphon was describing the unusual history of that strange land, and the Barrier Maker was a critical factor in Iftel's long isolation. *(Storm)*

Heal-All
The vine of a medicinal plant. Vanyel bought a cloak clasp adorned with a metal sculpture of entwining Heal-All enclosing a beryl the same shade of green as a Healer's robes as a gift for Randale, and a matching pendent as a present for Randale's lifemate, Healer Shavri. *(LHM)*

Healer Green
The color of the robes worn by a fully qualified Healer. *(BV)*

Healer-Adept
A rare Adept who can also Heal, especially blighted

lands. They are specially trained to use both Mage and Healing powers in concert. Healer-Adepts generally are taught one-on-one by another Healing Adept. Firesong, Moondance k'Treva, and Darian Firkin were all Healer-Adepts. *(Owl, LHM, Winds)*

Healers

They combine standard medical skills with a Gift for healing the sick and injured, particularly for accelerating the body's natural healing process. Healers have special Gifts of Empathy as well as Healing, and some possess other special abilities to assist them. Devan's Gift, for instance, is the treatment of traumatic injuries. Healers wear emerald green uniforms, while Healer-trainees wear pale green. Specialties among Healers include Healer-Herbalists, Mind-Healers, and so on. Most cultures employ their talents. Even Karsites used Healers, but didn't allow them to work outside the Sunlord's temples. Karsite priests hunted down and killed unaffiliated herbmen and wisewomen. Midwives, however, were ignored in Karse as unimportant practitioners who treated only women. When Kerowyn went to Valdemar, she learned their Healers wore green exclusively, a custom she strongly approved; it made them easier to spot on a battlefield. *(BV)*

Healers' Collegium

Located in Haven, it is part of the Collegium Complex along with the Bardic and Heraldic training centers, and includes a hospital with small, well-aired rooms for patients, classrooms, and an herb garden for botanical cures. *(BV)*

Healer's Hill

At the bivouac at Urtho's encampment at Ka'venusho, this was located past the surgeons' tents, and held common tents used as infirmaries and treatment centers. *(Gryphons)*

Healing-Meld

A joining of Herald and/or Herald-Mage energies with a Healer's to increase the Healer's strength. When Healer Andrei weakened while trying to save Vanyel in the

Grove Temple, Savil, Jaysen, Mardic, and Donni added
their powers to his. The meld produced a euphoric sense
of peace among the participants. *(LHM)*

Heartstone
An artifact of powerful magic created by Tayledras
Mages, it is a crystal-laced boulder taller than a man,
glowing with life and energy. Its purpose is to collect the
energy running from nodes and ley-lines surrounding a
Vale under proper direction so that no warped magic
will be left behind to harm the surrounding land. It is
also a Vale's repository of power, drawn on by the
Vale's Adepts to power spells, including the Veil protecting the Vale, weather-working, and other necessary
magics. The Tayledras use a Heartstone as a focus to
collect, concentrate, and improve ancient and often
harmful magic. A Heartstone was hidden within the Lineas palace, anchoring a deadly fault line lying directly
beneath the city. The Heartstone in k'Sheyna Vale was
sabotaged and fractured during the attempt to drain it
before moving it to a new location. The flawed stone's
surface glowed with red and gold tracings. It distorted
everything in the Vale, and attracted unwelcome magic
and Change-beasts. Heartstones were shielded by the
Hawkbrothers wherever possible, and thus many survived the great Mage-Storms. The stone in k'Vala Vale
was a tall, smooth spire of rock that glowed like a lan-
tern, creamy alabaster in color and texture. Starfall set
up what was to become k'Valdemar's Heartstone and it
took four years to draw enough magic from the area's
ley-lines to heat water for the Tayledras' popular soaking pools and to establish magical sentries, basic shields,
and other protections. When Vanyel conceived his plan
to relieve the burden on Herald-Mages and enlarge the
protections of Valdemar, he linked the energies of all
the Heralds to a node beneath Haven and created a
Heartstone there. *(BV)*

Heartwood
Snowfire's father. *(Owl)*

Heavens
In Valdemaran cosmology, there are five. *(Arrows)*

Hedge-mages

Also known as hedge-wizards. Generally untrained or informally trained practitioners of the craft who draw on earth magic and other natural sources to power their spells. They usually help the common people, though their powers are limited. For example, a hedge-wizard can encourage rain to fall in a given place or repel a storm to shield ready-to-harvest crops from damage, not by creating the rainstorm, but by moving an existing one around a bit. Because of the nature of their craft, hedge-wizards do most of their spellcasting out of doors. There were two hedge-wizards on the Sunhawks' payroll: Oreden and Jiles. Kethry convinced them earth-witchery was more valuable than straining to do High Magicks, for which they had no talent. Hedge-magery, like water finding, often could be more useful to a mercenary company than calling down lightnings, but a general long-standing scorn against such lesser sorcerers persisted. *(BV)*

Hedge-priests

Well meaning religious wanderers who have no set temple. *(Oath)*

Hedric

Lord Marshal of Valdemar, he is on permanent assignment to the Palace. *(Arrows)*

Heinkeir Told-True

Shaman of the Snow Fox tribe who played host to Darian's expedition beyond the Great Pass. *(Owl)*

Helansevrith

A member of Mornedealth's nobility, head of the Green Faction, and archrival of Kavinestral, Kethry's treacherous brother. *(Oath)*

Hell

A place of punishment after death. The number of hells and the punishment meted out in them depended on the territory and religion. At Rathgar's Keep, the belief was in six hells. But when Kerowyn was Captain of the Skybolts, she compared hot conditions to the nine hells.

Some hells are fiery, others are frozen wastelands. *(Oath, Sword)*

Hell puppets
Ancar's line troopers, or so Wolfstone's Pack called them. They were conscripted soldiers enslaved by Ancar's blood spells. Killing them was an act of mercy as well as a battle necessity. *(Winds)*

Hellhorses
What Karsites called Companions before Karse's war with Hardorn and alliance with Valdemar. *(BB, Exile, Storm]*

Hellsbane
The Shin'a'in battlesteed Tarma acquired on her return to the Dhorisha Plains, and the horse's subsequent replacements. Kerowyn also rode a battlesteed from the Hellsbane's original line when she joined the Skybolts. She would go through three more before being Chosen. *(Oath, Sword)*

Hellspawn
Karsite epithet for Valdemarans, until High Priest Solaris decreed otherwise. *(Storm)*

Henlin
Master Magister and senior spokesman of the Master Craftsmen during the Mage-Storm planning sessions in the Compass Rose tavern. *(Storm)*

Henricht
The first Son of the Sun. *(Storm)*

Henrick (Father)
Priest at Haven's Temple of the Lord of Light (Karse's Vkandis) during the reign of Sendar. *(Exile)*

Herald
A person who is Chosen by a Companion. Heralds are called "The Arrows of the Queen," and serve as the Monarch's messengers and information-gatherers. They may also serve as emergency war leaders in times of crisis. Heralds form strong mind-to-mind bonds with their Companions. They have at least one Gift, which

training and the Companion bond enhances and develops to full potential. These Mind-magic Gifts replaced the Old Magic that used to exist in Valdemar. Incorruptible, self-sacrificing, and fair, the Heralds dispense the Monarch's justice and enforce the law. Every monarch of Valdemar must also be a Herald, as must the Heir; this ensures that a tyrant will never rule Valdemar. As a conscience and counselor, one Herald is always Chosen as Monarch's Own, bonded to a Grove-Born Companion stallion who never seems to age. Heralds are normally Chosen when they are in their early teens, with more boys than girls being selected for the arduous career. Four to five years of training generally follow (less for those Chosen as adults), and Herald's Whites are typically issued when the Herald is eighteen. A twelve- to eighteen-month internship with an experienced Herald is required before the candidate is qualified for full Herald status. Heralds are regarded with respect throughout the realm, though local superstitions may color the Heralds' reception; among the Holderkin, gossip depicted the Heralds as monsters of depravity, living sensuous, orgiastic, and luxurious lives. That belief, however, did not affect the results of the Heralds' dispensing of justice. Heralds not only relay the new laws to the people, but explain and interpret those laws as well, to make certain the common folk fully understand the enactments of Queen and Council. In all things, the Heralds are the ruler's eyes, ears, and limbs. Thanks to the exceptional nature of their Companions, there are no swifter messengers to be found; no ordinary horse can come close to a Companion's supernatural speed and stamina. A Herald and Companion are a unique force, a combined power that has held Valdemar together for centuries and enabled it to stand firm against invasion and evil magic. More than half of the Heralds Chosen die in the line of duty. *(BV)*

Herald Collegium
The Collegium courses are designed to prepare the Herald-trainees for fully qualified status in their field. A five-year curriculum is standard, but may be adjusted to suit the trainee's already-proven skills and/or age. All

students receive training in weapons, logic, law, history, etiquette, and survival skills, with specialized classes as needed. The Herald's Collegium is situated in a wing of the Palace, its entrance marked by massive double doors. The first level of the building contains classrooms. The second floor holds the dormitories and common room where meals are served. The third floor is the library and study area. Storerooms, the Housekeeper's office, and the kitchen are in the basement. The kitchen is connected to the common room by a dumbwaiter. Schedules for waking, classes, calls to meals, and so forth are regulated by bells. In the courtyard are stables for horses and Companions, and training grounds. Beyond the Terilee River lies the Companion's Field. *(BV)*

Herald Magic
What outsiders call the Heraldic Gifts. *(Arrows)*

Herald Whites
The uniform of a Herald. Students earn Whites after training is completed, but before serving their field internship. Formal Whites closely approximate court dress, they are made from fancy fabrics and decorated with white silk brocade on pure white backgrounds, or silver thread designs. The everyday dress of the Heralds riding circuit is more practical, and consists of white undershirts of wool or ramie, with overtunics and breeches, or split skirts for riding, all of which can be layered as the climate requires. White riding boots and white leather shoes are also a part of the Herald's Uniform. Capes and cloaks of various lengths serve for cold or inclement weather. Comfort and practicality are more important than style. Everyday Whites reflect the rigors and dangers of riding circuit, and are cut so that freedom of movement is guaranteed. Kerowyn and Alberich refuse to wear Whites unless Queen Selenay requests it, calling the outfits "Just Shoot Me" uniforms. *(BV)*

Herald-Mage
A Herald with mage powers, among them the Guardians of Valdemar in Vanyel's era. Operating the protective Web required four Herald-Mages, each one tied to a quarter of the realm. Eventually, when there weren't

enough Herald-Mages left to carry out the task, Vanyel had to devise the Web spell as another means of protection. He was the last Herald-Mage until Elspeth came into her powers. *(Arrows, LHM, Winds)*

Herald-trainee
Student Heralds who study at the Collegium in Haven and wear gray uniforms. They have duties at the Collegium, including kitchen duty, laundry, sewing and cleaning in addition to their studies. They may also be assigned to duties of the Queen's choosing, including acting as servant/liaison to an ambassador. *BV*

Heraldic Circle
During Vanyel's time, the circle consisted of the Monarch's Own, Seneschal's Herald, Lord-Marshal's Herald, Speaker for the Heralds with trainees, Speaker for the Herald-Mages, Speaker for the Heralds on Circuit, plus the Monarch and Heir. Currently it is the term used for the entire collective of Heralds. *(BV)*

Heraldic link
As Vanyel proved, he could not only establish a "line" to all the Mages, with whom he shared magic, but also with every living Herald in Valdemar, by virtue of their being Heralds. This link is wrought through the Companions. Herald-Mages shared magic with Heralds lacking the Mage-Gift through all the Companions as well. Vanyel speculated this was the link King Valdemar was searching for when he first created the kingdom's Guardian Web-spell to protect his realm from ill-intentioned outsiders. *(LHM)*

Herb-witches
Also known as herb-wizards, they rank a grade below true Healers and serve the common folk on a basic level. The witches, however, are available in isolated regions where Healers are often difficult to find. *(Owl, Winds)*

Herbalists
Low-level healers skilled in identifying and using the curative powers of herbs and other vegetative remedies. *(Owl)*

Herd-sister
Shin'a'in term for mares trained as battlesteeds. Hellsbane and Ironheart were herd-sisters. *(Oath)*

Herdahl (Leftenant)
An officer in the Karsite military, he was a tool of the false Voices of Sunlord Vkandis. Herdahl was envious when Alberich was promoted ahead of him. *(Arrows)*

Herewan
Third Form instructor at the Merchants' School. He ignored obvious signs that his students were being mercilessly bullied by the Sixth Form. *(BB)*

Hero of Stony Tor
One of the laudatory epithets the Bards have given Vanyel in their songs. *(LHM)*

Hertasi
Lizard folk created before the Mage Wars, they have an incredible urge to be useful. Current mythology claims that Mage Urtho made them in ancient days. In Urtho's time, it was believed that an even more ancient mage was responsible. Urtho did breed a larger race of *hertasi*, known as *tyrill*, that still survives in Iftel. *Hertasi* are one of the five sentient races who live and work in harmony with the Kaled'a'in and Tayledras. Many *hertasi* share Vales with the Hawkbrothers, digging burrows in the ground rather than living in tree-top *ekeles*, exchanging their services for food, protection, and warmth—a very important thing to a cold-blooded race. Though smaller than humans, *hertasi* are strong for their size, extremely clever, and well-spoken. When happy, they carry their tails high. They come into season once a year; consequently, they like to tease humans about their continuous breeding habits. They do not see well at night, but have excellent day vision. Some *hertasi* live in caves near marshes; others have hillside homes in tunnels shored with timber and simply furnished. They grow rice, breed frogs, hunt, and fish. Some take care of the Vale's human and nonhuman inhabitants, doing everything from creating clothing and cleaning and cooking to serving as scribes and historians, all of it done beautifully with

great attention to detail. Many *hertasi* are master craft-workers, and all have a love for ornamentation. Nothing irritates a *hertasi* more than an ugly, under-decorated outfit, except possibly a badly cooked meal. They have a fondness for humans with style—Firesong always had *hertasi* lining up to serve him. *Hertasi* weapons include half-sized bows and arrows, fish spears, sickle-shaped daggers, quicksand, and sinkholes. The race seems to have something like a hive-mind; at any rate, information available to one *hertasi* seems to immediately become common knowledge among all of the Vale's *hertasi. (BV)*

Heshain (Wizard)
The mage-lord who raided the Sisterhood of Spell and Sword complex, killing the fighters and everyone else not mage-talented and kidnapping the gifted girls. *(Winds)*

Hesten
One of Tarma's students, he began school with a bit of an attitude. Nobly born, he thought being a fancy swordsman was sufficient until Tarma educated him about the reality of fighting. *(Oath)*

Hevenbeck
A town in Valdemar's northern sector. Kris and Talia visited there twice during their circuit. Their first stop resulted in a startling judgment involving a parsimonious older couple and their servant. The second involved an attack by raiders from over the border, and finished in the grim aftermath of a bloody battle. *(Arrows)*

Heverd
One of Lord Rendan's gang members killed by Vanyel during the ambush. *(LHM)*

Heward (Father)
A young priest at Forst Reach's village. He didn't approve of the sanctimonious and restrictive Father Leren, according to Radevel, who agreed with Reward's judgement. *(LHM)*

Her'y
Shin'a'in term meaning "(is this not) the truth?" *(Oath)*

Hewerd
One of Lord Rathgar's loyal guards. After the attack on the bridal feast, the wounded armsman Heward told Kerowyn that the raiders were accompanied by a mage and a hypnotic fog. *(Sword)*

Hicanth
A spring flower which produces a heady scent. They grow in abundance in Queen Selenay's Palace Gardens. *(Arrows)*

Hielmarsh
A town southeast of Petras in Rethwellan. A deserted tower there was used as a torture chamber for Raschar's bespelled sister Idra. To keep curious peasants away, he spread rumors that the place was haunted. *(Oath)*

Hieratic script
Karsite writing. It has a short form, which Karal and Ulrich used for taking notes. *(Storm)*

High Court of Valdemar
At Haven, located in the Palace. Appointees from all of Valdemar's districts as well as the guilds gather to hear matters brought by the people to their representatives for the High Court to decide. The Monarch, Monarch's Own, Heir to the Throne, Seneschal, and Heraldic representatives also attend. Among all the Great Courts of nobility in the realm, this is the true court, the one where the real business of governing is done and important social contacts are made. *(LHM)*

High Feast
A fancy dinner put on by a noble or royal for an important occasion. The bridal supper for Kerowyn's brother was one, and it was a struggle for Rathgar's small staff to provide the required number of courses for such an event. *(Sword)*

High Magick/Magic
A concentrated and specialized sorcery practiced by Courtly mages. *(Oath, Winds, Storm, Sword)*

High Spur Road
The road that branches off the Pelagiris Road and leads to Lythecare. *(Winds)*

High Table
The table at noble houses where the most exalted personages sit. The one at Forst Reach's manor-keep was raised on a dais a hand span above the rest of the room and set at the head of the lower table. From its vantage point, Lord Withen Ashkevron ruled, overlooking all those seated below. *(LHM)*

Highjorune
Capital of Lineas, it was the stronghold of the Remoerdis clan until their massacre. Vanyel discovered that the city was built on a dangerous fault. A Heartstone was placed above the fault to keep it stable and prevent earthquakes. Over a long period of time the Heartstone would heal the fault unless too much power was drained from the stone, in which case earthquakes and eruptions would result. It is the Remoerdis Clan's duty to protect this Heartstone located in the palace. *(LHM)*

Hildre
One of Ouenten's mages whose specialty was identifying and counterfeiting mage auras. Hildre intercepted a mage message from one of Prince Ancar's commanders, enabling Daren to thwart the attack Ancar was planning on Kerowyn's troops. *(Sword)*

Hiring Fairs
Where traveling laborers come seeking local employment. When Talia was contemplating running away to avoid being forcibly married, she remembered the hungry, desperate look of the out-of-work men haunting Sensholding's Hiring Fairs; and she recalled that she had never seen any women among those seeking employment, which was not encouraging for her plan of hiring herself out as a menial. *(Arrows)*

Hiring hall
Established in various cities, they are meeting places for those seeking employment and potential employers, and collect a fee for the service. Most are simply halls lined

with benches on each side with a desk at the end opposite the door. Tarma and Kethry stopped at a hiring hall when they arrived at Mornedealth. *(Oath)*

Ho Play
A traditional and very boring stylized enacting of traditional stories, the Haighlei art form was of little interest to most who attended the Evening Court. Nevertheless, custom demanded that it be staged at prescribed intervals during the year. *(Gryphons)*

Hob
The blacksmith and unelected leader of a half-abandoned Hardornen village where Elspeth and her escort spent a night. *(Storm)*

Hob
Healer-trainee, he was stocky, blond, over-eager, and a little self-conscious. He and his Healer mentor saw to Lavan's recuperation after the school fire. *(BB)*

Holard
Kerowyn's wiry little orderly, a native of the Valdemaran-Rethwellan border mountains. He advised her to wear sheepskin boots plus two pairs of wool socks to protect her feet when she headed into that territory. *(Sword)*

Holderkin
A puritanical, patriarchal border folk dwelling in the southeastern corner of Valdemar. Originally, the Holderkin were from outkingdom, in Karse. Talia's family had settled in Valdemar less than two generations before Talia was Chosen as Herald. Holderkin discourage knowledge of outsiders and merely tolerate the intrusion of the Heralds and Valdemaran rule. They fled from religious persecution in Karse and are determined to cling firmly to their own ways in their new land. In their belief system, a patriarchal god and a passive, submissive goddess govern mortal lives. Their land is stony and difficult to farm, and raiders attack them every winter. Nevertheless, they scorn help, even from Healers, so many injuries and illnesses end in unnecessary deaths. Their hard lives dictate cultural patterns. The males over the age of

ten are higher in rank than all women. Adolescent marriages are the norm, to hurry reproduction and make certain there are offspring to continue the Holderkin ways. A Holderkin household consists of the Father, his First Wife and Underwives, all unmarried sons and daughters, and the Father's Mother, if she is widowed. One household may combine with others into a Holding, or exist alone as a Steading. *(Arrows)*

Holka Creek
Place outside of Shonar where one of Tremane's scouting parties had an encounter with a spiderlike Mage-Storm Change-creature. *(Storms)*

Hollybush Tavern
The tavern' in Haven owned by Skif's Uncle Londer. It was a low class dump that served food made from the discards of better taverns and beer that barely passed for drinkable. *(TT)*

"Holy Kreeshta"
Exclamation of alarm. *(Gryphon)*

Holy Lerence
A highly regarded famous religious figure of the past. The maid Reta, in telling Vanyel the terrible history of the Houses of Remoerdis and Mavelan, said she wondered if that was what Holy Lerence meant when he said, "The sins of the fathers shall be taken up by the sons." *(LHM)*

Honeybee
Master Sun-priest-Mage Ulrich's mule. She was very steady, but with a "sting" in her hind hooves. *(Storm)*

Hooters
A mercenary company. Karsite bandits overran their winter quarters and killed the civilians while the Hooters were putting down a rebellion in Ruvan. The incident created a lingering hatred of Karsites, as the "bandits" were suspected of being regular army, and the Hooters weren't anywhere near Karse or threatening that land at the time of the massacre. *(Winds)*

Hopeless
Ugly, big war mare, partner of Graceless, trained by Beaker and Jodi and used in breaking other horses. *(Oath)*

Horn
A town on the Trade Road leading from Haven to the Karsite border. As Vanyel jokingly noted later in his career, the peacock he used to be got lost somewhere south of Horn. *(LHM)*

Horned Hunters
One of the Imperial peoples. Some were soldiers serving with Tremane's forces. A shamanistic sect, they wanted to turn a corner of their barracks into a permanent sweat house; they also requested permission to go on dream quests and hold ritual fastings during the long snow-bound winter at Shonar. *(Storm)*

Hostel
In Hardorn, they are always on the main road and in the main square of a town, with a Guardpost close by. The hostels look like inns, but the signs outside always have the symbol of a wheat sheaf and a crown. When Talia and Kris were on their ambassadorial mission to Hardorn, they were instructed to stay at one of the hostels every night. The establishments were an innovation begun by King Alessandar, intending them to serve as a courtesy to those moving about his realm on official business. Court officials, envoys from other countries, and clergy were all given free and unlimited use of the facilities. *(Arrows)*

Hounds
The Hardornen symbol of fidelity. Tremane's temporary throne, a theatrical prop, had originally been decorated with carvings of Imperial wolves, which Hardornen artisans converted to hounds. *(Storm)*

Hounds, The
Two stars that chase the sun at dusk. They provide a regular clock for the evening hours on clear, cloudless nights. *(Arrows)*

House of Healing

An intensive-care hospital located in Haven. Cases too severe to be treated elsewhere are brought here as a last resort. *(Arrows)*

House of Scarlet Joys

A brothel, one of three in Brether's Crossroads. Kethry took a room there and invited Tarma to join her, as it was the least likely place that bandits would look for them. *(Oath)*

Hovan

Healer apprentice with the Skybolts, he put something in the lamp oil used in Captain Kerowyn's tent; it made the lamp smoke, but kept out the bugs. *(Sword)*

Hover-sled

Related to a carry-basket. Magically operated, it floats at half man-height. These were used during the Mage War for moving troop supplies and during the evacuation to carry what the refugees would need beyond the Gates. *(Gryphon)*

Howell

Cloth Merchants' Guildmaster. He attended one of Lady Chitward's parties, and insisted on giving Lavan a package of tools suitable for an apprentice in the trade: a lens for examining a fabric's weave, a rule to determine thread count, scissors, etc. Howell's hands were permanently stained by indigo dye. *(BB)*

Hulda

The Adept mistress of Ancar, his ally, and teacher in black sorcery. She was voluptuous, with violet-colored eyes, good features, and long dark hair. She was also an agent of Emperor Charliss, and was sent to infiltrate Hardorn and later to spy on Valdemar. She told Ancar she would train him to be an Adept and promised him that he'd have dominion over seven kingdoms, including Valdemar. Her plan was to become Elspeth's nursemaid and turn her into enough of a brat that she would never be Chosen. Ancar would then offer marriage to Elspeth and take Valdemar. Hulda's plans were ruined when Talia was Chosen as Queen's Own and discovered that

Hulda was responsible for Elspeth's behavior. Lord Orth-allen warned Hulda of her imminent arrest, so she fled back to Hardorn. Talia would meet her again and learn part of the truth when she was captured and tortured during an ambassadorial mission to Hardorn. Hulda fell out of favor with Ancar because she could not or would not deliver what she had promised him—dominion over the kingdoms surrounding Hardorn. Hulda was also arousing suspicions in her true employer, Charliss, so he sent a second agent to Hardorn to analyze the situation and eliminate her if necessary. When Elspeth and her comrades stormed Ancar's castle, Hulda tried to flee through a Gate with this agent. In desperation, Elspeth killed them both. *(Arrows, Winds)*

Huur
An eagle owl bondbird. Snowfire's second bondbird and Hweel's mate. *(Owl)*

Huur
Winterlight's bondbird, a tuft-eared owl. *(Winds)*

Hweel
Snowfire's primary bondbird, a short-eared eagle-owl. His mate is Huur. *(Owl)*

Hydee
An Errold's Grove teenager, and one of Shandi's circle of girlfriends. *(Owl)*

Hydona
Gryphon Master mage whose name means kindness. Larger than her mate Treyvan and mother to a pair of gryphlets, she took over from Darkwind when he was having problems training Elspeth to become an Adept. Hydona and Treyvan were the advance guard sent by the Kaled'a'in Clan k'Leshya to investigate the appropriateness of the Vale area for settlement by a group from White Gryphon. When k'Sheyna Vale became open, they got permission to move their people into it. *(Storm, Winds)*

Hyllarr
Crested hawk-eagle of bondbird breeding, wounded and

captured by a blood-path mage, then rescued by Darkwind, Elspeth, and the k'Sheyna *hertasi*. After Vree killed the bondbird construct that held Starblade in thrall to Falconsbane, Elspeth thought that Hyllarr would be a natural bondbird for Starblade to help him recover from the damage Mornelithe had inflicted upon him. Hyllar agreed, as he was injured and wanted to bond with someone who would provide him with company and care. *(Winds)*

Hyron (Bard)
Speaker for the Bardic Circle on the Queen's Council. He supported King Alessandar's marriage proposal for Elspeth's hand, and Talia noted Bard Hyron was one of the Counsellors most eager for Lord Orthallen's approval. After the battle with Hardorn, however, the Bard's loyalty was confirmed. Talia told him his Circle would be invaluable in the future, because the Bards were Valdemar's only repository of knowledge about the old magic. *(Arrows)*

Hyrryl
Shaman of the *kyree* Hot Springs Clan, a snow-white beauty with eyes as blue as a Companion's. *(LHM)*

Hywel
The chief of the Ghost Cat tribe's son who followed the Ghost Cat Avatar out of the tribe's encampment, hoping to find a magical cure for his little brother Jendey, who had contracted Summer Fever. Hywel had prayed for help, and received it in an unexpected form when he was captured by Kelvren the gryphon, taught the Tayledras language by Tyrsell the *dyheli*, and interrogated by Darian and Keisha. Keisha discovered the cause of Summer Fever and cured Hywel's brother. According to custom, Hywel was now indebted to Keisha and Darian. To discharge his debt, he led them safely through the Northern territories on a search for Darian's parents. *(Owl)*

Ibram (King)
He was the previous Emperor of Shalaman's kingdom. Shalaman's mother was his First Consort; his third consort was Noyoki's mother, and Noyoki was her last son. *(Gryphon)*

Ice Wall Mountains
Far to the north of Valdemar, the Wall lies near Crookback Pass and beyond the wilderness of the Forest of Wendwinter. This was where Vanyel died fighting Leareth. *(Arrows, LHM, Owl)*

Iceshadow k'Sheyna
K'Sheyna Elder. *(Winds)*

Icolan Ar Perdin
A dour little man, he was Lerryn Twoblades' second-in-command in the Skybolts. When the Skybolts split up after the Karsite army's breakthrough, Kerowyn went with Icolan's group. Icolan died on that mission, clearing the way for Ardana to take over the Skybolts. *(Sword)*

Idra (Captain)
Third in line to Rethwellan's throne, she renounced her hereditary rights to become a mercenary. She formed the Sunhawks twenty-five years before Tarma and Kethry met her. A muscular, athletic-looking woman, Idra had mouse-gray hair, a heroic face, and was a born horsewoman. Her fellow mercenary Devaril called her "Old Horseface," and her brother Stefansen's nickname for her was "Dree." Idra was well-respected by her

country, so when a dispute erupted as to which of her brothers, Raschar or Stefen, would inherit the throne, she was called home. Originally she was in favor of the eldest, Raschar, but changed her mind and supported Stefen instead. Before she could publicly declare her choice, Raschar drugged her and took her to Hielmarsh, where he and his men raped and tortured her. She managed to get a knife and kill herself to end the pain. Tarma and Kethry discovered what had happened, rounded up the Sunhawks, and captured Raschar for judgment. They called Oathbreaker on him and released Idra from the Havens long enough to exact her revenge. *(Oath)*

Idry

Unpartnered Companion and Florian's younger sister. She was first to volunteer for the mission to Urtho's Tower, and was An'desha's mount for that arduous journey. *(Storm)*

Iftel

Country north of Hardorn and east of Valdemar, it is isolated and unassailable, and protected by an unbreachable force barrier. It has always been a mystery, even though Iftel has an ambassador in Valdemar. Its land is guarded by Vykaendys, a proprietary and powerful deity, the same as Vkandis of Karse. The god created the impenetrable barrier around Iftel, and only those invited or priests of the Sun God can penetrate it. The people of this country served in Urtho's Third Army, and survived the ancient Cataclysm by fleeing to Iftel by Gate. Afterward, they lacked the magic power to go elsewhere. Only a few traders have been permitted to cross the border into the country. However, those who want to leave are allowed to and generally describe the country as boring. Ancar made one attempt to invade Iftel which ended with his armies transported en masse back to his capital and their memories of Iftel wiped clean. Mages who accompanied them vanished. Now, with the approach of a new Cataclysm, Iftel and its deity have decided to aid the new Hardornan alliance, and have sent a wing of gryphons to join King Tremane's forces. Tashiketh, the wing's leader, explained that Iftel uses blood-sport games to choose its warriors and that those who flew to Hardorn were all champions. Their rankings in the contests also determine the gryphons' hierarchy and Iftel's tax distributions. The countries of Iftel, Valdemar, Karse, and Hardorn now have binding peace treaties. *(BV)*

Igan Horstfel

A Tradeguildsman, he was a conspirator in the slave raids which harassed the fisherfolk in the Lake Evendim district. *(Arrows)*

Ikala

Younger son of a Haighlei King. In his kingdom, Ikala is twentieth in the line of succession behind Crown Prince Nbubi. He elected to go to White Gryphon and join the Silvers, and became a good friend of Silverblade. *(Gryphon)*

Ikan Dryvale

Justin Twoblades' shieldbrother, who worked with him as a guard for the jewel Merchants Guild. During one off-season they paid Tarma to give them sword lessons. He helped rescue Kethry from Wethes Goldmarchant. Afterward, Ikan helped Kethry obtain a highly favorable settlement from the Mornedealth council. *(Oath)*

Ilderhaven

A town in Hardorn where Heralds Kris and Talia accumulated damning information about the ambitious Prince Ancar. *(Arrows)*

Ilea (Healer)

An exceptional Healer, wife to Herald Pol, and mother of Elenor. A strong-minded and beautiful woman who has given much in the service of Valdemar. *(BB)*

Ilvan

Torchbearer in Lady Myria's village. Myria was tied to the stake to be burned for the murder of her husband. He was going to light her pyre, until Tarma and Kethry arrived to save her. *(Oath)*

Imperial Seal
The official seal of the Eastern Empire. Tremane illegally held an exact duplicate of the original, a copy made while he was assigned to the Imperial Secretariat under Emperor Charliss. The seal must be applied with magic, leaving a holographic impression of the Wolf Crown as its authentication. Tremane used it to forge orders allowing him to empty an Imperial depot. *(Storm)*

Indra (Lady)
She was Herald Jeri's mother, and a notorious nag. Indra was particularly eager for her daughter to be named Heir pro tempore, should it become necessary to disqualify Princess Elspeth from the succession. Lady Indra hoped to control Jeri's vote in Council, a prospect to make everyone else at Court shudder. *(Arrows)*

Ink
Tremane had a supply of the special ink used only for official Imperial documents. The fluid contained tiny flecks of silver and gold that confirmed that it was the ink of an Imperial scribe. *(Storm)*

Inn of the Green Man
The seventh tavern Vanyel looked into in his guise as "Valdir the Minstrel" on his mission to Highjorune. Owned by threatening and slatternly Bel, it was not an attractive venue, but it seemed like a good place for "Valdir" to begin gathering information. *(LHM)*

Intelligencers
Prince Ancar's spies. *(Arrows)*

Internship
A newly graduated Herald undertakes twelve to eighteen months additional training in the field in the company of a senior Herald. The intern rides a sector with that partner, learning by doing Herald duties on the circuit. *(Arrows)*

Irenia Jadrevalyn (Queen)
Mother of handsome and spoiled Prince Karathanelan of Rethwellan. *(Sword)*

Iresh
Master Cloth Merchant to whom Samael Chitward is apprenticed. *(BB)*

Iron Throne
Made from the personal weapons (axes, swords, lance points, etc.) of all the monarchs deposed or conquered by the Eastern Emperors, the Throne is six feet tall, four feet wide, and so heavy it has not been moved in centuries. *(Storm)*

Ironheart
Shin'a'in battlesteed, sixteen hands tall, a herd-sister to Hellsbane. When Tarma acquired mares on the Dhori-sha Plains, she decided Ironheart would be a good replacement mount for Kethry's mule, Rodi, that was left with the Liha'irden herds. Like all battlesteeds, Ironheart was trained to fight with or without a rider. That was fine with Kethry, who tended to tumble off her mount if the going got bumpy. On foot, the sorceress could work magic without distraction while Ironheart guarded her back. *(Oath)*

Ironoak
A wood nearly as tough and indestructible as steel, it is a popular construction material in Valdemar. In Haven, outside of the granite Palace and nobles' houses, structures are mostly ironoak. *(Arrows)*

Irrl
One of Firesong's *kyree* academic teachers—Tarrn reminded him of Irrl. *(Storm)*

Isa (Madame)
Keeper of the *House of Scarlet Joy* at Brether's Crossing. She willingly harbored Kethry and Tarma there because the bandits the sorceress and swordswoman were hunting had abused her girls. Madame Isa wanted the brutes repaid and permanently removed from her town. *(Oath)*

Isak
Master Artificer whose specialty was mechanics and

clockwork. He helped a student with the boiler project at the Palace. *(Storm)*

Isda
Shin'a'in term meaning "have you (ever) seen (such)?" *(Oath)*

Isend
Court Lady in a constant fashion war with the Duchess Abel, to the discomfort and/or amusement of those around them. *(BB)*

Ismay (Lady)
Lord Breon's wife, a competent and strong-minded woman, and quite capable of organizing their manor's defense against invaders. *(Owl)*

Isrel (Underwife)
Underwife of Sen, she was dominated by Firstwife Keldar of Talia's household. The woman looked meekly to the Firstwife for approval in everything she did and said. *(Arrows)*

Istal
Vanyel's tutor at Forst Reach. He had assigned the boy a book on tactics which included the wisdom of Herald Seldasen on fighting, which went counter to what Lord Withen and Armsmaster Jervis taught. Citing the book got Vanyel in deeper trouble then he already was. *(LHM)*

Istan
Felwether townsman who was inclined to defy Tarma and go ahead and light the pyre set to burn the accused Lady Myria. The local priest, however, finally persuaded Istan to give way. *(Oath)*

Isten (Herald)
Herald with a round face and dark, curly hair. *(BB)*

Istren
Kerowyn's Shin'a'in second cousin, a horse-trainer. He came to Bolthaven with Sa'dassan and Tale'sedrin's shaman-in-training, Kra'heera. Young and enthusiastic,

Istren has his father's dusky golden skin and black hair and mother's green eyes. *(Sword)*

Ividian

Mage serving in Urtho's forces with the Sixth Crimson. When the division was trapped in an ambush (which their commander, Shaiknam, had been warned about), Ividian made it possible for some troops to escape. Covering their retreat cost him his life, a loss that outraged Vikteren. *(Gryphon)*

Jacinth
Night-blooming flowers that grow in Companion's Field. *(Arrows)*

"Jackals of Darkness"
A Shin'a'in reference: "Making such speed as if one were pursued by the Jackals of Darkness." *(Oath)*

Jacona
Throne city of the Eastern Empire, and the location of Crag Castle. *(Storm)*

Jacony
An aged beggar and old hand at his trade. He took Kanshin in and trained him as an apprentice. The partnership lasted until Jacony suggested maiming the boy so he would look pathetic and thereby gain more alms. *(Gryphon)*

Jadrek
Archivist of Rethwellan, a middle-aged scholar with sandy, graying hair, gray eyes, and a physical impairment that makes movement painful. According to Captain Idra, he was the only completely honest man at Court. His father used to amuse Idra and her older brother with tall tales, paying attention to them when no one else had time for two children. On the rare occasions when Idra mentioned her past, she spoke fondly of him and Jadrek. Remembering those comments, Tarma and Kethry sought out the Archivist as a likely ally when they went in disguise to Rethwellan's capital looking for

the missing Idra. Jadrek was instrumental in finding Prince Stefan and putting him on the throne. During this adventure Kethry and Jadrek fell in love. They eventually married and had a large brood of children. *(Oath)*

Jadrek the Younger

Kethry's son by Jadrek, and the shaman of the Tale'sedrin Clan. After the disastrous raid on Rathgar's Keep, Kethry appealed to her son to send her someone who not only could act as bodyguard to the survivors but train replacement troops. Jadrek the Younger obliged with Lyla Stormcloud. *(Oath, Sword)*

Jadrevalyn

The family name of the ruling dynasty of Rethwellan. King Stefansen was succeeded by his son Megrarthon, who was followed by his eldest son, Faramentha. *(Oath, Sword)*

Jadrie

Eldest daughter of Kethry and Jadrek, an excellent horsewoman and aspiring swordswoman. *(Oath)*

Jadus (Herald-Bard)

Served as King Sendar's bodyguard in the Tedrel Wars. Jadus lost his leg trying to defend the King during its final battle, and was unable, despite superhuman efforts, to prevent the King from being killed, something that haunted Jadus throughout his long life. The Herald-Bard was an elderly man, long retired, who became one of Talia's greatest friends and teachers. Jadus lost a leg in the battle with the Tedrel Mercenaries while in King Sendar's service. He blamed himself for not saving the King's life, even though Jadus was terribly wounded in the same ambush. The Herald was really never in any position to rescue the King, despite his sense of guilt. Jadus's Gift was Thoughtsensing, and he responded at once when he detected the lonely Talia lurking out in the hall near his rooms, listening to him playing his harp. Not only did he befriend and encourage the still-uncertain young Queen's Own and leave her his precious harp in his will, he aided her in uncovering plots against Valdemar. In return, Talia's presence brought him out of the aimlessness of his retirement and gave renewed meaning to his last years of life. *(Arrow, Exile)*

Jahan (Herald)
Herald in the reign of King Sendar, taught by Alberich upon his arrival in Valdemar. *(Exile)*

Jakem
Blacksmith of Errold's Grove. He did nearly all of the village's metal work except for fine objects such as needles and pins. He was a huge man, balding and paunchy. *(Owl)*

Jakir
One of the *dyheli* stags who volunteered to go on the northwestern expedition searching for news of Darian's parents. *(Owl)*

Jaman (Commander)
He served Grand Duke Tremane in Hardorn. Jaman was in charge of Sector Four, where his units were fighting against the local underground militia. He wrote exceptionally clear and detailed reports. *(Storm)*

Jan
Palace gardener, and one of Talia's information sources among the servant staff. *(Arrows)*

Jana
One of Quenten's assistant mages, and a Farseer. *(Sword)*

Janas (Father)
Hardornen priest. He was one of the few clerics left capable of testing a would-be monarch for earth-binding sense after Ancar's destruction of Hardorn. The ceremony consisted of touching Tremane's temple and uttering a single, penetrating, bell-like tone. This temporarily froze movement and drove out emotion. If a candidate had the power, he would involuntarily produce a harmonizing tone, and the candidate's earth-sense would become active. *(Storm)*

Janna
Kethry's disguise as a brown-haired, generously endowed wench. *(Oath)*

Jarim shena Pretara'sedrin
After Querna was murdered, Jarim temporarily acted as the Shin'a'in envoy to Valdemar. Quick-tempered and inexperienced, he wanted to launch an immediate attack on the Empire's base in Hardorn. In addition, he was very suspicious of Karal, accusing the grieving and overburdened young Karsite of being a traitor. *(Storm)*

Jarmin
One of Bazie's fences for stolen textiles. He bought finer items for resale to the prostitutes of Haven. Jarmin gave Skif a place to stay after his home burned down. *(TT)*

Jasan
The Companion who Chose Prince Darenthallis during the crucial battle with Hardorn. *(Sword)*

Jaseen
Kestra'chern serving Urtho's forces. She was a thin, ethereal blonde, fragile in appearance, but very strong. *(Gryphons)*

Jass
Also known by the aliases Tain Kelken, Hodak, and Derial. He was a sell-sword who burned down Skif's home after killing Bazie. Hired by Guildmaster Vatean, he was most likely killed by him as well. *(TT)*

Jay
A loud, bossy bird. In Velgarth, they are scarlet-colored. They also mimic other birds' calls. *(Arrows, LHM, Winds)*

Jaysen Kondre (Herald)
Seneschal's Herald, he accompanied Savil through the Gate to the Leshara Holding on Sovvan-night and witnessed the terrible scene Tylendel had caused. Later, he aided Savil and Vanyel through the magical backlash following Tylendel's suicide. Originally disliking Vanyel, Jaysen eventually came to see the error of his ways and became his friend. Jaysen's Companion was Felar, and

may also have helped him past his initial bias against the younger Herald. It was Jaysen who urged Vanyel to find a way to change the Web-Spell so that it no longer required constant vigilance by the Guardians, to make the Heralds themselves Valdemar's true power source. Jaysen was the Northern Guardian of the Mage-Web until his death, when he bequeathed the position to Vanyel. *(LHM)*

Jedin (King's Own Herald)
The King's Own Herald, a "granite cliff of a man" with an extremely strong personality. *(BB)*

Jehan (Duke)
He hired a young, inept assassin to try to kill Melles. Jehan was second cousin to Charliss, and was hoping to eliminate candidates for the throne. He assumed that he would be the only logical choice if he had Melles killed. Instead he wound up on the receiving end of Melles' wrath. *(Storm)*

Jel'enedra
An affectionate Shin'a'in term meaning younger sister. Tarma's chief sword-teacher, a spirit warrior, called her that. *(Oath)*

Jel'sutho'edrin
A Shin'a'in word meaning "forever younger Clanschildren," which they use for their riding beasts. Tarma's teacher used the word to impress upon her the importance of the welfare of Kessira and Kethry's mule; the animals' well-being was just as vital as the women's own, especially in an inhospitable place. *(Oath)*

Jelthan (Lord)
New Speaker for the Central District, he was nominated by Lady Kester to replace Lord Orthallen. Kester pointed out that Lord Jelthan was young but had good ideas, and he had been Lord of his Holdings for fourteen years already because his father had died unexpectedly. She felt experience and common sense would balance Jelthan's relative youthfulness. *(Arrows)*

Jem
The aide Tremane assigned to Darkwind and Elspeth during their stay in Hardorn. *(Storm)*

Jemmie
Son of Talia and Dirk. *(Winds)*

Jendar
Another of Kethry's sons, a mage of Adept potential who chose not to lead the life of a Shin'a'in clansman. Instead, he took over the White Winds school his mother had founded and eventually moved it from Petras to Great Harsey in order to be nearer the capital. Clever and lucky, he enjoyed playing politics. When King Megrarthon died, it was Jendar who mentally relayed the message to Kethry so that she could break the news to Prince Darenthallis. During the same long-distance exchange, Jendar mentioned Valdemar's Heralds and the eerie effect the land had on mages and magic, information that helped Kerowyn later. *(Oath, Sword)*

Jendey
Hywel's younger brother. He was striken with Summer Fever, which Keisha managed to cure. *(Owl)*

Jenna
A young Errold's Grove resident, part of Shandi's teenage girlfriend circle. *(Owl)*

Jenna (Companion)
Companion to Herald Lores, she was confused almost to the point of catatonia on the night when Lores was deluded into believing young Tashir and his new Companion were a murderer and a demon respectively. Yfandes picked up Jenna's horrified panic as far away as Forst Reach and urged Vanyel into going to the rescue. Only after Lores realized what he was doing to Jenna by his brutal behavior did he abandon his attempt to destroy the "demon" Companion Leshya with a whip. *(LHM)*

Jerard Stonesmith
A trade guildsman and abettor of the Lake Evendim pirates and their slaver allies. *(Arrows)*

Jeri (Herald)
When Weaponsmaster Alberich decided to retire, Herald Jeri was his successor in teaching the fighting classes. Nobly born, she could have had the rank of Countess if she had not

been Chosen. Because of her background, she grew up with
the benefit of private tutors, including those specializing in
weapons and fighting. Her preferred weapon was the rapier.
Herald Jeri was a potential nominee for Royal Heir during
the period when there was uncertainty about Elspeth being
Chosen. No one would have objected to Jeri's holding that
rank; but her mother, Lady Indra, was a notorious meddler
and inevitably would have battled daily with Jeri regarding
her votes in the Council. That alone was a heavy mark
against her being selected for the position. *(Arrows, Winds)*

Jerlag Gate
Near where the Second Wing of Urtho's forces were
overrun by Ma'ar's troops. The last of the Wing's
wounded were brought to safety via the Jerlag Gate.
(Gryphon)

Jernini
Silver gryphon of the goshawk type. *(Gryphon)*

Jervac
A helpful Gate Guard at Mornedealth. *(Oath)*

Jervain
A drug which dulls the Gift-senses and permits Healing
of injured Heralds. Healer Andrel used it on Vanyel to
ease the overwhelming impact of the young man's
blasted channels. *(LHM)*

Jervan/Jerven
Gryphon son of Hydona and Treyvan. *(Storms, Winds)*

Jervis (Armsmaster)
Armsmaster of Forst Reach. A blond, crag-faced former
mercenary, totally indebted to Lord Withen Ashkevron
for his position. He was commanded to break Withen's
eldest of fey manners and "make him a man." Jervis
became the brutal oppressor of the teenage Vanyel, who
was unfit for the hack-and-bash fighting style the armsmaster taught. Though Jervis broke Vanyel's arm in a
practice bout, years later he was able to satisfactorily
explain his actions, winning Vanyel's trust. He also won
the trust of Tashir Remoerdis when Vanyel brought him
to the family home for safekeeping when the boy was

in danger. Jervis befriended the frightened child and helped solve the mystery surrounding the slaughter of his family. As reward, he was made the Lord Marshal of the March of Lineas-Baires where Tashir was now Baron. Jervis would later marry Melenna, who was made Castelaine at that same time. *(LHM)*

Jesalis
Curly-headed blonde giggler, one of Vanyel's admirers at Court. *(LHM)*

Jesolon
One of Kalink's neighbors. Skif used part of his wall to scale Kalink's wall. *(TT)*

Jess
Bandit, part of Rendan's gang of ambushers. He was slain by Vanyel. *(LHM)*

Jessamine
Kestra'chern. Amberdrake considered her as a replacement for Silver Veil, who would have to retire from public service once she married Shalaman. *(Gryphon)*

Jessamine
Botanical that covers the bitter taste of sleep herbs put in tea. *(Gryphon)*

Jesto-vath
A shielding spell which seals out bad weather and heats the interior of a tent or room. Kethry set one around the Sunhawks' infirmary as well as the tent she and Tarma shared.

Jethry
An orphaned gypsy baby, temporarily adopted by Ifor Smithwright of Berrybay. Talia placed the child with the mindhealed Weatherwitch Maeven, curing her guilt and soothing her loss after the death of her own infant. *(Arrows)*

Jewel
Hertasi assisting the Healers in Ka'venusho. *(Gryphon)*

Jewel Merchants' Guild
They employed Justin Twoblade and his shieldbrother Ikan Dryvale as caravan guards. *(Oath)*

Jiles

A hedge-mage with Lord Leamount's forces. He and fellow mage Oreden went with the Sunhawks along the secret trail around the Jkathan rebels' stronghold. *(Oath)*

Jillian

Inane, flirtatious young woman residing at Haven. Vanyel hoped her father would marry her off soon because she had no common sense, the moral fiber of a hound in heat, and if left to her own devices would sleep her way around the Court. *(LHM)*

Jillian (Herald)

A Herald with a reputation for being sexually enthusiastic. *(Arrows)*

Jinian

Hawksnest youngster, age twelve, a budding orator who took herself a bit too seriously. Tarma's granny-story about the Snow Demon scared her, and perhaps taught her a lesson. *(Oath)*

Jirkin (Herald-trainee)

Herald-trainee. *(BB)*

Jisa (Herald)

Vanyel's daughter by King's Own Herald Shavri. The world believed Jisa was King Randale's child out of wedlock. He and Shavri kept secret the fact that Randale was sterile, in case a royal marriage alliance should present itself. Though Shavri was lifebonded to Randale, she desperately wanted a child, so Vanyel conspired with the pair to fulfill her desire. Jisa's empathic Gifts began manifesting when she was six. She matured into a level-headed and very determined young woman who made up her mind to marry Treven, the Heir Presumptive. Eventually she became King's Own Herald and Queen Consort, but the moment of her Choosing was put off because her mother's Companion Taver would Choose her on her mother's death. *(LHM)*

Jisette Jelnack

Tyron's mother, and the wife of the Silversmith Guildmaster. She became obsessed with punishing Lavan after her son's death, refusing to accept the truth of Tyron's cruelties. When she became uncontrollable, King Theran held Judgment and sentenced her to lifetime confinement in the Cloister of Kernos Sequestered. *(BB)*

Jkatha
The country south of Rethwellan, it borders the Dhorisha Plains. Its capitol is Throne City. It was ruled by Queen Sursha, who needed the help of the Sunhawks to help her regain the throne from her greedy brother-in-law. Kethry was from Mournedealth in Jkatha and Kata'shin'a'in is also located in that country. *(Oath, Winds)*

Jo
Villager Phellip's small son. Like many others, Jo believed war was exciting and glorious, but Vanyel showed him how terrible and personal it really was. *(LHM)*

Jodi
Sleepy-eyed, deceptively quiet Sunhawk scout. A pale blonde aristocratic mapmaker, her other specialties were subterfuge and assassination. A good knife-fighter and archer, she avoided positions of command. Her mount, Lightfoot, was a grey mare with battlesteed blood. Jodi was one of the infiltrators who sought a back door to the Jkathan rebels' stronghold. She retired and became a horsetalker. *(Oath)*

Jodri
One of Bazie's former gang members who moved south to be on his own. *(TT)*

Joffer
One of the White Gryphon mages summoned by Snowstar to search magically for Tad and Silverblade. *(Gryphon)*

Joffrey (Captain)
Leader of the Wolflings mercenary company. *(Oath, Sword)*

Johen
A Herald trainee assigned to act as Ulrich's aide while the ambassador was at the Palace. *(Storm)*

Jolene (Companion)
Companion of Herald Evan. *(BB)*

Jon
Guard posted in the New Palace wing, which holds the Queen's and Court's suites. *(Arrows)*

Jon Hapkins
Proprietor of the Virgin and Stars Tavern. *(Arrows)*

Jonis Revelath
The legal counsel for half the high-ranking nobility of Mornedealth and Ikan Dryvale's father. *(Oath)*

Jonaton
An elderly mage, bent and wizened. Part of one of the new groups put together to defend Valdemar, he was teamed with a Herald and a Sun-priest. *(Winds)*

Jonne
Border Guardsman who guided Vanyel through unfamiliar territory and later became the Herald-Mage's lover for a time. An accomplished fighter, Jonne was described as "rather sweet" by Yfandes. *(LHM)*

Jonny
Former entertainer at Bel's *Inn of the Green Man* in Highjorune. As Minstrel Renfry told Vanyel, Bel broke the boy's hands out of pique, ruining his livelihood. Renfry used that sad event to warn Vanyel, who was replacing Jonny, to watch himself when Bel was in one of her drunken rages. *(LHM)*

Jonotan (Herald)
One of the younger Heralds whose recent circuit had taken him on patrol at Lake Evendim. He joined Pol's group for supper in the Collegium. *(BB)*

Jons
One of Lord Leamount's sentries. He was ordered to fetch Leamount's squire in order to round up food and drink for Tarma after her grueling search for a secret trail. *(Oath)*

Jonti
A young *dyheli* stag who, with his twin Larak, volunteered to go along on Darian and Wintersky's forest tracking search. *(Owl)*

Joserlin Corby
A dissolute young lord, and the leader of a gang of palace rogues. One of Corby's crew was used as a tool to ensnare the naive Princess Elspeth into a potential blackmail situation. *(Arrows)*

Joserlin Corveau
A fosterling at Lord Withen Ashkevron's keep, he was adopted as heir by Withen's cousin. Joserlin was sent to Forst Reach to learn how to govern the family holdings. *(LHM)*

Joshe (Herald)
The Seneschal's Herald to King Randale, and not comfortable in the position. Young and nervous, he often asked others to check his figures before he reported to the Council. His Companion was Kimbry. *(LHM)*

Jostumal
Shin'a'in term meaning enemy, literally, "one desiring (your) blood." *(Oath)*

Journeyman Mage
Lower in rank and magical powers than an Adept or Master, able to use only personal power for magics, rather than tapping into external energy sources. *(Oath, LHM, Winds)*

Journeyman spell
A self-testing promotion spell of the White Winds School, it calls upon the mage's personal power and the Lesser Wind of Fire and Earth, the Stable Elements. If that wind rises from the south, it's a good omen. It circles the mage three times and leaves more power than it took to bring it into being. *(Oath)*

Joyeaus (Herald)
Lord Marshall's Herald during the reigns of Sendar and Selenay. *(Exile)*

Judeth (General)
The daughter of a stonemason, she was commander of the Fifth Company during Urtho's War. Loyal to the end and beyond, she was the highest ranking officer to come through the Kaled'a'in Gates before the Cataclysm. In its

aftermath, she became the military leader of Amberdrake's group of refugees and resolved to find them a home that never could be taken by siege. It was Judeth who proposed building a new city of cliffside terraces on the coast of the Western Sea, a city that would be known as White Gryphon. Later, she helped create the Silvers and became a member of the Council. *(Gryphon)*

Judgment
The reading, interpretation, and enforcement of the laws of Valdemar. On rare occasions, the King may hold a public Judgment, as happened in the case of Jisette Jelnack's insane obsession with Lavan. *(BB)*

Jumay (Guildmaster)
Guildmaster and Council member who complained because Vanyel's plan of recruitment for the military forces was taking so long to produce a seasoned army. *(LHM)*

Justen
One of the artificer students helping with the boiler project. He was the most seriously injured when it exploded, and lost his legs below the knees. Always enthusiastic, as soon as he had partially recovered, he began making plans for building replacement prostheses. *(Storms)*

Justen (Herald-Mage)
A Herald-Mage whose Prime Focus stone was a ruby. He was part of the Guardian Web in Vanyel's time. *(LHM)*

Justice Glyph
A mage sign that appears above the head of one on whom justice has been rendered. Kethry used a justice glyph to sign her work on Lastel Longknife. She judged him a rapist and cast an illusion upon him to make him appear as a woman. The glyph prevented another mage from taking off the spell. *(Oath)*

Justin Twoblades
A free-lancer who worked for the Jewel Merchants' Guild, and a former member of Idra's mercenary company, he was a weathered-looking blond with short hair. He was shield-brother to Ikan Dryvale. Hadell of the Broken Sword Inn led both men to where Tarma was

engaged in weapons practice. Justin offered to pay her for lessons, and she agreed. After helping put Stefen on the throne in Rethwellan, he became a fighting instructor at Tarma's school. His wife was Estrel. *(Oath)*

Justus

Talia's older brother, a golden-haired angel in appearance, in reality a sadist who scarred her hand with a poker when she was only nine years old. He was later killed during a border raid a year or two after Talia was Chosen. His cruelty, and the refusal of the Holderkin adults to believe Talia's side of the burning incident, taught her to be excessively cautious when she went to the Collegium. She was fearful of ever trusting adults again, and was especially wary of handsome men, such as Herald Kris. *(Arrows)*

Justyn

Wizard of Errold's Grove. A true Mage during the war, he was injured during an heroic stand. He never fully recovered from his head wound, and could no longer handle the earth- and Mind-magics that he had formerly used reliably. Sent to Valdemar's frontier, he served Errold's Grove as healer and hedge-wizard. A thin, dark man, he sounded pleasant but tired to his young apprentice, Darian Firkin. Justyn seemed to Darian to be a failed and pitiable old pensioner. But when the Blood Bear barbarians attacked the town, Justyn marshalled enough of his old powers to delay the tribe at the bridge with a Final Strike, trying to give the villagers time to escape, and nobly and willingly sacrificing himself to that end. Errold's Grove erected a statue in his memory. *(Owl)*

Jylen

Hertasi Lyam's lady friend/lover. *(Storm)*

Jyllian

One of the numerous fosterlings and cousins living at Forst Reach in Vanyel's youth. *(LHM)*

Kadessa

A grasslands rodent so greedy that, given a surplus of food, it would eat itself to death. It is also known for hoarding anything and everything it finds in its nest tunnels. The term "kadessa" is an insult, implying that one is an avaricious miser. *(Oath)*

Kaika

A Bard and the daughter of Herald Pol and Healer Ilea. *(BB)*

Kala

A Ghost Cat warrior who shared in the sweat lodge adoption ceremony with Darian and Herald Anda. *(Owl)*

Kalanel

The name of the Consort-Goddess of Sunlord Vkandis, her worship disappeared from Karse many years ago, and her statue has vanished from its place beside Vkandis in the Temples. *(Storm)*

Kalink

A rich grain merchant Skif robbed. The man had very little sense and kept a trophy wife and a mistress. Skif broke into his home and robbed his wife of most of her jewelry. *(TT)*

Kava

A hot beverage popular with Hardornens and at Tremane's camp in Shonar. *(Storm)*

Kal she li de'gande, orm she li de'gande
A Shin'a'in oath between close friends, it translates to "I swear my sword to you, I swear my hand to you." Kira, Jadrie, and Meri swear this oath to each other before the twins are kidnapped. *(Oath)*

Kalchan Galko
Skif's cousin and Lender's eldest son. He ran the *Hollybush* tavern until he was injured in a raid there. He died three months later while in the prison infirmary, never waking up from his coma. *(TT)*

Kaled'a'in
After the Great War and Cataclysm, divided into two groups, under the direction of their Goddess, to become the Shin'a'in and the Tayledras. She asked the Shin'a'in to take stewardship of the Dhorisha Plains because they shunned magic and would not be tempted to use Urtho's magic devices, which were buried in the heart of the Plains. The Goddess gave the Tayledras the job of using magic to cleanse the Pelagiris and lands west of Lake Evendim, lands that were tainted by the sorcery of the Great War. Partnered with specially bred bondbirds, the Tayledras created Heartstones, which collected and tamed the mage-energies of damaged areas, and built protected Vales where they lived until the area was safe. They then drained the Heartstone and relocated elsewhere, beginning the cleansing process anew. *(BV)*

Kaled'a'in Lady
A term for the Goddess, otherwise known as the Star-Eyed. *(Gryphon)*

Kaled'a'in Messenger Bird
Colorful, small, chattering counterparts of the humming-birds who carry messages for the Tayledras. *(Owl)*

Kal'enedral
Called Swordsworn by outClansmen, their name actually means both Children of the Sword and Her Sword Brothers. Blood feud is forbidden within the Clans, and only Kal'enedral are permitted to take vengeance on outlanders. They swear oath in the following order: first, in service to the Goddess of the New Moon and South

Wind; second to the Clans as a whole; and third to their particular Clan. The Swordsworn to the service of Kal'-enel, the Goddess as Warrior, wear dark brown garb unless on blood feud, in which case they are clad all in black. Certain special Kal'enedral wear midnight blue. They are sworn not only to the Goddess as Warrior but also to the Crone and they serve all the clans. They are referred to as Scroll-sworn, and guard the Wisdom of the Shin'a'in, the clans' collective memories, woven by shamans through thousands of years into rugs that convey the thoughts and emotions of the weavers. The vows of the Swordsworn of all kinds demand them to be chaste and celibate. The Kal'enedral train nightly with the Veiled Ones, the *leshya'e* Kal'enedral, spirits of Swordsworn who have died, but continue to manifest in this world to serve their Goddess. *(BV)*

Kal'enel
The Warrior aspect of the four-faced Goddess, literally, Sword of the Stars. She is also called Enelve'astre, or Star-Eyed, and Da'gretha or Warrior. *(Oath)*

Kalinda
Herald Shion's cousin and an incurable gossip. *(Winds)*

Kalira *(Companion)*
Lavan's Companion and the daughter of Satiran, who was Pol's Companion. Kalira Chose Lavan when he was in the Healers Sanctuary recovering from burns and trauma. Her Chosen had the Gift of FireStarting, but no control over it. Kalira provided that control by life-bonding to Lavan, the only case of Companion and Chosen lifebond in Valdemar's history. When a Karsite assassin at the Battle of White Foal Pass killed her, Lavan lost whatever had been holding him sane and in this world. He ravaged the Karsite army and the entire pass in revenge, dying in the resulting FireStorm. *(BB)*

Kally
A Gryphon in the Silvers and Reesk's partner. *(Gryphon)*

Kandace
A middle-aged Healer at the Healing Sanctuary and an expert in working with sick children. *(Owl)*

Kanshin

He was a thief in the Haighlei Empire. His father was a master ditch digger, but Kanshin had no intention of following a career of honest work. He started as a beggar apprenticed to Jacony, but struck out on his own after the old man planned to maim the boy to make him a more effective mendicant. With treachery and skill, Kanshin worked his way up to a form of power in his chosen field, earning enough from his theft to buy slaves and luxuries. He might have continued undetected if he had not formed a partnership with Noyoki, a man who was plotting to kill his brother, the king, and rule in his place. Kanshin sold his services to the traitor and when Noyoki was discovered, Kanshin was also captured and his mind stripped. *(Gryphon)*

Kantis

The child guise used by Vkandis to prepare the children in the Tedrel encampment for their lives in Valdemar.

Kantor *(Companion)*

Companion of Weaponsmaster Alberich, (though called Silver in the short story introducing these characters in *Horse Fantastic*). Disguised as an ordinary white horse, Kantor snuck behind the lines in Karse and rescued Alberich from being burned as a witch, a result of Alberich's untrained use of his Gift of ForeSight. *(Arrows)*

Karal Austreben

Secretary to Ulrich, the Karsite Ambassador to Valdemar, and a young Priest of Vkandis, he was claimed for the Sunlord by the Priests when he was nine. Sent to the Children's Cloister, he demonstrated great scholarly abilities and was chosen as an apprentice by Ulrich. A true god-touched soul, Karal was instrumental in bringing together the disparate elements that eventually united to end the Mage-Storms. He was sent a Firecat, Altra, as a sign of Vkandis' favor and to help him with the heavy destiny he faced. In the crisis of the Mage-Storms, Karal discovered that he was a Channel, someone able to become a conduit for more magical energy than even an Adept can handle. Karal served as a Channel three times during the struggle to end the Mage-Storms and avert the Cataclysm.

The last time, when he controlled the energy of one of
Urtho's devices, he was blinded as a result. He now teaches
at Haven's Collegium, sharing his knowledge of Karsite
culture and language with the Heraldic trainees. *(Storm)*

Karanel

Two sets of twin gods and goddesses, Kerenal and Dina,
Karanel and Dara, appeared in a story told by Need.
(Winds)

Karathanelan Jadrevalyn (Prince, Consort)

Prince of Rethwellan, father of Elspeth, first husband of
Queen Selenay, son of Megrarthon and Irenia. A
younger son of the royal house of Rethwellan, he came
to Valdemar's court shortly after Queen Selenay had
assumed the throne. She was instantly infatuated with
the handsome, cultured young prince and rushed into
marriage with him. Trouble soon began when he insisted
on reigning as equal consort even though no Companion
would Choose him. Karathanelan schemed to become
King, despite the law, planning to usurp Selenay's
throne. Thanks to Weaponsmaster Alberich's Gift of
Foresight, Queen Selenay was saved and the plotters
who intended to ambush her were killed, among them
the Prince himself. The official story was that he and his
friends were killed in a hunting accident. Fortunately,
Karathanelan's brother, King Faramentha of Rethwellan, was willing to accept that account even though he
knew the truth. He shed few tears over his despised
sibling's demise, and kept relations between his realm
and Valdemar cordial. *(Arrows, Sword, Exile)*

Karden (Master)

The owner of an isolated, stench-producing tannery in
the valley beyond a Hawk's Nest supply village. *(Oath)*

Karelee

One of Ikala's casual bed partners. *(Gryphon)*

Karis (Armsmaster)

He was the old Armsmaster of Deveran Remoerdis. As
Reta told Vanyel, Karis had been retired and took to
teaching young Tashir, protecting the boy as much as he
could. The Armsmaster gave the boy a place to hide

when he was abused and an adult to look up to who was sane, stable, and fond of him. A good man, he was killed in the Palace massacre at Highjorune. *(LHM)*

Karles (Companion)
Shandi's Companion. *(Owl)*

Karli
A young woman raised in Westmark. Her stepfather, who was abusing her and her siblings sexually, murdered her when she tried to escape from him by arranging to leave town with Trader Evan. *(Arrows)*

Karly
A trooper with Urtho's forces, he was often rude to Amberdrake. *(Gryphon)*

Karry
A Perlin falcon who was Starblade's first bondbird. When Falconsbane captured Starblade he gave Karry to Nyara to eat. *(Winds)*

Karse
A kingdom on the southeastern borders of Valdemar and often at war with its neighbors. After Herald-Mage Vanyel turned a Karse mage's demons back onto their own country, the Karsite priesthood outlawed magic. The reaction developed into a holy crusade under the leadership of a young zealot known as the Prophet. Magic was allowed only within the priesthood and under the direction of the Prophet; all others with Gifts were burned in the Cleansing Fires. During the reign of King Theran, Karse's army seemed to be unstoppable until Lavan Firestorm destroyed them in the Battle of White Foal Pass. Heralds and their Companions were declared demons before this time in Karse, but the army's destruction by fire, a tool they used so often to terrorize others, frightened them enough to keep them out of Valdemar for another hundred years. During the reign of Valdemar's King Sendar, Karse hired a nomadic nation of mercenaries to attack Valdemar. Sendar was killed defending the realm and his daughter Selenay assumed the throne and finished the task, teaching Karse another severe lesson. Ancar tried to invade Karse, but

got no more than a few leagues over the border when the land itself began opposing him. Sun-priests summoned demons to attack his armies, and scores of men vanished every night. When a woman, Solaris, became Karse's High Priest, Ancar lost even the small bit of land he had gained earlier. Solaris changed the country by abolishing the corrupted Black Robes who began the terror and Cleansing Fires. She had the backing of their God Vkandis and his Firecats; something the country had lost during the Burning Times when even Karsites were sacrificed for Blood-magic. Solaris stopped the slave trade, the dealing of narcotics, and demon summoning. She also formed an alliance with Valdemar, inducting Talia as an honorary priestess, and then formed an alliance with Hardorn under King Tremane's rule. *(Arrows, LHM, Storm, Winds)*

Kash
A hired thug Guildmaster Vatean used to kidnap children for resale to slavers. *(TT)*

Kat (Herald)
A Herald mourned by Vanyel on his return to Haven from Karse, she was one of his many friends who had died in the line of duty. *(LHM)*

Kata'shin'a'in
Lying just beyond the crater wall of the Dhorisha Plains in Jkatha, it is the regular venue for Shin'a'in trade, especially horse fairs. It is a city of thousands of brightly colored tents. Those on the downwind outskirts belong to beast sellers, then inward are the sellers of beast equipment, and further toward the center are leather workers. More inward are the makers of glass, metal, and stonework, then the tents of textile merchants. Closest to the core are sellers of foods and consumables. The core of the city has no shops, only the residences of year-round inhabitants, and some inns. After the trading season, the tents are gone, leaving only blowing leaves and memories, and a few permanent buildings where a huge city had stood days earlier. *(Oath, Storm, Sword, Winds)*

Ka'tesik
A spring on the Dhorisha Plains. The Hawkbrother

Tarma and Kethry met in the Pelagiris Forest told them
Clan Liha'irden was camped near there. *(Oath)*

Kathal
A Shin'a'in term that means "go gently." *(Oath)*

Katran
Lady Myria's very protective older companion, Katran
was especially angry that Lady Myria had been injured
during childbirth because Myria's husband was too parsimonious to hire a Healer to attend her. *(Oath)*

Ka'venusho
The Kal'enedral name for Urtho's Tower. *(Gryphon, Storm)*

Kav
A popular beverage in the Eastern Empire. *(Storm)*

Kaven
A member of Ancar's Elite Guard who visited the traveling Faire. He was the first in his group to sample Firesong's cure-all, and found it good. *(Winds)*

Kavinestral Pheregrul
Kethry's brother, eight years her senior, he was handsome, lazy, and spendthrift. He sold his sister into marriage to the sadistic Wethes Goldmarchant when she was
barely twelve. By the time Kethry returned to
Mornedealth, Kavin was head of the powerful Blue Faction among the city's Fifty Noble Houses. *(Oath)*

Kayka
He was an unpartnered Companion stallion who volunteered to be the mount of Lo'isha, the Sworn-Shaman,
on the mission to Urtho's Tower. *(Storm)*

Kayla (Weaponsmaster)
The weaponsmaster at the Collegium during Vanyel's
time. *(LHM)*

Kechara
A misborn gryphon with a loving personality and an unusually long-range Gift for Mindspeech, her name meant
"beloved" or "darling" in Kaled'a'in. She was the result
of Urtho's attempt at improving the gryphon species, but

was never able to fly and had the intelligence of a nestling. Urtho felt he was protecting her by keeping her hidden in his Tower so she would not be discriminated against. Skandranon found her there and befriended her. Concerned for her welfare, he convinced Urtho to let him care for her and brought her through the Gate with the Kaled'a'in after Urtho's death. Eventually, Kechara was adopted by Skan and Zhaneel and assisted the Silvers with her powerful Mindspeech. She was a quarter the size of Skan, with a small head, long wings, and dusty buff-gray color feathers. *(Gryphons)*

Kechara
A Tayledras endearment. *(Owl)*

Kedd (Herald-trainee)
One of the Herald-trainees taught by Herald Pol. Kedd's Gift was Animal Mindspeaking. *(BB)*

Kedrick
Tremane's cousin and heir, he was left in charge of the Duke's estate when Tremane was assigned to head the Empire's Hardornen operation. *(Storm)*

Keenath
He was Tadrith's twin and a gryfalcon like his mother Zhaneel. He was small, with light peregrine coloring, and stubby, dexterous handlike claws. Ill-equipped for fighting, he decided to train as a trondi'irn. *(Gryphon)*

Keeper
Title for the supervisor of the Children's Cloister in Karse. The youngsters feared his wrath, which was likely to descend upon them for any infractions of the rules. *(Storms)*

Keeper's Crossing
A village in Hardorn where Talia and Kris stayed in the hostel during their ambassadorial mission. It was at this inn that Talia was served the goatsfoot mushrooms that temporarily disabled her empathic ability. *(Arrows)*

Kef Hairlip
One of Lord Rendan's cutthroat gang. *(LHM)*

Kefta
Tarma's uncle, who displayed his rarely performed sword dance to celebrate the clan's success at the Summer Horse Fair. He died the night that her clan was destroyed. *(Oath)*

Keighvin (Monarch's Own Herald)
Talamir's predecessor as Monarch's Own Herald. *(Arrows)*

Keileth
Master of the Merchants' School. *(BB)*

Keisha Alder
Healer of Errold's Grove and k'Valdemar Vale. In addition to her Healing Gift, she also had the Gift of Empathy. She discovered cures for the diseases afflicting the Northern Tribes, and eventually become famous as a Wisewoman among them. Romantically involved with Darian, and sister to Herald Shandi. *(Owl)*

Keitel
He was the skinny young apprentice of Imperial mage Sejanes. *(Storm)*

Kelcrag (Lord)
Brother-in-law of widowed Queen Sursha of Jkatha, he opposed her regency and began a civil war. His initial assault drove Sursha and her supporters out of Throne City, the capital, but did not defeat her. Mercenaries, including the Sunhawks, were hired to supplement the Queen's forces against Kelcrag's bluecoat rebels. He was defeated and killed. *(Oath)*

Keldar (Firstwife)
She was the Firstwife in the Steading where Talia was born. Keldar heads a family that includes eight Underwives, but her voice rules the roost. Following the cultural patterns of the repressive Holderkin society, she did her best to break Talia's rebellious spirit while Talia was still a child. *(Arrows)*

Kele
A Shin'a'in term that means "onward." *(Oath)*

Kelee
A *hertasi* artisan who made the ring Elspeth gave Darkwind out of silver, crystal, and Gwena's intricately braided tail hairs. *(Winds)*

Kelethen
A *hertasi,* the personal attendant to Urtho. *(Gryphon)*

Kellan (Companion)
Savil's Companion. *(LHM)*

Kelles
One of the gods in the Velgarth pantheon. *(Oath)*

Kellwood oil
Used in massage treatments for muscle strains or as a prelude to amorous activities. *(Arrows)*

Kelmskeep
Lord Breon's manor and stronghold, the nearest defensible place to Errold's Grove. Its walls are three stories high, with guard walks on top and observation towers at the corners. Inside the manor's crenellated walls, there are civilized comforts and manicured gardens. *(Owl)*

Kelreesha Trondaar
His gryphons served with the Sixth Wing of Urtho's forces. Zhaneel attached herself to his group without waiting for assignment. *(Gryphon)*

Kelsie
The maid at the Chitward town house who brought food to Lavan when he was sick. *(BB)*

Kelsy (Herald)
Herald who was newly trained in Mage-Gift, and part of a weather control group. *(Winds)*

Keltev
Talia's brother, he used to tease her about wanting to become a Herald. He was growing up to be as cruel and sadistic as his elder sib Justus until his brother was killed in a border raid while trying to prove his bravery. The shock of his death made Keltev shape up nicely. *(Arrows)*

Kelvren
Silver Gryphon, Skothkar, "The Brave," Scout of the k'Vala gryphon wing and later a valued member of k'Valdemar Vale. Trained by the Kaled'a'in in White Gryphon, he is young, but a very capable fighter. *(Owl)*

Kemak
Ma and Pa Kemak, as Sunhawk Kyra called them, were the proprietors of the Wheat Sheaf Inn in Petras. *(Oath)*

Kemoc (Herald)
A potential candidate for Heir to the throne of Valdemar if Princess Elspeth wasn't Chosen. *(Arrows)*

Kendrick (Lord)
Joserlin Corveau was originally fostered in that Lord's Holding, and as a result admires both Kendrick and Armsmaster Orser. *(LHM)*

Kendrick Gorley (Lord)
The drunken petty despot of Viden, he hired prison scum and operated a protection racket, bullying local merchants and shaking down travelers like Tarma and Kethry. In Bard Leslac's version of events, however, Gorley became a "Wicked Overlord" and a powerful foe. He challenged Tarma while he was drunk and died when a misstep while he was lunging toward her caused him to fall and strike his head on the fireplace. *(Outh)*

Kentroch (Father)
A Kasite Sunpriest who was one of Alberich's early mentors. *(Exile)*

Kephira
A stimulant used by Mornelithe Falconsbane. *(Winds)*

Keplan
Master of a Leather and Furrier's Guild in Hardorn, he was a Town Councillor in a community a day's ride out from Shonar. Keplan was part of the delegation proposing that Tremane go through with the ancient earth-binding ceremony and become Hardorn's king. *(Storm)*

Kera (Herald)
A Herald stationed on the Karsite border. When the

anti-mage crusade began in that hostile neighboring land, Vanyel needed to contact her to assure himself that she was well and to get information from a Valdemaran operative on location. *(LHM)*

Keren (Herald)

A riding instructor at the Collegium, she was Talia's long-time friend and surrogate mother. Her twin, Teren, not only Mindspoke with her, but also with his Companion, Wythra, and Keren's Companion Dantris as well. Herald Talamir, who was Queen's Own before Talia, was their grandfather. Keren was raised in the Lake Evendim sector and had experience rescuing people from ice-choked waters; it was this training that saved Talia when she nearly drowned in the river. Lifebonded with Herald Ylsa until Ylsa's death, and then with Herald Sherrill. *(Exile, Arrows, Winds)*

Kerenal

Need told the story of the two sets of twin gods and goddesses, Kerenal and Dina, Karanel and Dara. *(Winds)*

Kerithwyn (Healer)

A Healer Talia brought back to Waymeet to treat the plague victims there. Normally residing at a district Healers' Temple, Kerithwyn agreed to stay until everyone stricken with snow fever was cured. *(Arrows)*

Kerle

He was one of Vanyel's many cousins and fosterlings residing at Forst Reach. *(LHM)*

Kern

Grandfather of the young mother threatened by the colddrake queen, he willingly sacrificed his life in hopes that she and his grandchildren would have a chance to escape the monster. *(LHM)*

Kernos

God worshipped in Valdemar and also known as Kernos of the Northern Lights. His acolytes are a martial order of fighting monks. Worship is organized in Temples, where good works may be performed, such as distribution of food to the poor, and in cloistered religious retreats devoted to prayer. They favor the Heralds. Many oaths, some of them vulgar, are sworn in Kernos's name. *(Arrows, BB, LHM)*

Kerowyn

Nicknamed Kero, she was Kethry's granddaughter, by her youngest girl, Lenore. While still a teenager, she won fame rescuing her brother Lordan's kidnapped bride Dierna. Her Godmother Tarma, the *kyree* Warrl, and the sword Need assisted her. A ballad was written about the rescue, entitled "Kerowyn's Ride," which would haunt her the rest of her life. With Need now her own, Kero was trained by Tarma in swordwork and fighting skills, while Warrl trained her in the use of her Mindspeech Gift. Upon completion of her education, Kerowyn joined with the mercenary company Skybolts, and eventually became its Captain. She was lifebonded to Herald Eldan, whom she rescued from a priestess' burning fires in Karse. It was an unusual romance because she saw little of him for the next ten years, but conversed with him every night by Mindspeech, thinking she was merely dreaming. Kero was afraid becoming a wife would diminish her, and resisted the lifebond for fear of losing her identity. Kerowyn was instrumental in the defeat of Ancar when Valdemar hired the Skybolts to help them in the war. During the final battle, Kero's battlesteed Hellsbane was killed and she was Chosen by Sayvil. Queen Selenay rewarded the Skybolts by giving them a town of their own, and making them part of Valdemar's official army, with Kero as their Captain. As a Herald, Kero rarely wore Whites because she felt they made her a target in battle. After moving to Valdemar, she was able to continue her affair with Eldan in person. Kerowyn trained Elspeth in swordwork and passed Need on to her. She also led Valdemar's forces to Errold's Grove when it was unclear if the barbarians coming into Valdemar were friend or foe. *(Owl, Storm, Sword, Winds)*

Kertire

A dark beauty, one of the inane gigglers who became part of Vanyel's admiring circle at Court. *(LHM)*

Kessira

Tarma's Shin'a'in saddlebred mare. Like all of her kind, she ran free and was trained nearly from birth to come only to her owner. When Tarma and Kethry returned to the Plains and acquired the battlesteeds Ironheart and Hellsbane, Kessira was left there to be pampered and maintained for breeding among the Tale'sedrin herds kept by Liha'irden caretakers. *(Oath)*

Kester (Lady)

A Valdemaren Councillor, she was speaker for the West and ruler of the Lake Evendim area. *(Arrows, Winds)*

Kestra

A Shin'a'in term meaning "casual friend." *(Oath)*

Kestra'chern

Among the Kaled'a'in, a person trained to aid in the healing of the spirit, mind, and body. Their skills are massage, aromatherapy, herbal remedies, therapeutic baths, sexual therapy, and counseling. Serving as confidants and advisors to their clients, theirs is a highly respected profession among the Kaled'a'in, and should not be confused with prostitution. *(BV)*

Kethra

A Shin'a'in shaman, Healer, and an adopted Tayledras Wingsib. While working to cure Starblade, she became his lover and lifemate. *(Winds)*

Kethren

Justin and Estrel's baby. *(Oath)*

Kethry, or Kethryveris Pheregrul

Known most commonly as Kethry, she grew up in Mornedealth as a member of one of the Fifty Noble Houses. After her parents died, her brother Kavin sold her in marriage to the rich, ambitious, and perverted Wethes Goldmarchant. Her old nurse smuggled the girl out of the sadist's house. Kethry's magical powers began manifesting in nightmares of her ordeal, so the nurse took her to the nearest White Winds mage-school for help. When Kethry first met Tarma in Brether's Crossing, she was a Journeyman mage wandering the country, offering her services to those who were in trouble, and dealing with the geas of her enchanted sword named Need. This sword enabled Kethry to defend herself and other women by taking over her body and giving her warrior gifts. After a chance meeting, Kethry joined forces with Tarma to destroy the brigands who slew the Tale'scdrin. When the task was done, the two women swore an oath to become *she'enedran,* blood-sisters. This meant that Kethry would become the clan mother of Tale'sedrin and preserve Tarma's clan. Together the pair would defeat demons, save women in peril, and decide the fate of kings. Kethry married Jadrek, Rethwellan's Royal Archivist, and produced a large family. Tarma, Kethry, and Jadrek founded a school of magic and war that trained the future rulers of the Rethwellan and Jkatha, as well as any number of other students. They also adopted children and took in fosterlings to rebuild the Tale'sedrin Clan. *(Oath, Sword)*

Kettlesmith
A town Talia visited on her way from Sensholding to Haven. A Roadguard instructed her to stop there and pick up food for the final leg of her journey. She assured Talia that the dayguard at Kettlesmith knew of Holderfolk, liked children, and would be very helpful to a confused young traveler. *(Arrows)*

Keyjon
A sorceress born of mage-talented parents and spoiled throughout childhood and adolescence. Her own talents were small, but her one true Gift was the ability to steal spells and powers from others. She wanted to make firebirds her slaves, and would torture and kill to achieve her goal. *(Oath)*

Khamsin
A benign Other-Planar creature that resembles a jewel-bright desert lizard standing erect. Intelligent and wary, it can be hired for a piece of fruit to scout out potential magic for a sorcerer. *(Oath)*

Khimbata
The capital of Emperor Shalaman's Haighlei Kingdom,

It is the most northerly of the Black Kings' cities and is two weeks sail down the coast of the Western Sea from White Gryphon. *(Gryphon)*

Kiela
A young blonde Herald who had recently been riding circuit in Staghorn Forest. *(BB)*

Kilchas (Herald-Mage)
Noted as the best Mindspeaker in the Circle, he was the Herald-Mage anchoring the South in the Guardians' Web-Spell. He was an offensive combat mage and his hobby was astronomy. He apparently fell from his rooftop observatory when observing astronomical phenomena, but in reality was murdered by the Dark Mage Leareth. His Companion Rohan died simultaneously in Companion's Field. *(LHM)*

Kili
An old Makaar leader with a prominent black and white crest. He was a familiar antagonist of Skandranon, and one he often taunted. *(Gryphon)*

Killing Trees
Located in the Forest of Sorrows, Herald-Mage Vanyel's ancient curse had long protected Valdemar against any invasion from the north. The trees of Sorrows would spear, squeeze, and drop on those who were evil, killing them. The curse was lifted when Vanyel was lost in a power-meld during the final solution of the Mage-Storms. *(Arrows, Owl, Storm)*

Kilmer
An Errold's Grove resident and a member of the Fellowship. *(Owl)*

Kimbry (Companion)
Companion of Seneschal's Herald Joshe. *(LHM)*

Kimel
Head of King Sendar's Personal Guard. *(Exile)*

Kin of Vkandis
A community of religious worshippers in Karse. Under the new rules decreed by Solaris, the Kin should be

guided to those in need, as young priest Karal was to An'desha. *(Storms)*

Kindas Sun-Kindler
A deity worshipped in Hardorn, his sect is a rival to that of Tembor Earth-Shaker. *(Arrows)*

Kingsmen
What the people beyond Valdemar's northern borders call the Heralds, Guards, and other agents of Valdemar's monarch. *(LHM)*

King's Arms
A tavern in Haven that served low quality but edible food and drink. Its owners had no love for the *Hollybush* tavern. *(TT)*

King's Tower
What Hardornens started calling Tremane's residence in Shonar after he was bound to the land and properly crowned. *(Storm)*

Kira
The ten-year-old daughter of Archduke Tilden, and Merili's fraternal twin. The twins had an unusual upbringing, tutored at age three by a retired acrobat and at six by a professional dancer. *(Oath)*

Kitten-paw flowers
A plant normally found only in Karse, and a common herbal remedy for headache. *(Storm)*

Kla'heshey'meserin
A Gryphon Kaled'a'in term meaning Clan k'Leshya, The Lost Ones, or the Spirit Clan. *(Winds)*

Klaus (Leftenant)
A fellow officer of Alberich's in the Karsite military. Klaus was his senior in years of service, though not in experience, and was resentful when Alberich was promoted to Captain before him. *(Arrows)*

Kleimar
A region of Valdemar rife with old-fashioned prejudice, including a bias against the *shay'a'chern*. Seneschal's

Herald Jaysen in Vanyel's time was from that area. *(LHM)*

K'Leshya

A Kaled'a'in Clan, the only one not named for a totemic animal. Its name means "Spirit Clan." The Clan developed an especially close relationship with Urtho's created creatures and the other non-human races. Amberdrake joined k'Leysha when he came to Ka'venusho; his family was lost in the devastation caused by Ma'ar, and k'Leshya became his new kinship group. After the Cataclysm, k'Leshya traveled further into unknown territories than any other Kaled'a'in Clan. They went through two Gates, not one, and continued their migration all the way to the Western Sea. In the time of Queen Selenay, Treyvan and Hydona arrived outside of k'Sheyna Vale, seeking land for colonizing by surplus k'Leshya members. Their arrival was a distinct shock to k'Sheyna, who never expected to see any members of the by-now legendary k'Leshya Clan. Spirit Clan humans are more genetically diverse than most Tayledras Clans; some have round faces, some green or brown eyes, and some are blond or redheaded. *(BV)*

Knowles Crossing

A town on the Heralds' northern circuit. *(Arrows)*

Kobold

A mischievous spirit of mines and caves. The Collegium's Cook, Mero, insisted kobolds were playing pranks on him whenever things turned up missing in his kitchen, even though he knew it was actually the young Herald-Trainees teasing him. *(Arrows)*

Koil

Known as Widow Koil, she and her children made paper and fabric flowers to sell. *(TT)*

Korad

One of Urtho's Generals. *(Gryphons)*

Korwain

An artist in Haven who had a brief affair with a noble-woman. *(TT)*

Kra'heera shena Tale'sedrin
Kerowyn's Shin'a'in cousin and an apprentice shaman. When Valdemarans arrived at Bolthaven, Kra'heera wanted Kerowyn to talk to them in their own language so that he could read their minds and decide if they were worthy to receive ownership of Shin'a'in bred horses. She suspected he was also responsible for supplying Geyr with mastiffs out of the Pelagiris Forest. *(Sword, Winds)*

Krashak
A demonic creature inhabiting Valdemar's Pelagir Hills. The krashak was twice a man's height, had four arms, with a face like a boar, taloned hands, no genitals, nipples, or navel, and was the color of clay. Jadrek also told Prince Roald how to get rid of it; High Magick was vulnerable to Earth Magick, in this case salt, moly, and Lady's Star. Throwing these into the krashak's eyes and mouth would make it disintegrate. *(Oath)*

Krawlven
One of Ma'ar's rebirth names. *(Winds)*

Krawn
He was Stormcloud's bondbird, a white raven, and a talkative jokester. *(Winds)*

Krebain
An evil mage who was advancing from the western lands, brutally encroaching on Tayledras territory and the land held by peasants under Tayledras protection. Krebain was a blood-mage who grew in strength from every victim he took. A Change-child, he was graceful, slim, and very tall with white-blond hair and blue-black eyes that were slitted like a cat's. Vanyel killed him in a battle at Covia after Krebain confessed to the murder of Staven Frelennye, the twin of his lover Tylendel. Wester Leshara had hired him to kill Vanyel as well, but when Krebain saw how beautiful Vanyel was, he wanted Vanyel for himself instead. Defeating Krebain was the turning point in Vanyel's decision to be a Herald. *(LHM)*

Kreeak
Wintersky's bondbird, a little sharpshinned hawk. *(Owl)*

Kreel
Firestorm's bondbird, a broad winged female cooperi-hawk half Vree's size. *(Winds)*

Krethes
A Shin'a'in term that means "speculation." *(Oath)*

Kris
Prince of Valdemar and Princess Lyra's twin, he is the son of Queen Selenay and her Consort Daren. *(Winds)*

Kris (Herald)
A student of history, law, and administration, he hoped to replace Dean Elcarth when the elder Herald retired from the Collegium. Kris's Gifts were FarSeeing and Mindspeech. His Companion was Tantris. Kris was the second son of Lord Peregrine, one of the Seneschal's chief assistants, and his mother organized the resupply of Heralds' Waystations throughout the realm. Lord Orthallen was Kris's uncle, and used that relationship to try to influence him. Kris was one of the potential candidates for Heir if Queen Selenay's child wasn't Chosen. When Talia was ready to begin her internship, it was Kris who was chosen to be her mentor. His uncle planted ideas that Talia was unfit to be Queen's Own and this weighed heavily on his mind when he saw that Talia had no control over her Gift of Empathy. Kris decided to train her, and got his chance to do so when they were snowed in at a Herald's station while on circuit. The stress led to a romance that put Kris at odds with his best friend Dirk, whom he knew to be in love with Talia. By the time Talia was trained and their circuit completed, they decided to become platonic friends. On a subsequent mission into Hardorn, Kris and his Companion were murdered by Ancar's troops while Talia was captured. *(Arrows)*

K'tathi
One of Scout Wintermoon's two bondbirds, a large snow-winged owl like his partner Corwith. *(Winds)*

K'Treva
One of the Tayledras Hawkbrother Clans. Their territory was located near the edge of the Pelagir Hills. K'Treva Vale, like all Tayledras settlements, is dedicated to cleansing and removing old and evil magic from the land, making

it fit once more for humans and for animals that were displaced from their original haunts by ancient sorcery and the malevolent creatures spawned by that magic. K'Treva Vale is a teardrop-shaped canyon altered by Tayledras magic to shelter it from the weather and maintain a perfect climate. There are other clans scattered throughout the length of the tainted lands, among them k'Sheyna, k'Chona, and k'Vala. The k'Treva Clan adopted Vanyel and his aunt Savil as Wingsiblings. *(LHM)*

Kuari
Darian's bondbird, he was an eagle-owl and the fledgling of Hweel and Huur. *(Owl)*

Kulath
A Shin'a'in term meaning go find. *(Oath)*

Kurhanna
The tribal name given to Darian Firkin after the sweat lodge adoption ceremony. In the language of the Ghost Clan, it means night walker. *(Owl)*

K'Vala
A Tayledras clan that was once decimated by a blood-path Adept who sculpted himself into a child's form. He played on the clan's emotions until he trapped them. When this happened the clan's territory lay on the Eastern Shore of the Great Crater Sea, which outlanders know as Lake Evendim. *(Winds)*

K'Valdemar
A new Vale in Valdemar built where Starfall's original outpost near Errold's Grove had been. Snowfire brought Darian to this small place, not yet classed as a Vale, as a refugee from the barbarian attack. Years later, when they returned from k'Vala, Darian found k'Valdemar was now a true Vale, with impressive works constructed by the *hertasi,* including pools and ekeles, though until the Heartstones were fully charged they wouldn't have a weather-ameliorating shield. The Vale now serves as an embassy. *(Owl)*

K'Varda
The collective name for the Mage-Clans of the Tayledras. Their mission is to identify places where the

magic creatures of the Pelagirs may live in peace, and then take the magic out of places where they do not live and make that land safe for human habitation. The k'Varda guard the Pelagirs from despoilers, just as their cousins, the Shin'a'in, guard the Dhorisha Plains. *(LHM)*

Kyanshi
A Tayledras couple-dance for the experienced. Its steps and movements are difficult if one is young and only used to the patterns of children's round dances. *(Owl)*

Kyldathar (Companion)
Companion to Herald-trainee Neave. *(Arrows)*

Kyle Osterham
The woodcutter of Errold's Grove. *(Owl)*

Kyliera Grove Brendewhins
A fluttering talkative relative of one of Lady Treesa's court ladies. *(LHM)*

Kylla
One of the numerous progeny housed at Forst Reach, Kylla was the baby who kept getting out of the nursery, usually without a stitch on. *(LHM)*

Kylleen
A gryphon, one of the Silvers serving with the fishing fleet. *(Gryphon)*

Kyllian
A famous Fireflower Mage. Wizard Justyn had a badly painted portrait of him on the wall. Too old to take part in battle during the Great War, he served as rear-line instructor to young Herald-Mages and as a Healer, saving Justyn's life among others. *(Owl)*

Kynan
A veteran Skybolt briefly considered for command after Ardana Flintcye's expulsion. Kynan lacked Kerowyn's training in tactics, logistics, and supply, and couldn't work with mages. Also, what command expertise he had stopped at groups larger than a squad. *(Sword)*

Kyndri (Herald-Chronicler)
Herald-Chronicler in Vanyel's era. The information

Kyndri recorded told Elspeth that old descriptions of the incredible powers available to a strong mage like Vanyel were not Chroniclers' hyperbole, but the truth. *(Winds)*

Kyra

One of Tarma's scouts. Kyra was an expert with bow, knife, tracking, and riding. She was also Shieldmated to Rild. When the Sunhawks were stalemated during the Jkathan civil war, Kyra knew the country, had kin in the region, and remembered a way to get around the entrenched rebels in their hilltop fortress. *(Oath)*

Kyran (Bard)

A Bard, and the lover of Queen Elspeth the Peace-maker. Vanyel pointed out to Randale that Elspeth could have married Kyran after the death of Randale's grandfather, but did not for the same reasons of duty to the state that prevented Randale and his lifebonded Shavri from marrying. *(LHM)*

Kyree

Larger than any true wolf, a *kyree*'s shoulder is as high as a man's waist, with a bread and wolflike head with a rounded forehead, forward-facing eyes, and enormous jaws. As intelligent as a human, *kyree* are Mind-speakers. The *kyree* have three sexes: males, females, and neuters. Pack life centers on the breeding males and females, leaving the neuters at loose ends, so they tend to be great wanderers and historians. *(BV)*

Kyril (Seneschal's Herald)

On permanent assignment at the Palace, he occasionally teaches at the Collegium. His Gift is Farspeaking. He taught Talia the Arrow-Code. *(Arrows, Storm, Winds)*

Kyrith (Companion)

The original Grove-Born Companion who Chose King Valdemar's Herald in the first days of the special bonding between the magical creatures and the realm's governors. *(Arrows)*

Kyrr

Dawnfire's bondbird, she was a red-shouldered hawk. While they were in full-bond, Dawnfire was trapped in Kyrr's body and captured by Falconsbane. *(Winds)*

Lada (Companion)
A Companion who was in foal, and was expected to
have a difficult birth. She Chose Wrenlet with less than
two moons gestation left. *(BB)*

Lady-Fountain
A fountain in Tailor's Court that's a Haven landmark.
It vents down a culvert to Breakneedle Street, or did
until it was diverted into a cellar gathering room at the
Virgin and Stars Tavern, the third-year Bardic students
favorite meeting place. *(Arrows)*

LadyTrine
The Rethwellan term for the triple Goddess aspects of
Agnetha, Agnira and Agnoma. *(Sword)*

Laeka
Hadell's daughter, a stablegirl at the Broken Sword
Inn. *(Oath)*

Laika (Herald)
She served as a spy in Karse during the Tedrel Wars,
and after the last battle of the war was instrumental in
saving and bringing to Valdemar the abandoned children
collected by the Tedrel Mercenaries. *(Exile)*

Laine
Hywel's mother, a member of the Ghost Cat Clan, and
the chief's wife. *(Owl)*

Laisfaar
Once a thriving trade town near the Pass of Stelvi, it

was captured by Ma'ar's forces and its citizens enslaved. *(Gryphon)*

Laj'ele'ruvon

A Tayledras word for a knowledge-seeker. The dying Firefalcon Clan shaman Jadrie found by the riverside was one of those. *(Oath)*

Lake District

Annexed by Tashir Remoerdis when he assumed the vacant throne of Lineas-Baires, the Lake Evendim people and their envoys are touchy and proud. When they arrive at Haven, they insisted on being greeted by King Randale as full provincials, or they would be grievously affronted. *(LHM)*

Lake Evendim

A huge lake located at the western edge of Valdemar, which the Kaled'a'in call the Great Crater Sea. The site of Ma'ar's stronghold during the Great War; when his tower was destroyed by Urtho, the resulting crater eventually filled with water. It is now a thriving area with many fishing communities that harvest the giant sturgeons that live in the lake. *(BV)*

Laker

A Skybolt scout assigned to accompany visitors from Valdemar to Bolthaven's guest house. He was given that task because he spoke their language, and might have learned information by listening to their conversations. *(Sword)*

Lakshe

A procurer of boy whores in Khimbata's sordid street trade. He offered to take Kanshin on as part of his stable, but Kanshin declined. *(Gryphon)*

Lallis

A young woman of Errold's Grove, Lallis was the boldest of the teenage girls, and was notorious for flaunting her assets. *(Owl)*

Lance of Hope

The name for the daily beam of sunlight which shines

through the Eye in the Temple of Vkandis in Karse. *(Storm)*

Lancir (Queen's Own Herald)
He was the Queen's Own Herald to Elspeth the Peacemaker, and was an expert on reading people's inner nature. A Mindhealer, he came through Tylendel's MageGate with Savil and Jaysen on Sovvan-night to try to help with the tragedy Tylendel had caused. Afterward, Lancir and his Companion Taver volunteered to stay behind to deal with the surviving Lesharas. *(LHM)*

Landon Castle
A castle located near Valdemar's eastern border with Hardorn. Selenay and Elspeth had been there, and Elspeth decided it would make an excellent Gate terminus. After Elspeth built the Gate (her first), the Queen and Darenthallis Gated directly to the castle to finish the last details of the war with Hardorn after Ancar's death. *(Winds)*

Landric
A farmer devoted to the Wheel-Bound religion, whose members believe that atonement is necessary to repair evil done in this life or an earlier one. Like all of that sect, Landric wore a five-spoke wheel branded on the back of his left wrist. He offered Tarma and Kethry shelter when they passed by, and it was from him they learned of the monster ravaging the countryside and of the reward offered for its slaying. *(Oath)*

Langenfield
A town on the Heralds' northern circuit. *(Arrows)*

Lanz
A young Healer with Urtho's forces, he answered to Senior Healer M'Laud, who sent Lanz to Amberdrake to learn about kestra'cherns. *(Gryphon)*

Larak
A young *dyheli* stag and Jonti's twin. One of those who volunteered to go with Darian and Wintersky on their forest tracking hunt. *(Owl)*

Larap
He was one of Bazie's apprentice thieves who took off on his own before Skif's arrival. *(TT)*

Lareen
The *dyheli* doe who carried Nyara to Falconsbane's stronghold. *(Winds)*

Larence
One of Vanyel's pack of cousins. *(LHM)*

Larsh
One of Tarma's students. *(Oath)*

Laryn
One of Kethry's and Jadrek's twin sons, younger than Jadrie but older than Jadrek Minor. *(Oath)*

Lashan
The human name of the spirit that inhabits Need. Over the millennia she forgot her true name. Need was crafted by the mage-smith Lashan of the Sisterhood of Spell and Sword, who forged twelve special swords every year. These swords would not rust, break, or lose their edge. There were set-spells on them for each season: Spring, calm; Summer, warding; Autumn, healing; Winter, luck. Once every four years she made only eleven swords. The twelfth she forged to include all four spells, and waited for someone in the Sisterhood to prove herself an intelligent and moral fighter. To that woman she would present the sword as a gift. When the Wizard Heshain massacred most of the order, Lashan invoked the gods and magic and sacrificed herself on the special twelfth sword, becoming one with the weapon, which was renamed Need. *(Winds)*

Lasha'Kaladra
This is the Tayledras word for Companion. *(LHM)*

Lasleric
An outlying town in Rethwellan. Tarma, disguised as Arton, split up King Raschar's forces by ordering some to "Lay a false trail to Lasleric." *(Oath)*

Lastel Longknife
A bandit who used his Gift of Mind-magic to fool people

into thinking he was someone familiar and trustworthy. He was the leader of a gang that raided merchant trains and raped and killed any captured women. Tarma and Kethry were hired to find out who was commiting the crimes and bring them to justice. When they discovered Lastel was responsible, Kethry cast an illusion on him, causing him to look like a woman, signing her work with a justice glyph. They tied him to his horse and sent it off to the bandits' camp, where they assumed he too would be raped to death. Unfortunately, he escaped and sought revenge by allying with Thalhkarsh, a demon they had defeated earlier. The demon transformed Lastel into a real woman so Need wouldn't harm him. Lastel's spirit was swapped into Kethry's body during a fight, but she regained it when the High Priest of Anathei rescued her. It is unknown what happened to Lastel's spirit, as the demon occupied Lastel's female form, but it most likely found the fate it deserved. *(Oath)*

Lastern
The man claiming to be the Son of the Sun, reduced to ashes by Vkandis when Solaris became the true one. *(Storm)*

Lavan Chitward, or Lavan Firestarter/Firestorm (Herald)
Later known as Firestarter and Firestorm, he was the son of a cloth merchant and a fine needleworker, but was not interested in following the family trade. He was sent by his parents to the Merchant School instead. Bullies there made his life miserable. The situation came to a head when, during a beating, Lavan's Gift manifested, killing the boys who had attacked him. Kalira Chose Lavan at this crucial juncture, and kept his Gift under control. Their bond was unusual—they were lifebonded in addition to the normal Companion/Chosen bond.

When the war with Karse escalated, Lavan went to the front lines and used his Gift in Valdemar's defense, though he was never comfortable killing—until a Karsite sneak attack blinded his teacher Pol. At the battle of White Foal Pass, Lavan and Kalira held back a large force of Karsites until an assassin killed Kalira. Enraged at the loss of his lifebonded, Lavan sent the entire valley up in flames, killing nearly all of the Karsite forces and himself. *(BB, Arrows)*

Laureate
The title given to the reigning member of the Bardic Circle. The Laureate wears the coronet during official ceremonies and has the right to attend Council meetings. *(Arrows)*

Lauren (Bard)
A full Master Bard, Lauren played the gittern and was accomplished at Healing-music, using it to try to ease the bone aches of his long-time friend, Kemoc. *(Oath)*

Law-Keepers
The official title of the Haighlei mages. *(Gryphon)*

Law-Slayers
A Haighlei slang term for criminals. *(Gryphon)*

Laylan (Companion)
Rubrik's Companion. *(Storm)*

Leafspear
The Tayledras elder who united Snowfire and Nightwind in formal partnership. *(Owl)*

Leamount (Lord)
The rough-hewn provincial noble that Queen Sursha selected as General-in-Chief to lead her forces against her usurper brother-in-law Declin Lord Kelers. *(Oath)*

Leana
A volatile noblewoman, she was the focus of much concern at court. Leana had a hot temper and her husband of one year was having an affair. It was feared that she might do something reckless, and that sooner or later a violent confrontation was likely to take place. *(BB)*

Leander
The name of one of two morning stars visible from Valdemar, the other is Lythan. *(LHM)*

Leander
The miller and baker of Errold's Grove. *(Owl)*

Leareth

One of the incarnations of Ma'ar, he took the Tayledras word for "darkness" as his name. Lord Rendan's gang knew him as Master Dark. Leareth is the Mage in Vanyel's fever dreams, an evil and too-perfect mirror image of Vanyel himself. In later dreams, after Vanyel has lifebonded to Stefen, Leareth reappears, and though the details of the dream have changed, the menace of the Dark Mage is still powerful. He is at the core of the prophetic visions which the Tayledras tell Vanyel are possible futures, though not inevitable ones. Leareth had been operating in the northern lands for a very long time, at least before Queen Elspeth was born. Desiring to expand his territory into Valdemar, Leareth attempted to subvert the Heralds, but without any success. He decided to destroy them one at a time, beginning with the Herald-Mages, who represented the biggest threat to him. He is responsible for the fact that no children with Mage-Gift have been Chosen in Valdemar for some time; Leareth has been killing any children who exhibit such Mage-Gifts while they are too young to be Chosen, disguising the attacks as accidents or illnesses. When Leareth prepared to invade Valdemar, he gathered his forces of black armored men and strange beasts and marched them down a Mage-made pass through the mountains to Valdemar's border. To abet his strength, Leareth employed other mages, and he sent these before him to confront Vanyel at Crookback Pass. When the Herald-Mage had defeated each of the enemy mages, Leareth offered his temptations to Vanyel. When the Herald-Mage refused his offer, he attacked, knowing Vanyel's strength was partially spent and would no longer be a match for his own. He did not count on Yfandes returning to combine her powers with Vanyel's in a Final Strike to destroy Leareth and his army and save Valdemar. *(LHM)*

Leech-blade

An ensorceled weapon designed to steal life gradually if it does not kill outright. A scratch can be fatal, and removing it without using the proper counterspell can be equally deadly. *(LHM)*

Leeside Park
A popular park in Haven known for recreational riding; in winter its central pond is used for skating parties. *(BB)*

Leland
A young mage who attempted to summon and bind the imp Talhkarsh from the Abyssal Planes. By mistake he called the powerful and dangerous demon Thalhkarsh, and paid for the error with his life. *(Oath)*

Lellian (Bard)
A Bard who specializes in music for funerary ceremonies. *(Exile)*

Lena
The niece of the silk merchant Grumio, his only heir, and the sole survivor of his brother's plague-ravaged family. She was captured by bandits along with a dozen other maidens while traveling with one of her uncle's packtrains. He had no hope she was still alive, but hired Tarma and Kethry to take revenge on those who kidnapped Lena and other young women. *(Oath)*

Lendori
A group of people with a dispute which King Randale needed to rule upon at Vanyel's request. The Lendori were offered a contract to supply the Valdemar Guard with mules if they in turn ceded water rights to Balderston. *(LHM)*

Lenne (Master)
The Master of the Tanner's Guild Hall in the supply village outside Hawk's Nest. Formerly a herder, he had a strong love for the land, and because of that had a great loathing for Master Karden's noxious neighboring tannery. Lenne was being magically poisoned by Karden, but Kethry discovered the means of the attacks and turned the poison back on the poisoner. *(Oath)*

Lenore
Kerowyn's mother, who died three years before Lordan's wedding. The youngest of Kethry's children, she disliked the Plains and exhibited no mage talent. Fostered with the Lythand family, she was suited for lady-

ship and nothing else, much to Kethry's disappointment. At first courted by the repulsive Baron-to-be Reichert, Lenore escaped his clutches when Rathgar showed up at the Keep. She fell madly in love with him, and other than his hostile attitude toward mages, he was perfect for her. *(Sword)*

Leodhan (High King)
The ruler of Predain, he was killed by the fear-spell dyrstaf, clearing the way for Ma'ar to take control of Leodhan's realm. *(Gryphons)*

Lerchbush
Valued medicinal plants that grow in thickets. Keisha harvested their buds by taking every third one and sealing the knife cut with pitch to heal the plant and encourage its further growth. *(Owl)*

Leren Benevy (Father)
Priest for the Ashkevron estate during Vanyel's time, he was a cleric of the narrowest religious outlook. Father Leren once attempted to kill Vanyel, but Armsmaster Jervis stopped him, saving Vanyel's life. Father Leren confessed to working for the Mavelan family, but he was also controlled by some other evil power. He was killed while in his cell, his stomach torn out by an unknown assailant, before that power was located. *(LHM)*

Lerry
A young Herald who had been riding circuit in the Fells, he joined Pol's group for supper at the Collegium to trade gossip. *(BB)*

Lerryn Twoblades
The son of Justin Twoblades and the Captain of the Skybolts when Kerowyn joined the mercenary company. He didn't look like a fighter, but Lerryn was whipcord and steel over bone. His brown eyes missed nothing, and his foppish curls covered a good brain. He could ride any horse in camp, including Kerowyn's battlesteed, which was a surprise both to the mare and Kerowyn. Lerryn wore a silver pin of two crossed swords bisected by a lightning bolt as his badge of rank. He was killed

by the Karsites along with one of the groups of Skybolts that had split up to try and lose their pursuers. *(Sword)*

Leshara

The family involved in a mortal feud with Tylendel Frelennye's family. The matter had been escalating for some time, with raids and counter-raids and wizards hired to do revenge work. The head of the Leshara family was Wester, whose youngest son was killed during a raid by the Frelennyes. To get back at his enemies, he hired a conjuror to convince Tylendel's recently widowed mother that the spirit of her husband was trying to contact her. Her desire to reach the other side and join him drove her insane and led to her death. Tylendel's worst foe at Court was Evan Leshara, who tried to get information from Vanyel he could use against the Frelennyes. When that was unsuccessful, the Lesharas arranged an ambush, killing Tylendel's twin Staven and precipitating a crisis that led to Tyndale calling up *wyrsa* into the Leshara stronghold on Sovvan-night. Evan Leshara died in that onslaught, and Tylendel in its aftermath. It took all the skill of Queen's Own Herald Lancir to settle the feud between the surviving members of the two families and end the senseless vengeance. *(LHM)*

Leshia (Queen)

The daughter of King Tavist, Queen of Valdemar. *(LHM)*

Leshya

A Kaled'a'in and Tayledras word meaning "spirit." See K'Leshya. *(Gryphon, Winds, LHM)*

Leshya (Companion)

The true name of the Companion who Chose Tashir Remoerdis, though the young stallion was so traumatized by the events that occurred when he arrived in Highjorune that he couldn't communicate it. Yfandes and the others referred to the Companion as Ghost until he could compose himself and provide them with his name. *(LHM)*

Leshya'e

The Shin'a'in term for a helpful spirit. Used particularly

with the *leshya'e* Kal'enedral and in reference to avatars of the gods, among them Companions. *(Oath)*

Leshya'e horses
What the Shin'a'in call Companions. *(Winds)*

Leshya'e Kal'enedral
Spirit Swordsworn and Teachers of the living Swordsworn. They are spirits who can be quite solid and real, as their students learn painfully during their lessons in swordplay. Their voices have a hollow quality, they dress in black and are veiled. Tarma was trained nightly by these *leshya'e* Kal'enedral when she was not indoors. *(Storm, Winds)*

Leslac
The Bard who was the bane of Tarma and Kethry's lives, though Warrl rather liked him. Leslac wrote a famous song, "Threes," which described Tarma's and Kethry's victory over caravan raiders. The ballad annoyed them with its exaggerations and inaccuracies, and made it difficult for them to get work. He irritated Tarma further by composing "The Sword-lady." Intended as a love tribute, it had the opposite effect on her. Tarma generally referred to it as "That Song." King Stefansen and Herald Roald helped their friends get revenge by maneuvering the troublesome Bard into a "sword-point" marriage in Valdemar. *(Oath)*

Lesser Battle Magics
When opposing armies' mages have exhausted their Great Battle Magics, they resort to lesser ones. In these, neither can see what the other is doing, and neither can let down their guards and shields long enough to recharge or to try any remaining Greater Spells. *(Oath)*

Lethe
A highly narcotic wine, it was the downfall of an aged half-blind mage that the ensorceled Lastel Longknife hired to remove the spell placed on him by Kethry as punishment for his crimes. *(Oath)*

Lethra
One of Sewen's sargeants. *(Oath)*

Levand (Page)
The page boy who brought Dean Elcarth the alarming news that a riot had taken place between the Bardic students and the Unaffiliates over the Lady Fountain prank. *(Arrows)*

Leverand
One of the first kings of Rethwellan went to this mage school. He bespelled the Royal Archives of the kingdom, ensuring that what was written therein could not be altered or removed. *(Oath)*

Levinbolt
A sorcery-directed attack of pure energy which can be deflected harmlessly by a skilled mage or a well-trained student mage. *(LHM, Winds)*

Levris
An elderly veteran, he was the Quartermaster assigned to the offices of the Guard during Queen Selenay's reign, in charge of issuing supplies for Herald missions. *(Arrows)*

Levy (Master)
The Master Artificer who worked with Master Tam to study the area around Haven for anomalies. He sent out teams to measure, collect, and collate information, trying to fight the Mage-Storms with science. Levy was a mathematician, and worked out a prediction of the Mage-Storms' time sequence and the places where waves of magic would intersect to cause Change-circles. *(Owl, Storm)*

Ley-lines
Invisible streams of magical power, they criss-cross the land and are only visible to those with Mage talent. Ley-line power is hard to control because the ley-line energy is moving. Masters and Adepts can tap into the ley-lines, and Adepts can change ley-line channels, thus using that power to strengthen nodes and build repositories of arcane energies. The Tayledras Adepts organize ley-lines to replenish their Vales' Heartstones. Other mages use ley-line energy to power spells. Energy not used will eventually drain away to the Void. *(BV)*

Leyuet

A Haighlei Truthsayer and King Shalaman's Chief Priest. Under strong religious auspices, Leyuet could read the soul of someone being questioned. Originally hostile to the strangers from White Gryphon, in time he became one of their allies. *(Gryphon)*

Liam

A young man in the traveling carnival who was assaulted by Ancar's Elite Guards. Gerdo, Sara and Firesong helped him come to terms with the incident. *(Winds)*

Liam (Healer)

A Healer who was part of the Court in Vanyel's time. When a messenger brought news of the Karsites new anti-mage campaign, Liam immediately demanded to know which Karsite priesthood was controlling the dangerous crusade. *(LHM)*

Liaven Cedrys

The son of Lady Cedrys of Briary Holding, he was interested only in weaponry and swordplay, but was forced toward a scholarly vocation by his book-loving mother. In the end, he ran away, joined a mercenary company, and was never seen again. *(LHM)*

Liers

A young courtier who waxed eloquent about his brother's bravery in battle, behavior which Vanyel maintained was stupidity, not valor. *(LHM)*

Life-debt

A very serious matter among the Northern tribes, it refers to a debt owed to someone responsible for saving that person's life. Unless it is repaid, the life-debt will hold back the bearer socially and personally in many ways; he cannot even court or marry until the debt is discharged. Hywel felt he owed a life-debt to Keisha and Darian for saving his brother and insisted that being their guide on the northern expedition was his life-debt duty. *(Owl)*

Life-energy lights

They illuminate the caves of the Hot Springs Clan of *kyree*. The glow balls are different colors, shining with the last life-energy of the *kyree* who created them for the benefit of their survivors. Blue lights were Mages, green were Healers, yellow were those who had been god-touched, and red those who primarily possessed Mind-magic. *(LHM)*

Lightfoot
The Sunhawk Jodi's mount, a cross-bred grey mare, part Shin'a'in, part mountain pony. Quiet as a shadow, she is a near-twin in appearance to Hellsbane. *(Oath)*

Lightwing
A Tayledras scout. *(Winds)*

li'ha'eer
A Shin'ai'in exclamation meaning "by the gods." *(Oath)*

Liha'irden
The Deer Clan of the Shin'a'in, their name literally means "deer-footed." They helped, healed, and protected Tarma after the slaughter of her own Clan, and were guardians of Tale'sedrin herds and assets while Tarma pursued her revenge and built her reputation. *(Oath)*

Lilly
The barmaid and sometime prostitute at Errold's Grove tavern who was slandered by village gossips. When the barbarians came, she served one of the invader's officers, both to preserve her life and to keep the barbarians' attention from the other girls. After the Blood Bear barbarians were defeated, she decided to leave Errold's Grove and go into business for herself as an inn owner so that she could make a clean start untarnished by her past. *(Owl)*

Lily
A kestra'chern with Urtho's forces. *(Gryphons)*

Lineas
An ally of Valdemar, it lies on the country's western border, with Baires to its north. Lineas' capital is Highjorune, the seat of its Palace, ruled by the clan Remoerdis, headed by Deveran. After a long period of strife, Lineas agreed to peace with Baires, sealing the

bargain by marrying Deveran to Ylyna Mavelan of Baires. The couple had a son named Tashir. After the incident at the palace when every Remoerdis except Tashir was killed, he became sole heir to both countries. A contract between Lineas and Baires stated that if one family died out by means other than provable assassination, then the heir of the other family would inherit both kingdoms. In reality, the Mavelans planted an assassination device they thought would also kill Tashir. When this failed, they accused the boy of murder and tried to take the throne. Vanyel discovered the device in his investigation of the incident and triggered it back onto the Mavelans, effectively wiping them out. Tashir now ruled both countries with the backing of Valdemar. When the Lineas' line of succession died out, the land was absorbed into Valdemar along with Baires. *(LHM)*

Linnay (Lady)
An ineffectual old noblewoman murdered by Hadanel-ith. *(Gryphon)*

Lion Lilies
A symbolic gift from a Haighlei monarch to a woman he regards highly. They are large, tawny gold flowers with a heavy fragrance. Three lilies signify interest, four a serious courtship, and a dozen, with an accompanying betrothal necklace, a firm proposal of marriage. *(Gryphon)*

Lion Throne
The traditional governing seat of the Emperor in Khimbata. *(Gryphon)*

Lionwind
K'Leshya's Clan Chief, and an "old soul." His parents were both shamans, and he is a Mindhealer. His mount is a warmare. *(Gryphon)*

Li'sa'eer
A Shin'a'in exclamation of highest surprise, literally, "by the highest gods!" *(Oath)*

Lisha (Herald)
One of the three Heralds serving as escorts for the k'Sheyna party. *(Winds)*

Liss
One of the Third Form students at the Merchants' School, she decided to follow the lead Lavan and Owyn set by boycotting the school dining hall to avoid their Sixth Form tormentors. *(BB)*

Lissandra (Herald-Mage)
The Herald-Mage who, with her Companion Shonsea, anchored the North in Vanyel's setting of the new Web-Spell. Lissandra had assumed Guardianship of the North along with her Whites. Close to achieving Adept status, she was also a specialist in alchemy, poisons, and antidotes. A victim of Leareth, she was killed in her lab, apparently from an accident involving the chemicals she was working with. Her Companion died at the same moment in the northern end of the Companion's Field. *(LHM)*

Little-death
A *kyree* ability to enter a trance that closely resembles death. Warrl used this trick to fool Thalhkarsh into believing he was dead. *(Oath)*

Little gods
A reference to ancestor veneration used in the Empire. In its higher form it honors all previous Emperors and their Consorts. Sometimes phrased as "the forty little gods" or "the hundred little gods," neither is an accurate number. *(Storm)*

Littles
Common Valdemaran term for children. *(BV)*

Locasti Perken
A member of the Haven City Guard, she was recruited to be one of Princess Selenay's Personal Guards during the Tedrel Wars. *(Exile)*

Lodella
Predatory creatures with fuzzy tails, dorsal spines, hairless heads, and a sensitivity to magic. Two of these creatures were attracted when Darkwind spellcast messenger birds, and had to be dealt with. *(Winds)*

Loden
A town on the South Trade Road near the border. During the Mage-Storms a bridge there was destroyed by the peculiarly violent weather assaulting Valdemar at the time. *(Storm)*

Loman Strecker
One of the Sixth Form bullies, nicknamed Loathsome by Lavan. *(BB)*

Londell River
The river that runs through the eastern edge of Errold's Grove, and the main watercourse serving the village. In addition, its banks provide clay for the town's pottery needs. *(Owl)*

Londer Galko
Skif's uncle, his mother's brother, who took in young Skif after his mother died—though only because he was hoping to make a profit out of the deal. Londer had his finger in many of the illicit activities that went on in the poorer parts of Haven. An abusive and venal man, Londer often commented that if Skif were not already on the school rolls he would have gladly sold him to the slavers. This was no idle threat—Londer had an arrangement with the slavers to use his warehouse for temporary storage of captives. Loader would sacrifice any member of his family if it would advance his fortunes in some way, and let his injured son die in jail to take the heat for the troubles at the *Hollybush* tavern. *(TT)*

Long Meadow
The main pasturage at Forst Reach. Lord Withen was outraged when his son Mekeal put sheep there, ousting his prize cattle. *(LHM)*

Long Walk, The
A euphemism for Death. *(BV)*

Lord Holder
A rank of nobility in Valdemar. Withen Ashkevron holds this title. His tenants farm for him and peasants hold their lands under his protection and governance. Withen often lectured Vanyel on his future duties as

Lord Holder, a title and job Vanyel was glad to eventually yield to his brother Mekeal. *(LHM)*

Lordan
Kerowyn's brother and Dierna Brodey's bridegroom. He was badly injured during the wedding feast massacre, though he eventually, thanks to Kerowyn and Kethry, recovered to wed Dierna. *(Sword)*

Loren
A Kestra'chern in Urtho's army assigned to work with the Healers putting together packs of supplies for evacuees going through the Gates to safety before the Cataclysm. *(Gryphon)*

Loren (Commander)
An officer who asked Urtho to reward one of the gryphons under his command. *(Gryphons)*

Loren (Master)
A teacher at the White Winds school when Kethry was training there. Mara Yveda once stole Master Loren's staff under the mistaken belief that it was magical. *(Oath)*

Lorenil (Companion)
Sendar's Companion, killed alongside King Sendar during the last battle of the Tedrel Wars. *(Exile)*

Lores (Herald)
King Randale's envoy to the Court of Lineas. A witness to events which triggered a massacre of the Linean royal house, or so it was assumed. Lores was spellbound and made to believe the sole survivor of the debacle, Tashir Remoerdis, was the culprit. Despite the fact that Tashir had just been Chosen by the Companion Leshya, Lores was determined to destroy both, thinking Tashir was a murderer and the Companion was a demon Tashir had summoned. The Herald's attack on the pair drove his own Companion, Jenna, nearly mad with her inability to act against her Chosen or to go to the aid of the ones Lores was striking with his whip. Vanyel and Yfandes were able to stop the Herald before it was too late. *(LHM)*

Loriganalea

The Haighlei word for lifebonded, which in their culture also means sacred and sealed by the gods. Trying to break such a bond would bring the curse of the ages on the perpetrator or anyone who helped him or did not aid the bonded ones. If the bondbreaker was a ruler, the curse would fall on his entire people as well as upon him. *(Gryphons)*

Loris (Healer)

A Healer who assisted Healer Kerithwyn in treating plague victims during Talia's internship in the northern sector. *(Arrows)*

Lorn and Rellan

A *hertasi* couple who had recently moved out of a water-line marsh home because it flooded every spring. They gave the empty tunnel to Nyara to use during her recuperation. *(Winds)*

Lorshallen

A Kestra'chern who took Amberdrake as his apprentice on Silver Veil's recommendation. Lorshallen was already old then and virtually retired. His Gifts were Healing and Empathy. *(Gryphons)*

Loschal (Mayor)

The Mayor of Trevendale, he was nominated by Talia to be Lord Gartheser's replacement as speaker for the North on the Queen's Council. *(Arrows)*

Losh

A Skybolt appointed to command the horse-archers after Dende was put on sick leave because of fever. *(Sword)*

Loshi

A *hertasi* who was particularly attached to Darian and Keisha. *(Owl)*

Losita

A Kestra'chern in the service of Urtho's army. On a day she had pulled a muscle, Gesten arranged for her usual clients to be treated by Amberdrake. *(Gryphon)*

Lothar (Prince)
The Ruler of Ruvan, he was often called "the Looney," although never to his face. After the disaster at the Temple of Thalhkarsh, Lothar decreed human sacrifice punishable by enslavement. *(Oath)*

Lother
Apprentice to Henkeir Told-True, the Snow Fox Clan's shaman. *(Owls)*

Lotte
One of the Palace Guards, she was recruited to be one of Princess Selenay's Personal Guards during the Tedrel Wars. *(Exile)*

Loverhawk
A Tayledras endearment. *(Winds)*

Low Magic
The collective term for basic sorcery and earth-witchery, often scorned by snobbish High Magic-users. Although Low Magic spells are not powerful, they are useful for tasks such as water-finding and fire-making, among other things, and can be very effective when judiciously applied. In addition, these spells are often functional when little other magic is. Low Magic is hampered during the dormant season, when there is very little ambient energy available. *(Oath)*

Lurchan
A luck-god whose sect makes cursed coins. Lurchan's followers try to plant the counterluck talismans on the unsuspecting. The only way to get rid of the cursed coin is to have someone accept it of their own free will. *(Oath)*

Lursten
The *hertasi* Darkwind assigned the task of providing Elspeth with a wardrobe more practical for the Vale than her Whites. *(Winds)*

Lyam
The *hertasi* secretary to Tarrn, the *kyree* scholar. They both came to the ruins of Urtho's Tower to translate the ancient texts found there. *(Storms)*

Lyam
One of Kethry and Jadrek's children, and Laryn's twin. *(Oath)*

Lyan
One of Kethry and Jadrek's children. *(Oath)*

Lyavor
A town near Viden where travelers prefer to stay to avoid Lord Gorley's traveler taxes. *(Oath)*

Lyer
Winterlight's daytime bondbird, a snow-eagle. *(Winds)*

Lyla Stormcloud
She was a half-Shin'a'in mercenary from the far southeast, beyond even the Dhorisha Plains. Her father was a Hawkbrother and her mother a Full Bard. Thanks to an arrangement with the Tayledras of the Pelagiris Forest, she came north with astonishing speed to assist Kethry. *(Sword)*

Lyle
One of Bazie's boys when Skif joined the thieves' gang. He was an excellent pickpocket, but he eventually met a farm girl and settled down to an honest life. *(TT)*

Lynnell (Bard)
She brought Stefen to the Bardic Collegium when he was barely ten. The bewildered boy had no idea why this strange woman wearing red robes had plucked him off the street corner where he was performing. Lynnell was embarrassed when she learned the boy thought she was a procurer and had kidnapped him to sell to a *shaych* bordello. *(LHM)*

Lyonnes (Lady) Kalthea
One of the nobles who opened her manor to provide hospitality for the k'Sheyna group on their way to Haven. *(Winds)*

Lyosha
One of the Second Wing gryphons serving Urtho. She tried to flirt with Skan, but at that stage he was too absorbed in watching Zhaneel to notice her. *(Gryphons)*

Lyr
A flat-voiced, colorless woman, the head of all Skybolt scout groups. When the fleeing mercenary company was forced to split up to evade the pursuing Karsites, Kerowyn ended up with twenty riders led by Lyr. *(Sword)*

Lyra (Princess)
Princess of Valdemar, and the twin of Prince Kris, she is the daughter of Selenay and Daren. *(Winds)*

Lyris (Countess)
An older noblewoman at Raschar's court, she was a good source of information for Tarma and Kethry in their quest to discover what had happened to Idra. *(Oath)*

Lysle
The Herald-trainee assigned to help Ambassador Ulrich at the Palace. *(Storm)*

Lysle
The *hertasi* who helped Vikteren to his tent after the mage collapsed from overwork. *(Gryphon)*

Lytha
The gryphlet nest mate of Jervan and daughter of Treyvan and Hydona. *(Storm, Winds)*

Lythan
One of the two morning stars visible from Valdemar. The other is Leander. *(LHM)*

Lythands
The neighbors to Kerowyn's family Keep. Kethry's youngest daughter, Lenore, was fostered with the Lythands, and returned trained as a lady and uninterested in anything but dreams of romance and an idyllic life as a Keep Lady. *(Sword)*

Lythecare
The Jkathan town where Adept Jendar lives, though the mage-school he founded is in the Rethwellan city of Petras. He prefers to live in Jkatha, nearer his Shin'a'in relatives. He also refuses to live in Kata'shin'a'in because its fall and winter climate is so dry, and it lacks the luxuries he demands. *(Winds)*

Lytherill
One of Treesa's ladies, and an incurable chatterbox. She cornered Starwind until his bondbird drove her away. *(LHM)*

Lythiaren (Queen)
Queen of Rethwellan, her Royal House had mages in its bloodlines. When the anti-mage crusade began in Karse, it was soon realized that Lythiaren and her kin and realm might be in danger along with Valdemar. King Randale ordered his Seneschal to draft a letter to the Queen to inform her of the situation, offering an alliance against their hostile neighbor. Randale insisted that the message be carefully worded because Lythiaren didn't entirely trust him after "that mess with the Amarites." *(LHM)*

M

Maeven (Weatherwitch)
A resident of Berrybay who accidentally drowned her illegitimate baby. She went mad as a result. This tragedy also awoke her latent gift of weather clairvoyance. Her fellow villagers pitied her but valued her predictions. Maeven, thanks to Talia's insight, was made whole again when she adopted the orphaned gypsy baby Jethry. When Kris and Talia visited Waymeet again, Maeven had retained her weather clairvoyance and her sanity, and was being trained by the local priestess of Astera to succeed her. *(Arrows)*

Maffie Olan
He was a young bully in Errold's Grove who beat up Dib Dawkin. *(Owl)*

Mage of Silence
One of Urtho's titles. *(BV)*

Mage-barrier
A shimmering curtain of magical energy which allows Hawkbrothers, their allies, and harmless wildlife in while repulsing everything else. *(Winds)*

Mage-craft
The art of using magic. *(BV)*

Mage-fog
k'Sheyna Vale ran into this magical effect in a valley just beyond k'Sheyna's wild territory. It was a mottled blue-white colored cloud, thick and oily, and too murky

to see through. The mist rose and fell in a wavelike motion, leaving brown and withered vegetation in its wake. It was caustic and deadly for wildlife or humans to breathe. A bachelor herd of *dyheli* had become trapped by the fog, but Nyara saved them. *(Winds)*

Mage-Gift
The term for supernormal abilities possessed only by sorcerers, which may also include the Gifts known to Heralds, such as Thoughtsensing, Fetching, and Empathy, but generally involves the power to reach into nodes or ley-lines, or to draw energy from the surrounding world and from other beings, and use that energy to power magic. *(BV)*

Mage-glyph
A mage's magical signature. *(Oath)*

Mage-light
Illumination without fuel that is generated by the mage's own will, it can be dim or bright according to need, and hovers without fuel or support wherever the mage commands it. *(BV)*

Mage-raven
The construct specifically designed by Leareth to attack and kill Herald-Mage Savil. When Vanyel froze time and replayed it to witness the scene, he saw a tooth-beaked raven with evil red eyes and powerful legs ending in feet with sharp, hand-sized talons. The creature, disguised as wood brought for Savil's fireplace, penetrated a warded and shielded room to get at its prey. After killing Savil, it sought out and killed her Companion, Kellan. *(LHM)*

Mage-sight
The ability to literally See mage powers or magic potential in a living being as a glowing aura. *(LHM, Winds, Owl)*

Magic
An unnatural action or force caused by powers outside those of ordinary human beings. There are four kinds of magic on Velgarth. The first is magic performed by Gifted individuals manipulating energy only they can see, like ley-lines or nodes. This is the kind of magic

used by Adept mages. The second kind of magic uses power that can be taken from other living things and the land itself, and is not dependent on a Gift to perform it, such as the magic utilized by blood-mages and hedge-wizards. The third kind of magic is Mind-magic—the paranormal abilities that Heralds have developed and utilized for centuries, including Fetching, Foresight, Far-sight, FireStarting, and so on. The fourth kind of magic in religious or shamanic magic powered by the interference of a deity in the natural world. Magic of all sorts is generally ranked according to whether it is Light or Dark, depending on the system of ethics involved in drawing the power for the magic, particularly for those who gain their power from other sources, and in how those working the magic use it. *(BV)*

Magnus
A child who lived in the village of Garthhold. He wanted to ask Vanyel how he had killed the colddrake, but the older woman tending the shaken youth shooed Magnus away, demanding that he let Vanyel recuperate. *(LHM)*

Magpie Clan
One of the Northern tribes. *(Owl)*

Maiden's Hope
A fragrant little deep-woods northern flower which blooms only for a week preceding and following Mid-summer's Day, a wreath of it was given out-of-season to Talia as a wedding present from Kris. *(Arrows)*

Maisie
The underage half-wit girl employed by Londer at the *Hollybush Tavern*. She was the sex-partner of Kalchan, and the reason he went to jail. After the raid on the *Hollybush*, Maisie was sent to the temples for care and education. *(TT)*

Makaar
The gryphons' vicious counterparts, cold-blooded flying beasts created by Ma'ar. They were designed to have short lives so that their breed would cycle through generations fast, enabling their creator to weed out defects quickly and experiment with new variants sooner. Ma-

kaar are completely obedient to their masters, and have no free will, no joy in life, and few emotions other than killing rage. They are faster than gryphons and have more endurance, but less intelligence. Even as they fought them, the gryphons pitied them. *(Gryphon, Storm)*

Makke
An elderly Haighlei servant assigned to the k'Leshya embassy from White Gryphon. She became very friendly with Zhaneel and the gryphlets. She was also a key source of information about the Haighlei Empire. *(Gryphon)*

Makus
The official cobbler of Errold's Grove. Known as Old Man Makus, he was one of the victims of the barbarian invaders. *(Owl)*

Mala
One of Tarma's Sunhawk scouts, she was wounded by an arrow while on patrol and taken to the company's Healer barely in time to save her life. *(Oath)*

Malcam
The *dyheli* stag Keisha rode on the northwestern expedition. *(Owl)*

Malken (Herald-trainee)
A nine-year-old Herald-trainee, Malken was Chosen by his Companion Hayke while very young. His powerful Gift of Foresight had awakened early, nearly driving him insane. After consultation with his Companion and the Collegium's specialist in Foresight, Herald Evan, it was decided to block the boy's Gift until he was older. *(BB)*

Mandatory Education Law
A law passed during King Randale's reign requiring that every child in Valdemar, highborn or low, was to be taught simple reading, writing, and numbers. Classes were to be held in the Temples in the mornings during winter from after harvest until first planting. This act made it the duty of each Lord Holder to ensure that the law was faithfully carried out. It signaled significant change in the lives of all Valdemarans. King Randale

was able to get this law passed because of the panic that resulted after the death of Queen Elspeth. Randale's argument was that an informed population that could read official proclamations would not be likely to panic. *(LHM)*

Manifestation

The term for an Adept mage's sorcerous image. Kethry's was a twenty-foot tall golden hawk with fiery wings. The enemy Adept she confronted in The Comb had a Manifestation of a winged snake, with scales and wing membranes glistening in shades of green and blue. The term is also used to describe the appearance of a deity or a deity's avatar. *(Oath, Storm, Winds)*

Manor-keep

The habitation of a local lord that usually includes a walled village and its surrounding farm fields and pasturages. *(Oath)*

Mara Yveda

A former schoolmate of Kethry's, Mara left the White Winds establishment in frustration, convinced that her fellow mages-in-training were hiding a talisman which would give its user complete mastery of sorcery. When Tarma and Kethry encountered her years later, she had gained the ability to shapechange into a bear, but at the cost of her sanity. She attacked Kethry, and Tarma killed her. *(Oath)*

Marak (Herald Lord Marshal)

The Lord Marshal's Herald during the reign of King Theran, he was badly injured during the initial battles on the Karsite front. Though expected to live, it was likely he would be out of action for a long time and might lose a leg, so he was replaced by Herald Turag. *(BB)*

Marble Office

Urtho's headquarters in his Tower. *(Gryphons)*

Mardic (Herald-Mage)

The protege of Herald-Mage Savil, Mardic was lifebonded to Herald-trainee Donni. Both Mardic and Donni were victims of a Karsite necromancer. In a desperate attempt to save a village under attack, Mardic and Donni called the flame generated by the mage to themselves, knowing it would result in a painful death. *(LHM)*

Margan
One of Tremane's mages posted outside Shonar. After the first Mage-Storm, he reported that circular pieces of land two and three cubits in diameter had been instantly transported from elsewhere: circles of desert, swamp, and forest now were in completely different locations. *(Storm)*

Margret (Housekeeper)
Savil's servant at Haven, she tidied up the Herald-Mage's rooms and was remarkably calm in the face of fallout from magic-working. *(LHM)*

Mariwell (Squire)
A very elderly Hardornen citizen who had intended to make an informal pledge and participate in the seisin ceremony with Tremane at Shonar, but had to delay his journey because of the hard winter. *(Storm)*

Marlina
One of the kestra'cherns who assisted with preparations for evacuating the noncombatants from Ka'venusho. *(Gryphon)*

Marsh-fever
An illness marked by bone aches and headaches. *(LHM)*

Master Bards
The most experienced Bards in the land, they are often members of the Bardic Circle. Along with their task of creating and preserving the musical heritage of the land, Master Bards write short dissertations on the derivation and meaning of popular songs, later used as teaching materials. Their writings were responsible in part for the suppression of the knowledge of magic in Valdemar. *(LHM, Winds)*

Master Dark
The name his hirelings gave their overlord Leareth. *(LHM)*

Master Spell
The spell cast by a self-testing mage of the White Winds School. It calls upon the Greater Wind of Air and Water, which are known as the Mutable Elements, and are much more difficult to control than the Stable Elements of a Journeyman's Spell. A Master Spell demands the ability and will to form the energy into mage-shapes named the Cup and the Mill. Its wind comes from all directions and enfolds the mage with a shell of force and shifting, opalescent light. *(Oath)*

Masters of Portals
The collective title of the Empire's mages. However, after the Mage-Storms began, they had great difficulty building and sustaining the Portals they were named for. *(Storms)*

Masters' Room
Presided over by Magister Henlin, it's where the Master Artificers meet and dine. Located in the Compass Rose Inn, it is separated from the main area by a curtain. *(Storms)*

Mavelan
The ruling family of Baires, a clan notable for its high number of mage-gifted members. Their leader is Lord Vedric, brother of Ylyna. Ylyna was given to Deveran Remoerdis of Lineas in a marriage alliance because she had no mage potential, and the Lineans abhor magic. After the massacre in the Linean palace, Vanyel's investigations led him to conclude the Mavelan Clan was behind it, wanting the Lineas lands so much that they risked a war with Forst Reach to obtain them. They were wiped out by their own assassination trap, which was meant to kill the entire Remoerdis family. *(LHM)*

Mavry (Herald)
Skif's year-mate at the Collegium. *(Arrows)*

Mayhew (Father)
He had passed along a warning to the boys and men of the village that the new Priestess Healer coming there knew how to defend herself. *(Oath)*

Ma'ar

Also known as the Mage of Black Fire, his full name is Kiyamvir, Urtho's mortal enemy, and his only equal in magic. Even as a youth, Ma'ar lusted for power, particularly over people. He united dozens of warring tribes, calling them his Superior Breed, and used them in his ruthless conquest of one realm after another. Defeated and about to be destroyed, he boasted that he had found a way to survive death, and would return again to torment Urtho's successors. He died in the explosion of his tower, which, together with the explosion of Urtho's tower, caused the Cataclysm. Ma'ar came back by usurping the bodies of his descendants, continuing his vendetta against gryphons and their allies. Two of his reincarnations were the Dark Mage Leareth and Mornelithe Falconsbane. (*Gryphon, LHM, Storm, Winds*)

Medren

The servant of Herald-Bard Jadus, he invited his master and Talia to share the staffers' Midwinter Eve celebration. (*Arrows*)

Medren Ashkevron, (Bard)

Mekeal Ashkevron's bastard son by Melenna, Lady Treesa's maid. When Vanyel discovered that Medren had the Bardic Gift, he convinced Mekeal to send the boy to the Collegium for training as a Bard. Medren spent his journeyman period in the wild northlands and returned to Haven by qualifying as Journeyman in the shortest time ever. Discovering Stefen's Wild Talent for singing away pain, Medren brought the young man to Vanyel in hopes Stefen's Gift could help the chronically ill King Randale. (*LHM*)

Meeren

The *hertasi* who adopted Darian and Keisha. (*Owl*)

Megan

The Garthhold village girl who brought tea to the Adepts while they were recovering from fighting the colddrakes. (*LHM*)

Megrarthon Jadrevalyn (King)

Son of Prince Stefansen and Lady Mertis. He was a baby

when Kethry and Tarma first saw him at Herald Roald's hunting lodge. Later, when Megrarthon became King of Rethwellan, he asked Tarma to train his youngest son, Darenthallis, in weaponry and warcraft. Megrarthon entered three state marriages, two of them loveless, and had a large brood of children, including eight daughters. His eldest son and heir, Faramentha, caused no trouble. Nor did the youngest son, Darenthallis. But the middle son, Karathanolan, was a spoiled bully who delighted in hounding Daren; Megrarthon was concerned that if the two remained in close proximity, sooner or later something serious, perhaps fatal, would happen to Daren. *(Sword)*

Megwyn (Companion)
One of Yfandes's foals. *(LHM)*

Meiline
A Karsite measurement of distance. For example, the Temple of Vkandis at Sunhame was four hundred meiline south of Haven. *(Storms)*

Melania
The White Winds Adept who taught Kethry to use magic. *(Oath)*

Melenna
Lady Treesa's maid, she was determined to seduce Vanyel. When that failed, and after he had left Forst Reach for Haven, she became involved with Vanyel's brother Mekeal, and bore him a bastard son, Medren. Years later, after she failed to win Vanyel a second time, she was appointed Castelaine of Tashir Remoerdis' palace at Highjorune in Lineas and eventually married Armsmaster Jervis. *(LHM)*

Melidy
Elspeth's original nurse, she had suffered what the Healers called a brainstorm, or stroke, two years before Talia's arrival at Haven. While Healers believed the elderly woman had completely recovered, Talia suspected Melidy had been left vulnerable. She discovered Hulda was dosing Melidy's medicine with powerful sleeping po-

tions and reinforced those with sly suggestions, giving Hulda complete access to the Heir. *(Exile, Arrows)*

Melles (Baron, Emperor)

A wealthy Baron at the Eastern Empire Court, titled but owning no lands. A ruthless, amoral, powerful Adept, Melles was both treacherous and merciless. A former chief Imperial assassin known as Emperor Charliss's Executioner, Melles had held a grudge against Grand Duke Tremane for decades, because when they were both army cadets, Tremane reported Melles' criminal behavior to their colonel, getting him thrown out of the corps. Years later, both were candidates for the Emperor's Successor. Tremane was chosen and given the task of successfully completing the stalled conquest of Hardorn, but was abandoned in Hardorn along with a large contingent of the Imperial Army when the Mage-Storms struck, and Melles was named High Lord Heir. Using his unique and terrible talents, Melles assured his rapid ascension as the twentieth Emperor to sit on the Iron Throne. *(Storm)*

Melly (Herald)

Instructor at the Collegium who taught History and Literature and also tutored the trainees who were having difficulties in those subjects. *(BB)*

Melody

A chestnut filly, she is the granddaughter of Vanyel's mare Star, the Herald-Mage's favorite mount before he was Chosen by Yfandes. Vanyel made presents of Star's children to kin and friends, and Melody was his gift to Bard Stefen. *(LHM)*

Menfree

A grateful Garthhold woman who found Vanyel after he had saved their small community from the colddrake queen. *(LHM)*

Menmellith

A small buffer zone between Rethwellan and Karse, it is located in a small valley surrounded by protective steep mountains. The area was granted semi-autonomous status by King Megrarthon shortly after his son Daren was born. After constant harassment by raiders from Karse, the Menmellith Council hired four mercenary Companies, one of which was the Skybolts, to eradicate these bandits. *(Arrows, Sword, Oath)*

Meralis and the Werebeast

A cautionary fable Tarma and Kethry used to convince the new bride Darthela that she was lucky to have a sensible husband like Sir Skolte. *(Oath)*

Mercenary Code

A code of ethics and behavior enforced by the Mercenary Guild that all honorable mercenaries follow. The tenets of the Mercenary Code include: the terms of a contract will be honored by both parties; bonded Companies must not pillage in their employer's country, and may pillage while in enemy territory only with a hirer's permission; bonded Companies cannot switch sides in mid-contract; promise not to instigate a mutiny against an employer; and won't fight for a suicidal cause. If a bonded Company or one of its members surrenders, they are permitted to leave the battlefield and retire to a neutral point to be ransomed by the Guild, with the amount it takes to ransom them to be deducted from their accumulated Guild dues. The Mercenary Code also includes the ritual of Oathbreaking and Outcasting, which requires a priest, mage, and honest man, all of whom must have suffered personal, irreparable harm at the offender's hands. One of the oldest parts of the Code involves the right of a Company that has lost more than half its officers and a third of its fighters to put the Captaincy to a vote from the ranks. When Kerowyn resigned, the Skybolts exercised that right, voting Ardana out and replacing her with Kerowyn. *(Oath, Sword)*

Mercenary Guild

This guild regulates licensed and bonded mercenaries. A bonded Company posts a surety bond with the Guild on top of each members' individual dues. The bond guarantees the entire Company will follow the Mercenary Code. Violations allow an injured party to collect damages, which are taken out of the bond. The Guild then exacts its own punishment, up to and including fines and a penalty forbidding an offender to hire bonded fighters again for at least a year. Guild members wear a Guild badge to advertise their affiliation and make sure that their rights are recognized and honored. During the reign of one of the Sons of the Sun, Karse kicked the Guild out and failed to honor the Guild Code. Under Solaris, the Guild is slowly reintegrating itself into the country. *(BV)*

Mercenary Guild Company

A registered and bonded commercial fighting outfit such as Idra's Sunhawks or Kerowyn's Skybolts. *(Oath, Sword)*

Merchants' School

A school created by the Merchant and Craft Guilds to educate their children with a curriculum unique to the Guilds' needs: for example, in-depth geography lessons with emphasis on the major trade routes and sociology lessons detailing the needs and wants of different cultures. Parents paid the school well and expected professional supervision and instruction in career choices. Instead, the schoolmaster and his subordinates ignored their charges and allowed the Sixth Form bullies to dominate the establishment. After the fatal accident involving Lavan Chitward, Heralds took over the school in the name of the Crown, reorganized the faculty, and reopened it with instructors and staff capable of fulfilling the charter of the school. *(BB)*

Meree

The *dyheli* Keisha rode from Errold's Grove to k'Valdemar Vale, and who exchanged information with her on herbs and healing. *(Owl)*

Merili

Ten-year-old daughter of Archduke Tilden, and Kira's twin, she is gifted in languages, a graceful dancer, an accomplished needleworker, and has a strong interest in herbalism. Thought of by the boys at school as "Little Princess," she is already semi-engaged and life-bonded to Prince Albayah, the eldest son of Jkatha's Queen. *(Oath)*

Mero
The Collegium's Cook during Queen Selenay's reign, he was a good-hearted taskmaster whose kitchen helpers always got the best part of the daily meals. Mero came from Three Rivers and was a monotheist, very fond of quoting homilies from the famous Book of the One. *(Arrows)*

Merthin
One of Vanyel's many cousins. *(LHM)*

Mertis (Lady, Queen)
Prince Stefansen's wife and the mother of Megrarthon, his first son, she truly loved her husband, and was a skilled and intelligent helpmate to him in regaining his rightful place on the throne. *(Oath)*

Mertun
One of Melles' secretaries, he was assigned to organize requisitions of beasts of burden and vehicles after the Mage-Storms began to worsen. *(Storms)*

Messenger birds
Brightly colored avians with small, plump bodies and a noisy cry. They were excellent mimics, and could repeat a message exactly as the sender gave it to them. They were used as messengers in the enormous camp surrounding Urtho's Tower and by the Tayledras. *(BV)*

Mical (Herald)
His youthful bout with Bard-trainee Adain shattered one of the Collegium's expensive mirrors in the training salle. Mical learned his lesson that day about taking life seriously. As a young Herald-Trainee, he was very athletic, and became part of Alberich's Herald-trainee team responsible for thwarting the assassination of Queen Selenay. Mical faced near-certain death as he tried to block Norris's death-blow aimed at the Queen. He succeeded in blocking the blow, and survived. Partnered with Companion Eloran. *(Exile)*

Midsummer Gathering
A celebration among the Northern Clans where they all assemble once a year under a flag of truce. It is an opportunity for the tribes to trade, learn from one another,

and meet potential mates. It was called off after the Summer Fever struck, and resumed only after the cure Keisha discovered became widely available. *(Owl)*

Midsummer's Eve
Usually associated with a day of ribald celebration, it is also Talia's birthing day. Among the Holderkin, Midsummer's Eve is associated with taboo and arcane things. Keldar Firstwife thought Talia's birthing day was a possible explanation for the child's intractable behavior. *(Arrows)*

Midwinter Fairs
These begin the day after Midwinter Feast, and run for the next seven days. *(BB)*

Midwinter Feast
On the winter solstice, a large feast is traditionally held for friends and families. *(BB)*

Midwinter Festival
Also known as Midwinter Holiday, the winter solstice is celebrated throughout most of Valdemar with gift-giving and parties. The revelry at the Palace lasts three months, with Collegium classes suspended and family visits arranged. The actual festival takes place for two weeks in the middle of the general period of rejoicing. *(BV)*

Migration, The
The term the White Gryphon population gave to their long trek via two Gates which eventually brought them to the western coast. *(Gryphon)*

Mind-magic
What outlanders call Valdemar's magic. *(Oath, Storms)*

Mind-mate
Warrl's nickname for Tarma. *(Oath)*

Mindspeaker
The term for someone who can communicate directly to another person's mind without verbal speech. Many Heralds are able to do this. The majority of those with the skill form their strongest Mindspeaking bonds with their Companions. Also known as Mindspeech, the skill is closely related to the talents known as Mindtouching,

Mindreaching, Mindcalling, and Farspeaking. *(Arrows, BB, LHM, BV)*

Minstrels
Performers who lack the Bardic Gifts, but who have sufficient musical talent to be in demand as performers strictly on the basis of the sound of their music. They haven't the mind-Gift that allows true Bards to sway the audience's thoughts by manipulating them, and achieve their fame and livelihood based solely on their musicianship and charisma. *(LHM)*

Miranda thorn
An assassination tool created by Ma'ar and used by Conn Levas as a poison dart on Urtho. It has no antidote, and causes hallucinations and great pain before the victim finally dies. *(Gryphon)*

Mirilin (Herald)
One of Princess Selenay's mentors, he asked her to accompany him as he dispensed justice in the civic courts in the city of Haven. Partner to Companion Estan. *(Exile)*

Mirror-egg
A Mind-magic technique Herald and Heir Roald taught Kethry. The mirror is an egg-shaped shield that is completely reflective on the inside. In Valdemar, Heralds use it when a trainee with the Projective Gift refuses to lock his mind-Gift down or uses it harmfully; inside the mirror-egg, everything projected is reflected back at the projector. Kethry found a way to adapt the technique magically as a Mage-trap and used it to trap Raschar's mages before they could attack the troops fighting to avenge Idra and put Prince Stefanson on the throne of Rethwellan. *(Oath)*

Misborn constructs
Mage-created beasts that chased Elspeth, Skif, Gwena, and Cymry from the Plains. These constructs looked like cattle with horny plates covering their bodies. Each was as tall as a warhorse, with swept-back horns, slitted eyes, fangs, clawed hooves, and front legs that move like a dog's. *(Winds)*

M'laud
Senior Healer of Urtho's forces. *(Gryphons)*

Mocker-birds
A bird common throughout Forst Reach, its call varies between a shriek and pleasant singing, and often imitates sounds the bird has heard. *(LHM)*

Moll
The drunken cook at the Hollybush tavern. *(TT)*

Mona (Herald-trainee)
One of Lan's classmates in Herald Artero's Field Investigations course. *(BB)*

Monarch's Own
The title of the Herald Chosen to become the closest friend and advisor of Valdemar's ruler. The position has existed since the first days of the Herald-Companion relationships, and it is a position of such special trust that it requires an extraordinary Herald to fill it. A new Monarch's Own is Chosen by the Companion of the last Monarch's Own Herald to occupy that position, which is held for the Herald's lifetime. The character strength and honesty of the Monarch's Own is the reason why Valdemar has suffered so little strife through the centuries, compared with its neighboring kingdoms. A monarch with such a trusted friend is much better able to withstand the stresses of ruling and steer a moral course in difficult times. *(LHM, Arrows)*

Moon-Steeds
In Valdermaran religion, they are the magical horses that draw the Lady's Chariot. *(Arrows)*

Moon-days
A term that refers to the time of women's menstruation, it is also known as the Moon-time. *(BV)*

Moondance k'Treva
A Tayledras Healer-Adept. He was born as Tallo, and brought to the Pelagirs by Savil when he was a young man. Tallo discovered he was a Mage by reading books. He fell in love with a gleeman, and called down lightning to frighten his lover after he was rejected by him. The

lightning went out of Tallo's control and killed the gleeman, so the horrified Tallo tried to take his own life.
Savil found the dying boy and took him to the Hawkbrothers to be healed. Tallo gradually came to forgive
himself, and took the use-name of Moondance. Moondance lifebonded to Starwind, and was one of Vanyel's
Tayledras teachers. Moonwind came to Forst Reach to
save Vanyel from an ensorcelled leech-blade. While
there, he was able to make Withen Ashkevron forgive
Vanyel for his sexual orientation, and reach out to embrace his son. Moondance and Starwind adopted and
raised one of Vanyel's children, Brightstar. *(LHM)*

Moon-flower
A botanical which can be made into a powder controlling a woman's moon-days, and also prevents pregnancy. *(Sword)*

Moon-trout
These were a special treat for Zhaneel, who was very
fond of the fish—preferring them fresh, by which she
meant still wiggling. *(Gryphon)*

Moonmist k'Sheyna
A Tayledras scout who ran into a basilisk on her patrol. *(Winds)*

Moonpaths
The name for the Shin'a'in spirit realms. Any clan member who seeks the paths with unselfish intent and concentration can walk them at night under the full moon.
Swordsworn can walk the Moonpaths any night and can
call and be answered by *Leshya'e* Kal'enedral, the spirit-
warriors. Shamans may also walk into this spirit world
whenever they choose and speak with any spirits there,
if any are willing to reply. *(BV)*

Moonshadow
The infant daughter of Snowfire and Nightwind. *(Owl)*

Moonsong k'Vala
A Tayledras Adept who directed Tarma where to find
the Liha'irden Clan, and predicted Kethry's future relationship with Need. *(Oath)*

Moonwing
The Tayledras mage who, after the k'Sheyna Heartstone disaster, changed her use-name to Silence and became a recluse. *(Winds)*

Mornedealth
The Jkathan city where Kethry grew up. Bounded by forests, timber is its staple in trade. The outer walls, two stories tall and as strong as stone, are a monument to ingenious wood-workers. These towering barriers were designed to keep forest beasts out, especially in winter. *(Oath)*

Mornelithe Falconsbane
The last incarnation of Ma'ar, a powerful, ruthless blood-path Adept, who lived during the reign of Queen Selenay. His name is Kaled'a'in, meaning "Hatred-That-Returns," emphasizing the many times he has been reborn throughout the centuries since he was destroyed by the gryphon Skandranon, since then, he has always sought revenge, particularly on gryphons and descendents of the Kaled'a'in, the loyal allies of his ancient enemy Urtho. Other incarnations include Leareth, the mage Vanyel destroyed, along with his Dark Servants, during a Final Strike. Ma'ar found a way to hide his soul in the nether planes after death, waiting until one of his descendants learned and cast the Firespell. He would then steal the descendant's body, destroying its soul and substituting his own so that it could live again. Falconsbane took the body of a young Shin'a'in runaway named An'desha, but this time the victim's soul stayed in place, hiding from Mornelithe. During this life, Mornelithe fathered, experimented on, and abused the Change-child Nyara. He tested alterations upon her that he later employed on his own stolen body. His final form combined the features of a man and lynx, with tawny-gold hair, canine teeth, and gold-green slit-pupiled eyes. Mornelithe was responsible for the enslavement of Darkwind's father, Starblade, forcing Starblade to crack the k'Sheyna Vale Heartstone in an effort to steal its power for his own purposes. With the help of Nyara, Skif, Firesong, the Avatars of the Shin'a'in Goddess, Darkwind, Elspeth, and the sword Need, An'desha escaped his prison and reclaimed his body. Firesong chased Mornelithe's soul

into the nether plain and tore it apart, killing Ma'ar forever. *(Winds, Storm)*

Mount Thurlos
Along with Dellcrag, it marks a pass infamous in Valdemaran legend, the site of the last Herald-Mage Vanyel's valiant final stand against the hordes of Dark Servants and Leareth. *(Arrows)*

Mountain sickness
Caused by traveling at higher altitudes and the drop in barometric pressure, the symptoms are nausea, headaches, and shortness of breath. *(Owl)*

Movat
One of Urtho's Generals. *(Gryphons)*

Movement, The
Also known as the Citizens for Rights Group in the Empire, they tried to establish reforms in the Eastern Empire. Melles ordered his agents to use propaganda and rumor to establish him as "The People's Friend" and Emperor Charliss as "The Tyrant," to confuse the Movement and subvert its goals to his own. *(Storm)*

Mudders
The type of horses Lord Ashkevron loaned to Darkwind and Nyara for their ride to Haven. They are sturdy, duncolored, and big-boned with rough coats. They work well in mud. *(Winds)*

Muleteer
One of Hulda's seemingly endless stream of bedmates, all chosen for their physical prowess. He was dimwitted but had plenty of stamina. Ancar selected him for these qualities, and had him deliberately placed in Hulda's way so she would be occupied while Ancar pursued his own plans. *(Winds)*

Murfee
Also known as Old Man Murfee, he was the deceased owner of the inn at a small supply village near Hawk's Nest. *(Oath)*

My Lady
The beloved instrument of Herald-Bard Jadus, it was a

superbly made harp which he willed to Talia upon his death. As a wedding gift, Talia was looking for a harp for Herald Dirk, when she discovered the curious history of "My Lady." Originally created as the masterwork of a Master instrument builder, twin harps were commissioned by a pair of identical twin Master bards. The two harps were created out of the same tree, at the same time, and crafted by a master to be as identical as any two instruments could possibly be. After the death of their original owners, the two harps were separated, and one came into the hands of Herald Jadus and, after his death (Herald) Talia. Once she learned the story, Talia launched an extensive search, and was able to find "My Lady's" long-lost sibling, and reunite the pair of harps, providing a priceless and unique wedding gift for her beloved Herald Dirk. *(Arrows)*

Myrgan
One of Ouenten's apprentice mages, he was assigned to find a weapon that could strike Ancar's chief sorcerer. *(Sword)*

Myria (Lady)
Accused of slaying her husband, she was about to be burned at the stake in the village of Felwether when Tarma and Kethry rescued her. The lady was eventually exonerated by the efforts of the two oath-sisters. *(Oath)*

Myrim (Healer, Councilwoman)
The speaker for the Healer's Circle in council, she was not a supporter of Lord Orthallen, nor was she wholeheartedly in favor of the proposed marriage alliance between Valdemar (Elspeth) and Hardorn (Ancar). She was cautiously in favor of the betrothal if the Heir stayed at the Collegium until her training was complete. Her caution turned out to be warranted. *(Arrows)*

Myste (Herald-Chronicler)
The current keeper of the records of Valdemar, she wore bifocals and was romantically involved with Herald Alberich. Elspeth asked Myste to translate one of the Collegium's ancient mage books into modern language for her. *(Exile, TT, Winds)* Note: Myste bears a profound physical resemblance to Mercedes Lackey, as well as sharing her nickname. Hmmmm . . . *(BV)*

Nada

A Holderkin woman married to an abusive man, she was beaten every night and wore high-necked tunics to hide the bruises. She served as an example for girls like Talia, who feared what marriage might mean to a Holderkin female. *(Arrows)*

Mala Karcinamen

A junior-ranked Healer attached to Kerowyn's troops. *(Owl)*

Nandy Lutter

The most notorious gossip in Errold's Grove, she and her husband Derrel owned the only shop in town. They were also the only residents who regularly went to the outside world for trade goods the town could not make, giving them a monopoly on selling certain items to the village. *(Owl)*

Naril (Lady)

The noblewoman who ruthlessly toyed with Dirk's emotions to get to Kris. The Court beauty manipulated Dirk shamelessly, making him fall in love with her, then cruelly rejected him, nearly driving him to suicide. *(Arrows)*

Nathen (Herald)

A Herald posted to assist the fisherfolk of Lake Evendim, he was seriously injured fighting off a slaving raid by pirates. He impressed the Queen's Council when he reported that the brigands abetting the slavers were people Valdemar had previously banished. Nathen presented inarguable proof of a conspiracy involving many highborn and highly-placed people in the western sector. *(Arrows)*

Natoli
Herald Rubrik's daughter, she was a student artificer dedicated to the pursuit of science and engineering, and was romantically involved with, as well as intellectually attracted to, the Karsite envoy Karal. *(Storms)*

Neave (Herald)
A Herald-trainee Chosen by Companion Kyldathar, he was Talia's classmate in their Herald's Magic instruction group. His Gift was Projection. Before coming to Valdemar, Neave's early life had been a horror of physical and sexual abuse, which he inadvertently projected into the dreams of the other Herald trainees. He later developed this into a weapon, projecting those memories into the minds of evildoers. *(Arrows)*

Need
A magical, nearly indestructible short sword created in a desperate and successful sacrifice so long ago that the times of its origin have been lost from living memory. The blacksmith mage Lashan forged it, working into its metal powerful spells and prayers. She impaled herself on the blade when it became necessary to save the young female acolytes of her faith by joining her soul and the steel she'd forged into one spirit. Need serves only women, and refuses to strike or kill them. Need supplies whatever her wielder lacks: Adept-level mage skills when she is in the hands of a trained fighter, superb fighting skills when used by a sorceress. She will also heal anything short of a death-wound. When Need encounters the successor to her present handler, she awakens and sings. As that woman draws the blade, writing as fine as any scribe's flares crimson along its length. The words are always in the reader's own language, and state "Woman's Need calls me, as Woman's Need made me. Her Need must I answer, as my maker bade me." A deep bond is formed between sword and wielder, and Need sometimes drives that wielder into deadly danger in her eternal quest to succor womankind. She can be

resisted and reasoned with, as Kerowyn discovered, but the bond and her strength are so powerful that parting with her causes agonizing pain, as Kerowyn also discovered. Kethry received the sword from Baryl Longarm; years later, when Kerowyn sought help from Kethry to save Dierna, the sword "spoke" for Kethry's young grandaughter. Need gave the inexperienced Kerowyn both fighting ability and mage skill, enabling her to defeat her enemy. In later years Need chose Elspeth and then Nyara. Need was destroyed when she was channeling energy during the Mage-Storm solution at Urtho's Tower, and the resulting explosion scarred Firesong's face and arms horribly. Karal and An'desha saw the spirit of the woman who had been Need on the Moonpaths after they recovered from their exertions at Urtho's Tower. See Lashan. *(Oath, Storm, Sword, Winds)*

Needleworkers' Guild
One of the Crafts groups, it dealt with seamstresses and embroiderers. The Guild helped throw a party to welcome the Chitward family to Haven. *(BB)*

Nemor
The Arch-priest of Anathei of the Purifying Flame. A philosopher and true believer, Nemor longed for a really challenging being which he could convert from evil to good, and thus prove the tenets of his religion. He got his chance with Thalhkarsh. After Nemor saved Kethry and Tarma's lives in the battle with the demon, he took Thalhkarsh back to his temple for reeducation. *(Oath)*

Nera
A *hertasi* Elder of the enclave at the marsh in k'Sheyna territory, he enjoyed playing the role of an eccentric old creature. *(Winds)*

Nerissa (Herald)
Also known as Nessa, she was noted for her amorous conquests, and often teased about them. Despite her success in attracting men, she panted for a chance to ride Circuit with Herald Kris, regarding him as "the lure of the unattainable." To shake her off, Kris eventually let her "attain" him once. *(Arrows)*

Nerya

A fourteen-year-old girl at Forst Reach, and one of the few females the traumatized Tashir Remoerdis wasn't afraid of. Vanyel suggested that he should go out riding with her. *(LHM)*

Nes

A Shin'a'in term meaning "bad." *(Oath)*

Nestor (Lord)

The lord of Laverin, and speaker for the West, he was involved with the pirates who had raided the shores of Lake Evendim. *(Arrows)*

Nether Planes

The plane where natural magical energy, which flows through various dimensions like water, eventually ends up. In these Planes, everything is chaos and energy. From here it is thought that magic flows back into the World Plane of living things, repeating the cycle. It's also where Ma'ar and his incarnations fled whenever the stolen bodies they inhabited died. There Ma'ar hid his disembodied personality in a pocket amid the planes, waiting for an opportunity to seize another hapless descendant's physical form and be reborn again. Also called the Void. *(Storm, Winds)*

Neutrals

These Mages refused to take sides during the War. They were flamboyant and chose to perform magic whenever and wherever they could with no regard for consequences that might affect the innocent. Their selfish actions and refusal to commit to the side of good caused conflict with Urtho. *(Gryphons)*

Nevis

A bisexual young courtier at Haven, he broke Tylendel's heart by seducing the Herald-Mage trainee. Nevis then went to Savil and accused Tylendel of being the seducer; fortunately she knew the opposite had been the case. As Vanyel overheard from Court gossip, Nevis was a problem to both sexes, and everyone at Court was glad when his family finally called him home. *(LHM)*

Nevis
One of Tremane's numerous aides. *(Storm)*

Night-singers
A common insect in Haighlei once trapped and caged to provide a night sound that was popular in the gardens, but whose popularity had since been superseded by night-singing birds. *(Gryphon)*

Night-trumpet
A scented plant native to Haighlei. *(Gryphon)*

Nightbird
Nightwind's sister, a Kaled'a'in who teased Darian and her friend Summerdance for "hitting it off so quickly." *(Owl)*

Nightfire
A Tayledras formerly named Starfire, one of the mages involved in the Heartstone accident. Afterward, Starfire became Nightfire and was obsessed with studying the stone's remains, spending every waking moment trying to determine what caused the disaster. *(Winds)*

Nightjewel
A Tayledras mage paired with Iceshadow in the circle that gathered to destroy the rogue Heartstone at k'Sheyna Vale. *(Winds)*

Nightsky
A Tayledras who left the windows of her high-level *ekele* open on a windy day, and came back to find her belongings strewn all about the room. *(Winds)*

Nightwind
A Kaled'a'in trondi'irn who came with Kelvren to k'Vala Vale and eventually became Snowfire's lover and pledged mate. She is dark haired—as she had not practiced much magic or lived in a Vale with a Heartstone, thus her hair was not bleached white like most Tayledras. *(Owl)*

"Nine-Days King, The"
A theatrical favorite with Imperial audiences, the storage depot Tremane raided held scenery, props, and costumes for putting on a production of that play. This equipment

became very useful when Tremane was crowned King of Hardorn. *(Storm)*

Node

A repository of magic power that may be tapped by a mage at a price paid in control and mastery of will and focus. The node concentrates energy flowing to it from hidden ley-lines deep beneath the ground. The advantage for a mage in using a node is that drawing on a node's accumulated power saves the use of the sorcerer's personal energy and boosts his ability to wield magic. Where two or more natural lines of magical force meet in a node, the power is so strong that only Adepts can control the pooled energy. A lesser practitioner of magic attempting to tap into that source would be unable to touch the power at all, or would be engulfed and destroyed by it. Heartstones are used by Tayledras, mage created super-nodes where many ley-lines collect, and where the energy lines from the surrounding area are relocated to drain off the land's excess magical energy. The Heartstones store energy for the needs of the Vales, to be drawn off as needed by the Vale's mages. *(LHM, Storm, Winds)*

Norris Lettyn

A skilled and talented actor recruited by Lord Orthallen to teach the art of seduction to spoiled young Rethwellen Prince Karathanelan, so that the Prince can first marry, then control, and finally kill Queen Selenay. Norris is killed in the final assassination attempt on the Queen. *(Exile)*

Nort Halfden

A young Valdemaran foot soldier in the Tedrel Wars. *(Exile)*

Norten

One of the engineers at Haven, Master Henlin delegated Norten to go with Bret and Levy and take the bad news about the strengthening Mage-Storms to Queen Selenay. *(Storm)*

North-Province, bride

Elspeth felt like one after Quenten exchanged her Valdemaren and Rethwellan coins for jewelry and told her to wear all of it, as North-province brides often carry their entire dowries on their necks. *(Winds)*

North-needle
The Velgarth term for a compass, which was used by the Silvers when magical direction-finding did not work. *(BV)*

Nos
A Shin'a'in term meaning "it is." *(Oath)*

Noyoki
Also known as the Nameless Brother, the Disgraced One, the One With No Honor. The word *noyoki* literally means "no one," in Haighlei. The last son of King Ibram's Third Consort, he is King Shalaman's half-brother. He had mage powers as a child, and was sent to priest school to be trained, but misused his Gifts and was to be rendered magically impotent as punishment. However, the Cataclysm struck down the priest assigned to cleanse the boy, and Noyoki escaped with his mage powers intact. Grown to manhood and consumed with jealousy and resentment, he plotted to overthrow his brother. When he was discovered, his mind was wiped clean, but his body left alive and put on display as punishment and warning. *(Gryphon)*

Nyara
Falconsbane's Change-child daughter, slave, and pawn. She was experimented upon by Falconsbane while he occupied An'desha's body. Attractively catlike, she was slim with a triangular face, small chin, pointed ears with tufted ends, short sable-colored hair, upswept eyebrows, golden-yellow eyes with slit pupils, low, husky, purring voice, and retractable fingernails. Many of these traits changed and she became more human in time, thanks to the intervention of Need and the avatars of the Star-Eyed Goddess, as Nyara's reward for helping to defeat her father. Nyara had stolen bits of magic-learning from Mornelithe, and gained a small bit of power. He had let her keep her Mage-Gift so that he could use her as a repository of energy gained from his blood-path sacrifices; she couldn't use the energy, but he could draw on

it by hurting her, making magic without needing to touch any sources on the Tayledras lands which might attract the attention of their mages. Originally believing his manipulative lies, Nyara regarded herself as worthless and evil. Only with the loving care of her mate Skif, her teacher Need, and others could she finally emerge from her monstrous father's shadow and become her own woman. *(Storm, Winds)*

Oath of Sword and Hand
A Shin'a'in pledge of mutual friendship and support that is a vow sacred to the Star-Eyed Goddess. Jadrie had sworn this oath to Kira and Merili before their abduction. *(Oath)*

Oberdorn
The city in Ruvan where Lastel Longknife sought release from the curse Kethry had placed upon him. He hired a drug-addicted mage to petition Thalhkarsh to break the spell that made him appear as a woman. However, the mage was killed and Lastel was made into the demon's slave. Tarma, Kethry, and the priest Nemor later defeated Thalhkarsh. *(Oath)*

Oden (Duke)
The Collegium Weaponsmaster whom Kayla assigned as Vanyel's instructor, warning that he would find the Duke no easy teacher. In contrast to Vanyel's previous lessons, however, Oden was an artisan with a blade, and he and Vanyel got along very well, and Vanyel eventually became a superb swordsman and very effective with almost any weapon. *(LHM)*

Odo
Weaponsmaster of the Collegium during King Theran's reign, he understood the need to be strict and tough in order to save trainees' lives on future assignments to dangerous territories. *(BB)*

Official Chronicles
Kept in the capitol of the Eastern Empire, Tremane's scholars could find nothing in the official chronicles of the Empire relating to Mage-Storms in the past. *(Storms)*

Old Charcoal
This was a nickname the Sixth Wing allegedly gave Aubri in the days of Urtho's War, as a fighter notorious for drawing firestrikes. *(Gryphon)*

Old City
The permanent section of Kata'shin'a'in, as opposed to the tent-city. *(Winds)*

Old Palace
This was once the center of government at Haven. The stone-floored building dated back to the Founding by King Valdemar. The most ancient section was still used for Herald's quarters until a more recent wing was constructed. *(LHM)*

Olek Gelcress
Tansy Gelcress's husband, a neighbor of the Alders' in Errold's Grove. *(Owl)*

One-Eye Tham
A beggar in Oberdorn who told Arch-priest Nemor that the mendicants once used the old Temple of Duross as a meeting hall, but later left it empty because it was too cold and damp in the abandoned structure. *(Oath)*

Ophela
A Karsite ascetic who was noted as being blind and deaf to anything other than Vkandis and Karse. *(Storm)*

Order of the Brotherhood of Perpetual Indulgence
A tongue-in-cheek classification applied to hedonists, particularly those fond of sexual dalliances. *(LHM)*

Order of the White Winds
The school of magic in which Kethry trained. Its disciplines mandate self-knowledge and self-mastery. The heart of its teaching is that no negative ties be permitted to bind the sorcerer in any way, because immoral, negative bonds of fear, hate, or greed will drain a mage of needed energy. *(Oath)*

Oreden
A hedge-mage with Lord Leamount's forces who went with the Sunhawks on their end-run around the Jkathan rebels. *(Oath)*

Orsen Brodey (Lord)
Father-in-law of Kerowyn's brother Lordan. Orsen's daughter Dierna was abducted on the eve of her wedding and saved by Kerowyn. The family emblem was the red deer. *(Sword)*

Orser (Armsmaster)
Lord Kendrick's armsmaster, he taught Joserlin Corveau weaponry skills. *(LHM)*

Orser (Companion)
Herald Liam's Companion, he told Yfandes and others about Treven's and Jisa's marriage, which was met with general approval among the Companions and the people of Valdemar. *(LHM)*

Orthallen (Lord)
The Lord of Wyvern's Reach, most senior Council member and Chief Councillor to the Queen, and to her father before her. His benevolent facade concealed a man determined to acquire power at any cost, including the lives of those closest to him. He was Herald Kris's uncle, and took advantage of that relationship to plant suspicions of Talia in the younger man's mind, suggesting that Talia was using her Gift of Empathy to manipulate the Queen and Princess Elspeth in matters of state by influencing their feelings. He was the probable sponsor of Hulda, though the records to prove that vanished before anyone could check them. Lord Orthallen was an eager proponent of Elspeth's betrothal to Prince Ancar of Hardorn. Ancar was secretly working with Orthallen, promising him the throne of Valdemar when Hardorn conquered the country, though he had no intention on delivering on that promise. When Talia discovered this, she trapped Orthallen into revealing his true intentions. Furious, he tried to kill Talia, but was killed by Elspeth instead. There are strong indications that Orthallen was responsible in part for King Sendar's death, Talamir's death, an attempted seduction of Elspeth by a young courtier, and

several of the illicit industries troubling Valdemar, particularly the slave trade. *(Arrows, Exile, TT)*

Ortrech (King)
King of Karse, though his role was largely ceremonial. Real power in Karse lies with the Sunpriests in the Temple of Vkandis. *(Exile)*

Orven (Herald)
He served as a spy in Karse during the Tedrel Wars. *(Exile)*

Orwind
The translator whose edition of *Grindel's Discourses on Unnatural History* was preferred by Jadrek and Herald Roald. *(Oath)*

Osberg
One of Gregoth's raiders, he stole the amber necklace Dharin gave Tarma for a betrothal gift after participating in slaughtering the clan. Later, when Kethry and Tarma killed the murdering bandits, Tarma reclaimed her property. *(Oath)*

Osen (Father)
He was the priest at Forst Reach who died when Vanyel was only four, but the boy remembered him fondly and recalled how willing Father Osen was to answer questions and not be judgmental. *(LHM)*

Oskar
Host of the *Bottomless Barrel*, the Oberdorn inn where Tarma and Kethry stayed. *(Oath)*

Osten Deveral
A tradeguildsman and a secret ally of the Lake Evendim slavers and raiders. *(Arrows)*

Other-Planar
Dimensions that touch, but are not part of, the human world. Sorcerers can summon creatures from there and coerce aid from them, if the sorcerer's will is strong enough. *(Oath)*

OtherSenses
An ability to be aware of presences and energy currents

beyond those detectable by normal means. OtherSense can be used by a powerful mage despite the attempts of others to shield against it. *(LHM)*

OtherSight
Mage-Gift which can See potential deep-buried Gifts in seemingly untalented persons and is similar to Mage-sight. *(LHM)*

OtherWinds
Currents of power in Planes separate from the one inhabited by humans. On the night of the Highjorune palace massacre, Vanyel and Yfandes felt the stirring of the monsters responsible along the OtherWinds. *(LHM)*

Ourra
A *kyree* who didn't know the sheep he'd been feeding on belonged to anyone. He frightened the neighboring village by prowling it at night, but was merely curious. When the local priestess gave him a tongue-lashing for eating livestock, Ourra was deeply embarrassed. Thus arose the legend of the Demon-Wolf of Hastandell. *(Oath)*

OutClansmen
A term the Shin'a'in use to refer to those who are not Shin'a'in. *(Oath)*

Outcasting
An ancient ritual in the Mercenaries' Code, it condemns an oathbreaker and is a death-curse. *(Oath)*

Outer eyes
A Shin'a'in shaman's Gift similar to Mage-sight, the ability to probe the nature of beings at a distance and discern if they possess Gifts. *(Oath)*

OutKingdom
A term Valdemarans use to refer to all other kingdoms. *(BV)*

OutLands
What the Tayledras and Shin'a'in call the lands other than their own. *(BV)*

OutLanders
What the Tayledras and Shin'a'in call people who are from outside their own lands. *(BV)*

Outpost Five
The remote post in the territory jointly claimed by Haighlei and White Gryphon. It is twice as far from White Gryphon as the other outposts. Patrolling and exploring that area is the responsibility of the Silvers. The region is a rain forest climate, with heavy morning fog and daily thunderstorms. *(Gryphon)*

Oversight
How a Healer sees the world, alive with a web of light, color, and energy. With this Gift, a Healer is able to tell if plants are thriving, or if people are ill. Once her Gift was opened, Keisha learned there were many kinds of Oversight, and many ways to use this special way of looking at the world. In the texts Gil Jarrad had given her to study, Oversight was referred to as Mage-Sight or Healing-Sight. *(Owl)*

Owain (Priest)
A middle-aged priest of Astera who performed the marriage ceremony of Valdemar's Heir Presumptive Treven and Jisa. Owain stated that because the pair were lifebonded, in his judgment it would be a sin and blasphemy not to unite them. *(LHM)*

Owyn Kittlekine
A leatherworker's son, he was one of Lavan's Third Form classmates at the Merchants' School. *(BB)*

Page, The

An inn in Highjorune which caters to *shaych* customers. Its proprietor had an arrangement with other establishments along the street, such as Bel's *Inn of the Green Man*; she and the other inns didn't sell boys and *The Page* didn't sell girls. *(LHM)*

Pahshen (Companion)

Dethor's Companion. *(Exile)*

Paintbox-birds

Haighlei avians, the ones that inhabit the capital gardens are tormented by simie. *(Gryphon)*

Palimpsest

A parchment or other piece of writing material on which the old writing had been rubbed off to make room for new. *(LHM)*

Palinor (Lord)

The Seneschal and a councilman of Valdemar. Herald Kyril is his assistant. *(Arrows, Sword, Winds)*

Palisar

The Haighlei Speaker to the Gods, and one of King Shalaman's advisors. *(Gryphon)*

Pandemonium, The Great Mage

The stage name and role Firesong adopted when he worked undercover as a carnival performer in Hardorn during the mission to kill Ancar. *(Winds)*

Panjir
The town where some of Ma'ar's troops were holding a defensive position. Against all logic, Garber sent an aide to order the gryphons to fly a suicide mission, supporting an attack on Ma'ar's well-entrenched forces. *(Gryphon)*

Pass of Stelvi, The
The scene of a great battle in the Mage Wars, and a terrible defeat for Urtho's forces. A split valley lies beyond the pass and the captured town of Laisfaar, opening the way into the heart of Urtho's realm. *(Gryphon)*

Pass-through
An invisible door, a common mage trick. One led into Starwind k'Treva's Work Room and was guarded by a set-spell which would only admit certain persons. Kethry used a pass-through to disguise the door between her room and Tarma's when they were plotting the downfall of Raschar. *(LHM, Oath, Winds)*

Patris (Healer)
The Mindhealer assigned to the OutLanders' defenses on the Gyrefalcon's Marches. *(Arrows)*

Pawell
A Sunhawk scout killed in a skirmish. Kyra replaced him, and since Pawell had no relatives or shieldmate to claim them, Tarma gave her his horse, gear, and tentmate. *(Oath)*

Peace of the Goddess
A Holderkin term for religious vocation; for a female, it meant a lifetime in the Temple Cloisters, covered in clothing from head to toe and forbidden to leave the premises or to speak. *(Arrows)*

Pedron's Wolves
A mercenary fighter group attached to Urtho's forces. *(Gryphon)*

Pelagir Hills
A range of hills lying west of Valdemar and harboring a variety of strange creatures that the magic-using Tayledras Clans worked to render harmless. The region was little understood and very feared. The Pelagirs were a

remnant of the world left in magic-riddled ruins after the ancient Mage Wars. From time to time, malevolent and unwelcome things escape from the Hills' hidden recesses and move into areas protected by the Tayledras. *(BV)*

Pelagiris Forest
The massive wilderness at the base of the Pelagir Hills, it was created during the first great Mage-Storms of ancient times. The Tayledras have spent more than a thousand years working to cleanse it. Always dangerous, after the Mage-Storms it became a terrible place indeed, riddled with Change-circles and strange and unnatural beasts roaming the vast woodland. *(BV)*

Pelagiris Road
Elspeth and Skif rode this route south of Valdemar. It led from the hills to the High Spur Road, and on into Lythecare. *(Winds)*

Peleun (Commander)
He once led Emperor Charliss' Imperial Guards, and was loyal because he was under a geas. *(Storms)*

Pellion d'Genraves (Patriarch)
Head of all of the many and varied religions in Valdemar, he presided over Selenay's coronation. *(Exile)*

Pelsin (Herald)
A Herald who aided the Healers Kerithwyn and Loris during the plague crisis at Waymeet. *(Arrows)*

Peluverr
The senior gryphon in Kelvren's Wing. *(Owl)*

Penchal
An artist in Haven. *(TT)*

People of the One
They settled around Crescent Lake and are unusual in that they are monotheists in the polytheistic Valdemaran world. Their holy writings are contained in *The Book of the One.* *(LHM, Arrows)*

People of the Plains
An OutLander term for the Shin'a'in. *(Oath)*

Perchi
An insult meaning "common prostitute." *(Gryphon)*

Peregrin (Lord)
Herald Kris's father and one of the Seneschal's chief assistants. *(Arrows)*

Peregryn of Adair (Baron)
One of the few members of Hardornan nobility to survive Ancar's purges. When Peregryn came to Shonar to pledge fealty to King Tremane, the young baron was only fourteen, but already battle-hardened and well bonded to and respected by the fighters and people who followed him. He was charismatic, so much so that it was clear that deeds that Bards could sing about had brought him through Ancar's wars, and many more such deeds lay in his future. His lands of Adair were in the northern part of Hardorn, close to Iftel. *(Storm)*

Perry
A spoiled rotten page at Rathgar's Keep. *(Sword)*

Petar
Potboy at the *Inn of the Green Man*. *(LHM)*

Peter Ringwright
A Valdemaran tradeguildsman and co-conspirator in the secret alliance between the slavers and the Lake Evendim pirates. *(Arrows)*

Petras
Capital city of Rethwellan. *(Oath, Storm, Sword, Winds)*

Phellip
Having survived a colddrake attack, he was worried about further trouble, based on previous experience. Vanyel could hardly blame him. *(LHM)*

Pheregrul
Kethry's family name; the Pheregruls were members of the Fifty Noble Houses of Mornedealth. By her father's day, the name was an empty title. The House estates had dwindled to a decaying mansion in the Old City and the family perks to little more than an open invitation to Court functions and permission to hunt in the Royal Forests. *(Oath)*

Phoenix
A Haighlei legend of an Air-Spirit and Fire-Spirit combined. The legend became the basis for a classic dance performed at the Palace called, "Phoenix Dancing with Dragon." *(Gryphon)*

Phryny
The astronomical body that Herald-Mage Kilchas planned to study the night he died, while watching the conjunction between Phryny and Abcrdene's Eye, a celestial event which only occurred once in a hundred years. *(LHM)*

Piel
Shandi's most romantic and least sensible suitor. After Shandi was Chosen, he mooned about brokenheartedly, making a pest of himself. In his foolish posturing and fantasizing, he stood out in the rain until he caught cold, and then expected Keisha to cure his ills. *(Owl)*

Pig and Potion
A tavern in Carter's Lane in Petras, it offered good food, fine drink, and various forms of accommodations. The inn was especially noted for its excellent brewmaster. *(Oath)*

Pig and Stick
A tavern in Highjorane in Lineas where Minstrel Renfry worked. Vanyel, in his disguise as Valdir, had looked there in hopes of getting a job, but Renfry's presence chased him off. Later, the two men struck up an acquaintance and Renfry was surprisingly helpful and sympathetic to the threadbare character Vanyel was portraying. When Vanyel fled Highjorune, he went to *The Pig and Stick* looking for the older man. Renfry tipped him off on how to escape the city, and coaxed the tavern's cook into supplying the Herald-Mage with food for his journey. *(LHM)*

Pillars of Wisdom
They stand at either side of the gates between this world and the world of the Dead, invoked during the death-curse ritual against an Oathbreaker. Formed of ethereal glowing mist and bracketing the Gate of Judgment, the

Pillars allow those wronged by the Oathbreaker to return long enough to find just revenge. *(Oath)*

Pine Forest

The only name given to a location on the Guard's maps, a heavily wooded area east of White Foal Pass near the Karse border that Lord Marshal Weldon speculated was the place where the Karsites would try to flank Valdemar's army and press forward their invasion. He assigned Lavan to hold off the attack there, using whatever means necessary to stop the Karsites. *(BB)*

Pires Nieth

A Blood Mountain Master mage in Ancar's pay. The bastard son of a noble family, he briefly assumed the crown of Hardorn until he discovered that the Eastern Empire's army was pouring over the border, when he abandoned the crown and fled. *(Winds)*

Poidon

A *hertasi* who demonstrated for Skan a backspin pointe dance maneuver his species regularly used at Harvest Festival. Skan adapted the move for aerial combat. *(Gryphon)*

Poison-vellis

A plant to be avoided. Forst Reach fosterling Jyllian compared Vanyel's aloof behavior to one reacting to poison-vellis. *(LHM)*

Pol (Herald)

A teacher at the Collegium and the Herald present when Lavan was Chosen, Pol was married to Healer Ilea, and their daughters were Healer-trainee Elenor, Bard Kaika, and Healer Amaly. The daughter of his Companion Satiran, Kalira, became Lavan's Companion. Fortyish, of medium height, Pol possessed a little bit of every Heraldic Gift in a weak yet active form. This made him extremely valuable in teaching new trainees until they were ready to work with a Herald mentor who would further develop their Gifts. Pol befriended and taught Lavan Chitward all he knew about being a responsible Herald. Lavan never wanted to use his FireStarting Gift on a human until Pol was attacked and blinded by a Karsite assassin. After the Karsite army was burned to ash along with Lavan, Pol accompanied Elenor and a few of Lavan's friends to the spot where Lavan was killed and nurtured a firecone tree there in memory of the Herald. *(BB)*

Polda
A town that proved to be an important defensive battle site in the Mage War. The Sixth Wing gryphons fought there. *(Gryphon)*

Poldara
A Valdemaran town Kubrick might have had to detour to if Loden's bridge fell. *(Storm)*

Poldarn
The drunken thief who taught Kanshin his trade. *(Gryphon)*

Polden (General)
One of Ma'ar's officers. *(Gryphon)*

Pomera
A fruit served in k'Sheyna Vale. *(Winds)*

Ponjee
A village Tarma and Kethry were trying to reach on one of their journeys, hindered by the bad luck talisman they had acquired. *(Oath)*

Portal
A Mage Gate created by the internal energy of a powerful Adept. It must be constructed by one person, and is entirely dependent upon him or her to erect both entrance and exit, as no two people see the same place in exactly the same way, and building a portal is a precise weaving of magic, though others can feed the gate-builder power. *(BV)*

Potter
A village built by a community of workers in clay, it was so small it was no more than an isolated cluster of buildings around a public well. Guildmaster Egon and his kindred and workers lived in this tiny settlement, churning out works of art in pottery. *(Oath)*

Power Stone
One of Urtho's most important magical artifacts. *(Gryphon)*

Power-nexus points
The term Ancar used to describe nodes. *(Winds)*

Power-poles
Falconsbane wanted to construct these with the ley-lines he tried to steal magically from k'Sheyna Vale. Poles are produced by a mage's own energy or energy from another mage's body. *(Winds)*

Power-theft
Some mages can tap and steal power from others whose Gift is weaker than theirs. As a crime, it falls under the provenance of the clergy, and ranks between rape and larceny. *(LHM)*

Preadeth
One of Falconsbane's mages who was sacrificed to acquire the power-pole. *(Winds)*

Preatur (Lord)
Father of an uncommonly beautiful and seductive daughter whose presence wreaked havoc among Valdemar's Guard at Court. King Randale issued orders, via Herald-Mage Vanyel, for Preatur to either marry off his daughter or take her home, else the Crown would find a husband for her. *(LHM)*

Predain
A neighboring realm of Tantara, and Amberdrake's homeland. As a boy, Amberdrake was sent to study in Predain. Ma'ar became Prime Minister to Predain's King, until the monarch died without an heir. Ma'ar then became the country's Warrior-King and began his conquests. *(Gryphon)*

Presen (Herald)
A Herald who assigned Princess Elspeth to attend city court as part of her duties as Herald intern. *(Sword)*

Pretera
A Shin'a'in term meaning "grasscat." *(Oath)*

Pretera'sedrin
The Children of the Grasscats, a Shin'a'in Clan. *(Oath)*

Pretor (Herald)
A Herald who died in the line of duty, he was one of the many familiar faces now gone when Vanyel returned from his mission to the Karsite border. *(LHM)*

Priestess of the Sunlord
A servant of the main Karsite divinity. Prior to Solaris's times they were not permitted to wear the gold robe of their hierarchy's top rank. *(Sword)*

Priests' Staff
After the miracle of Solaris at Midwinter, the staffs of the false Karsite priests turned brittle and disintegrated. The staffs of the true priests burst into bloom. Ulrich's staff was covered with flowers. *(Storms)*

Prime-focus
A stone used by a mage to assist his spell casting. The stones match and amplify resonances from the mage. Like harmonics of a note, a mage will have a variety of stones that suit his or her personal vibrations. The stone that most closely matches is ranked as the primary, followed by the secondary, and so on. The most effective prime-focus stone should be large and flawless. Often a mage will be able to work better with a large clear secondary stone than a smaller or flawed primary focus stone. Herald-Mage Vanyel had always worked with a secondary focus stone until Stefen gave him a large flawless piece of amber, the Herald-Mage's preferred prime-focus stone. *(LHM)*

Privilege Tax
A remission in part of the taxes due for a community which has contributed a citizen to the Heraldic Circle. *(Arrows)*

Prophet, The
She was a Karsite fanatic who claimed to be the religion's original Prophet reborn in a female's body to prove the Deity's Oneness. She brought Vkandis Sunlord's immense wooden shrine to the final battle of the Karsite War against Valdemar to inspire the troops. That

gave Kerowyn a chance to finish the Prophet's reputation, and the war, by sending the shrine up in flames. *(Storms, Sword)*

Prophet-King
A young zealot, probably no more than twenty years old, who rose to become the leader of the Karsite antimage crusade. The Prophet's exhortations set his entire country upon a killing spree, giving rise to the Cleansing Fires. Some of his agents even tried to penetrate Valdemar. *(LHM)*

Protea
Kestra'chern assigned to attend a group of *tervardi* little ones during the evacuation of Urtho's camp. *(Gryphon)*

Provost-Marshal
The dignitary heading the Herald's Collegium, he has special powers to enforce discipline as well as to secure prisoners before they are brought to trial. As part of his duties, he maintains the infamous book containing Herald-trainees' demerits. The Provost-Marshal's main function is to coordinate between Collegia, Court, and Haven's municipal authorities, smoothing out any problems concerning town and government. *(Arrows)*

Prytheree Ford
A Holding west of Forst Reach, beyond the untamed woodlands. *(LHM)*

Pyreen
Dyheli doe assigned to carry a magical decoy and move as though she were an object being transported and escorted by a heavily guarded caravan. *(Owl)*

Qorthes
The capital city of Baires. *(LHM)*

Queen's Own
See Monarch's Own

Quenta
A translator of *Grindel's Discourses on Unnatural History.* *(Oath)*

Quenten
A White Winds Master-class mage who served under Kerowyn in the Skybolts and became their chief mage. *(Owl, Sword, Winds)*

Querna shena Tale'sedrin
Emissary from the Tale'sedrin Shin'a'in to Valdemar and a Swordsworn history-keeper, she was killed along with Ulrich when Tremane ordered the assassination of Valdemar's envoys. *(Storms, Winds)*

Quorn
One of Falconsbane's underlings sent to gather information about Ancar. *(Winds)*

Racing Clubs
The divisions among the offspring of the Fifty Noble
Houses of Mornedealth. They began as racing clubs: the
Blues, Greens, Reds, Yellows, and Blacks, but competi-
tion among the clubs degenerated into duels and
crime. *(Oath)*

Racky Loder
A Shonar area youngster who took sheep out of town
to graze and was among the children lost in the Mage-
Storm blizzard until Tremane led a rescue party to save
them. Racky was later appointed to be one of King
Tremane's pages, helping to carry the train of the long
theatrical cape that the new king had to wear on special
occasions. *(Storm)*

Radevel
One of Vanyel's cousins who took over the training of
Forst Reach's novice fighters when Jervis moved on.
(LHM)

Radiance
A title of respectful address to the Son of the Sun.
(Storm)

Raebuck
A cervine prized by gryphons as prey. *(Gryphon)*

Raf
A pickpocket with Bazie when Skif was in the gang. He

was caught and served time as a prisoner on the border with Karse. *(TT)*

Rafe (Herald)
A Herald with Farsight and Mage-Gift, he was trained by Treyvan as part of a weather control team. *(Winds)*

Rafe Alder
One of Keisha's five brothers. *(Owl)*

Rag and bone men
Responsible for sweeping out fireplaces and ovens in prosperous homes. They sell the ashes to soap-makers and tanners, and the ends of logs to the poor for their fires. *(TT)*

Ragges
One of Kero's spies who worked undercover in Hardorn. *(Winds)*

Rainbird dance
A Shin'a'in custom where maidens wave scarves during the dance. *(Storm)*

Raindance
A Tayledras scout. *(Owl)*

Rainlance
One of the Tayledras Elders who solemnized the joining of Snowfire and Nightwind. *(Owl, Winds)*

Rainstar
A Tayledras Adept. *(LHM)*

Rainwind k'Vala
A k'Vala Vale Tayledras scout whose bondbird is a falcon. *(Owl)*

Rainwind k'Sheyna
A Tayledras scout with a permanent limp. *(Winds)*

Raival leaves
Foliage of trees in Valdemar known for the spectacular golden hue it turns in the autumn. *(Arrows)*

Ralf
A palace groom, and one of Talia's friends. *(Arrows)*

Rana (Herald)
A character in a story Elspeth told Skif to discourage him from tailing her like a mooncalf, thinking he was in love with her. *(Winds)*

Rana Trilvy
A pregnant Errold's Grove resident. Keisha spent a lot of her time calming the new expectant mother's nerves, especially as the birth became imminent. *(Owl)*

Randale (King)
The grandson of Queen Elspeth the Peacemaker, son of Herald-Mage Darvi, King of Valdemar during Vanyel's time. Life-bonded to Healer and Herald Shavri, he slowly succumbed to a long wasting ailment. In the year before Randale's death, his unbearable pain was kept at bay by Bard Stefen's Gift, prolonging his life. Despite his pain, Randale grew from the young boy who assumed the throne unexpectedly after his father's early and unexpected death to become a superb monarch. *(LHM)*

Randel
The bridegroom of Lord Baron Dudlyn's granddaughter. *(Oath)*

Randel's Raiders
A mercenary Company Idra served with before she formed the Sunhawks. *(Oath)*

Randon (Lord Marshal)
The Lord Marshal of Valdemar, and a Councillor during Queen Selenay's time. *(Arrows)*

Ranolf (Healer)
Pol's son-in-law, wed to Amaly, and a Healer like her. *(BB)*

Raschar Jadrevalyn (King)
Heir to the Rethwellan throne, he killed his sister Idra and attempted to kill his brother Stefan to be sure of his position. Stefan opposed Raschar's reign, so Idra came home to help decide who should inherit. Originally she was for Raschar, but she changed her mind to Stefan when she saw the tyranny Raschar planned for the king-

dom. Before she could declare her vote, Raschar kidnapped, raped, and killed her. He met his death at Idra's hands when she was temporarily brought back from the dead by an Oathbreaker Ceremony led by Tarma, Kethry, and Jadrek. *(Oath)*

Rashi (Herald-trainee)
A Herald-trainee and the son of a pigkeeper, he was skilled in certain protective spells as yet unmastered by the rest of Treyvan's magery class. *(Winds)*

Raslir
He was Kerowyn's orderly in the Skybolts who had one arm, but was a talented masseur. *(Sword)*

Ratha
She was the sister of Wendi, one of the adolescent girls at Court. *(LHM)*

Ratha
One of the species making up Urtho's Third Army, which fled far northward to the land that was to become Iftel. The *ratha* are to mountain cats what the *kyree* are to wolves. *(Gryphon)*

Ratha (Companion)
He was Eldan's Companion, and helped Kerowyn rescue his Chosen from a Karsite priestess. *(Sword)*

Rathgar
Kerowyn's father and the ex-commander of a mercenary company. *(Sword)*

Raven Clan
One of the Northern tribes, their land lay beyond Snow Fox and Wolverine territories. Darian's parents became members of this clan after being transported there by a Change-circle. *(Owl)*

Ravenscroft
A prominent noble house of Valdemar where Governess Gaytha was from before she became Housekeeper at the Collegium in Talia's time. *(Arrows)*

Ravenwing
A Tayledras scout and Wintersky's lover, her bondbird is a cooperi hawk. *(Owl)*

Ravenwing
A Tayledras maker of feather masks. Darkwind has a collection of her artistic creations hanging on the walls of his *ekele*. *(Winds)*

Ravenwing
A shaman during the time after the Cataclysm when the Kaled'a'in returned to their homeland, which had been turned into a blasted crater, and made the decision to divide the tribes. Her clan was Taylesederin, foremost in demanding that magic be eliminated from the people's lives. She began the shamanic weaving, set up regulations for shamans and their apprentices for every clan, and created Kal'enedral. Her Seeking and Calling evoked the Goddess to grant the Plains to the Shin'a'in, naming the blood sacrifice they must pay for that gift. *(Winds)*

Ravinia (Herald)
An old friend of Mirilin, she has the Gifts of Animal mindspeech and Mindspeech. *(Exile)*

Reaycha
A young gryphon paired with Talsheena. They were assigned to handle the points farthest from the power web during the effort to bring down Falconsbane. *(Winds)*

Red Fox Tribe
A Northern Tribe raided by Wolverine warriors, who crippled the men and carried off the boys and young women. *(Owl)*

Red Nose Inn
A ramshackle tavern outside Haven's west wall. *(LHM)*

Redel (Lord)
Vanyel's fellow student at Weaponsmaster Kayla's training school and a master of the light sword. *(LHM)*

Redhawk
Kaled'a'in Senior officer of the young Silver Gryphons. *(Owl)*

Redoak
A young Kaled'a'in mage on the rescue team to find Silverblade and Tadrith. *(Gryphon)*

Reesk
A gryphon in the Silvers, partnered with Kally. *(Gryphon)*

Refectory
The enormous dining hall at the Collegium. *(BB)*

Regen (Herald)
Vanyel's deceased friend from among the Heraldic circle. *(LHM)*

Regin
A human Silver who led the search party which included Amberdrake and Skan. *(Gryphon)*

Regyl
Wethes Goldmarchant's house mage assigned to control the captive Kethry. *(Oath)*

Reichert (Lord Baron)
An ambitious and amoral power grabber, as a young man he courted Kerowyn's mother, Lenore. His niece would eventually marry Lenore's son. Tarma and Kethery suspected he was behind the attack on the Keep before the wedding. *(Sword)*

Reindeer People
A nomadic tribe living in the far northern part of the Empire. *(Storm)*

Reine (Countess)
Prince Roald made a deal with Tarma to force Leslac into marriage with this Countess, thus getting the Bard out the Tarma's hair, in exchange for some prime Shin'a'in horses. *(Oath)*

Releigh
He was Commander of Lord Marshal Weldon's troops on the Karsite front.

Rellan and Lorn
A *hertasi* couple who had recently moved out of a water-

line marsh-side home because it flooded every spring. *(Winds)*

Relli
A Skybolt known to be a clotheshorse, she was Shallan's lover. *(Sword)*

Relnethar (Lord)
A Lord of Karse in the time of Queen Selenay. *(Arrows)*

Remoerdis
The ruling family of Lineas whose palace was in Highjorune. *(LHM)*

Rendan (Lord)
Leader of the bandit gang that ambushed and tortured Vanyel. They were hired by Master Dark (Leareth). *(LHM)*

Renfry
Minstrel employed at *The Pig and Stick* tavern along The Row in Highjorune. He helped Vanyel escape the city. *(LHM)*

Renthan
One of Falconsbane's mages sacrificed in his master's attempt to create his own power-pole. *(Winds)*

Renthorn
One of Ma'ar's incarnations. *(Winds)*

Renton
A kestra'chern whom Amberdrake tried to assign to best advantage during the evacuation from Ka'venusho. *(Gryphon)*

Replicators
Imperial mages who use magic to duplicate letters and documents. *(Storm)*

Resley the Liar
One of Lord Rendan's bandits killed in the ambush of Vanyel. *(LHM)*

Restil (Prince)
He was King Valdemar's son and Chosen by Companion Steladar at the beginning of the Herald-Companion rela-

tionship. It was the first instance of the Heir to the throne being Chosen, proving his worthiness to wear the crown. *(Arrows)*

Reta
The former maid to Deveran Remoerdis's mother, she became Ylyna Mavelan's maid when the young woman was married to Deveran. *(LHM)*

Rethaire
A Herbalist-Healer in the Sunhawk mercenary company. *(Oath)*

Retham
A member of the Silvers. *(Gryphon)*

Rethwellan
The country south of Valdemar and west of Karse. Petras is its capitol. Rethwellan is ruled by the Jadrevalyn family, important allies to Valdemar, who have assisted in the fight against Hardorn and Karse on several occasions. It is also where Kethry and Tarma have their school. Quenten also has a mage-school there, in the city of Bolthaven. Mages and mercenaries are prominent in the country and protected by guilds. *(Oath, Sword, Winds)*

Reva
A Court beauty, prominent on the social scene when Vanyel first arrives in Haven. *(LHM)*

Reva
She was Veth's mother and the wife of Covia's Headman Garth. *(LHM)*

Reven (Lord-Marshal)
The Lord-Marshal of Valdemar during Randale's time. *(LHM)*

Revenie
A town in Valdemar whose temple children's choir serenaded Kerowyn with the song "Kerowyn's Ride," much to her chagrin. *(Sword)*

Ri
A kitchen drudge at the *Inn of the Green Man* in Highjorune. *(LHM)*

Riannon Silkedre
A kestra'chern whose skills were slightly inferior to Amberdrake's. *(Gryphon)*

Ricard (Lord Patriarch)
He was a religious leader of Valdemar and a member of the Council in Selenay's time. *(Storm, Winds)*

Rides-alone
A Kaled'a'in mage and one of Snowstar's team searching for the lost Silvers. *(Gryphon)*

Rild
Shieldmate of Sunhawk scout Kyra. *(Oath)*

Rilei
A kestra'chern who assisted with the preparations for the evacuation from Ka'venusho. *(Gryphon)*

Rinan
A Red Fox tribeswoman and one of three widows of the slain shaman. *(Owl)*

Rio
A *hertasi* and Healers' assistant. *(Gryphon)*

Rites of Dark Desires
The name for worship concocted by Thalhkarsh when he subverted the citizens of Delton. *(Oath)*

Riverford Farm
A large estate upstream of Errold's Grove that was attacked in the first wave of northern men and monsters, and its population wiped out. *(Owl)*

Road, The
This is what the Holderkin call the South Trade Road. *(Arrows)*

Roadguards
The auxiliaries of Valdemar's regular army who wear bright blue uniforms marked with the insignia of a crossbow and arrows. The road-guards keep watch at towns

and the realm's borders, and aid travelers in need. *(Arrows)*

Roald, (King, Herald)
Selenay's grandfather, he found Tarma, Kethry, and Jadrek half-frozen beside a trail over The Comb and brought them to the safety of his hunting lodge. At the time he was Prince of Valdemar and hiding Prince Stefanson of Rethwellan from his brother. *(Oath, Winds)*

Roan
A Shin'a'in saddle-bred gelding and Tarma's parting gift to Daren when he returned to Petras after his father's death. *(Sword)*

Robin (Page)
A very young and bookish fosterling from Gyrefalcon's Marches sent to Court to become a page. Talia arranged for him to study at the Collegium and have permission to enter the library and introduced him to Dean El'-carth, and the two scholarly souls became fast friends. *(Arrows)*

Rodi
Kethry's mule before she began riding battlesteeds. *(Oath)*

Rogare
Shaman of Gray Wolf clan. *(Owl)*

Rohan (Companion)
Companion to Herald-Mage Kilchas. Rohan died when his Chosen did, and the other Companions found him in the far corner of the Companion's Field. *(LHM)*

Rojer Klinseinem (Lieutenant)
He was a Lieutenant and Undersecretary in Ancar's officer corps. Agents smuggled him out of Hardorn, and he told them how his people were disappearing in large numbers. The missing were being used in blood-sacrifice rites by Ancar and his blood-path mages. *(Winds)*

Rokassan
Alberich developed this persona among the taverns of Haven so he could blend in with the crowds and gather information. *(TT)*

Rolan (Companion)
Companion to the Monarch's Own. He Chose Herald
Talamir after Talamir's Companion, Taver, died in the
Tedrel Wars while they were trying to rescue the King.
When Talamir was murdered, Rolan Chose Talia after
a two-month search. Though he and Talia were not able
to communicate in words since she did not have a strong
Mindspeech Gift, the bond between them was exceptionally strong. Talia could see through her Companion's
eyes at will, no matter where he was, and he was always
able to feel her presence in his mind. Like all Companions to the Monarch's Own, Rolan is a Grove-Born stallion and never seems to age. The strongest and perhaps
the wisest of all the Companions in Selenay's reign, he
also has the strongest Mindspeech of all the Companions, and can receive messages from incredible distances.
(Arrows, Winds)

Rolf (Herald)
The advisor to Herald-Mage Savil, he helped her rescue
Herald-trainee Tylendel after the mindlink assault in the
Grove when Tylendel's twin brother, Lord Staven, was
murdered. *(LHM)*

Rolf Dawson (Master)
A instrument maker and inventor Vanyel sought out at
the Forst Reach Harvest Fair while looking for the right
lute for his nephew, Medren Ashkevron. Not only did
Dawson have a lute perfect for Medren, he also sold
Vanyel a twelve-string gittern. *(LHM)*

Rory Halfaxe
Kethry's would-be suitor. After the incident at Viden,
she and Tarma, knowing Rory was at the nearby town
of Lyavor, led their pursuers onto his backtrail. *(Oath)*

Rovenar
Skif slept in the Rovenar family crypt to escape the mid-
day summer heat and inadvertently became eavesdrop-
per to treachery. *(TT)*

Row, The
A string of inns and taverns lining a street in Highjorune, the Linean capital. The establishments varied

from well-maintained to filthy, and offered various types of entertainment. *(LHM)*

Royal Valdemaran Guards
The guards to the queen, they wear uniforms of dark blue and silver. *(Arrows)*

Rris
Torrl's enthusiastic young *kyree* cousin and an oral historian, he helped the Tayledras by babysitting the gryphlets and assisting the scouts. *(Storm, Winds)*

Rrrillia k'Treva
Tervardi singer and mate to Sarrrsee. *(Owl)*

Rubrik (Herald)
The Herald sent to Valdemar's border to escort the new Karsite ambassador and his secretary to Haven. Rubrik was a veteran of the border wars, and as a result was partially paralyzed and used a cane. His daughter was Natoli, an Artificer student, and his Companion was Laylan. *(Storm)*

Rudi
An innkeeper of Selina who hired Kerowyn as his bouncer after she resigned from the Skybolts. *(Sword)*

Ruins, The
The home of Hydona and Treyvan, and a place of old, tame magic with half a dozen ley-lines under it. There is a power node far beneath the ruins, which connects to the ley-lines of k'Treva Vale. *(Winds)*

Runes of coercion
These are Rune symbols drawn by a blood-mage to place an individual under his power. *(Winds)*

Rusi and Severn
A Hardornen couple in exile but who returned to their ruined home. They acted as guides for Elspeth and Darkwind. *(Storm)*

Ruvan
Ruled by Prince Lothar, it is a small country east of Rethwellan. The cities of Delton where Thalhkarsh was summoned, and Oberdorn, where he was defeated, are

there. The Sunhawks also have a mercenary town located there called Hawk's Nest. *(Oath)*

Ruvon
A member of the Errold's Grove's Fellowship community, he offered to send Shandi's things to her at Herald's Collegium with a trader who was dealing in the Fellowship's products. *(Owl)*

Rynee (Mindhealer)
Though not a Herald herself, Rynee possessed the same Gifts for Mind-healing that Heralds Talia and Patris did, and during their absence could watch for stress and distress among the Heraldic Circle. *(Arrows)*

Ryvial (Herald)
The Herald sent to search Vatean's house after it was discovered Vatean was involved in slavery and kidnapping. *(TT)*

Sadar
A fragrant Haighlei wood used for making chests and other furnishings. *(Gryphon)*

Sadullos
A Shin'a'in term that means "safer." *(Oath)*

Sa-hai
A Shin'a'in term meaning "(you're) right." *(Oath)*

Saffy
A resident of Errold's Grove; Ida's daughter, suggested as a Healer's apprentice to replace Wizard Justyn. *(Owl)*

Saint Keshal
Called upon by the Skybolt Shallan in one of her numerous oaths and curses. *(Sword)*

Salle
A practice room for weapons training. *(BV)*

Salten Sea
The Sea on the east coast of the Eastern Empire. *(Gryphon, Storm)*

Sanctuary
A quarantined area in the forest where Healers could isolate the sick among the Ghost Cat clan and the incoming northern pilgrims. The route to the Sanctuary was hidden deep in the woods and was only known, as far as the northerners were concerned, to the "holy"

dyheli. This prevented new pilgrims from kidnapping a Healer to take back with them. *(Owl)*

Sand-demon
Tarma tells Kethry she fights like one of these creatures when she's wielding Need. *(Oath)*

Sandaar
A fire elemental that Herald-Mage Vanyel sent into the face of the enemy mage who attacked his mother. The sandaar did not kill the attacking mage, but the distraction gave Vanyel time to ready other magic weapons. *(LHM)*

Sandar
One of Vanyel's cousins, he was scornful of the boy's regal airs. *(LHM)*

Sandar Giles
Mayor of the city of Shonar in Hardorn. A thin, dark young man, he escaped being conscripted by Ancar because he was frail and had a club foot. *(Storms)*

Sania
She was the shieldmate of Varny. Both women were former Sunhawks and each had a daughter, but neither girl was interested in becoming a mercenary. *(Oath)*

Sara
The wife of Gerdo, the contortionist with the traveling carnival. The couple took Liam in after the boy was attacked, sympathizing with his situation because Sara had gone through the same thing at one time. *(Winds)*

Sari
One of Shandi and Keisha's teenage circle of friends. *(Owl)*

Sarnedelia (Lady)
A Rethwellan noblewoman who was an enthusiastic rider, and welcomed Kerowyn's innovation of exchanging skirts for sensible breeches. *(Sword)*

Sarrrsee k'Treva
Tervardi singer who performed at Snowfire and Nightwind's bonding, mate to Rrrillia. *(Owl)*

Sartra (Companion)
Unpartnered Companion and Senta's twin. *(Storm)*

Sar'terixa the Mad
One of the later evil embodiments of Ma'ar, this time in the stolen body of a young Kata'shin'a'in mage. *(Storm)*

Sathen
The *hertasi* who usually tended Starblade's *ekele*. *(Winds)*

Savil Ashkevron (Herald-Mage)
See Ashkevron, Savil

Sayvil (Companion)
The Companion who Chose Kerowyn on the battlefield. *(Owl, Sword)*

Sa'dassan
Kerowyn's Shin'a'in adopted cousin and one of the horse trainers who came to Bolthaven to trade, rather than to the regular Horse Fairs. *(Sword)*

Scarlet lamp
A lamp used to mark a Shin'a'in priest tent, and also brothels in Brether's Crossroads. *(Oath, Winds)*

Scarlet-crested firebird
A species found in the far northern region of Valdemar. One of them brought Firesong a black rose after the proto-Gate was mysteriously hijacked to Haven. *(Winds)*

Scrub
The derisive nickname Tyron gave Lavan. *(BB)*

Scrying Bowl
A bowl that Master or Adept mages use to communicate, which shows the images of whomever they are communicating with. Its use is very draining and as obvious to other mages as setting off fireworks. *(Sword)*

Scrying stone
An Adept mage's long-distance viewer. *(Winds)*

Se
A Shin'a'in term meaning "is/are." *(Oath)*

Search
The term for a Companion's journey when looking for a new Herald-trainee to bond with. *(Arrows, Oath, Owl)*

Seashan
A tribal name of one of the Northern clans. Keisha could gather no mental image of the totemic animal they were named for. *(Owl)*

Season, The
Winter at the Imperial Court, when revelry, intrigue, gossip, marriage-brokering, and jockeying for power occurred. *(Storm)*

Second Emperor, The
He was one of the rulers of the Eastern Empire, and was known for setting up the Empire's law system, basing it on heavy monetary penalties suited to each crime. *(Storm)*

Sectors
The various territorial and political divisions within Valdemar. The areas are kept linked to Haven through the Heralds' circuit rides as they tour the sectors either singly, in pairs, or teams. The Border sectors are generally the most dangerous. *(Arrows)*

Seeing
A Heraldic Gift, also known as FarSeeing, that allows the Gifted to see other places in their mind. *(LHM)*

Seejay/Ceejay
See Ceejay

Seeking and Calling
A ritual undertaken by Shin'a'in shamans to call for divine aid. The answer they receive explains the price the Goddess demands for her gifts. *(Winds)*

Seisin
An ancient Hardornen ritual where the King was presented with the soil of his country, which was then mixed with his blood to sanctify it. It signified the monarch's bond with his land and gave Hardornen nobility a chance to swear fealty to their new ruler by offering a piece of their own territory for the ritual. In the course

of the ritual, the earth-bound monarch would reveal any problems in the vassel's lands. *(Storms)*

Sejanes
The oldest mage in Tremane's entourage and his most trusted advisor, he'd been with Tremane since the Duke was a boy and loved him like a father. *(Storm)*

Seldasen (Herald)
A famous Herald and swordsman; Vanyel read about his adventures. *(LHM)*

Selenay (Queen)
The monarch of Valdemar, she is the daughter of King Sendar and mother of Princess Elspeth, Princess Lyra, and Prince Kris. She is married to Prince Darenthallis, the former Lord-Martial of Rethwellan, and now Royal Consort. Assuming the throne after her father was killed during the Tedrel Wars, she led Valdemar to victory. Afterward, Selenay fell in love with and married Prince Karathanelan of Rethwellan, Elspeth's father. Dissatisfied with his role and seeking the throne for himself, he plotted to become King by having Selenay assassinated and taking the throne by force. Alberich discovered the plot, and Karathanelan and his co-conspirators were killed during the attempt. Selenay met Darenthallis in the heat of battle against Hardorn, and the two were lifebonded. They were then married and had the twins Lyra and Kris. *(Exile, Arrows, Storm, Sword, Wind)*

Selina
The town where Kerowyn sought out a Guildhall after her resignation from the Skybolts. *(Sword)*

Selina Ironthroat
A prosperous female free-lance mercenary Elspeth and Skif met in a tavern. Elspeth struck up a quick acquaintance with the woman and, to Skif's horror, went pub-crawling with her. *(Winds)*

Sella
A Silver, a gryphon, he served as one of Shalaman's personal guards. *(Gryphon)*

Selwin (Herald)
He was a Herald posted to a Skybolt garrison town on Valdemar's eastern border. They sent him to the Council with alarming news of a magical attack on their position. *(Wind)*

Semon
One of the Artificer students working on the Mage-Storm problem at the Compass Rose. The Change-rabbit captured after the third Mage-Storm almost bit Semon's hand off. *(Storm)*

Sen
Talia's father and the master of Sensholding. *(Arrows)*

Sendar (King)
He was Queen Selenay's father, killed by an assassin in the final battle of the Tedrel Wars. *(Exile, Arrows)*

Sendlewood
A fragrant material used in oils to massage the body or to protect linen and bedding from insects in storage. Sendlewood comes from a slow growing tree that has tiny purple and white flowers. Distilling the powdered heartwood and roots produces the oil. The lumber is used in the construction of temples and palace throne rooms. *(LHM)*

Seneschal
The person in a Royal Household in charge of all domestic arrangements and ceremonies, and who handles certain administrative and judicial functions. As the Seneschal is the Chief Steward of Valdemar, his Herald is steward of the Heraldic Circle and is one of its more important members. *(Arrow)*

Sensholding
The Holderkin Steading which was Talia's original home. Sensholding and its repressive, polygamous culture had been Talia's entire world until she was Chosen. That upbringing left her completely unprepared for the freedom, noise, and bustle of settlements along the Trade Road, let alone the size and excitement of Valdemar's capital city. *(Arrows)*

Senta (Companion)
An unpartnered Companion and twin of Sartra. *(Storm)*

Sentlewood
A scent often incorporated into perfume Tarma's Clan used to anoint themselves. *(Oath)*

Sentry-mode
The stance taken by a Shin'a'in battlesteed which has been given the command to guard. *(Oath)*

Serais (Councillor)
Head of the Imperial Tax Collectors. *(Storm)*

Serens
Also known as Pappa Serens, he was the owner and proprietor of the *Broken Arms* tavern. *(TT)*

Seri
Urtho's *hertasi* servant. *(Gryphon)*

Serina
One of Vanyel's aunts. *(LHM)*

Servants of Darkness
Also known as the Dark Servants, they were an evil army guided by the invading sorcerer Leareth. Vanyel held back their hordes at the pass of Dellcrag and Mount Thurlos long enough to save the Kingdom. *(Arrows)*

Servants of the Warrior
The Spirit-trainers who serve the Goddess as Warrior by training her Swordsworn. Such instructors taught Tarma by night, instilling in her the skills she needed to survive her quest. They are what she will become should she die while under Oath. *(Oath)*

Set-spell
A spell that recognizes certain specified individuals and allows them entrance to protected areas. *(LHM)*

Seven Corey Swordmaids
The way Lissa referred to herself and her fellow students at Trevor Corey's school for single warrior women. She promised to lead the seven to her brother Vanyel's rescue if he was being mistreated at Court. *(LHM)*

Sewen
Captain Idra's second in command, handfasted to Shayana Healer-Priest Tresti. *(Oath)*

Shadow Stalker, The
See Ashkevron, Vanyel

Shadow-Lover
A euphemism for death, to embrace the shadow-lover. *(LHM, Oath)*

Shadowdancer, Lythe
One of a pair of early Heralds that Talia read about in tales and legends. Lythe Shadowdancer was lifebonded to Rothas Sunsinger and their romantic story thrilled Talia as a child, when she dreamed of becoming a Herald. *(Arrows)*

Shadowstar
A Tayledras scout who offered Darkwind food at the Council meeting and teased him about his appetite. *(Winds)*

Shaiknam (General)
He led the Sixth Wing East of Urtho's forces and was notorious for having little regard for his fighters except as living weapons. He failed as a general, and decided to turn traitor by joining Ma'ar and becoming a spy and internal saboteur. *(Gryphon)*

Shakras
Their hides are used to make soles for boots used by Tayledras scouts. *(Winds)*

Shalaman (King)
In the Haighlei Empire there are Six Nations of the Black Kings. Shalaman is King and Emperor of the nation closest to White Gryphon. *(Gryphon)*

Shallan
A Skybolt scout whose lover, Relli, was killed in the rout during bandit eradication operations for the Menmellith Council. After the Skybolts were reformed under Kerowyn, Shallan was named co-commander and lieutenant of the specialists. *(Sword, Winds)*

Shallan (Herald)
Field trial herald; her students are called her brood.
(LHM)

Shaman/Shamaness
In the Shin'a'in tribes they are known as the Wise Ones,
and wear headdresses adorned with two tiny antelope
horns. They usually have the power of magic, and are
more learned than average Clansmen. Each shaman or
shamaness is also a keeper of outClan knowledge.
(Oath)

Shaman of the Eclipse
A Mage and Shaman of the Eclipse Cult with the Wolverine barbarians attacking Raven village. He wore the
same kind of medallion, an eclipse painted in scarlet, as
the shaman who led Blood Bear warriors in the attack
on Errold's Grove years before. He also shared that shaman's rough power and urge for conquest. *(Owl)*

Shamanic dowsing
A ritual that enables a mage to look for something, or
something missing. Snowstar used the technique with a
map to find the area of rain forest where magic was
nullified. *(Gryphon)*

Shamanic weaving
The tapestries kept in a secluded building in Kata'shin-
'a'in and guarded by the Scroll-Sworn Warriors of the
Goddess, open to use by the shamans of all the clans.
The weavings were made by the Shin'a'in shamans from
the moment of the sundering of the tribes after Urtho's
War, and preserve the whole history of the clans, including the emotions felt by participants in the events recorded. The weavings are a permanent method of
keeping Shin'a'in memories of important events alive.
(Winds)

Shamile
Herb used in tea making, it serves as a strong tranquil-
izer. Talia drank it often in the early days of her internship to relieve stress. *(Arrows)*

Shan
A fur trader who had traveled among the northern bar-

barians and taught Snowfire what he had learned about them. *(Owl)*

Shandi Alder (Herald)

Keisha's younger sister, Chosen by Companion Karles as a teenager. Her Gifts are Empathy and Foresight, and she has strong mundane talents for needlework and making friends. Romantically involved with the Tayledras plant expert Steelmind. *(Owl)*

Shanse (Minstrel)

A minstrel who had stayed for a time at Forst Reach and praised Vanyel's good ear for music. The comments gave the boy hope and fostered his dream of escaping his unhappy home to become a Bard. *(LHM)*

Sharissa (Herald)

The Herald who led the Guard unit that rescued Lavan and Kalira from ambush by Jisette Jelnack's hired thugs. *(BB)*

Shavri (Herald-Healer)

King's Own Herald, a Healer, and King Randale's life-bonded lover. She would not marry him because that would prevent any chance for Randale to make a valuable alliance marriage outside the realm, and because she was terrified of the prospect of having to rule Valdemar—something she would have to do if she survived him as a wife and Consort. But Shavri's desperate desire for a child led her to persuade the couple's mutual friend, Herald-Mage Vanyel, to sire her daughter Jisa. Healer Shavri kept secret Randale's sterility, and the world believed that the girl was Randale's. Shavri could not, however, keep secret the knowledge that Randale was slowly dying of a wasting illness. As Randale's end drew nearer, Shavri opened all her Healing channels, giving him everything she could of her strength, aware that it would mean her death when he finally succumbed. Shavri feared ruling so much that it threw her into terrible emotional turmoil when Jisa married Randale's Heir, Treven. She became reconciled to the match in the end, but could never understand Jisa's willingness to accept the responsibility of ruling Valdemar. Grove-Born Companion Taver had Chosen Shavri after the death of

Queen's Own Herald Lancir, and when Shavri died, Taver Chose Jisa. *(LHM)*

Shaya
A Kaled'a'in term of endearment. *(Winds)*

Shayana
A sect of Healing priests which makes no distinction of gender. Tresti, a female attached to the Sunhawks, was a priest of Shayana. *(Oath)*

Shaych
A shortened form of *shay'a'chern,* a Tayledras term meaning preferring partners of the same sex in romantic relationships. By the time Vanyel returned from his mission to the Karsite border, *shaych* had become common slang throughout Valdemar. *(BV)*

Shaydra
A Tayledras term of endearment. *(LHM)*

Shay'a'chern
A Tayledras term for same-sex orientation. These relationships are fully accepted among the Tayledras. In Valdemar this very old word has been shortened to *shaych,* but retains its original meaning. *(BV)*

Shuy'kreth'ashke
A Tayledras term meaning beloved lifebonded person of the same sex. *(LHM)*

She'chorne
A Shin'a'in term meaning homosexual, it does not have negative connotations among the clans. *(Oath)*

Sheda (General)
An Imperial officer and one of Tremane's predecessors in the campaign in Hardorn. Tremane wondered if, like General Sheda, he should press on despite increasingly difficult obstacles. *(Storm)*

She'enedra
A Shin'a'in term for lifebond friend, or the Oathbound, two-made-one. Blood-sisters make a cut in their palms, then clasp hands. For Tarma and Kethry, the Goddess

healed these cuts into silver scars, a sign of their bond.
(Oath)

Sheka
A Shin'a'in term for horse droppings. *(Oath)*

Shelana
The warleader of Liha'irden Clan in Tarma's time, and
the one who taught the children swordwork. *(Oath)*

Shelass
Murassa Emperor of the Haighlei five hundred years before the time of Shalaman. It was he who decreed that the
kestra'chern were to be taken into the Empire. *(Gryphon)*

Shena
A Shin'a'in term meaning "of the Clan," literally, "of
the Brotherhood." *(Oath)*

Sheran
A Gryphon fighter rescued by the Third Wing just before the battle at Stelvi Pass. She had been captured and
tortured by Ma'ar's forces. *(Gryphon)*

Sherisse (Lady)
A noblewoman at Shalaman's Court. She fell under the
influence of the hated Lady Fanshane and as a result
became a man-hating, reclusive drunk, eventually dying
young. *(Gryphon)*

Sherrill (nicknamed Sherri) (Herald)
A senior instructor at the Collegium, her Companion
was Silkswift. Sherri was detailed to act as Talia's guide
when the newly Chosen girl had just arrived at the Collegium. Before she was Chosen, Sherill had lived her life
packed together with a large family. They were fisherfolk
on Lake Evendim, and Sherrill spent her youth either
on a boat or in a longhouse with her entire family and
her many uncles' families. Chosen right off a fishing
boat, Sherrill could not read or write when she was
brought to the Collegium. She also believed, as do most
fisher folk, that too much bathing was bad for one's
health, and objected to the daily bath required by the
Collegium. She helped Keren rescue Talia when the
Blues threw her into the river. After Ylsa's death, Sher-

rill lifebonded with Keren. Sherri remained Talia's staunch friend and supporter throughout their lives. *(Arrows)*

Shesti
A Shin'a'in term for "nonsense." *(Oath)*

Sheyna
A Tayledras term meaning "brother." *(Winds)*

Shield-Wall
A magical barrier placed by the god Vykaendys around Iftel. It is constantly renewed by earth-magic, which is why there is very little magic to spare inside Iftel's borders. *(Storm)*

Shieldbrother
The term used for good friends among mercenary companies or armies. *(Oath)*

Shielding
In Mind-magic it is the process by which an Empath or one Gifted with ThoughtSensing protects herself from an overload of other people's everyday emotions or thinking. Dean Elcarth taught Talia to imagine an impenetrable wall around her mind, and make it vivid enough to screen out the surrounding babble. He also told her not to hesitate to drop the shield if she suspected danger as her inner Gift might well be her best advance warning. In traditional magic, it the process of building barriers to magical energies. *(BV)*

Shieldmate
The term for a military or mercenary company partner who is also one's lover. *(Oath)*

Shin'a'in
Dark-haired, golden-skinned, blue-eyed nomadic peoples of the Dhorisha Plains, related to the Tayledras; they guard the Dhorisha Plains as the Hawkbrothers guard the Pelagir Hills. The Shin'a'in are noted for horse breeding, especially their warsteeds. Each clan is advised by their Elders, a group consisting of a Healer, a Shaman, a Warleader, and a Clan Chief. Wary of outsiders, the Shin'a'in are close-knit and friendly within their own

elaborate inter- and intra-Clan relationships. Except for dark-clad Swordsworn devotees, Shin'a'in prefer bright garments and are very fond of music, preserving their history in song. The only time most Shin'a'in leave the Dhorisha Plains is to trade in cities like Kata'shin'a'in. Shin'a'in forsake magic, except for Shamanic magic, and Gifted children are either trained as Shamans, sent to the Hawkbrothers, or have their Gifts sealed off. *(BV)*

Shin'a'in bows
Small but powerful weapons made of laminated wood, horn, and sinew. They fire small sharp arrows that cannot penetrate good armor, but can find every weak spot in a common soldier's war-gear. *(Oath)*

Shion (Herald)
One of the three Heralds diverted from Circuit duty and assigned to escort the ambassadors from k'Sheyna, she annoyed Elspeth with her endless curiosity. *(Winds)*

Shkar
The warrior leader of the Blood Bear barbarians who invaded and captured Errold's Grove. *(Owl)*

Shonar
The town in Hardorn where the Imperial Army was headquartered during the Mage-Storms. It eventually became Tremane's capital. *(Storm)*

Shonar Council
Tremane worked out conflicts between the town and the military to everyone's mutual satisfaction with the Shonar Council. They established a list of infractions and punishments based on the Imperial Code, which were then impartially enforced. *(Storm)*

Shonar Manor
The former residence of a Hardornen noble who was probably killed by Ancar. Grand Duke Tremane made it his headquarters; it was the best available lodging for him and his officers, though its comforts were far inferior to those of his own estate back in the Eastern Empire. *(Storm)*

Shonsea (Companion)
Herald-Mage Lissandra's Companion, who died at the northern end of Companion's Field, apparently having fallen and broken her neck at the same instant her Chosen died in an accident in the alchemy lab. Both were probably murdered by Leareth. *(LHM)*

Shoveral (Lord) ·
One of Lord Leamount's commanders, assigned to guard his western flank during the final attack on Kelcrag's forces. Shoveral's standard was the badger, suiting his military style of implacable defense. His ability to attack was untested, but he ordered a charge and his troops took advantage of a hole in the enemy's line. *(Oath)*

Shyrestral
A gryphon, one of Tashiketh's ambassadorial group from Iftel. *(Storm)*

Siara
Generic Imperial term of respect. *(Storm)*

Sifyra
A *dyheli* stag and Snowfire's mount. *(Owl)*

Sigfrid
A red-robe priest and mutual friend of Treyvan and Ulrich. *(Storm)*

Sigil
A vowelless representation of a Companion's name, it is carved into a Companion's saddle and on the skirting. A Roadguard at Horn pointed out Rolan's sigil to Talia and explained its meaning to her while she was traveling to Haven. *(Arrows)*

Signal-towers
They were built in Hardorn to serve as an early-warning system. Based on fire-tower architecture, but with massive mirrors on top that could be used to transmit coded messages as a series of light flashes to other signal towers. It generally took a fraction of the time to transmit a message via signal tower relays than it would with traditional couriers. Ancar had signal-towers built at regular intervals all along Hardorn's major roads. Signal-

towers had the advantage of being non-magical and therefore immune to the arcane effects of the Mage-Storms, though they were subject to the whims of weather. *(Arrows, Storms)*

Silence

An adept whose original use-name was Snowfire, she was badly hurt in the Heartstone disaster, and afterward became an unsmiling, tragic recluse. After her recovery, she went with Kaled'a'in Adept Summerfawn to find k'Sheyna's new homeland and prepare to build a Gate. When she returned she was smiling, and no longer silent. *(Winds)*

Silence Bell

This bell was rung in the *Compass Rose* whenever someone needed to make an emergency announcement. *(Storms)*

Silkswift (Companion)

Herald Sherrill's Companion. *(Arrows)*

Silver (Companion)

Companion Kantor crossed into Karse and allowed himself to be captured as war-booty. Vkandis priests gave the stallion to the newly promoted Captain Alberich as a reward for his service. Alberich treasured the beautiful horse, whom he named Silver, even though he was troubled by Silver's shining white coat, which he felt was so visible that it could be a disadvantage in battle. Also, white horses were considered unlucky in Karse, as they were associated with the witch horses of Heralds. Alberich had a latent precognitive Gift that was discovered by the Karsites, who condemned him to death for it, giving him to the fire. Silver rescued Alberich from his burning prison and brought him to Valdemar, where he revealed his real nature (Companion), and his real name (Kantor). Heralds took the newly Chosen Alberich to Haven to become a Herald himself. *(Arrows)*

Silver Gryphons

Named for the silver badges shaped like gryphons worn by the members, this is the policing organization of White Gryphon, formed from the remnants of fighters and soldiers who managed to make it through Urtho's Gates before the Cataclysm. The Silvers serve both military and police functions, and are the fighters, guards, scouts, and constables of their city. *(Owl, Storms, Gryphon)*

Silver Veil
A kestra'chern, and later wife to King Shalaman. Her platinum hair reached the ground and trailed behind her as she walked, and is the reason for her name. When fleeing her home land of Therium during the Mage-Wars, she took in young Amberdrake and taught him her trade. She apprenticed Amberdrake to her friend Lorenshallen and traveled further south to the land of the Black Kings. The Haighlei call her Ke Arigat Osorna, which means silver veil. *(Gryphon)*

Silver sticks
Writing implements manufactured by the Haighlei. *(Gryphon)*

Silverbird
A Tayledras weaver who made the pledge ceremony robes for marriage. *(Owl)*

Silverblade
Daughter of Amberdrake and Winterhart. Named Windsong as a child, on her twelfth birthday she announced her name change. Silverblade is now a warrior attached to the Silvers and Tadrith's partner. She has some Empathic ability, but must touch the subject before she can read feelings. *(Gryphon)*

Silverfox k'Leshya
Kestra'chern with the k'Treva clan, he came to Haven with the first floating barge group of the Kaled'a'in. Silverfox was a member of one of the k'Leshyan Disciplines. He had been assigned to learn if Firesong, among others, had been affected by the aftermath of the Mage-Storms. This was a serious concern, since, according to ancient records, extremely sensitive mages were often affected so in the days of Ma'ar and Urtho. In time he and Firesong become life mates. *(Storm, Winds, Owl)*

Silverhorse
Clan chief of the Taylesedrin after the Cataclysm, and a
strong opponent of magic in all forms. *(Winds)*

Silversmith Guild
Jelnack was its Master in Haven in the reign of King
Theran, but lost his position as a result of his insane
wife's vendetta against Lavan Firestorm. *(BB)*

Silverswan
One of the Tayledras Elders who solemnized the bonding of Snowfire and Nightwind. *(Owl)*

Simie
Small, furry, human-looking creatures which inhabit the
gardens throughout Haighlei. They enjoy tormenting
paintbox-birds. *(Gryphon)*

Sisterhood of Spell and Sword
The ancient order that mage-smith Lashan served so
long ago that no one knows exactly what or where it
was. The order's stronghold was a huge, sprawling group
of wooden buildings that looked very much like Quenten's mage-school. Without a town or stockade, only forest surrounded the Sisterhood's retreat. Flat roofs
topped the structures, and a square-knot pattern was
carved above all of the doors. The Sisterhood was part
temple, part militia, and part mage-school. Its disciples
worshipped four deities—two sets of twins: Kerenel and
Dira, Karanel and Dara: Healer, Crafter, Fighter, and
Hunter. *(Winds)*

Sisters of Agnetha
They worship one aspect of the Goddess. Dierna Brodey
was sent to the Sisters' cloister when she was eight to
be taught the womanly arts. *(Sword)*

Sixth Crimson
Part of General Shaiknam's and Garber's troops, they
were led into an ambush which Shaiknam's scouts had
already informed him of and were wiped out. *(Gryphon)*

Skandranon Rashkae
The most famous gryphon ever, the Black Gryphon, and

the ally of Urtho in ancient times. He was the strongest and bravest of the gryphon race. His exploits over his long life have never been equaled in all of the long history of gryphons. He discovered and broadcast to all gryphons the fertility spells needed to create offspring. He killed Ma'ar after Urtho was assassinated, he founded White Gryphon after the Cataclysm, and served upon its council. His children grew up strong and clever and became famous in their own right. He was the mate of Zhaneel, father of Tadrith and Keenath. (*Owl, Gryphon, Winds*)

Skif (Herald)

Skif lost his father young, and his mother when he was barely nine. He became the responsibility of his venal and amoral uncle, Londer Galko, who put Skif to work in his miserable tavern, the *Hollybush*. Skif woke up early and got the fires at the tavern started and water hauled in from the well while dodging blows from the other tavern workers, then spent his mornings in school and his afternoons stealing food to eat, finishing off the day by working in the tavern at night until it closed in the wee hours of the morning. Skif eventually ran away from his uncle and became a member of a gang of petty thieves headed by a former Tedrel mercenary named Bazie. He and the other boys lived as a family—the only one Skif had known after the death of his mother. When Bazie and his boys were killed in an arson fire, Skif swore that he would find the person responsible and take revenge in their names. After being Chosen by his Companion Cymry, Skif found a new family with the Heralds. He and Alberich broke up a slavery ring and Skif discovered his purpose in the world, as a Herald. Skif's mate was the Change-child Nyara, Mornelithe Falconsbane's daughter. Skif met her when accompanying Elspeth on a mission to find mages for Valdemar. (*Arrows, Storms, TT, Winds*)

Skolte (Sir)

A scrawny, middle-aged, but quite clever nobleman who hired Kethry and Tarma to escort his wife Darthela to Fromish before winter set in. (*Oath*)

Sky-mother
A Hardornen deity associated with the Earth-father and represented by the color blue. *(Storm)*

Skybolts
A mercenary company, they were noted as mounted scout-skirmishers. Lerryn Twoblades, the son of Justin Twoblades, was Captain of the bonded outfit, and was willing to hire Tarma's student Kerowyn. After Lerryn and his second officer were killed in the war against Karse, the company was almost ruined by the inept leadership of Ardana Flinteyes. Kerowyn was elected Captain, and under her guidance the Skybolts enjoyed ten years of expansion and prosperity. She arranged the Skybolts into four combined companies, each with a pair of lieutenants. The largest group was the light cavalry, followed by horse archers, and together these comprised two-thirds of the outfit. The remaining third was divided between scouts and specialists: messengers, saboteurs, two Healers and their four aides, three mages, and six apprentice mages. Company uniforms were silver and grey tabards bearing the device of crossed lightning bolts on the sleeve. The Skybolts used Bolthaven in Rethwellan as their winter quarters, until they were deeded a town in Valdemar, which was renamed Bolton, as reward from Queen Selenay for helping to defeat Ancar's forces. After Kerowyn was Chosen, the Skybolts remained in Valdemar and were added to Queen Selenay's official forces. *(Sword)*

Skydance
A Tayledras scout whose bondbird, Raan, killed one of the forest intruders when Darkwind was attacked. *(Winds)*

Skyr
The hawk-eagle bondbird of Starfall's Healing-Adept father. Starfall used Skyr's talons as tokens to adopt Nightwind and Darian into the k'Vala clan. *(Owl)*

Skyseeker k'Treva
A Hawkbrother fond of garish designs Darkwind imitated in his disguise as a carnival worker. *(Winds)*

Skyshadow
A Tayledras scout whose bondbird was Eere, a second-year suntail hawk-eagle. *(Owl)*

Smoke
Leftenant Alberich of Karse's former mount, killed a few weeks before Alberich was promoted to captain and given the white stallion Silver as a replacement. *(Arrows)*

Snow Demon
A creature that first appeared during an unusually cold winter four generations before Tarma's time, and was killed by one of Tarma's teachers, another Kal'enedral, who also perished in the fight. The history-song of the battle is a favorite among the Shin'a'in. *(Oath)*

Snow Fox Clan
One of the northern tribes friendly with the Ghost Cat peoples. *(Owl)*

Snow Fox
The avatar of the tribe that bears his name. He is the size of a small pony and has milky-blue, catlike eyes, a sharply pointed muzzle, and blunt, pointed ears. To onlookers his furry body seems misty white and translucent. Tiny fragments of white light, like twinkling stars, dance around him like dust motes in sunlight. *(Owl)*

Snow fever
A dangerous and sometimes fatal disease known in Valdemar's northern sectors. It generally shows up immediately after the first few snowfalls and is gone by Midwinter. Its symptoms are high fever, delirium, a red rash, and swelling under jaws and arms. Treatment is imperative, and trained Healers are required if one hopes to avert numerous deaths from this plague. *(Arrows)*

Snow-rose
A gift Vanyel made as a reward for a chirra that had carried his packs through a blizzard. *(LHM)*

Snow-wren
A brown bird with a gray cap, native to Valdemar. Dean

Elcarth reminded Talia of a snow-wren with his gray hair and chipper behavior. *(Arrows)*

Snowfire k'Vala
The Hawkbrother who rescued Darian Firkin from capture by invading barbarians and adopted the boy as his younger brother. He was also Darian's first teacher in magic. Snowfire was married to Nightwind, the father of Moonshadow, and his bondbirds were the mated eagle-owls Hweel and Huur. *(Owl)*

Snowlight
A Tayledras woman who conceived twins by Vanyel so that Starwind k'Treva and Moondance could adopt one of them, the boy who became Brightstar. Featherfire, the girl, remained with Snowlight. *(LHM)*

Snowstar
Tayledras scout who called for mage help in evicting a basilisk from his patrol area. *(Winds)*

Snowstar
The Kaled'a'in Adept, Snowstar, was the official go-between for the mages and Urtho. He also helped lead the evacuation before the Cataclysm, and became a member of White Gryphon's council. *(Gryphon)*

Soaproot
A natural cleanser, it is often planted among the water-weeds near the Herald Waystations. Heralds use it to wash soiled clothing and themselves. *(Arrows)*

Sofi (Companion)
Companion to Herald Destria. When Destria was circuit riding in Valdemar's northern district and broke her legs while rescuing children from a flood, Sofi got her Chosen and the youngsters to safety. *(Arrows)*

Sofya (Herald)
A Herald Courier Vanyel met at an inn on his way to Forst Reach for a vacation. Sofya's Companion is the stallion Gavis. *(LHM)*

Solan
Hardornen soldier posted to the message tower on the Hardorn-Valdemar border. Solan and his captain dem-

onstrated to Kris and Talia the message-relay system King Alessandar's realm used, which involved towers, light, and reflection devices. *(Arrows)*

Solaris (Son of the Sun)
The High Priest chosen Son of the Sun by the god Vkandis himself. She reformed the corrupt black robe priests and returned Karse's worship to the original writ and rules of Vkandis. Solaris was also responsible for eliminating the cleansing fires, slavery, prostitution, and the production of narcotics. *(Storms, Owl)*

Solstice fires
They are lit at Midsummer Solstice and part of ancient rituals that include maidens leaping over the flames. *(Sword)*

Son of the Sun
The title given to the Supreme High Priest in the Karsite religion, who is also the temporal and spiritual leader, and military commander under the guidance of Vkandis. *(BB, Storm)*

Sondri
She was a maid at the Forst Reach manor-keep. *(LHM)*

Song-carving
What the *kyree* shaman Hyrryl called Bard Stefen's singing for the entertainment of the Hot Springs Clan of *kyree*. *(LHM)*

Songlight
A Tayledras mage assigned to help the scouts. Though injured, Songlight still attended the Council by Mind-touch and relayed to others who couldn't be there. *(Winds)*

So'trekoth
Shin'a'in term for a fool who will believe anything, literally, "gape-mouthed hatchling." *(Oath)*

Soul-bond
A magic link similar to a geas. Need has a Soul-bond with her chosen bearers. *(Winds, Oath, Sword)*

Southford
A village in Hardorn visited by Kris and Talia during their ambassadorial trip to that country's capital. *(Arrows)*

Southron Keep
One of Valdemar's Great Courts. Bards and minstrels often dream of attaining a permanent spot at such a place. *(LHM)*

Sovvan Feast
A harvest festival held on Sovvan-night. According to the old folks, a successful Sovvan hunt meant good luck for the entire winter. *(Oath)*

Sovvan-Night
A harvest festival celebration filled with partying and superstitious rituals. It is also a night of honest wariness and respectful traditions such as putting candles in darkened windows. Tradition holds that on Sovvan-night the veil between this plane and the Otherworlds is thin. *(LHM)*

Spangera
A town in Hardorn where army stragglers managed find shelter behind the fortifications before the worst of the Mage-Storms struck. *(Storm)*

Spears of the Law
The Haighlei Royal Police and Guard. *(Gryphon)*

Special Council
A resistance government of Hardorn after the Empire had moved into their territory. It was a disorganized group of about thirty nobles who had survived Ancar's purges, plus the heads of Guilds and one member who claimed to speak for Hardorn's mages. There was no single leader. *(Storm)*

Special Messenger
Heralds appointed as messengers on Royal command, they wear a silver-arrow insignia. *(Arrows, Winds)*

Speed-healing
A technique trained Healers resist using because of the severe strain on the patient's reserves. With speed-

healing, intense exhaustion and buildup of fatigue poisons mean the patients must sleep frequently, and they experience considerably more pain than they would with normal-rate healing. *(Arrows)*

Spell of the True Sight
A spell that keeps the mage who casts it from being fooled by illusions. *(Oath)*

Spider-Priestess
A religious order of eunuchs who wear female garb. Sewen volunteered to convince the Bard Leslac that Tarma was a Spider-Priestess. The idea was to make Leslac stop writing outrageously flattering songs and hanging around Tarma in hopes of becoming her lover. *(Oath)*

Spirit of Truth
A painting representing the Spirit of Truth hanging in Haven's High Temple; it reminded Vanyel of a demented angel, and of Bard Stefen. *(LHM)*

Spirit-sword
What the Hawkbrothers called Need. *(Oath)*

Spongetoad
An amphibian that soaks up vast amounts of water in the rainy season, swelling to several times its normal size, then survives on the stored water supply during the long summer drought. *(Arrows)*

Stable Elements
The elements of Fire and Earth; their Lesser Wind is invoked by a Journeyman mage's testing spell. *(Oath)*

Staferd's Colddrakes
A mercenary company camped next to the Sunhawks during the siege against Declin Lord Kelcrag. *(Sword)*

Star
Vanyel's mare, a delicately boned black palfrey. She was a gift from his mother, Lady Treesa. *(LHM)*

Star-Eyed, The
The Shin'a'in Goddess, also known as She of the New Moon and South Wind. Her eyes are the spangled dark-

ness of the sky at midnight. Raven-haired and tawny-skinned, her forms/faces are: Maiden, Mother, Warrior, and Crone. While the Maiden and Mother claim the Clan, the Warrior claims the Oathbound and Sword-sworn, and the Crone claims Healers. *(Oath)*

Starblade k'Sheyna
A Clan Elder and a Adept mage, he was estranged from both his sons, Darkwind because he became a scout and wouldn't use magic, and Wintermoon because he had no strong mage skills. Starblade was captured and subverted by Falconsbane, his bondbird Karry killed and replaced by a hawk-sized crow. The spell tying him to Falconsbane was broken when Nyara revealed the compulsions and Vree killed the crow that held them in place. Starblade's new bondbird was Hyllarr, a crested hawk-eagle. He also acquired a lover, the Shin'a'in shaman healer Kethra, who helped him recover from his mental and physical wounds. *(Winds)*

Starfall
Tayledras Adept, Elder, Leader, and father of the Healing-Mage Firesong. His bondbird was a cooperi hawk. Starfall worked hard to build the Heartstone of what was to become k'Valdemar Vale. *(Owl)*

Stargem
A member of Amberdrake's lost family. *(Gryphon)*

Starsinger
A member of Amberdrake's lost family. *(Gryphon)*

Starsong k'Sheyna
A Tayledras scout and a former lover of Wintermoon. *(Winds)*

Starwind k'Treva
An Adept Tayledras and Speaker of the k'Treva Hawk-brothers. Starwind's bondbird was a white gyrfalcon, Asheena. Herald-Mage Savil studied magery with Starwind and became his Hawksister. Lifebonded to Moon-dance kTreva, the couple adopted and raised Vanyel's son, Brightstar. *(LHM)*

Staven
Shin'a'in word for "water." *(Oath)*

Staven Frelennye
Lord Holder of Frelennye, Tylendel's twin, and his elder by an hour. The boys were always closely mind-linked, a fact that enabled them to know of each other's danger or pain. Staven was intensely involved in the Frelennyes' long-running feud with the Leshara clan, and when he died in an ambush, Tylendel felt his death and almost went mad, triggering a fierce psychic storm that damaged the Temple Grove. Tylendel's grief over Staven's murder was overwhelming, and had tragic consequences. *(LHM)*

Steading
A Holderkin one-family property. A man and his Firstwife are expected to eventually move out of his Father's Steading and set up their own. *(Arrows)*

Steelmind
A Hawkbrother whose name was given to him by an older Tayledras who admired the young scout's ability to gather information. Steelmind traded plants, herbs, and seeds at the Errold's Grove market. He also delivered herbal remedies to Keisha from his vale's Healer. While he was participating in Darian's expedition to the north, he and Shandi fell in love. Steelmind's bondbird was a buzzard. *(Owl)*

Stefansen Jadrevalyn (Prince, King)
The King of Rethwellan. Kethry, Tarma, and Jadrek helped put Stefan on the throne after Stef's brother Raschar had seized it for himself through murder and treachery. Stef was declared an outlaw the day his brother Raschar was crowned. Stefansen, his wife Mertis, and their baby son found refuge at Herald Roald's hunting lodge in Valdemar. They were left alone there until Kethry, Tarma, and Jadrek arrived, bringing with them the legendary Sword That Sings. The Sword identified Stefansen as Rethwellan's rightful ruler, obligating him to fight for his throne. *(Oath)*

Stefen (Bard)
Stefen had been kidnapped by Bard Lynnell and brought

to the Collegium when he was only ten. Until then, he had been in the dubious care of an elderly drug addict, Berte, playing on street corners. At eighteen, Stefen was Medren Ashkevron's roommate, and Medren noticed that when he was ill and Stefen played, his pain went away. The Bardic Council studied Stefen's skills after he had successfully demonstrated his talent by aiding the seriously ill King Randale. As a result of this and his natural ability for all three Bardic Gifts, he was advanced to full Bard status. Stefen had a crush on Vanyel and set out to win his affections. It took some time to gain the trust of the over-worked Herald-Mage, but Stefen was successful. The two spent many hours together, and became lifebonded. Stefen became willing to dare any danger and go wherever Herald-Mage Vanyel was to be. Moonwind discovered that Stefen was actually the reincarnation of Tylendel. When Vanyel died, Vanyel left Stefen the life-long task of convincing the people of Valdemar that they could survive without Herald-Mages, and that the skills of regular Heralds would serve to protect the kingdom. In the end, Stefen went to his natural death in the Forest of Sorrows a contented man, and joined Vanyel and Yfandes guarding the Forest of Sorrows and later in the Havens. *(LHM, Winds, Storms)*

Steladar (Companion)
One of the original three Grove-Born Companions, he Chose King Valdemar's son. *(Arrows)*

Stella Harthorn
Villager who unfairly accused Lilly of profiting from Errold's Grove's occupation during the barbarian invasion. *(Owl)*

Stellat Shoots
A plant that clusters at the foot of a mother tree like a town at the foot of a Lord's Keep. *(Oath)*

Stenchbeetles
An odorous pest, they inhabit some of the southern woodlands of Valdemar. *(Arrows)*

Stormcloud
The Tayledras scout who is Darkwind's oldest and best

friend. His Mage-Gift was not enough to qualify him for the Council. His bondbird was a white raven, Krawn, a talkative joker. *(Winds)*

Stormwing k'Sheyna
A captive Hawkbrother Adept caged by the sorceress Keyjon. Guardian of the firebirds, he refused to help her enslave them. *(Oath)*

Stormwing
An Adept who couldn't join Starwind's search for a colddrake swarm set loose near the k'Treva vale because she was pregnant. *(LHM)*

Stranger's Gate
A town's entry where non-citizens register their names, origins, and business with Gate Guards. In Mornedealth, Stranger's Gate linked the town to Trade Road and was wide enough for three wagons to pass side by side; it had an ironwork portcullis as well as massive bleached wood doors. *(Oath)*

Strategy Room
Located in Urtho's Tower, its most prominent feature was a table-sized contour map of the war zone. *(Gryphon)*

Street of the Chandlers
A Mornedealth lane where a faked traffic blockage forced Kethry down an adjacent alley where she was abducted. *(Oath)*

Sturgeon, Giant Lake Evendim
A white-fleshed freshwater fish that lives in the deep rivers of Valdemar. Normally a large fish, the specimens that live in the magic-tinged waters of Lake Evendim grow into true giants. The tough fisher folk hunt the sturgeon with harpoons and harvest the roe for caviar and the bladder stones for cleaning purposes. *(LHM)*

Sturgeon Stones, or Cleaning Stones
White stones found in the swim bladders of the giant Lake Evendim sturgeon. These are valued for their ability to remove any kind of stain or mark from white leather, and each year the fisher folk pay part of their

taxes to the crown in sturgeon stones. A cleaning stone is included in each Herald's field kit. *(LHM)*

Sulemeth (King)
The Haighlei Emperor of the nation of Ghandai. Two of his sons are part of Shalaman's bodyguard. *(Gryphon)*

Sulma Farle
Urtho's Field Commander during the mission to disable the "stick" weapons of Ma'ar's troops. *(Gryphons)*

Summer Horse Fair
The Shin'a'in chose a town to hold their annual horse fair in every year, but change it from time to time based on sales and safety issues. *(Oath, Sword)*

Summerdance
A young Tayledras woman who flirted with Darian as soon as she met him, and became his first real girlfriend at k'Vala Vale. Apprenticed to Steelmind, she studied plants and herbs, and their uses. *(Owl)*

Summerfawn
A Kaled'a'in Adept who went with Silence/Snowfire to find k'Sheyna's new homeland. A Gate could not be built unless the anchors had seen the place and could visualize it as a terminal. She was the one who remained at the new site to anchor that Gate, sending Snowfire back to anchor the k'Sheyna Gate, lessening the burden on both Adepts. *(Winds)*

Summerhawk
She was with the k'Leshyan delegation which came to Haven, and part of the Husbandry Discipline. Notable as a good cook. *(Storm)*

Summerhawk
A Kaled'a'in trondi'irn who accompanied Judeth to Khimbata with the Silvers. He is a strong Mindspeaker. *(Gryphon)*

Summersky
A Tayledras scout who relieved Darkwind when he patrolled with Elspeth. *(Winds)*

Summerstar
A Tayledras scout. *(Winds)*

Suncat Trevavyska
A member of the Falcon Clan, he was a Councilman in the ancient times when the Kaled'a'in divided into two peoples. *(Winds)*

Sun Throne
The Sun throne is reserved exclusively for the High Priest of Karse, speaker for Vkandis. *(BB, Storm)*

Sun-Lord Resoden
A deity worshipped in Jkatha, Kethry punished an ex-apprentice mage-turned-robber by putting a geas on him to build walls for Sun-Lord Resoden. *(Oath)*

SunDescending
A Karsite holy service conducted at the end of each day by one of the Voices of Vkandis. *(Arrows)*

SunHeart
A Karsite version of walking the Moonpaths. The seeker must be in the sun-exposed Temple or must go out into the open sunlight and wait for the God's answer to his prayer. *(Storm)*

Suncloud
A Tayledras scout sent to fetch extra Gate-guards when Herald-Mage Savil arrived in the Vale unexpectedly. *(LHM)*

Sundered Kin
To the Shin'a'in, these are the magic users known elsewhere as the Hawkbrothers or Tayledras. *(Winds)*

Sundering of the Clans
The division of Kaled'a'in into the Shin'a'in and the Tayledras after the end of the Mage Wars. *(Winds)*

Sundisk Pectoral
A very ancient symbol, as old as Karse itself, worn only by the Son of the Sun. *(Storm)*

Sunfeather
A Tayledras scout. *(Winds)*

Sunhame

Karse's capital and the site of Vkandis Sunlord's first and largest Temple, called the Throne of Vkandis. *(Storm)*

Sunhawks

A top mercenary company formed by its captain, Idra, and composed of specialist troops: skirmishers, horse-archers, and trackers. Its colors were brown and golden-yellow. Tarma hired on with them as scout and Kethry as mage, with Warrl as a bonus. The Sunhawks' repute was so high that monarchs often negotiated contracts in person with Idra. *(Oath)*

Sunleaf

A k'Vala scout whose bondbird is a forestgyre. *(Owl)*

Sunlord Vkanda

An early name for the Karsite god, his is the official state religion of Karse. In the time of Vanyel, Vkandis was referred to as Vkanda. *(LHM)*

Sunpriest

A member of the religious establishment serving the god Vkandis in the nation of Karse. *(BV)*

Sunsdale

An about-to-be-attacked Karsite village which appeared to Alberich in a vision. He led his soldiers to Sunsdale's defense and destroyed the bandits who had hoped to convert the town into an impregnable stronghold after killing most of its residents and enslaving the rest. This brought Alberich to the attention of the priests, who pronounced him a witch for possessing the Gift of Foresight, and sentenced him to death by burning. *(Arrows)*

Sunsguard

Karse's military, reorganized when Solaris became High Priest. *(Winds)*

Sunsinger, Rothas

One of a pair of early Heralds that Talia read about in tales and legends. Rothas Sunsinger was lifebonded to Lythe Shadowdancer, and they were separated by a tragic curse, she confined to the night hours, he to the daylight. They had many adventures before finding the means to break their curse. Their story is well-loved by the people of Valdemar, and many versions of their life and wanderings exist. *(Arrows)*

Sunsong
A Tayledras Adept, still recovering from moving some firebirds to a sanctuary at the time Starwind needed help in coping with the colddrakes, and thus excused from being asked. *(LHM)*

Sunstone
A Tayledras scout whose bondbird is a falcon. *(Owl)*

Sun's Ray
Talia's Karsite priestly title after she was adopted into their order. *(Storm)*

Suras
One of the three *hertasi* who attached himself to Darkwind when he moved back into the Vale. *(Winds)*

Suriya
One of Hadanelith's victims at White Gryphon. *(Gryphon)*

Sursha (Queen)
The widow of Jkatha's King and his appointed regent for their three children. Civil war erupted when her brother-in-law, Declin Lord Kelcrag, opposed her. Sursha chose Havak Lord Leamount as her General-in-Chief. He and the Sunhawks won the war for her. Her eldest son is likely to wed Merili of Rethwellan. *(Oath)*

Swan
She was one of the Chesters' milch cows. White, and with a nasty habit of using her tail to sting anyone milking her who hadn't warmed his hands before touching her udder, as Lavan found out the hard way. *(BB)*

Sweetsprings
The first town Talia came to when Rolan took her to Haven. A roadguard and a kindly innkeeper befriended her there. *(Arrows)*

Sword that Sings, The
The subject of an ancient story Jadrek found in Rethwellan's chronicles. Legend said the sword could determine the country's lawful ruler. Idra sought permission to leave the capital on the pretext of a hunt for the missing Sword, but was using the story to find Prince Stefanson. Raschar the Usurper gave his approval. Though he wanted the Sword himself, to prove he was the rightful monarch, he was sure she was using the tale as a ruse to get to Stefan, so he caught and killed his sister before she could leave town. Kethry and Tarma came upon the weapon beside a skeleton in The Comb. Kethry sensed magic on it and took it with her. Later, at Herald Roald's lodge, Stefansen unsheathed the Sword, and it sang for him, the true king. *(Oath)*

Sword-dance
Strenuous and whirling, it is performed by men of the Shin'a'in Clans. It should properly end in a calculated sprawl and a pretense of utter exhaustion. *(Oath)*

Sworn One
A Shin'a'in who is Kal'enedral or pledged to the Goddess. *(Oath, Storm)*

Sylvan (Herald)
A mathematics instructor at the Collegium. *(Arrows)*

Syrtin
Lady Myria's newborn son. Giving birth to him left her in poor health because her stingy late husband would not hire a Healer to attend her. *(Oath)*

T

Tadrith Skandrakae
Son of Skandranon and Zhaneel and Keenath's twin. He was a goshawk-type gryphon with broad gray wings and short ear tufts. He joined the Silvers with dreams of doing something spectacular but very different from the heroic deeds his father was famous for. Like his partner Silverblade, he felt smothered by his parents and was eager to accomplish something on his own, and succeeded magnificently. Tad joined the gryphon fighting wing known as the Silvers. On his first mission he was lost in the wilderness along with his partner Silverblade, and had to fight off a pack of vicious, magic-absorbing *wyrsa*, then survive in the jungle despite his injuries until help came. *(Gryphon)*

Tahk
The stablemaster at the Palace in Haven. *(Storm)*

Tailor's Court
A street in Haven and the site of the Lady Fountain. *(Arrows)*

Talamir (King's Own Herald)
Talamir was the Queen's Own Herald in the first years of Queen Selenay's reign. During his years as a regular Herald, he was one of the two Heralds who got Alberich over the border from Karse. Talamir served Selenay's father, King Sendar, in the Tedrel Wars, and he was trying to protect the King, along with Jadus, when his first Companion, Taver, was killed. Jadus lost his leg and

King Sendar perished in the same attack. Talamir almost died of pain and guilt, but was chosen by Rolan to be Queen's Own and survived, though it was said half of his heart was already in the Havens with Taver. When Selenay took the throne, the elderly Talamir was uncomfortable advising a young and headstrong female ruler, and was unable to prevent Selenay from contracting an impetuous marriage to Prince Karathanelan of Rethwellan, the father of Princess Elspeth. When, under the manipulations of Nursemaid Hulda, Elspeth behaved so badly that her selection as Heir was in doubt, Talamir was on the point of proposing that she be fostered with his remote kindred. He died before the plan was put in place, and it was later confirmed that he was poisoned. Herald Teren and Herald Keren were his surviving grandchildren. *(Exile, Arrows)*

Talen
The *dyheli* who served as Keisha's mount on her ride back to Errold's Grove. *(Owl)*

Talesar (Lord)
One of Lord Breon's rude guests at the celebration where Darian was made a knight. *(Owl)*

Tale'edras
See Tayledras

Tale'sedrin
The Shin'a'in name for Tarma's clan, Children of the Hawk, which was nearly wiped out by bandits. Tarma was the only survivor, and became Kal'enedral to seek revenge, aided by the White Winds sorceress, Kethry. As Tarma's blood-sister, Kethry was Oathbound to raise the clan banner again because the Swordsworn Tarma had taken a vow of celibacy. The mage and her husband Jadrek produced seven children to form the core of the reborn Tale'sedrin, thus the clan became known as The Clan that Would Not Die. *(Oath, Storm, Sword)*

Tale'sedrin token
The size of a coin, it is metallic on one side, enameled on the other, and bears the image of a gold-feathered hawk. Given by the Kal'endral to OutLanders they deem

worthy, it grants passage through the Dhorisha Plains. *(Winds)*

Talhkarsh

The true name of the imp a young sorcerer named Leland meant to summon and bind to his will, but he called instead upon the demon Thalhkarsh, a fatal mistake. *(Oath)*

Talia Sensdaughter (Queen's Own Herald)

Talia grew up as one of the Holderkin, a puritanical border group which discourages knowledge of outsiders. When Talia turned thirteen she fled her family and an arranged marriage and ran to a secret hiding place in terror and grief. She heard the unmistakable sound of a Companion's bridle bells and tumbled from her cave to fall at the hooves of Rolan, who Chose her. This would prove to be the turning point in Talia's life. She was now Monarch's Own Herald and in charge of the taming of the brat, Princess Elspeth. Talia uncovered a plot by nursemaid Hulda to keep Elspeth from being Chosen, and was able to end the conspiracy and turn young Elspeth into a giving and loving girl. Talia's gift of Empathy was combined with Healing, thus making her a Mind-Healer. She used her Gift to calm the troubles of the Queen and all the Heralds. Talia became close to everyone in the Circle after letting go of the insecurities she'd learned in her Holderkin upbringing. She was especially close to Herald Kris and Herald Dirk. Talia was assigned to ride her trainee circuit with Kris, and during it was thoroughly schooled in using her Gift, after a near-breakdown out on the far end of Valdemar. After completing her internship, Talia and Kris were sent on a doomed mission to Hardorn to check out Ancar's suitability as a possible spouse for Elspeth. During Ancar's coup Kris was assassinated and Talia was captured and tortured. Prince Ancar and Hulda were plotting to take over Valdemar by marrying Ancar to Elspeth and then subverting the Princess, but Talia was able to keep Valdemar's royals out of Ancar's hands. Dirk rescued Talia from certain death by using his Fetching powers amplified by the Companions and Elspeth's Farsight. Talia lived to enjoy her lifebond with Dirk. They were married and had a son named Jemmie. After the marriage, Dirk and Talia were sent on a diplomatic mission to Karse to meet with Solaris, the new Son of the Sun. Solaris declared Talia to be an honorary Priestess of Vkandis upon the advice of her Firecat Hansa. A later mission sent them to Rethwellan to seek help from King Faram. They received help in the form of Kerowyn and her Skybolts, and the Rethwellan Army under the leadership of its Lord Martial, Prince Darenthallis, who would become a Herald himself and Queen Selenay's Consort. *(Arrows, Storm, Sword)*

Tallen-flowers

These bloomed around Master Lenne's tannery, and acted as a warning of pollution. If the tallen sickened and died, Master Lenne knew there was a problem, and would fix it before worse damage was done. *(Oath)*

Tallo

Former name of Moondance k'Treva. He talked with Vanyel and revealed that, like the younger man, he had been a misunderstood youth, both *shay'a'chern* and having his magical Gifts appearing early, frightening his family. Unlike Vanyel, however, Tallo was of humble birth. Rebelling against parents who did not understand what was happening to him, Tallo ran away with his lover, a member of a travelling troupe of gleemen. A quarrel loosed Tallo's untrained Mage-Gifts, killing his friend, and a remorseful Tallo tried to kill himself. Found by Savil, who brought him to Starwind, Tallo was gradually transformed into the Healer-Adept Moondance. *(LHM)*

Talon-sheath

A metal claw-guard that fits over a gryphon's talons to protect them against weapons. The sheaths make walking awkward, but prevent crippling combat injuries. *(Owl)*

Talsheena

Reaycha's young gryphon partner (gender unspecified) in the campaign to defeat Falconsbane. *(Winds)*

Taltherian wine
An excellent strong wine. Alberich gave Skif his first glass. *(TT)*

Tam
Lord Withen's chief stableman and his most trusted horse trainer. *(LHM)*

Tam (Master)
One of the Artificers, she and Master Levy were assigned by Magister Henlin to go to the Queen and present the Craftsmen's plan of counterattack on the storms. *(Storm)*

Tamar
A Sunhawk that took over Tarma's scout patrol while she looked for a secret path around Declin Lord Kelcrag's stronghold. *(Oath)*

Tamas
One of Sewen's sargeants. *(Oath)*

Tammas (Herald)
Herald in the reign of King Sendar, he was taught by Alberich upon his arrival in Valdemar. *(Exile)*

Tamsin
Lady Cinnabar's lifebonded mate and a Healer in Urtho's camp. *(Gryphon)*

Tan Twoknives
One of Lord Rendan's band of cutthroats. *(LHM)*

Tandere Cycle
A Bardic song supposedly written by the same Bard who created "Blood Bound." *(LHM)*

Tangle-cord
A rope weapon one throws to trip an opponent. *(Winds)*

Tansy
A young mother of two toddlers entranced by the colddrake queen in the Pelagir village of Garthhold. Her husband was killed by the monster and her grandfather sacrificed himself to save them by sticking a pitchfork into the side of the colddrake queen. This broke the

enchantment and freed his granddaughter, enabling Vanyel to save her and her children. *(LHM)*

Tansy Gelcress
Good neighbor of the Alders in Errold's Grove, married to Olek Gelcress. *(Owl)*

Tantara
A land far from the Kaled'a'in Clans. Amberdrake's family volunteered to live there in the city of Therium so that the Kaled'a'in would have agents in the north. When Ma'ar took over the neighboring realm of Predain and moved against Tantara, Amberdrake's family was caught in the war, and he never saw them again. *(Gryphon)*

Tantras (Herald)
Also called Tran. The Herald who volunteered to be the non-active anchor while the Herald-Mages reset the Guardian Web, knowing that if there was an accident, he would die. His Companion was Delian. *(LHM)*

Tantris (Companion)
The Companion to Herald Kris, who nicknamed him Fairyfoot. Tantris was killed along with Kris by Ancar's troops. *(Arrows)*

Taran Shire
A seasoned gryphon trainer at Ka'venusho. *(Gryphon]*

Tarma shena Tale'sedrin
Once a talented young woman on the eve of marriage to a good man she loved, with a voice that was the pride of the Shin'a'in clans, Tarma's life changed forever after a vicious bandit attack. Her voice was ruined when the bandits raped, strangled, and left her for dead during her Clan's massacre. She became Kal'enedral, bonded to the Goddess, a sexless Swordsworn Warrior determined to pursue revenge as the sole survivor of the massacred Stooping Hawk Clan. Trained by spirit-servants of the Goddess and aided by the mage Kethry, Tarma won her revenge. The bandits all died, and the women who defeated them became *she'enedra,* or blood-sisters. It was through Kethry, who, as *she'enedru,* was a member of the clan, that Clan Tale'sedrin lived once more.

For the rest of her life Tarma traveled with Kethry. They helped put Prince Stefansen, the rightful king of Rethwellan, on the throne, and they trained his descendants in a school where Tarma taught the students swordfighting while Kethry taught magic, and Kethry's husband, Jadrek, taught scholarly subjects. After Tarma and Kethry retired and turned the school over to Kethry's son, they helped Kethry's granddaughter Kerowyn save her brother's fiancé when she was abducted from her wedding feast, and took Kerowyn and Darenthallis, prince of Rethwellan, on as students. *(Oath, Sword)*

Taroc
A popular tavern game. *(BB, Oath)*

Tarres
A hedge-wizard with the Skybolts, he went with Lerryn Twoblades' group when the company had to split up to lose the enemy forces pursing them. Kerowyn and the second group could have used Tarres' skills to counter the enemy mage chasing them. *(Sword)*

Tarrn
A neuter *kyree* historian, he was the Compiler of Chronicles, which were then interpreted in his accompanying Commentaries. Outside of White Gryphon, he was the finest scholar in the ancient Kaled'a'in tongue. *(Storm)*

Tashi
A girl who was part of Vanyel's mini-Court, she had a crush on Tylendel. *(LHM)*

Tashiketh Pral Skylshaen
Leader of the gryphon wing from Iftel. Like the rest of his kind, he was heavier than a k'Leshyan gryphon in beak, neck, and chest. *(Storm)*

Tashir Remoerdis
The son of Deveran, he was the only survivor of the massacre at the palace. He escaped to be Chosen by the Companion Leshya and became the ruler of Lineas-Baires and a staunch ally of Valdemar. *(LHM)*

Taver (Companion)
The Monarch's Own Companion, he was the Companion

of Lancir, who was Queen Elspeth's Own, then Chose Healer Shavri, the lifebonded of King Randale. When Randale and Shavri died, Taver Chose Shavri's daughter Jisa, the wife of King Treven, maintaining the link of Companion and Monarch's Own. Taver was also the name of the first Companion of Talamir, who was killed in the Tedrel wars. *(LHM)*

Taving (Lord)
A councilman and the representative for the South who wondered if the Karsites were just biding their time until they could launch a new crusade, attacking Valdemar and invading his lands first. *(LHM)*

Tavis of Brengard
A high-ranking western nobleman who was secretly helping the Lake Evendim pirates. *(Arrows)*

Tavist (King)
He was Valdemar's Monarch in the era of the Arvale-Zalmon negotiations. The son of Queen Terilee and father of Queen Leshia, his reign was a quiet one, devoted to studied diplomacy. *(LHM)*

Tay
A kitchen drudge at the *Inn of the Green Man* where Vanyel sought employment, Tay was one of the menials who suffered as a result of Bel's hangovers. *(LHM)*

Tayledras
The mysterious and secretive people who dwell west of Valdemar in the Pelagir Hills. They were once part of the Kaled'a'in, but the Tayledras and the Shin'a'in Clans were sundered from each other after the Mage Wars, with the Tayledras choosing to use magic to cleanse the lands poisoned by Mage-Storms, and the Shin'a'in choosing to forego magic forever, except for shamanic magic. The Herald-Mage Savil was one the few outsiders who knew the Tayledras. She was adopted as a Wingsib into a Hawkbrother Clan and studied with one of their Adepts, Starwind k'Treva. So little-known and semi-mythical were the Hawkbrothers that children at Forst Reach had been warned for generations to "be good, or the Hawkbrothers will get you." It was therefore a

tremendous shock when two Hawkbrothers came through a Mage-Gate to the Holding and spent several days within the borders of Valdemar. Tayledras dwell in shielded Vales, magically modified areas alive with greenery and warmed by hot springs. Individual Tayledras dwellings, called *ekele*, sit high upon enormous trees whose growth is augmented and speeded by magic. Because the Tayledras Mages manipulate high levels of magical energy, their work with the powerful nodes bleaches out their hair and eyes, leaving them with silver hair at a very early age. Even Tayledras who forego magic and work as scouts or artisans have silver hair by the time they are thirty—a result of living in the magical energy of the Vales. Tayledras scout dress consists of jerkins and breeches dyed to match the forest. The Tayleras Mages wear wondrous outfits of embroidered and beaded fabric, often made of silk. Almost all Tayledras are accompanied by uniquely-bred and mind-linked bondbirds. The Vales also have populations of other sentient races associated with them—including *hertasi*, *kyree*, *tervardi*, and *dyheli*. By the time the Mage-Storm Crisis was over, the Tayledras Vales were firmly allied with Valdemar, and were engaged by Queen Selenay to help rid the country of the bad effects left behind by the Change-circles. *(BV)*

Tedrel Companies

Alleged mercenaries, they were really an entire nation of freelancers sent by Karse to fight Valdemar. After their defeat, the Tedrels looted Karse on their way home. Karse unsuccessfully complained about their behavior to the Mercenary Guild. *(Sword)*

Tedrel War

A conflict that occurred fifteen years before Talia came to Haven. Karse hoped to conquer Valdemar without actually declaring war on it. To accomplish that, Karse hired an entire nation, the Tedrel mercenaries, to attack Valdemar. Selenay's father King Sendar was killed by an assassin during the fighting, and Selenay, who had barely completed her Herald's training, assumed the throne and defeated the invaders. *(Arrows, Sword, Winds, TT, Oath)*

Tedric
A hired sword who worked for traders Tarma's Clan had dealt with. Tarma thought a guard using Mind-magic and accompanying Grumio's packtrain looked familiar, like Tedric. *(Oath)*

Tedric (Herald)
A Herald pensioner posted in Berrybay, he led the rescue team when Talia and Kris were snowbound in the Forest of Sorrows. *(Arrows)*

Tel
The cook at the *Pig and Stick Inn* of Highjorune, whom Minstrel Renfry persuaded to pack food for Vanyel before he left. *(LHM)*

Telemaine
The captain of the Haven Guards, he was originally in charge of the investigation into the deaths at the Merchant School. *(BB)*

Teleson
A long-distance communication device, also known as a mind-mirror, it was found in the hidden room beneath Urtho's tower, and enabled the party at the ruins to communicate with Haven and Karse. Operating by amplifying Mindspeech, the device used resonance from an arrangement of crystals. Requiring very little magic to function, the teleson was self-sustaining once started. It had a round crystal lens mounted on top, which showed the image of a distant speaker. A thin, distinct voice emerged from a gray metal box holding the crystal cradled in a quarter-moon-shaped depression. *(Gryphon, Storm)*

Teleson set
An amplifying metal lacework headband sometimes worn by Kelvren which assists communication between him and the Tayledras, since his Mindspeech is not particularly strong. *(Owl)*

Teleson-spell
A spell which assists a mage in speaking mind-to-mind. *(Storm)*

Telica
One of Hadanelith's victims in White Gryphon. *(Gryphon)*

Tell Alder
The middlemost of Keisha's five brothers. *(Owl)*

Tell-Me-True Spell
The Karsite equivalent of a Valdemaran Truth-Spell. *(Storm)*

Tembor Earth-Shaker
A god worshipped in Hardorn whose sect rivals that of Kindas Sun-Kindler. *(Arrows)*

Temple High Sanctuary
The most imposing structure in Talia's hometown of Sensholding. She used to be awed by it, thinking it the grandest building imaginable, but when she arrived at Haven, she learned it was really rather small and threadbare. *(Arrows)*

Temple Row
The street in Delton where Thalhkarsh's temple was located. *(Oath)*

Temple Servant
Among the Holderkin, the Goddess's servants had less freedom and more duties than the Temple's Handmaidens, and literally lived and died in their assigned Cloister corridors. *(Arrows)*

Temple and Priory of Thenoth
Thenoth was the lord of the beasts, and his followers care for injured, sick, and aged animals. Skif worked at the Thenoth temple in Haven just before he was Chosen. *(TT)*

Temple of Belden
A charitable order comprised of four priests and six novices. Beel was a novice in the small temple, which educated children as one of its charitable acts. *(TT)*

Temple of Kernos
The spiritual center in Haven. Excess food from Midwin-

ter Feasts of wealthier families is taken to the Temple
and distributed there to the hungry poor. *(BB)*

Temple of Thalhkarsh
Raised in one night by the demon who promoted itself
to godhood, it was adorned with obscene statues. Rites
of Dark Desires were held there, conducted by Thalhkarsh's high priest, an apprentice mage he controlled.
(Oath)

Temple of Ursa
A temple outside Petras that contained an escape tunnel
from the royal palace. The usurper Raschar used this
tunnel to flee the Sunhawk-led uprising on Midsummer
Night. *(Oath)*

Tenavril (Magister)
A writer of philosophy, he is regarded as an authority
on demons. *(Oath)*

Tent shrines
Religious shrines to the Star-Eyed Goddess, they are
identical in every Shin'a'in camp. Four simple tiny
wooden altars sit against the tent's walls. To the east
stands one to the Maiden, containing her symbol, a single fresh blossom in spring and summer, burning incense
in fall and winter. The Warrior's altar is at the south
wall, adorned with an ever-burning flame. The Mother's
altar stands to the west and holds a sheaf of grain. The
Crone dominates the north side, and her emblem is a
smooth black stone. Prayers are always sung to these
deities, not spoken. *(Oath)*

Teren (Herald)
Herald Keren's twin brother and Queen's Own Herald
Talamir's grandson. His situation is unusual in that he
wasn't Chosen at the same time as his sister but seven
years later. Teren is completely devoted to the Heraldic
Circle, and in later years he replaced Elcarth as Dean
of the Collegium. *(Arrows, TT, Winds)*

Terill (Queen)
Queen Terill was the mother of King Tavist of Valdemar. *(LHM)*

Terilee River
The main river in the southern half of the kingdom, it parallels the South Trade Road for much of its length. *(Arrows)*

Terthorn
An acquaintance of Barlen's who tried to cook some snails in white wine and discovered that the remains produced an intense red dye. *(Owl)*

Tervardi
A sentient birdlike race created by Urtho and his predecessors. They are magnificent singers, especially noted for their amazing trills. Their eminently defensible treetop homes gave the Tayledras the idea of building *ekele*. *(Owls, Storm, Winds)*

Ter'hala
A black-clad Kal'enedral, his blood-feud was with the deceased Mornelithe Falconsbane so it would never be completed. He dressed in black because he was too old to change. *(Storm)*

Te'sorthene
A Shin'a'in word meaning "heart-friend or spirit-friend." *(Oath)*

Tevar
King Theran's younger brother and an Orienteering instructor at Heraldic Collegium, Tevar's specialty is wilderness survival. He is an expert on Valdemar's flora and fauna. *(BB)*

Teyll-deer
The name of the natural deer of the Pelagiris. *(Winds)*

Thalhkarsh
A demonic spirit summoned from the Abyssal Planes when a foolish mage named Leland made an error in his incantation. Thalhlarsh took over a temple in the city of Delton and demanded sex and blood sacrifice from his followers. Tarma and Kethry thought they had defeated him, but he was recalled into being in the city of Oberdorn by an old enemy of theirs named Lastel Longknife. Tarma and Kethry nearly died battling him

at his new temple. Nemor, a priest of Anathei of the Purifying Flame, saved them and captured Thalhkarsh, who was taken to the priest's temple for safeholding until they could re-educate him. *(Oath)*

Thayer (General)
The commander of the Imperial Army, a no-nonsense officer with a raspy voice, the result of a youthful injury. *(Storm)*

Theela (Herald)
Herald in the reign of King Sendar, she was taught by Alberich upon his arrival in Valdemar. *(Exile)*

Theran (King)
The King of Valdemar during Herald Lavan Firestarter's time. In addition to his intelligence, natural ruling abilities, and commanding presence, he also looked like a King. He sentenced Jisette Jelnack to permanent incarceration with the Cloistered Order of Kernos Sequestered. *(BB)*

Therium
A city in Tantara where Amberdrake's family were living as agents for the Kaled'a'in. When he returned there, fleeing from Ma'ar's invasion, they had disappeared. *(Gryphon)*

Thesa (Healer)
The Healer who worked to bring Dirk back from the crisis caused when he used his Fetching Gift at extreme range to save Talia, which pushed his strength to its limits. *(Arrows)*

Thiera (Saint, The Immaculate)
A Saint of Valdemar venerated for her purity and resistance to worldly temptations. *(LHM)*

Third Army
Urtho's army before the Cataclysm, afterward it became the population of Iftel. Its human members served a god who decreed magic power would be held by priests only. Accompanying the humans to their new home were gryphons, *kyree, ratha, tyrill,* and *dyheli. (Storm)*

Thomlan Vel Cercian
A wealthy merchant whose home Skif robbed and vandalized. *(TT)*

Thorinna
A friend of Lady Treesa's who gave her a set of horrible plaster cherubs, which were broken when the screaming of Treesa's women panicked the untrained young mage Tashir. *(LHM)*

Thornton
A town in Valdemar where an old man, accompanying himself on the hurdy-gurdy, insisted on singing "Kerowyn's Ride" for her. Meant as a compliment, it irked the Captain; as she had perfect pitch, most amateur singers offended her. *(Sword)*

Thoser (Brother)
A priest of Anathei that questioned a young woman who claimed the forbidden worship of Thalhkarsh had been renewed in Oberdorn's old temple of Duross. *(Oath)*

Three Rivers
The Collegium cook Mero's hometown. It is also home to a cultural group that believes there is only one god, an oddity among the polytheistic peoples of Velgarth. The sect's teachings are contained in their oft-quoted *Book of the One. (Arrows)*

Throne City
The capital of Jkatha. During their civil war rebels drove the kingdom's rightful ruler, Queen Sursha, out of Throne City. *(Oath)*

Throwing spike
A Shin'a'in weapon usually worn in a wrist sheath. *(Oath)*

Thundersnow k'Sheyna
The Tayledras scout who went to Dawnfire's *ekele* to see if she wanted to go hunting, and found her dead. *(Winds)*

Ti'aeva'leshy'a
Considered a forest spirit by superstitious villagers, it is

a snow-white ghost bird with faint blue-gray markings. *(Winds)*

Tilden (Archduke)

The Archduke of Rethwellan and King Stefansen's former horsemaster, he holds estates on the Rethwellan/Jkatha border. He married his former bodyguard and fathered several daughters. Among them is a scholarly girl named Arboli who is older than the twins, Kira and Merili, and three younger girls. *(Oath)*

Tildy

Kethry's old nurse, she rescued Kethry from Wethes Goldmarchant when Kethry's brother married her off for money. Tildy also took Kethry to the White Winds school when the girl's mage Gifts began manifesting. *(Oath)*

Tilredan

The *dyheli* stag who carried packs on Wintermoon's and Skif's expedition to find Nyara. *(Winds)*

Tival

A city in the Eastern Empire. When cargo from Tival arrived in Jacona, Melles tricked Commander Peleun into investing against it, as he believed it contained products he had already cornered in the market. *(Storm)*

Tobe

A boy of Shonar, Tobe and four other youngsters got lost in a mage-blizzard and were rescued by Tremane. Tobe, along with Racky Loder, later became one of Tremane's pages. *(Storm)*

Tobe

A hard-bitten Skybolt who objected to Lyr's plan to lead her small band of scouts across the border into Karse. *(Sword)*

Tom Kalley

Leader of Errold's Grove's militiamen. The Blood Bear barbarians who raided Riverford Farm wiped out him and his entire force. *(Owl)*

Tori

The housekeeper at the Collegium who supplied Heralds

and trainees with special things if properly notified, such as properly altered Formal Grays suitable for Lan's Midwinter outing. *(BB)*

Tor'Getha
The chief Healer of An'desha's old clan, he was quick to jump to conclusions and look for enemies outside his own folk. Jarim reminded An'desha of Tor'getha. *(Storm)*

Townchit
A small brass token marked with the name of the town of issue, it is given to a Herald, along with supplies and services, as a record for the tax authorities at Haven. The courtesies signified by the townchit qualified the community for certain tax abatements. *(Arrows)*

Trade-tongue
The merchant language the Shin'a'in use in dealing with outLanders. *(Oath)*

Trana Farane
A prostitute in Haven, and sister to Desi Farane. *(TT)*

Tran-dust
A narcotic that induces dreamy clumsiness, slows reflexes, and confuses the user's senses. *(Oath, Winds)*

Transmuting
The rare mage power of transforming a spell already cast into another. Need possessed the power to Transmute, and was able to change Falconsbane's attack on the gryphlets into a spell that cleansed them of his tampering. *(Winds)*

Trap-spell
A magical snare set in advance around an enemy sorcerer, it requires only a signal from the mage who set it to trigger it, and trap the enemy mage. *(Oath)*

Tre
A swarthy Skybolt scout, the twin of Gies. Capable at handling a squad, Tre couldn't work with mages and lacked the expertise to become Captain of the Skybolts after Ardana's ouster, which was one of the many reasons Kerowyn was elected to the job. *(Sword)*

Tree-hare

An animal similar to a rabbit, but with short, tufted ears, long claws, and a flexible, bushy tail. Tarma and Kethry dined on them during their journey to visit the Hawk-brothers. *(Oath, Owl)*

Treelion

A creature that was one of the possible dangers in the forest area Wintermoon and Skif explored. They did not encounter any, however. *(Winds)*

Tremane (Duke Tremane Gyfarr Pendleson of Lynnai)

The Imperial Grand Duke once named as Charliss' Successor, Tremane was the Emperor's cousin several times removed, and was sixteen when his father first brought him to court. A Master mage, he worked as an Imperial scribe, and successfully completed cadet training. Tremane's Duchy of Lynnai bordered Hardorn, so Charliss put him in command of Imperial forces there as a test of worthiness, with the promise to train him as Heir if he was successful in conquering Hardorn. Tremane was intelligent, cunning, and facile in changing his tactics to suit the situation at hand, but his greatest virtue, according to Charliss, was his good luck. Tremane inspired great loyalty in his followers, both military and civilian. When the Mage-Storms began, Tremane and his army were cut off from communication with the Empire. Forced to survive on his own, Tremane established a central encampment at the town of Shonar, rounded up sufficient shelter and rations to get his troops through the winter, and worked with the people of Shonar to establish order and prosperity. His actions so impressed the people of Hardorn that they eventually asked Tremane to become their king, once it was ascertained that he had the gift of earth-sense and was willing to be bound to the land. Tremane entered into alliance with Valdemar, Rethwellan, Iftel, the Tayledras, the Shin'a'in, and others, presenting a solid and resolute border to the Eastern Empire and working together to end the Mage-Storms. *(Storm)*

Trenor

A little gelding palfrey Karal requisitioned from the

Temple herds and named after his younger brother, who exhibited many of the same nervous mannerisms. *(Storm)*

Trenor Severik
A rich man in Haven who had his collection of silver miniatures stolen. *(TT)*

Tresti (Healer)
A Journeyman Healer with Idra's Sunhawks, and a Healing Priestess of Shayana handfasted to Idra's second-in-command, Sewen. *(Oath)*

Trevale
A town on the East Trade Road between Haven and the border with Hardorn. Herald Talia and Herald Kris stopped overnight at an inn there while on their ambassadorial mission to King Alessandar's country. *(Arrows)*

Tre'valen shena Tale'sedrin
Kra'heera's apprentice, he was assigned to stay in k'Sheyna Vale to investigate why the Star-Eyed chose a Tayledras to become her avatar. Tre'valen gradually fell in love with the now ethereal Dawnfire. He sacrificed himself to save Starblade from Falconsbane and was also transformed into an avatar. *(Winds)*

Treven (Herald, King)
Grandson of Queen Elspeth the Peacemaker and Heir Presumptive of Valdemar to King Randale. Cousin to King Randale, and Herald Tantras' more distant cousin, Treven was a powerful Mindspeaker, and well trained in government and executive power. He had acted as his father's right-hand man at their border barony since he was nine. When it became apparent that Randale would never have a son, Treven was selected as Heir, and his training as a Herald was accelerated. Treven was lifebonded to Jisa, supposedly the daughter of King Randale and the King's lifebonded Healer Shavri, though actually Herald-Mage Vanyel was Jisa's father. In time, Jisa and Treven married, Treven took the throne, and Jisa became the King's Own Herald, and Treven's consort. *(LHM)*

Trevor (Herald)
The Seneschal's Herald during the reign of King Theron. *(BB)*

Trevor Corey (Lord)
Teacher of sword-ladies who wish to join the Guard. *(LHM)*

Trey/Torey Alder
One of Keisha's brothers. *(Owl)*

Treyvan
A gryphon, the mate of Hydona and father of Jervan and Lytha. A Master mage with a sly sense of humor, Treyvan is also a powerful fighter. Treyvan and his mate were sent by their clan k'Leshya to scout for a new home in the Pelagiris Forest, and they settled near k'Sheyna Vale. They helped train Darkwind and Elspeth in their mage abilities and were instrumental in the early defeats of Mornelithe Falconsbane. Eventually they went on to serve as k'Leshya's envoys to Valdemar, and helped fight the Mage-Storms. *(Storm, Winds)*

Triumph Gate
The main gate out of Hardorn's capital onto the main highway. Trader Evan took this route to meet with Rolan and leave Hardorn. *(Arrows)*

Trondi'irn
A k'Leshya Discipline, a trondi'irn is a Healer as well as a special caretaker for non-human creatures, particularly gryphons. Trondi'irn handle all the things the non-humans cannot do for themselves, and act as healers when necessary. *(Owl, Gryphon, Storm, Winds)*

Truth Spell
A spell used when necessary by the Heralds, the only residents of Valdemar trusted with the skill. The truth spell uses the air elemental *vrondi*. It is invoked by the Herald mentally reciting a cantrip nine times and envisioning a wisp of fog with blue eyes enveloping the person being examined. The First Stage Truth Spell reveals whether or not the speaker is telling the truth. The Second Stage Truth Spell forces him or her to answer any question truthfully. *(BV)*

Truth-Finder General
The official title of Hardorn's Grand Inquisitor. *(Winds)*

Tuck Chester (Herald)
See Chester, Tuck

Tuli (Herald-trainee)
A fellow student at the Collegium with Elspeth who was involved in discovering where Elspeth was disappearing to. *(Arrows)*

Turag (Herald)
The Lord Marshal's Herald, he was a battlefield replacement for Herald Marak, who had been one of the early casualties at White Foal Pass. *(BB)*

Twin Suns School
This mage school taught that demonic beings were created purely of evil forces, in opposition to the belief of Anathei's followers. *(Oath)*

Tylar
One of the human Silvers, he almost lost his composure when the Silvers arrested Hadanelith. *(Gryphon)*

Tylendel Frelennye (Herald-Mage-trainee)
Herald-Mage Savil's protege and the son of her heart, and Vanyel's life-bonded lover until his death. Tylendel's Gifts appeared wildly and dangerously when he was nine, beginning with ThoughtSensing, Fetching, Empathy, and the Mage-Gift. Only his twin brother Staven had the nerve to stay with him until they were under control, as the brothers had been mindlinked since birth. Tylendel's beloved twin brother, Staven Frelennye, was murdered in an ambush by the Leshara Clan. Maddened by the pain of losing him, Tylendel hatched a plan to eliminate the Lesharas, with Vanyel's help. In the course of carrying out his revenge, Tylendel was repudiated by his Companion Gala, who died protecting the Leshara clan. Tylendel, unable to bear the pain, committed suicide. The Companions accorded Tylendel full Heraldic status, and rang the Death Bell in his honor. Bard Stefen had Tylendel's reborn soul. *(LHM)*

Tyler (Father)
The amiable and non-repressive priest who served Forst Reach after the late and unlamented Father Leren Benevy. He was attacked by the seemingly deranged hedge-wizard Vanyel brought to Tyler for treatment. The devious mage stabbed Father Tyler, then attacked Lady Treesa and wounded Herald-Mage Vanyel with a leech-blade before being captured. *(LHM)*

Tyreena's Blessed Ass
An oath the normally ladylike Yfandes swore when Bard Stefen apologized to her for running away. *(LHM)*

Tyrill
Native to Iftel, they are a larger race of *hertasi* created by Urtho. According to Tashiketh, they breed very rapidly. *(Storm)*

Tyron Jelnack
Leader of the Merchants' School Sixth Form bullies. His father was Grand Master of the Silversmiths' Guild. Lavan nicknamed the boy "Tyrant." When Tyron tried to administer a brutal and unmerited punishment on young Lavan, Lavan lost control of his then dormant FireStarting Gift and burned Tyron and his comrades to death. *(BB)*

Tyrsell
A king stag and leader of the k'Vala *dyheli*, like all king stags, he was an extremely powerful Mindspeaker, with the ability to mentally control his entire herd. Also like all king stags, he was able to force-teach humans foreign languages in a matter of moments by impressing the language on their mind. Tyrsell became a Great Lord of State when he was chosen to lead the splinter *dyheli* herd to the new k'Valdemar Vale. *(Owl)*

Ulrich

Karal's master and mentor in Temple service. Ulrich was a Sun-priest mage, a black robe scholar, an advocate of the reforms of Solaris, and one of her most trusted aides. He was appointed envoy to Valdemar in an effort to negotiate a lasting peace between the long-feuding countries. Ulrich was murdered in Valdemar by a device planted by an assassin employed by the Eastern Empire. *(Storm)*

Unaffiliated Students

Also known as the Blues, they are a mix of serious scholars, Artificers, and courtiers' offspring who are allowed to attend classes at any of the three Collegia. Blues generally have a sponsor in the Court or among the three Circles of Heralds, Bards, or Healers. Blues fall into two groups, the Scholars and the Artificers. Some of the Blues are too busy with their studies to cause mischief, while other less serious students—particularly the highborn ones—are ripe for trouble, and are sometimes little better than thugs. *(Arrows, Storm)*

Uncle Silverhorn

A member of Amberdrake's lost family. *(Gryphon)*

Uncleansed Lands

The Tayledras term for the Pelagir Hills. The strange things found there include dangerous thinking plants and other unnatural leftovers from the ancient Mage-War and Cataclysm. *(Storm, Winds)*

Underwife

Any wife ranking second or lower among the Holderkin households. Those who adapt fully to the role feel they have it easy because they are not required to make decisions regarding the Steading; that is the responsibility of the Firstwife. In addition, becoming an Underwife is sometimes a guarantee of a more comfortable lifestyle; it means the household is already well established, and scrimping and hoarding are no longer necessary. *(Arrows)*

Unkindly Ones, The

Name for the Imperial deities who punish hubris. *(Storm)*

Upvale

A region famous for its wines. A member of the cadet branch of one of Mornedealth's Fifty Noble Families had just come into an excellent Royal Grant, the revenue on the Upvale wines. With visions of becoming a real aristocrat, he hired Kethry to check his newly acquired racing stable for harmful glamours. *(Oath)*

Urtho

Also known as The Mage of Silence, he was one of the most powerful Adepts in the history of Velgarth. Urtho was an artist and an inventor; his work included the creation of many complicated mechanical and magical constructs, but his greatest love was the creation of beauty, whether in the form of jewelry or of new sentient species, including the gryphons, the *tyrill* form of *hertasi*, and possibly firebirds. When the evil Adept Ma'ar tried to enslave his creations and the people around him, Urtho reluctantly became the leader of an army against the dark mage. He was betrayed by two of his own commanders, and poisoned by an agent of one of them in a successful assassination attempt. Urtho's Healers slowed the eventual outcome, but could not save his life. With his last hours ebbing away, Urtho sent Skan with a destruction device to Ma'ar's tower after evacuating his people away from Ma'ar's grasp and far from the destruction Urtho knew was coming in his own lands. Urtho's death would destroy his own Tower, a safeguard to prevent his constructs from falling into the wrong hands. The resulting double explosion caused what was to become known as the Cataclysm, and its echoes in Queen Selenay's reign resulted in the Mage-Storms. Excavations at the ruins of Urtho's Tower unearthed the device that stopped the Mage-Storms and prevented a second Cataclysm. *(Owl, Gryphon, Storm, Wind)*

Urtho's Tower

Located near the center of what is now the Dhorisha Plains, the ruins of Urtho's Tower resemble a snow-covered stub of melted rock protruding from a rolling hill, remarkable only for its immense size. In ancient times, the Tower was the headquarters of Urtho, the Mage of Silence, who fought the evil Ma'ar with incalculable magic energies, causing the Cataclysm. Weapons, workshops, and other arcane tools were buried deep beneath the crumbling structure, and recovered by mages and artificers who were seeking a solution to the Mage-Storms. *(Gryphon, Storm)*

Use-name

Most Tayledras choose a use-name more descriptive of their adult natures than that given them at their birth. Blood-path Adepts also adopt one to to hide their birth or true names and prevent enemies from spellcasting and thus learning everything about them, including their evil past histories. *(Winds, Owl, Gryphon)*

Ustil

A green vegetable that Herald Dirk despises. *(Arrows)*

Vai Datha
A Shin'a'in expression for "resignation or agreement," literally, "there are many ways." *(Oath)*

Val, also Valan/Valyn
Lord Breon's son and heir, his betrothed was Belinda. Val had unrealistic ideas of what battle was all about until Darian told him the realities. *(Owl)*

Valdemar
Kingdom in the world of Velgarth founded by the followers of Baron Valdemar, who were fleeing the tyranny of the Eastern Empire. Leading his people to the lands that now form the Kingdom of Valdemar, Baron Valdemar established his realm in the most northwest sector of the civilized world, an event marked on the Valdemaran calendar as the Year Zero. The nature of this realm's origin made it a welcome refuge for other exiles and law-abiding fugitives from elsewhere in Velgarth, hence the capital's name, Haven. Such a patchwork of languages and cultures would be difficult to rule were it not for the Heralds and their Companions, who ensure that the country's monarch and its Heralds are well-trained, well-meaning people working for the good of Valdemar. Valdemar's motto is "No one way is the true way." *(BV)*

Valdemar (Baron, King)
Baron and mage who led his people westward out of tyranny in the Eastern Empire and became king of the land which took his name. He was accompanied by his

wife and his seneschal, who were also mages. Baron Valdemar worried that his country would become just as tyrannical as the Eastern Empire if he could not find a way to insure that every monarch would be incorruptible. He petitioned to the Gods and Goddesses to help him prevent that, and received his answer in the form of the Companions. *(BV)*

Valdir (Minstrel)

A scruffy disguise Vanyel used to do undercover work. *(LHM)*

Vale

The equivalent of cities among the Taleydras. Each Vale is home base for a group of Kaled'a'in or Tayledras. The Vale's core is a magic-storing Heartstone. Once a Vale is fully established, it is protected by a shimmering magic curtain called a Veil set up around its perimeter. This Veil filters out undesirable natural things, like predators and cold weather, producing a lush, semitropical climate within, and serves as a warning net by letting those within the Vale know if it has been breeched by any unknown life-force. A Vale community consists of humans, *hertasi, dyheli,* gryphons, *kyree,* and *tervardi.* Human dwellings are called *ekele,* homes made of natural materials and designed to blend into the surroundings. Frequently these *ekeles* rest high in trees or are built into rock faces. In addition, there are gardens, bathing pools in a variety of temperatures, communal kitchens and eating areas. Meandering paths through the Vale are marked with colored stones to indicate directions and destinations: reddish stones lead to the Vale's entrance, black to private *ekeles,* green to water sources, and gray to the common areas. *(LHM, Winds, Owl)*

Vallen

The Guard-Captain with Elspeth and Darkwind's escort from the Vale to Haven once Elspeth finished her Mage training. *(Winds)*

Valley-node

A source point of great magical power. One lay under Starwind k'Treva's vale in the Pelagir Hills. The magic energy flows along lines like rainwater to streams. Wherever the streams connect, there was a concentration of energy called a node. The Tayledras can sometimes direct the course of such streams and move the magic from places where the ancient Mage Wars left it to other places where it will be useful. They also build their strongholds over these powerful areas. Tayledras Adepts can draw from the energy, while most outlanders can neither sense nor use them. Savil and Vanyel were among the rare exceptions to this. *(LHM, Winds)*

Vanyel Ashkevron (Herald-Mage)

The legendary Last Herald-Mage of Valdemar. A troubled youth, he came to Haven reluctantly, but became a well-adjusted young man with the help of his first love Tylendel, his aunt, Herald-Mage Savil, and his aunt's Tayledras friends. When Vanyel lost Tylendel in a tragic series of events, all of Vanyel's potential Gifts—Mindspeech, Fetching, Empathy, Mage-Gift, Farsight, Foresight, FireStarting, Bardic—were blasted fully open during a backlash of mage-energy of immense power. The terribly wounded Vanyel was Chosen by the Companion Yfandes. He healed, learned to control his powers, and became a Herald-Mage. Ambivalent about his new calling at first, he soon embraced his mission to protect his Queen and country from the enemies of Valdemar. He expanded and stabilized the Web connecting the Heralds, and cast the spell that protected Valdemar against foreign mages by having the *vrondi* watch them. Vanyel lived a heroic life serving Valdemar that ended when he sacrificed himself in a Final Strike to defeat the Dark Mage Leareth at Crookback Pass. His spirit haunted the Forest of Sorrows for hundreds of years after his death, joined by the spirits of his second love, Stefen, and his Companion Yfandes. As the Mage-Storm crisis reached its peak in Selenay's reign, he took an active role in solving it, and after it was over, he was released from his guardianship of The Forest of Sorrows to go with Stefen and Yfandes to the Havens. He had four children: Jisa, Brightstar, Featherfire, and Arven. His descendants include Elspeth and the royal line of Valdemar beginning with Jisa, and a large number of

Tayledras Mages, including Firesong. *(LHM, Storms, Winds)*

Vanyel Demonrider
Karsite epithet for the Valdemaran Herald-Mage Vanyel. He was able to turn back the most terrible demons and monsters that the Karsite priests could summon. Ironically, Vanyel used the demons against their summoners, which earned him the title King of Demons. When he returned the demons to their summoners, Vanyel started a chain of events that produced a cascade of changes in Karse, not all of them good. *(Storm)*

Vanyel's Curse
A spell laid upon the Forest of Sorrows by the legendary Herald-Mage, it was actually a guardianship of the borders of Valdemar by the spirits of Vanyel, Stefen, and Yfandes. The curse created the Killing Trees and kept the northern barbarians from using the Great Pass to reach Valdemar. The curse was no longer in effect after the Mage-Storms. *(Arrows, Owl)*

Vapor Demons
Many of Errold's Grove folk superstitiously believed that these ghostlike creatures existed in the Pelagiris Forst. *(Owl)*

Var'athanda
A Shin'a'in term that means "to be forgetful of." *(Oath)*

Varianis
Herald Kris's sexual partner in his early days as a Herald. *(Arrows)*

Varny
Sania's shieldmate and a former Sunhawk, she left the mercenary group after losing her left eye in battle. She now lives with Sania and their two daughters at Hawksnest. *(Oath)*

Varrir
Transparent creatures from the Ethereal Plane. The dying King Randale reminded Vanyel of one of these. *(LHM)*

Vasely
One of the Sunhawks who came to Petras in response to Kethry's call, seeking vengeance for Captain Idra. *(Oath)*

Vatean (Guildsmaster)
Guildsmaster for the traders, and friend of Lord Orthallen. His respectable façade concealed a vast empire of illicit activity, including serving as the ringleader for the slavers that were kidnapping children in Haven. He also hired Jass to burn down one of his own slum properties to avoid fines. Skif's surrogate family died in that fire. Skif eventually killed him with a knife in the eye. *(TT)*

Vaul (Lord)
An older soldier who helped Prince Darenthallis adjust to the cruel realities of military command early in his career as Lord Martial. *(Sword)*

Vault, The
A repository of ancient tools and weapons under Urtho's Tower. *(Storm)*

Vayshe'druvon
A Tayledras term for guard, scout, and protector; Darkwind is one. *(Winds)*

Vedric Mavelan
The leader of the mage-gifted Mavelan family, he plotted to kill the entire Remoerdis clan in order to obtain access to the powerful node beneath the Baires castle. He was killed with the rest of the Mavelans by his own assassination trap. *(LHM)*

Vega
Jadrek's gentle palfrey, formerly the property of Lady Mertis, who gave Vega to Jadrek when he, Kethry, Tarma, and Warrl set forth on their return trek across the Comb. *(Oath)*

Veil
The magic energy barrier at the entrance of a Vale. It is transparent and permits Clan members and harmless wildlife to pass, but bars enemies and bad weather. Pass-

ing through the Veil creates a brief tingling sensation, as though lightning were building somewhere nearby. *(Winds, Owl)*

Velcher (Lord)
Tremane's spymaster. *(Storm)*

Velgarth
The continent on which Valdemar and its surrounding kingdoms are located. *(LHM)*

Vena
The apprentice of the mage-smith at the Sisterhood of Spell and Sword when Wizard Heshain attacked. Vena survived the massacre because she was herb-hunting in the woods. She was the first bearer of the sword Need. *(Winds)*

Vengeance of the Sunlord
What the Karsites call the Karsite military. *(Arrows)*

Vere Neshem
Harris's brother, and also a farmer in Errold's Grove. *(Owl)*

Verenna
Kerowyn's Shin'a'in mare, the only mount left at the Keep after the raider attack, because Verenna was always pastured, not stabled. *(Sword)*

Vernal Equinox Festival
A Valdemaran annual seasonal celebration that is observed with elaborate Court ceremonies. *(Arrows)*

Vertalays (Lord)
A courtier with the difficult task of dowering six marriageable daughters. Lord Vertalays was a wool and mutton merchant. His wife saved money by bringing the family to court during the winter season. This clever tactic meant they could cut fine figures by wearing court dress made from their own wool and embroidered by the Lady and her daughters. This allowed them to demonstrate the family's domestic skills to potential suitors. *(BB)*

Ver'Kal'enedral

Herald Roald, the future king of Valdemar, was given this title by the Star-Eyed Goddess. He became a minor legend among the Tale'sedrin because he was a good friend of Tarma, and visited the Plains often with his white spirit-horse. *(Oath)*

Ves'tacha

A Shin'a'in term that means "beloved one." *(Oath)*

Vetch

The Sunhawk scout Gerrold's horse. *(Oath)*

Vetch

One of the Silvers. *(Gryphon)*

Veth

Covia Headman Gallen's half-grown son, he inadvertently caught the results of Vanyel's fatigue and frustration and got knocked halfway across the village square. *(LHM)*

Veth

A Healer-trained herbalist, he supplied a remedy for Lan's dazzle headaches. *(BB)*

Veth Kethren

A legendary sword fighter who developed a graceful style of sword fighting for those without upper body strength. Vanyel successfully tried this fighting technique with his cousin Radevel, much to Armsmaster Jervis's dismay. *(LHM)*

Viden

The home of Lord Gormley, it is a town mentioned in Bard Leslac's heroic version of an unheroic clash between Tarma and a drunken belligerent. *(Oath)*

Vikteren

He served Urtho, passing as an apprentice mage or journeyman, though he was actually a Master. With Skandranon he relayed information from Urtho himself regarding the Gates and the coming Cataclysm. *(Gryphon)*

Virgin and Stars Tavern
Popular with the Collegium's third-year Bardic students, the tavern is owned by Jon Hapkins. *(Arrows, TT)*

Vkandis Medals
Gold disks blazoned with a sun-in-glory symbol and worn by Karsite priests as part of their ceremonial garb. *(Storms)*

Vkandis Sunlord
One of the numerous names for Karse's deity, he has manifested as a golden statue, flames, and lightning. Like the Goddess of the Shin'a'in, he is very actively and often quite visibly involved in the affairs of his people and Karse as a whole. *(BB, LHM, Storm, Winds)*

Vkandis' Flames
Colorful spun-sugar confections meant to resemble the real fires handed out to youngsters at the annual Feast of the Children. *(Storms)*

Vkandis' Light
What Karsites call the sun. *(Storm)*

Voice of Flame
A nimbus of fire that appears above the head of a priest and speaks through him. Fakery of this manifestation is possible, since Karsite priests are often mages as well as clergy. *(Storm)*

Voices of Vkandis Sunlord
A title borne by Karse's priesthood. Its leading members wear red and are the land's ultimate authorities. *(Arrows)*

Void
The Void lies outside the normal plane of existence. It was in the Void that Ma'ar hid his Sanctuary throughout the ages. Firesong returned there to study the damage he inflicted when he destroyed Falconsbane, and to see if the Mage-Storms were disturbing the fabric of that unreal place. *(Storm)*

Voorthayshen, Clan Keep
A Tayledras community whose structures make use of

natural elements, including trees, ferns, hot springs for bathing, and skylights for illumination. *(LHM)*

Vordon
Chief of Ghost Cat Clan. *(Owl)*

Vorn
A gryphon who is Salla's partner, and one of Shalaman's personal guard. *(Gryphon)*

Vor'kela
The Shaman of An'desha's clan and a rigid man, he was a large part of the reason the boy fled to Tayledras lands and came under Falconsbane's power. An'desha was certain that if Vor'kela learned of his Mage-Gift he would insist that An'desha become a shaman, a possible fate that appalled the youth. *(Storm, Winds)*

Vostel (Herald)
A Herald who had been burned by the full fury of an angry firebird, he was helped to heal by Talia in her days as a student. Vostel was posted to the Fallflower Healing Temple when word came of Herald Destria's plight—she had suffered the same sort of burns he had endured. Vostel was able to help Destria cope with the pain and self-doubts generated by her long and painful recovery. *(Arrows)*

Vree
Darkwind's bondbird, a large forestgyre strong enough to kill a deer or a man. He killed the raven that was holding Darkwind's father in thrall to Falconsbane. *(Storm, Wind)*

Vrisa Sensdaughter
Talia's much-loved sister, she married and became a Firstwife with three Underwives to command. When Talia went back to rescue the older woman from that life, Vrisa turned her back and made holy signs to ward off the danger posed by her own sister, who she now perceived as a demon. *(Arrows)*

Vrondi
Simple air elementals that cannot abide the emotional emanations associated with falsehood. Linked with the

Truth Spell, the *vrondi* produce a glowing blue mist forming a visible aura about the subject's head and shoulders. Vanyel summoned the *vrondi* in greater numbers than anyone ever had before and set them to watch throughout Valdemar for disturbances in the fabric of mage-energy lying over the land. This became a force detectable and intensely worrying to incoming mages. The *vrondi* would follow a mage if the mage was not a Herald, and watch that mage's every moment. The sense of being watched by thousands of magical eyes drove foreign mages nearly mad once they crossed into Valdemar, especially if they tried to use magic. Vanyel's *vrondi* spell was ended in the Mage-Storms. But the Truth Spell remains one of the most useful skills that Heralds have to keep Valdemar safe and well governed. *(LHM, Winds)*

Vuysher'edras
Brothers of the Wolves, one of the oldest of the Shin'a'in Clans. *(Oath)*

Vykaendys
The god of Iftel, also known as the Holy Sun, the same God as Vkandis of Karse. Vykaendys created the anti-mage barrier around Iftel after the Cataclysm's survivors found refuge there and prayed for protection from Ma'ar's mage-led forces. *(Storm)*

Vykaendys First Bryron Hess
Iftel's current Son of the Sun. *(Storm)*

Vysaka
Shin'a'in term for the Goddess-bond formed when the Swordsworn take the Oath. Its presence can be detected by an Adept, another Kal'enedral, and the Kal'enedral who has the bond. It is this bond that creates the shielding that makes Kal'enedral celibate and somewhat immune to magic. Tarma temporarily lost her bond while she was possessed by the demon Thalhkarsh. *(Oath)*

Vyusher
Shin'a'in term for "wolf." *(Oath)*

Wagon-families

Itinerant peddlers who travel across borders and have no home base. Trader Evan was from one of these families and helped spread word throughout Hardorn that Prince Ancar had assassinated his own father. *(Winds)*

Ward-off spells

They can be set as the first line of defense along a kingdom's border to discourage rather than hurt trespassers. The more intelligent the trespasser, the more likely it is to be affected by the spell. *(Winds)*

Warrior Within, The

The Shin'a'in believe in this inner voice that tells them what they must know. According to them, it is the source of all honor, faith, and prosperity under the Goddess. *(Storm)*

Warrl

A *kyree* summoned as a familiar by Kethry, he chose to bond to Tarma instead because they were alike—warriors and neuter, and Kethry already had Need. Warrl accompanied Tarma and Kethry on all their adventures, and trained Kerowyn in mind-speech. *(Oath, Sword)*

Wasting Sickness

A disease afflicting the Northerners and brought with them into Valdemar. Ghost Cat Clan called it Summer Fever, and knew no treatment or cure. The illness takes two forms, one that causes paralysis, and one that kills.

Keisha was able to track down the cause of the illness and destroy the source of the infection. *(Owl)*

Wayfarer's peace
A greeting announcing that the speaker comes with no evil intent and seeks only shelter. *(Oath)*

Wayfood
Dry travel fare carried in packs or obtained at supply stations on the road route. Wayfood is highly compressed and nutritious, but bland and hard to eat. The one exception to this rule is special bars of pressed grain, fruit and honey. They are tasty, but susceptible to spoiling, and are generally only issued to those on winter duty. *(Arrows)*

Waymeet
A northern town on Kris and Talia's circuit that was severely hit by plague. Kris helped the townpeople while Talia brought back Healer Kerithwyn to treat the stricken townspeople. *(Arrows)*

Waystations
Supply posts and shelters for the Heralds to use on their Circuits of Valdemar's outer sectors. Herald Kris' mother is responsible for managing the restocking and supplies in the Waystations. *(Arrows)*

Weatherwitch
Clairvoyants with a special Gift in long-range weather prediction, particularly of bad weather. Maeven of Berrybay developed the Gift as a result of grief and madness, but retained it when Talia helped restore her to sanity. *(Arrows)*

Web-spell
Also referred to as The Web, it was created by Vanyel because too few Herald-Mages were left to watch Valdemar's borders. In the past, four Herald-Mages, one for each direction, manned the Web-spell, patrolled the border, and reported trouble to one another. The Web was reset using the energy of focus stones as substitute sentries and feeding on and joining together the life-energy of all Heralds and Companions. The Web alerted all Heralds when there was danger. Thus, Heralds with

Foresight were able to make sure that the right Heralds with the right Gifts would be moved to the right places every time a threat to Valdemar crossed its borders. This Web-spell became permanent, the best way to protect Valdemar from any approaching danger, and ensured that any threat was responded to instantly. *(LHM, Winds)*

Webs of Time, The
The Shin'a'in tapestries incorporating the memories of those who lived through history, housed in a holy building in Kata'Shin'a'in. *(Winds)*

Weldon (Lord Marshal)
The Lord Marshal and leader of the forces at the Karse border. *(BB)*

Wendar
Keep Seneschal and the former scribe and accountant of Rathgar's mercenary company. *(Sword)*

Wendi
A courtier, her older sister Ratha had been fostered with Vanyel's mother. *(LHM)*

Werda
Elderly history instructor at the Collegium, replaced by Teren when she retired. *(Arrows)*

Werenton (Ambassador)
Representative to Haven from Hardorn. *(Exile)*

Wernar (Herald)
He joined Pol and other Heralds at the table near the fire for supper and to relay gossip from his recent Circuit near Torgate. *(BB)*

Western Sea
The migrating k'Leshya clan reached this vast body of water after traveling through two Gates and the wilderness beyond. It is the boundary of Velgarth and is a deep blue-green body of water stretching to the horizon. White Gryphon was built on its coast. *(Gryphon)*

Westmark
A town on the Herald's northern Circuit where Herald Talia had to judge a tricky murder case. *(Arrows)*

Westrel Keep
The family holding of House Leshara. *(LHM)*

Wethes (Herald)
He served as a spy in Karse during the Tedrel Wars.
(Exile)

Wethes Goldmarchant
A wealthy, abusive, amoral Mornedealth banker, he
wanted entree into the ranks of the Fifty Families and
Court. He got it when noble Kavinestral Pheregrul sold
him his young sister Kethry in marriage. Years after her
escape from her sadistic monster of a husband, Kethry
returned to Mornedealth as a trained mage, only to be
captured by Wethes. The confrontation with Wethes
taught Kethry that he was merely an aging, paunchy,
greedy coward, not the overwhelming monster of her
memory. With the help of Tarma and other friends, she
escaped and got revenge on her former tormentor in the
city's courts, having the marriage annulled and fining
Wethes heavily for his behavior. Wethes was publicly
humiliated, disgraced, and thrown out of the exalted circles that meant everything to him. *(Oath)*

Wheat Sheaf Inn
Operated by the Kemaks, this inn was a rendezvous
point in Petras for the revenge-seeking Sunhawks.
(Oath)

Wheat-smut
The only pharmacological remedy known for the dazzle-
headaches Bard Breda suffered. The concoction's main
ingredient is ergot, which can be dangerous, elevating
the blood pressure and inducing cardiovascular distress.
(LHM)

Wheel-bound
A religious belief that one pays for evil done in past
lives by performing good deeds in the present one. Landric the farmer was one of that sect and wore a five-
spoke wheel brand scar on the back of his left wrist to
show his faith. *(Oath)*

White Foal Pass
The pass lies near the shared border of Karse, Rethwel-

lan, and Valdemar, and was where the Karsites first invaded. When Vanyel told Herald Kera, who was posted in that dangerous area, to escape the growing anti-mage crusade brewing in Karse, he advised her to go over White Foal Pass. This is also where Lavan Firestorm made his last fatal stand against the Karsites. *(BB, LHM)*

White Gryphon
A cliff-built city on the edge of the Western Sea, laid out in the shape of a stylized gryphon and carved of the cliffs' snowy white stone. It took ten years to build the main part of the city. Nearly three-quarters of its citizens live in cave dwellings. Its population is made up of humans, gryphons, *kyree, hertasi* and *tervardi* who fled Urtho's keep during the final days of the Mage-Wars via a gate. *(Owl, Gryphon)*

White Winds School
This branch of sorcery had as its most famous leader a *hertasi* mage—Gervase, the Wizard Lizard, who lived for hundreds of years and built the school into its final form. Kethry studied magic at a White Winds school and founded her own school later on—founding a school being the obligation of any White Winds Adept. White Winds philosophy teaches that one never coerces Other Planar creatures and must not deal at all with entities of the Abyssal Planes, except to send them back or destroy them, if possible. The White Winds order believes that mage powers should be used for the greatest good. White Winds Graduates are wanderers who look for opportunities to do good and do not take permanent positions with a patron. *(Oath, Owl, Storm, Sword, Winds)*

White-Demons
A Karsite epithet for Valdemar's Heralds. *(Storm)*

Whitebird
Trondi'irn with the k'Leshya delegation to Haven. She chose to stay with the gryphons at the Palace rather than in Firesong's *ekele*. *(Storm)*

Whitefell
A pastureland south of Forst Reach notable for raising

sheep. Vanyel's brother Mekeal had put sheep in the Long Meadow against his father's wishes in an attempt to compete with Whitefell. *(LHM)*

Whitethorn
With Darian and Wintersky, he helped the *hertasi* build the *ekele* for Darian's teacher and staff. *(Owl)*

White Rider
A hostelry and tavern in Haven, it has a sign with a Herald and Companion on it. *(TT)*

White-shirts
A slang term the poor of Haven called the Heralds. *(TT)*

Willem
One of Bazie's former gang members, he made a large score and retired from thievery. He purchased a house with rooms to rent and was set for life. *(TT)*

Willem
A mage with Ancar's invasion force who acted as a mind-controller over the troops. *(Winds)*

Willi
Known as Scratcher, he was the Skybolts' bookkeeper. *(Sword)*

Willowbark Tea
A popular Valdemaran analgesic tea, willowbark contains salicylic acids and is effective in easing pain. *(LHM, Arrows, Storm)*

Windblade k'Treva
A Tayledras Gate-guard who Firesong sent to fetch tea and honey to revive the exhausted Herald-Mage Savil after Savil's abrupt arrival in k'Treva Vale. *(LHM)*

Wind Dance
A traditional Tayledras dance. Darkwind performed the wind dance at a Vale celebration. It consists of flowing movements, demanding the dancer be extremely strong and supple. *(Winds)*

Wind Lord
Another name for the God of Iftel, who takes an active hand in mortal affairs of Iftel. *(Oath)*

Windborn
Lady Windborn Soulshaper, Kethry's name for her Goddess. In an encounter with The Warrior, that aspect of the Goddess told her She was but another face of Lady Windborn *(Oath)*

Winddance
A Tayledras mage assigned to help the scouts, he was wounded in a fight with Change-wolves. *(Winds)*

Windshadow
A Tayledras scout. *(Owl)*

Windsteed
A member of Amberdrake's lost family. *(Gryphon)*

Wingsiblings
Also called Wingsister and Wingbrother, outlanders can become members of a Tayledras clan through a ceremony, and are addressed by this title. *(LHM, Winds, Owl)*

Winterhart
Mate of Amberdrake and mother of Silverblade, she was born Reanna Laury, and resided at King Leodhan's court until Ma'ar's invasion. Fleeing south, she joined Urtho's forces as a trondi'irn healer and adopted a Kaled'a'in name. Winterhart met Amberdrake and fell in love after initially disliking him when she sought his services as a kestra'chern. She was courted by King Shalaman in the Haighlei Empire, but turned him down because she was already lifebonded to Amberdrake. *(Gryphon)*

Winterlight
The oldest Tayledras scout in k'Sheyna vale. He originally held the position of Council Elder and Speaker for the scouts, but willingly gave that up to Darkwind. Winterlight flew two bondbirds, Lyer, a snow-eagle, by day and Huur, a tuft-eared owl, by night. When Darkwind resumed Adept Mage status, Winterlight was chosen once again to be scout leader. *(Winds)*

Wintermoon
Darkwind's half brother, one of two children of Star-

blade's contracted liaison with a k'Treva mage. Winter-moon had no mage talents and just enough Mind-magic to speak with his bondbirds, Corwith and k'Tathi. Be-cause of his lack of magic, he and Starblade were es-tranged. Wintermoon was a loner, and preferred to take the night-hunting patrols as a scout. *(Winds)*

Wintersky
One of Darian's oldest friends, he was a Tayledras scout whose bondbird was Tiec in *Owlflight* and Kreeak in *Owlknight. (Owl)*

Wisdom Keeper
Shamans sworn to the Crone aspect of the Star-Eyed Goddess. Called the Scroll-Sworn, they wear dark blue and protect the history and wisdom of the clans. *(Storm)*

Wisewomen
Practitioners of simple magic, they are sometimes called earth-witches. They draw on ordinary, natural sources for their small powers and serve as healers for remote villages and clans, just as hedge-wizards do. *(Owl)*

Witchlight
Another term for mage-light, it is a glowing orb that needs no source of earthly fuel but is kindled and main-tained entirely by sorcerous energy. *(Arrows, Oath)*

Wolf Crown
Worn by the Emperor of the East, it is a circlet of elec-trum inset with thirteen yellow diamonds. The design is of twelve wolves, eleven in profile to the viewer, five facing left, six facing right, and the twelfth as pack leader, gazing directly at an observer. *(Storm)*

Wolflings
The name of Captain Jeffrey's infantry, one of four mer-cenary Companies hired by the Menmellith Council. *(Sword)*

Wolfstone's Pack
A mercenary force that fought for Valdemar and Reth-wellan against Hardorn, recruited by Herald-Captain Kerowyn. *(Owl)*

Wolf's Head Ring
Worn by the Emperor and cast from the same mold as the center figure on the Wolf Crown, its eyes are topazes. *(Storm)*

Wolverine Tribe
A northern barbarian clan, the Wolverine had taken up where the almost extinct Blood Bear clan had left off by raiding its neighbors and taking young women and boys captive. Their shaman could tap into the power of the Eclipse, as Blood Bear clan's shaman had. *(Owl)*

Woodlark
The nickname Vanyel gave to his favorite instrument, a lute, when he was a boy. *(LHM)*

Woodlark
Dirk's pet name for Talia, he compares her to the elusive and shy bird. It is small, brown, and blends in with its surroundings. Remarkably pretty in its own quiet way, it has the most beautiful voice in the forest. *(Arrows)*

Woolly Ram
An inn at the Skybolt's winter quarters. *(Sword)*

Word of Opening
An Adept-controlled power spell designed to call an evoked spirit from beyond the Pillars of Wisdom and the Gate of Judgment. *(Oath)*

Work Room
Mage Adepts train their proteges to use their Gifts in these tightly shielded rooms. Savil's room was a circular chamber within the Palace, and its shielding was so ancient and powerful it actually muffled physical sound, keeping out even the Death Bell's tolling. Its walls were stone and the floor had an inlaid pattern of light-colored wood delineating a perfect circle. In time, the room became the heart of the new Web established by Vanyel. *(LHM)*

Working, The
The avatars's name for the use of Urtho's great device, channeled through Karal to strengthen the breakwater

against the Mage-Storms. They warned that this was only a reprieve, not a solution. *(Storm)*

World Plane
The plane containing the continent of Vergarth, this is where the energies and chaos of the Nether Planes are regenerated into streams of magical energy by living things. *(Storm)*

Wrenlet (Herald-trainee)
A recently Chosen Herald-trainee, she had not been at the Collegium more than a fortnight and had a heavy task ahead, as her Companion Lada was about to foal. *(BB)*

Wrightguild
The craft group that makes fine porcelain and stoneware. Egon, of the small settlement of Potter, was a Guildmaster of this guild. *(Oath)*

Writ and Rules of Vkandis
The Writ and Rules is the book Karsites follow to interpret the ways of Vkandis. For centuries corrupt priests used the writings to promote their own agenda. These laws were reinterpreted correctly by Solaris after her ascension. *(Storm)*

Wtasi Empire
It lies far to the east, on the Salten Sea. A few refugees from the Cataclysm reached there, and reported that it was devastated by the incredible double explosion when Ka'venusho and Predain were simultaneously destroyed. No Gates could then be erected to move supplies to the Empire, and it suffered greatly as a result. *(Gryphon)*

Wulaf
A shepherd and Valdemaran native of the area near White Foal Pass. He acted as Lavan's guide and helped him find an ideal observation post above the Pine Forest region. *(BB)*

Wulf (Herald-trainee)
Herald-trainee whose Gift is Seeing. *(Arrows)*

Wulfres (Count)
One of Jadrek's hoped-for contacts in Rethwellan's Pal-

ace circles. However, during preparations for the uprising, Tarma, in her disguise as Arton, had to leave her message with Horsemaster Tindel, because Wulfres was too suspicious of her disguise. *(Oath)*

Wulgra (Herald)
He was one of a number of familiar faces among the Heralds that Vanyel was missing when he returned from his mission to the Karsite border. *(LHM)*

Wyrfen Woods
They share a border with the orchards on Forst Reach's lands to the southeast, and are permeated by old magic. *(LHM)*

Wyrist (Lady)
A Councilwoman who speaks for the East, her governed area borders Karse and is vulnerable to threats from that direction. *(Arrows)*

Wyrsa
Created by one of the Old Adepts, they are a failed attempt to mimic *kyree* and are completely uncontrollable. Those who escaped into the rain forest near White Gryphon were changed by the Mage-Storms, becoming magic absorbers. In later times, these vicious creatures inhabited the Pelagirs and could, at enormous magical cost and risk, be summoned as arcane weapons. They were too powerful for even a Companion to fight unaided. The *wyrsa* were an evil-looking blend of snake and dog. They came in different colors ranging from black to yellow to white. They had scales in some strains, and dance in hypnotic patterns. The *wyrsa* travel in packs, share intelligence, and feed on mage energies. *(Gryphon, LHM, Storm, Winds)*

Wythra (Companion)
Herald Teren's Companion. *(Arrows)*

Yai
A Shin'a'in term meaning "yes." *(Oath)*

Yai Se Corthu
A Shin'a'in term meaning "two are one," the Oath-bound. *(Oath)*

Year-and-Day Handfasting
A border custom requiring young couples that wish to marry to live together first to ensure they are fertile before any formal union is allowed. *(Arrows)*

Yellowthroats
Songbirds that appear in Haven in spring, they have a warbling note. The males of the species try to outsing each other in territorial displays. *(LHM)*

Yfandes (Companion)
Companion to Herald-Mage Vanyel, she was the only adult Companion in Vanyel's time who had not Chosen, and had been unpartnered for over ten years. On the night of Tylendel's death, Yfandes Chose the boy, rescued Vanyel from the river and protected him until he was coherent enough to be entrusted to the Healers. She was patient but firm with Vanyel, becoming the devoted companion and support he needed. When Vanyel battled the Dark Mage Leareth, he sent Yfandes to carry his life-bonded mate Stefen to safety. Vanyel expected to die alone, but Yfandes returned to him after alerting the nearest guard post of the coming danger, and helped to destroy Leareth and his army. She guarded the Forest

of Sorrows with Vanyel and Stefen, and disappeared to the Havens with them when the final solution to the Mage-Storms was put into effect. *(Arrows, LHM, Storm)*

Yip Dogs
What Kaled'a'in call the annoying, small, and otherwise useless breed created by the Haighlei peoples that make a lot of noise and attract unwelcome attention. *(Owl)*

Yllyana
One of the ancient bearers of the sword Need. *(Winds)*

Ylsa (Herald)
A Herald-Courier, her Companion was Felara. Herald Ylsa and her Companion died in an ambush, yet she successfully completed her mission thanks to a powerful mindlink with Talia and other Heralds. She was lifebonded with Herald Keren. *(Exile, Arrows, TT)*

Ylyna Mavelan
The bride of Deveran Remoerdis of Lineas and mother of Tashir. The only potential treaty-spouse among the Mavelans of Baires to lack mage-powers, she was the only bride acceptable to Deveran. She was killed with the rest of the Remoerdis family by the assassination trap. *(LHM)*

Yonisse
One of Hadanelith's victims at White Gryphon. *(Gryphon)*

Yuthi'so'coro
A Shin'a'in term meaning "road courtesy," they are the rules followed by the nomads when traveling on a public road. *(Oath)*

Zado
The God worshipped in some quarters of Valdemar, Guildmaster Jumay of the Royal Council was an adherent of that divinity. *(LHM)*

Zaleka (Companion)
The Companion to Herald Arven. *(Arrows)*

Zalmon
A city in southwest Valdemar. *(LHM)*

Zaras
One of King Raschar's mages, he cast a spell on one of his apprentices to make him look like the King and sent him off with the rest of the court on a three-day hunt. Zaras and Raschar then hid in the Palace stables to ambush Captain Idra. *(Oath)*

Zendak
Ma'ar's name in one of his incarnations. *(Winds)*

Zephyr
Amberdrake's little sibling, whom he never saw again after the fall of Therium. *(Gryphon)*

Zhai'helleva or Zha'hai'allav'a
A friendly Tayledras or Shin'a'in parting wish that means "wind to your wings." The second version is Shin'a'in. *(Winds)*

Zhaneel
Skandranon's mate and the mother of Tadrith and Kee-

nath. During the War she was originally attached to Commander Loren's group. Not knowing what her origins were, she originally thought she was misborn, but she was actually a deliberate creation of Urtho. Amberdrake dubbed her a gryfalcon: small, lightly built, with a deep keelbone, narrow chest, no neck ruff, and humanlike hands which she used as fists in combat. She developed her own training course and techniques, and achieved quite a spectacular reputation among Urtho's forces. *(Gryphon)*

MERCEDES LACKEY

The Novels of Valdemar

To Order Call: 1-800-788-6262

Mercedes Lackey & Larry Dixon

The Novels of Valdemar

"Lackey and Dixon always offer a well-told tale"
—*Booklist*

DARIAN'S TALE

OWLFLIGHT
0-88677-804-2

OWLSIGHT
0-88677-803-4

OWLKNIGHT
0-88677-916-2

THE MAGE WARS

THE BLACK GRYPHON
0-88677-804-2

THE WHITE GRYPHON
0-88677-682-1

THE SILVER GRYPHON
0-88677-685-6

To Order Call: 1-800-788-6262

Tad Williams

THE WAR OF THE FLOWERS

0-7564-0181-X

To Order Call: 1-800-788-6262

TAD WILLIAMS

Memory, Sorrow & Thorn

"THE FANTASY EQUIVALENT OF *WAR AND PEACE*...
readers who delight in losing themselves in long complex
tales of epic fantasy will be in their element here."
—Locus

THE DRAGONBONE CHAIR
0-88677-384-9

STONE OF FAREWELL
0-88677-480-2

TO GREEN ANGEL TOWER (Part One)
0-88677-598-1

TO GREEN ANGEL TOWER (Part Two)
0-88677-606-6

To Order Call: 1-800-788-6262